BEST NEW AMERICAN VOICES 2003

GUEST EDITORS OF
Best New American Voices

Tobias Wolff
Charles Baxter
Joyce Carol Oates

BEST NEW AMERICAN VOICES 2003

GUEST EDITOR

Joyce Carol Oates

SERIES EDITORS

John Kulka and Natalie Danford

A Harvest Original • Harcourt, Inc.

San Diego   New York   London

Requests for permission to make copies of any part of the work should
be mailed to the following address: Permissions Department, Harcourt, Inc.,
6277 Sea Harbor Drive, Orlando, Florida 32887-6777.

www.HarcourtBooks.com

Library of Congress Cataloging-in-Publication Data available upon request

ISBN 0-15-600716-9   ISSN 1536-7908

Text set in Adobe Garamond
Designed by Lori McThomas Buley

Printed in the United States of America
First edition

A C E G I K J H F D B

CONTENTS

PREFACE

Where do writers come from?

No one knows what mixture of childhood reading and imagination, what combination of early happiness and sorrow creates writers, but the Best New American Voices series is proof that writers continue to arrive, even in the information age that so many predicted would spell the death of literature. Readers continue to develop as well, passionate readers who place high value on the imaginative and intellectual dimensions of fiction. They, too, gravitate to the series.

In this anthology we present the very best emerging short story writers, people—*young* people for the most part—who have devoted themselves to the craft of writing and specifically to the art of the short story. And it is precisely this forward-looking aspect—a commitment to publishing stories by new writers—that distinguishes Best New American Voices from other annuals.

For this, the third edition in the Best New American Voices series, we have again solicited nominations from graduate writing programs, arts organizations, workshops, and summer conferences. We do not accept submissions, nor do we cull stories from magazines and quarterlies.

It may not be clear where writers come from, but judging by past history, the writers included in *Best New American Voices 2003* are going somewhere, and fast. Previous volumes contain stories by writers who have since become more familiar names. We are gratified to see the successes of Timothy Westmoreland, Ana Menendez, David Benioff, and William Gay, for example. The authors of the fifteen stories that Joyce Carol Oates has selected for *Best New American Voices 2003* will likely be unfamiliar names—for now. A few of these writers make their debut appearances here, while one or two already have forthcoming books. We wish them all luck; they're a talented bunch. We'll *all* be watching.

We would like to thank Joyce Carol Oates for her careful reading (and rereading) of these stories; for her promptness, speed, and professionalism; and for her counsel and wise editorial suggestions. We really do consider ourselves fortunate to have had her serve as guest editor. We would like to thank our past guest editors, Tobias Wolff and Charles Baxter, for their continuing support for the series. To the many writers, teachers, and directors who are really the ones responsible for making this anthology a reality we extend thanks and congratulations. To name just a few others: We thank our editor André Bernard for his guidance and patience; Lisa Lucas in the Harcourt contracts department for making plain to us what did not seem at all plain; Margie Rogers, deputy managing editor at Harcourt, for her usual heroics; and our families and friends for their love and support.

—John Kulka and Natalie Danford

INTRODUCTION

Joyce Carol Oates

A spontaneous *swerve of engagement* draws us to certain works of art. Often we know nothing of the artist and so our expectations are neutral, blank; but there's an instant rapport, a visceral connection that captures our attention. It's appropriate that this volume is titled *Best New American Voices* since it's "voice" that draws us into prose fiction. Among these wonderfully diverse and imaginative stories, there are openings so compelling one can't resist wanting to know more, immediately:

> They are excavating the bodies at night, a few hundred yards away from our house. The bright halogen from the spotlights seeps through cracks in our closed windows and doors.
>
>   ("Everything Must Go" by Barry Matthews)

> In the end, my mother still knew a few things. She knew, for example, that telephones existed, that they had been a part of the world that she had been a part of.
>
>   ("Good" by Cheryl Strayed)

> Somehow the chickensnake had managed to climb up the twenty-foot steel pole and into one of the hollowed-out gourds the farmers had hung there as birdhouses for purple martins.
>
>   ("Chickensnake" by Brad Vice)

Four days before the UN Security Council resolution will turn Desert Shield into Desert Storm, the team waits for the scouts on the south side of a dust-covered washout deep in the Iraqi desert. Their operation is illegal, but necessary.

("The Storekeeper" by Otis Haschemeyer)

Of course, compelling openings are simply the way *in*. Once we're inside the fictional world we look for other qualities as well as voice. In choosing the final selections for this volume, out of thirty-five finalists sent to me by series editors John Kulka and Natalie Danford (who'd chosen those thirty-five from 350 nominations), I was looking for works of fiction that involve the reader in dramatically realized, emotionally charged situations of significance. I was looking for originality of expression and characterization. I might have wished for more formal experimentation and writerly playfulness, while acknowledging that contemporary times, even before the terrorist attacks of September 11, 2001, seem less amenable to subversive texts than such preceding, highly inventive decades as the 1960s and 1970s. Ours is an age of realism, in which memoir and memoirist fiction predominate.

Though there are several darkly surreal tales among these selections, the dominant mode is psychological realism. By "psychological realism" we mean, usually, the establishment of a central consciousness through whose perspective a story is narrated or unfolds; our involvement in the story depends largely upon the plausibility and worth of this central consciousness. Do we believe in him or her? Is the fictional world convincing? Unlike fantasy, realism derives much of its power from a skillful evocation of time and place. In this volume, settings and circumstances are deftly, often brilliantly, rendered and strike us as unquestionably authentic, whether the cancer wing of a hospital ("Good"), the Iraqi desert on the eve of Desert Storm

("The Storekeeper"), a residence for terminal AIDS patients ("The Year Draws in the Day"), Vietnam ("Peace"), an impoverished Alabama farm ("Chickensnake"), a backwater New Hampshire town that can't support a library ("Everything Must Go"), a farm residence for emotionally disturbed patients ("April"), or native New Guinea villages ("A Few Short Notes on Tropical Butterflies"). There are love-story variants that range from the breezily comic ("Circuits") to the mordantly melancholy ("Transparency"), and there are tales of confrontations with mortality that remain purposefully irresolute, proffering no formulaic happy endings ("The Good Life," "Who Is Beatrice?", "Under the Influence"). Even those stories that shade into the fantastic ("The Woman Who Tasted of Rose Oil," "At Celilo") are so convincingly rendered that the shift from realism to surrealism isn't intrusive. We read such fiction with little resistance to suspending our disbelief. We read with eagerness, pleasure, enlightenment.

I should note that in reading, and rereading, the thirty-five finalists passed on to me, I was struck by the high percentage of stories in which extreme or grotesque imagery figured. This leads me to conclude that, though this is an age of literary realism, it's also an age that perceives its possibilities without, one might say, an excess of youthful optimism. Perhaps what struck me most about the stories was, simply, their diversity. In even those stories not selected for the anthology there were often passages of startling, wayward originality; familiar situations were narrated in unfamiliar, odd tones; the seemingly predictable often turned out not predictable at all. Though it's frequently said by critics of writing workshops that there is a typical "workshop story," as there's a typical "workshop poem," the nominations to *Best New American Voices* suggest the reverse.

Writing is a visionary activity but it is also, perhaps more fundamentally, a craft. To be a writer isn't to compose words in the air, as in a dream; it's to commit oneself to the discipline of communicating with readers through a commonly shared language. The more involved one becomes in this craft, the more one is involved with a professional literary community of editors, publishers, book designers, printers. Writing may be initially an isolated activity, in fact like a dream, but it quickly becomes collaborative, if it is to have any existence beyond the immediate and ephemeral.

Of all collaborative creative efforts, the "workshop" is the most communal, as it's often the most democratic. Theatrical and musical works are commonly workshopped, and the tradition of young sculptors and painters apprenticing themselves to gifted elders surely originated in antiquity. Yet the question is often asked, naively and aggressively, "How can 'creative writing' be taught?" Though it's taken for granted that young people in music, art, and drama work with instructors, it seems somehow unnatural that young writers may want to work with more experienced writers in workshop situations. Obviously, there's a common misconception of what happens in writing workshops.

Creative writing isn't "taught" in any conventional sense of that term. No instructor can assign inspiration. We can't assign the basic principle of artistic creation, which is a mysterious and utterly idiosyncratic amalgam of ideas, energy, imagination, "talent." Most instructors assign exemplary texts for the workshop participants to read and discuss, but we don't assign formal papers on these subjects. (For my part, I usually assign two stories each week, a classic and a contemporary paired for aesthetic reasons.) Many workshops don't give standard academic letter grades (A, B, etc.); courses may be ungraded, or Pass/Fail. The experience of a writing workshop is unique to its time, place, participants, instructor. A workshop will take its shape and tone from the individuals who comprise it, and yet is more than the mere sum of its parts. Obviously, more advanced workshops require little formal guidance from the instructor; writers come to workshops highly motivated and knowing what they want to write. They know their intentions, but they don't know how an intense attentive readership of other writers will respond to their work. Younger writers tend to benefit from assignments that are precise yet general enough to allow for the expression of individual imagination. (Typical assignments I give in my first-level fiction workshop involve experimenting with genre: writing dramatic monologues, miniature narratives, self-portraits by way of metaphor, journal entries to be transposed into fiction.) The workshop instructor is probably most helpful when he or she guides the young writer toward powerful but unconscious material that can be shaped into coherent fictions. But it isn't possible, or desirable, to "teach" creative writing any more than one might teach another person to dream.

The most pragmatic instruction one can give in a workshop isn't abstract or ideological but editorial. In my workshops, we proceed with the assumption that we're a gathering of dedicated, highly professional editors on a magazine or literary quarterly. We aren't editors who have the luxury of rejecting: We "accept" all the material that's submitted to us, and our task, as editors, is to provide editorial advice to the writer that will allow for significant revision. I ask my fellow editors: Did you like this story? Would you want to read more work by this writer? If not, why not? Beyond such impressionistic responses, which are essential for the writer to gauge his effectiveness, we critique the manuscript in editorial terms: Is the story too long, too short, too slowly paced, too sketchy; is its tone appropriate to its subject; is the opening the most strategic opening; is the ending the very best ending, both a surprise and yet inevitable; is this the most effective sequence of scenes, or might the story be more dramatically rearranged; are there scenes in earlier drafts that have been dropped out; are the characters fully realized, and are their names carefully chosen; does the story achieve closure; does the story read smoothly;

are there grammatical errors, awkward sentences, repetitions, confusing passages, metaphors that don't work, misspellings? Such a system of procedure is called line-editing, which is analogous to having one's work examined with a very fine toothed comb. It can be exhilarating, exhausting, invigorating, inspiring. The surprise of many workshops isn't that there are good writers in them, for we expect this, but that there are natural-born, instinctive editors. These are the individuals whose comments are most eagerly sought. They may or may not be the most gifted writers, but the ability to self-edit, like the ability to self-criticize, is inestimable for a writer. It's my intention to provide training for editors as well as writers in my workshops, and I would guess that other instructors of workshops have similar aims.

Since the inauguration of the Iowa Writers' Workshop at the University of Iowa in 1939, writing workshops have proliferated in this country and, after decades of resistance, have become popular in England as well. Writers as diverse as Flannery O'Connor, John Gardner, Ray Carver, Jay McInerney, Mona Simpson, Joanna Scott, Madison Smartt Bell, and Pinckney Benedict are graduates of workshop programs, and writers of the stature of Bernard Malamud, Kurt Vonnegut, John Cheever, E. L. Doctorow, Toni Morrison, Grace Paley, Russell Banks, Tobias Wolff, Edmund White, and Michael Cunningham, among numerous others, have taught such workshops. There are good reasons for this: Writing is a very lonely and obsessive activity, and one does write, after all, with the hope of being read. In the workshop, one is assured of an attentive and usually sympathetic audience; one sees one's readers, editors, reviewers, critics face-to-face, and the solitary, obsessive activity may become demystified to a degree. (In my workshops, criticism is exclusively constructive. No cruelty or backbiting in the guise of "honesty." Enough of that will await the writer in the world beyond the workshop.) A workshop can be a dramatic and intellectually stirring arena for the exchange of ideas otherwise lost. There is no atmosphere quite so intense as a writing workshop when discussion is free-flowing, imaginative, and responsible, and when the work being critiqued is meritorious.

Henry James famously spoke of the "madness of art" and of the writer possessed by his writing, as by a dream, but we should remember that James was an exacting, professional writer with a keen awareness of the literary marketplace, even when he couldn't quite manage to satisfy its commercial demands; like his predecessor Edgar Allan Poe, who was a magazine editor and a reviewer as well as a writer, James saw himself as both an artist and a craftsman. Ultimately, it's probably true that a certain "madness" fuels art, and compels us to write in the face of possible, even probable, discouragement and hostility, and yet more immediately we can focus upon writing as a craft and a discipline; we can celebrate the amorphous literary world as a living culture comprised of individuals not very different from ourselves. The emerging writers of *Best New American Voices 2003* are a testament to the ongoing vitality, imagination, and richness of that culture.

BEST NEW AMERICAN VOICES 2003

CHERYL STRAYED

Syracuse University

GOOD

I.

In the end, my mother still knew a few things. She knew, for example, that telephones existed, that they had been a part of the world that she had been a part of. She yelled, "Answer the phone! Please stop the phone from ringing!" and then she sobbed and sobbed and asked why I was torturing her until she coughed and coughed and lost her breath and then gasped madly for it. (The phone was not ringing, but I put it in a drawer anyway.) She knew what an enchilada was. She demanded that one be gotten for her and heated up in the imaginary oven near her hospital bed. Given this, it would not be too much to suppose that she was aware of Mexican cuisine altogether. Likewise the existence of Mexico. Of Mexican people. Of *people*, though she did not, in the end, acknowledge them. She knew about cats and dogs and horses and believed them to be in the room with her. She hollered, "Don't sit on the bed or you'll squish Mister

Carpaccio!" She knew that there was rain, especially raindrops. She sang a song that featured them and waved her fingers to the melody. On the very last day she panted, "What! What!"

"What? What?" I asked, begged.

"Oh," my mother said and moaned. She swung her head mournfully in my direction. She opened her eyes: blue, beloved, uncomprehending as a buzzard's. "Now there you go again," she said. "Always interrupting me."

Before this, a couple of weeks before this, when she'd first been admitted to the hospital, she knew everything. She said, "For heaven's sake, open the curtains." She declared, "I'm not using any damn bedpan. I don't care. I'll die first! I still have my dignity, you know." How little she knew.

She slept. She woke. She tried to eat. She couldn't eat.

The radiation treatments had started decomposing her stomach and she vomited pieces of it up into a yellow pan that was clipped to the railing on the side of her bed. I had a lollipop from the health food store that was made of honey and ginger. I encouraged my mother to have a lick. She held it, shaking, brought it slowly to her mouth.

"Maybe this will make me feel better," she said. Large blisters had formed on her lips—burned by the acid of her stomach. "Ginger is what you should have when you're pregnant, by the way. It's a natural cure for nausea."

"I know," I said. "You told me." I stroked the top of her head. Her hair—she had hair—was sharp and dry like the weeds that grow flat along the cracks in rocks.

"Oh," she moaned. "Don't touch me. It hurts. Everything hurts. You wouldn't believe the pain." She closed her eyes; held the lollipop. "Let's sit and not say anything. That's what I want more than anything. Let's just be together and rest."

I was twenty-one, my mother forty. It was cancer, but not the way we'd imagined it would be. Adenocarcinoma stage four.

Everything went very quickly, but it took a dreadfully long time.

2.

There was a place called the Family Room where I went when I needed a break. Inanimate objects were everywhere you looked: a pair of plastic ficus trees in pots of jagged white rocks, seven pink paper butterflies taped to the window, a basket of nonelectronic handheld games. I rummaged through the basket and became obsessed with one in particular—a tray of inextricable cubes with letters. Everything you spelled had to be four letters long: *wand, toss, pond, burn, bask, wick, piss, fish.* And so it went.

On the wall of the Family Room, someone had painted a giant rainbow, and at the end of it, a pot of gold and a fat elf doing a jig. There was also an itchy orange couch, a refrigerator, a microwave oven with a bulletin board hanging above it, a coffeepot, and a water dispenser with one spout that was hot, the other cold.

I drank tea from a pointed paper cup and read the bulletin board. There were signs advertising groups for people with AIDS, with chronic fatigue; for parents of premature babies or twins; for drug addicts and anorexics. I read those signs each day as if I'd never read them before. I stood perfectly still and erect and I was acutely aware of my stillness, erectness. Grief had suddenly, inexplicably, improved my posture. It had also, more understandably, made me thin. These things combined to give me the sensation that I, too, had become an inanimate object. Something brittle, like the branch of a tree or a broomstick.

Usually I had the place all to myself. One day a man walked in. "Hello," he said, "I'm Bill Ristow."

"I'm Claire. Claire Wood." I shook his hand and held on to my empty paper cup, which was pliant and soft and wet as the petal of a lily.

Bill's eyes were hazel, sunken. He scratched his head with a pinkie finger. "My wife's in four-ninety. She's got cancer," he said. "Are you new here?"

"Kind of," I said. "My mom, she's been here a week. We didn't know anything. She had this bad cold and then all of a sudden it was cancer everywhere." I looked up at him, smiled, stopped smiling, went on. "Like three weeks ago they found it. And now the doctors say there's nothing they can do." I stared at the absurd green bumpers on the toes of my tennis shoes. I didn't know what I would or would not say. I didn't feel like I would cry. I had no control over either.

"Christ," he said and jingled the coins in his pocket. He was making coffee. The water fell one drop at a time into the pot. "Well, kiddo," he said, "I hate to say it but in a way you're lucky. It's no vacation to drag it on. Nance and I—we've been doing the cancer thing for six years."

He was older, but not old—my mother's age. I thought he might have been a wrestler in high school. His body was dense and wide, like a certain kind of boulder; his face, too—primitive. He wasn't good-looking, he wasn't bad looking. He took a mug that said WYOMING! from the cupboard and another one with a chain of vegetables holding hands and filled them both with coffee. He handed me WYOMING! without asking if I wanted it.

"You and me have a lot in common," he said.

I didn't say anything. I cradled the coffee in both of my hands. I didn't drink coffee, I didn't like coffee; but I held it anyway. With pleasure.

3.

"I was thinking about the time that I locked myself in the bathroom," my mother said.

"What time?" I sat with my knees pulled tightly up to my chest in the wide bay of the windowsill in her hospital room.

"You remember the time."

"I don't remember any time."

"I was furious with you. You were about six. I don't remember what you did. Probably a combination of many small things." She paused, looked over at me. Her beauty, even then, was like a Chinese lantern hanging in an oak tree. "It was just after I'd finally left your father. Anyway. Nobody tells you how it will be. I was so furious that I wanted to hurt you. I mean *do you physical harm*. Well I didn't *really*, and I wouldn't have, but right then and there I felt *capable* of it. They don't tell you that when you become a mother—and nobody talks about it—but everyone has their breaking point, even with children. *Especially* with children." She laughed softly. "So. I went and shut myself in the bathroom to calm down."

"That was probably good," I said passively.

"Oh, were you ever mad! Just seething. You couldn't bear that I wouldn't let you in. You hurled your body against the door with all your might. I thought you were going to hurt yourself. I thought you would break a bone. I had to come out so you wouldn't."

I hopped down from the window and went and stood at the foot of her bed and rubbed the tops of her feet. It was the only place I could get at freely, without the tangle of tubes and plastic bags of fluid and tall carts holding the machines that sat near her head.

We were quiet then. My mother fell asleep and I watched her face for signs of relief, which did not come. She held an expression of permanent tension and I could not discern if this was a new thing, or if it had been there all along, masked by the ordinary light of real life. Her chin hung slack, making the flesh beneath it baggy, but her mouth was strangely alert, puckered, and faintly streaked with vomit. I thought of the commercials of starving African children, the flies gathering at the corners of their eyes, the kids too weak to swat them away. How unbearable it was to see that, more so than anything else, more than all the other things, which were so much worse.

I got a T-shirt from my mother's duffel bag, wetted it with warm water, and wiped her face.

"Thank you, honey." She opened her eyes. In slow increments, she turned her head to face the window.

4.

The next day Bill Ristow and I walked to a place called the Lakeshore Lounge, a few blocks from the hospital. The bar was dark, windowless, lit with yellow lightbulbs and Budweiser signs. It was noon. We ordered vodka and grapefruit juice and sat in a booth. The only other person in the place was the bartender, an old lady with painted-on eyebrows who sat on a stool and watched television.

Bill told me that he grew up in Fargo and joined the army and went to Vietnam. He'd married his high school sweetheart, a woman named Janet, before he went overseas and by the time he'd returned Janet had a tattoo of a fire-breathing dragon on her ass and was running around with a man called Turner, who was the leader of a Manitoba motorcycle gang.

"Such is life," he said sipping from his drink. It meant something to him that we had the same kind of drink. He'd ordered a vodka and grapefruit to be polite. Initially, he'd asked for a beer. "Let me ask you this," he said. "You got a tattoo?"

I shook my head. He rolled up his sleeve and showed me the inside of his forearm: a cougar, ready to pounce.

"Take my advice and don't. It's a bad idea, especially for women."

"I've thought about it. Maybe a chain of daisies."

"Anyways," he said, "after all that with Janet, I took my broken heart to Alaska to work in a salmon cannery. Now that's good money. That's where I met Nancy. She worked there, too, but that's not where we got together. No, that was about five years later when I moved to Duluth to take a job—I schedule the ships that come in and out of the harbor—and I had never forgotten about Nancy, you know, I met her and never forgot her. Don't ask me why. And I knew that she was from here, so I thought why the heck not call her up? The rest, as they say, is history."

He asked where I lived, who my family was, whether I like the Minnesota winters or not, and if I'd ever been to Florida. He wanted to know what my favorite movie was, if I believed that life existed on other planets, if I ever wanted children.

"We were planning on kids, but then boom—Nancy has cancer." He looked around the room. There was a row of video games across from us repeating a display of wrecking balls and exploding rockets, automobile crashes and little hooded men wielding axes. "It's so nice to talk to you," he said.

"Yeah."

"There aren't many people you can talk to. People in this situation, so to speak."

"No."

"Nobody wants to hear it. Oh sure, they wanna know what they can do for you and so forth. That's nice. But no one really wants to hear about it."

"No," I said. I was sitting on my hands. I rocked forward every few moments to sip from my straw. A woman with a rash on her face came into the bar with a bucket of flowers and asked if we would buy some and we said no, but then Bill called her back and bought a bouquet after all: red carnations with a tassel of leaves and baby's breath. He set them beside him on the seat.

"I know exactly what you mean," I said. People had carved messages and names into the table. *Tammy Z,* it said in front of me, *cunt.*

"You go to bars much?"

"Actually, I just turned twenty-one."

"No kidding," he said and fished an ice cube out of his glass and tossed it in his mouth. "You seem older. I'd have guessed twenty-five. You strike me as a sophisticated lady. You've got a way that's grown-up."

He had a small, firm belly and a thick bush of graying hair on his head. The same tufts of this hair sprang from his eyebrows and nostrils and the backs of his hands. His ears were red and burly and stuck out like small wings. He reminded me, not unkindly, of a baby elephant, in a lordly, farcical way. He was the kind of man that other men did not know well enough to be threatened by sexually.

I crossed my legs. I rattled my ice. "We should be getting back."

"Well, it was nice to get away. Everyone's got a right to that from time to time." He raked his hands through his hair as if he were just waking from a nap. I was acutely aware of his body across the table, of my own pressing luxuriously back into the ripped-up vinyl.

He looked at me. He set his hands on the table and knocked on it with his knuckles. I reached out and put my hands lightly on top of his. He stayed still for a moment, then turned his hands over and laced his fingers into mine.

"Shall we?" he said after a while.

"Yes," I said in a nondescript foreign accent. "We shall."

5.

Bill's house was white on the outside and cloistered among a thicket of pines. It sat a few steps down from the sidewalk, but above everything else—the buildings of downtown Duluth, the lake. I could see the roof of the hospital far off. It was freezing. I was shaking, but impervious to the cold.

"The snow is sparkling like diamonds," I said, idiotically.

"Diamonds?" Bill smiled at me curiously.

"Yes. I mean the ice crystals. They're sparkling," I said and blushed. "I like the word *sparkle,* don't you? It's one of my favorite words."

"I can see what you mean. It has a ring," he said, guiding me onto his porch.

I wanted to take my clothes off as soon as possible, so I would stop being nervous.

Bill took me on a tour, as if he'd forgotten why I'd come. My boots echoed loudly wherever I went until I finally took them off and carried them around with me. He showed me the cabinets that he'd built, the place where there had once been a wall that he and Nancy had knocked down to let more light into the dining room, the hardwood floors they'd redone themselves. I oohed. I aahed. Every room was painted a different color, but none of the colors clashed. A cast-iron woodstove stood sentinel in the corner, unlit, with a small glass pane in the door and a gleaming silver handle. It looked like a person, as decorative woodstoves often do. A jolly old maid or Benjamin Franklin.

In the bathroom there was a bowl of stiff rose petals on a narrow shelf and a photograph of Bill and Nancy—both of them completely bald—with their heads tilted toward one another. I washed my hands and face with a bar of green soap that smelled like aftershave and then went into the living room.

"You like Leo Kottke?" he asked, holding a record, blowing on it, putting it on the turntable. "I thought we'd have some music. I've got all kinds of music. Country, rock, classical, bluegrass, jazz. You name it."

"Me, too. I mean that's what I like. All kinds." The skin of my face was tight from the soap. I sat down on a blue couch and instantly stood up again. "So come here," I said, smiling like a maniac.

He took my hair by the ends and pressed it to his nose and smelled it. He wound it around his fingers, pulling me toward him, to kiss me. His mouth was cool and shaking and strange, but nice. Nicer than anything. I shoved my hands into the back pockets of his jeans and felt his ass. "I'm glad I met you," he said.

"Me, too," I said. "Take this off," I said impishly, tugging at his shirt. He gathered both of my wrists in his hands and pulled me into his bedroom. The walls were the same color as the comforter on his bed: amber, with an edge of smoke.

"Now," he said, unbuttoning my shirt. We laughed awkwardly, pawed at each other. He bent down and kissed my breasts, bit my nipples tenderly. We teetered, finally, onto his bed.

"Do you have a condom?"

"No."

It seemed impossible that I would get pregnant. Nothing could take root. I knew it, he knew it. It didn't make any sense to think this, but we were right.

I watched his face while we fucked. It was haggard and tense, as if he were concentrating on something either very far or very near, as if he were attempting to remove a splinter or thread a needle or telepathically shatter a glass in France. He saw me watching him and then his face became animated again, wide-eyed and carnivorous.

"That was nice," he said afterward. We were lying on our backs on his bed. A mobile of fat chefs dangled above our feet. Over our heads was a birdcage without a bird. He turned on his side and placed his palm delicately on my stomach. He found my birthmark and petted it and outlined it with his finger as if he'd known me all of my life.

"Was that weird for you?" I asked.

"I wouldn't say that," he said.

"How do you feel then?"

"Like a million bucks," he said, then stood up, jerked his jeans on.

6.

"There's a lady down the hall who's a high school teacher," I said to my mother, even though it appeared that she was sleeping. I went to the window and stared out onto the street below: snow, cars, a slice of the lake. A long silence, and then my mother's low voice.

"What's her name?"

"Nancy Ristow."

"Is she a visitor or a resident?" She smiled, a small glorious smile.

"Resident. She's a history teacher."

My mother kept her eyes closed and we were silent for a long while. Then she said, "Ask her what she thinks happened to Amelia Earhart."

"Why?" I snapped.

"Well, you said she teaches history, right? History interests me. I'd be curious to know what her theories are. She might have a theory since she's in the know. I always liked Amelia Earhart." She opened her eyes and tried to push herself up to a sitting position against the pillows, the tubes swaying around her. "I think of her going off like that. Can you imagine? I mean, *can you imagine?* Having no idea what would happen? Imagine how brave she was. She was one of my personal heroes."

"Is," I said.

"What?"

"Is. She *is* one of your personal heroes."

"Well, yes," she said. "Is." My mother sat looking carefully at me. "Where have you been?"

"Nowhere. You were sleeping. I walked around."

She continued to look at me. Pale. Drained. Regal.

"*What?*"

"You've been somewhere."

"I *told* you."

"You're different."

7.

My affair with Bill lasted only four days, but we had a ritual nonetheless. After sex we dressed and drank warm apple cider and ate toast with peanut butter in the kitchen before we went back to the hospital. We told each other stories about the lovers we'd had. My list was short, but interesting and multiethnic and it also included a man who was surely gay. Bill got a kick out of this. He told me about losing his virginity with Janet in a closet where his mother stored cleaning supplies; Vietnamese prostitutes; a series of alcoholics in Alaska; and then Nancy. They went to Puerto Rico for their tenth wedding anniversary. They'd lolled in bed and made love and ate a bag of plums they'd bought on the street. In jest, Bill put one of these plums into Nancy's vagina and it sucked itself up inside of her and they couldn't get it out.

"Well, it came out eventually," he said, laughing, rubbing his face, laughing again, laughing so hard that his eyes filled with tears. I sat with him and smiled. I nibbled my toast. "Now there's something," he said, finally getting a hold of himself, wiping his tears away, "there's something you don't do twice."

8.

I caught glimpses of Nancy as I passed by her room. She had a position she liked: on her side, her thin hip a tiny triangle, her blond frizzy hair matted into a flat nest at the back of her head. Besides my mother and Nancy there were the old people. Old old. They were so old that no one knew them anymore, or, if anyone did, they came to visit only on Sundays. As I passed their rooms, I came to know them the way one knows the houses along a familiar street: the lady with a hole in her throat, the endlessly sleeping bald woman, the thrashing man tied to his bed, the other man who beckoned and yelled, "Jeanie! Jeanie!" when he saw me walk past until, finally, one day I stopped.

"Jeanie?" he said.

"Yes," I said. I stayed in the hallway, peering into his open door.

"Jeanie," he said.

"Yes."

"Jeanie."

"Yes," I said. I twisted my hands into the wrists of my sweater.

"You ain't Jeanie," he said at last, gently, as if he were sorry to hurt my feelings. "I know my Jeanie and you ain't her."

How impossible it is to hoodwink the nearly dead.

Often, I saw their private parts. Gaping and grappling among the sheets, musty and chafed, dimly shimmering like the rinds of hard fruit. I didn't care; they didn't care. Who cared? Nobody.

I never saw Nancy's, but I imagined it, that plum. Purple, red, and black; sweet, soft, and bruised. Held warm inside her, as if it were still there: a thing she would not release.

9.

Then she died, Nancy. I saw Bill in the Family Room the next morning, emptying his part of the refrigerator, clutching a paper bag.

"Hey," he said dreamily.

I shut the door behind me and locked it. I hugged him and the paper bag. He patted my back with his free hand. I'm sorry. I'm so sorry, I kept saying to him.

"It isn't what I expected," he said.

"What did you expect?"

He set the bag on the floor. "I'm not taking these. They're those frozen dinners. You can have them if you want."

"Okay," I said gravely. His face was pale and puffy. He smelled like worn-out peppermint gum and french fries. I hugged him again and cupped my hand around the back of his neck and he pressed into it the way a baby who can't hold his head up does.

"Look," he said almost inaudibly. "I feel that I should apologize."

"For what?" I let go of him.

"For what's gone on with you and me."

"There's nothing to be sorry about."

"I feel that I behaved badly," he said.

"No," I said.

"I didn't want to leave the room. They took her—her body—out after a couple of hours. People came to see her, to say good-bye. Her folks, her brothers, a couple of her best friends and then they took her away and I just didn't wanna leave, you know, the room."

"That's understandable," I said. I was holding myself, my arms crisscrossed around my waist. "I can see wanting that."

He sobbed. He made small whimpering noises, and then he found a rhythm and his cries softened. I rubbed his shoulders. He went to the sink and leaned deeply into it and rinsed his face and then dried it with a paper towel. He took several deep breaths. "Anyways, you know something? I never cheated on Nancy up until now. That's the truth. Maybe you don't know that, but thirteen years plus and I never cheated. I almost did once or twice, but I never followed through. That's normal human temptation. That can happen in any marriage. But I didn't do it. I honored the vows." His voice quavered and he took more deep breaths. "The vows meant something to me once upon a time." He paused. "And don't get me wrong. None of this is your fault. I hold you responsible not one iota. You're a beautiful girl. A top-notch young lady. I was the one married. It has nothing to do with you."

The bag of frozen dinners shifted without either of us touching it.

"It didn't take anything away from what you had with Nancy," I said. "I never thought that."

"No. Definitely not. My allegiance was always with her. No offense, Claire. I think you're wonderful. I mean, you are one very, very pretty girl. And smart, too. Kind." He clutched the edge of the counter with one hand. "And what am I when Nancy needs me the most? I'm a pathetic old man."

"You aren't old."

"No. Not old, but to you I am. I'm too old for you. I lost my morals."

I stared at the floor. A spoon had fallen there, crusted with hair and what looked like bits of chocolate pudding.

"Plus, what was I doing gallivanting around and meanwhile she's dying?"

"She was sleeping. She probably didn't even know you were gone."

"Oh, she *knew*. She *knew*." He put his hand on his forehead and pressed hard.

"We weren't gallivanting anywhere. We were at your house," I said softly. He stayed with his hand pressed to his forehead. I bent to pick up the dirty spoon and set it silently in the sink. It seemed the least I could do.

"Well," he said after a while. "I wish you the best. I'm hoping for a miracle for your mother."

"Thank you." I patted his hand on the counter and we looked at each other, serious as animals. He took my hand and kissed it and then pulled me into him and held me hard against him. His breathing was heavy and I thought he had started to cry again but when I looked at him, I saw that his eyes were calm and dry.

"Claire," he said, but didn't say anything more. His fingers began to slowly graze my throat, down over the top of my chest, over my breasts, barely touching me. Suddenly he grabbed my face with both of his hands and kissed me fiercely and then stopped kissing me just as quickly. "What am I doing?" he asked sadly. He pulled me to him and squeezed my ass, hips, thighs.

"Stop it then," I said. I unbuckled his belt, unzipped his jeans. I got down on my knees.

"This is completely wrong."

"Stop me then," I hissed. I took his cock in my mouth. I had the sensation that he was going to hit me; that he was going to smack the side of my head or yank me away by the hair. I also had the sensation that I wanted him to do it. I had never wanted a man to do this, but I wanted it then so that something would be clear, right, and that he would be the one to make it that way.

"Jesus," he whispered. He leaned against the wall and held on to it to keep himself up. I smelled his man smells, his cock smells: a sour salt, a sharp subaqueous mud. He came without a word and I swallowed and then sat back on my heels. I touched the hairs on his thighs, kissed one knee.

He reached for the sides of my face. "Oh," he moaned, "I can't stand up."

10.

"Something about you sitting in the window reminds me of when you were little," my mother said. "Sometimes I see your face and I can see just exactly what you looked like when you were a baby and other times I can see what you'll look like when you're old. Do you know what I mean? Does the same thing happen to you?"

"Yeah, I know what you mean." I pushed myself off the windowsill and pulled a chair up next to her, coiling my way through the IV lines.

"Yes," she said. "Come sit next to me." Her words were slurred from the morphine. Tomorrow she would become delusional. In three days she'd be dead. "That's what I'm glad of. That you're here with me. I'll never forget that you were here with me. And sitting the way you were, in the window, it made me think of that, of all the things, of you being little and everything and now being grown-up."

"Do you feel better?" I asked. "You slept for a long time. You slept for twelve hours straight."

"It was the same way as when you used to sit in that window in Pennsylvania. Do you remember the window seat in the apartment when we lived in Pennsylvania? Oh, you were too small then. You wouldn't remember. That was your spot. You liked to sit there and wait for the mail to come."

She paused. I thought she would have to vomit, but she didn't.

"You liked to see the mailman come and put the mail in the box and then you wanted to be the one to go and take it out."

"I don't remember." I leaned forward and rested my head on the bed. I would not be with my mother at the moment of her death. She would wait to die until she was all alone in her room and this would kill me. It would kill me for a long time.

"That's how you were," she said happily. "It's how you are."

"How's that?" I asked.

"The way I taught you to be. Good."

She lifted her hand from the bed. Softly, she stroked my hair.

ESI EDUGYAN

Johns Hopkins University

THE WOMAN WHO TASTED OF ROSE OIL

On the third day she came back. Lurching through the darkness, Philomena stubbed her knees against the room's veiled clutter, hissing *glory* with each new pain. Riled and sluggish, she tried to avenge these slights by wanly kicking what had had the gall to kick her first. When her knees finally met the bed frame, she sank gravely onto it and discovered that the mattress under her wasn't the one on which she'd passed thirty-four steady years of matrimonial slumber.

She ran a shaky hand along the flank. The once ripped strings were now tight as sutures. Philomena calmly drew back her hand and turned to glare at the black heap of her husband's form beside her on the bed. Over the years Francis had acquired the animal habit of burrowing; the yellow blanket he'd yanked over his face fluttered as he argued in his sleep. The end of his muttering was always punctuated by a sharp grunt, as if he'd declared he'd say no more. Philomena had once been charmed by his nighttime sermons, used to tuck a limp pillow under her armpit and watch as he shuddered and groused, wondering what strange affliction could so take hold of a grown man that he'd prattle on, hopelessly pained, even in his sleep. Over the years the ritual became less tasteful, and looking on him now made Philomena weary. She pursed her lips and, fully clothed, swung her heft onto the bed, lining up her ample hips against his thinner ones. Francis suckled his hollow cheeks, his teeth sitting on the nightstand, and curtly turned on his side as if to spite her.

Philomena stared briefly at the crown of her husband's head, then sat up to struggle from her clothes. Francis slept still as a pane of glass beside her. Philomena was wearing one of her best dresses, an august-looking thing of crushed lilac and frills, and as she fought it over her head she was struck by how parched her skin felt. Her joints were stiff; at fifty-nine there was nothing new in this. But her skin itself had always been pert—their neighbor, Joan Majors, often said, *My god, you've got the skin of a six-year-old. Taut as apples.* The sheets were cool, and Philomena rolled to cup her husband's body with her own. Sensing the motion, Francis rocked toward her, his face at a crisp distance, and in turning cut her knee with a sharp toenail.

"Glory," she muttered under her breath. She'd begun to back away tail first from Francis when he stung her again with a deft kick. "For the love of God, Frank," she said, "you could skin a deer with those toenails. Cut them."

Francis stiffened, the blanket falling calm against his ear. Then, as if he himself had been kicked, he drew his thin body up in bed and, thumbing the sleep from his one good eye, said, "Phila, that you?" His speech was muddy; he groped for his glass of teeth on the nightstand.

"Well, who else?" she said. "Or were you ex*pec*ting someone else?"

"I'm dreaming," he said. "I'm dreaming."

"Dreaming about a brawl, most probably. Do you have to act it out, too? I already killed myself on that stuff you got lined up by the window. Don't need to be clawed to death in my sleep, too, thank you kindly and good night."

"Phila..." Francis made an audible hesitation, then doubtfully reached out to touch her. He wheezed as he clasped her broad arm, and the way his fingers flinched gave Philomena the sensation of being tainted goods. "No," said Francis.

"Francis Enyia Torto, if you don't stop prodding me like—"

"You're gone, Philomena. You've been gone these three weeks, at least."

"Three days, maybe—play fair. Nancy decided she needed me with the kids after all, remember? I walked on up after supper, on *Fri*day. It's *Sun*day. And I'm back to find you in bed early, you sloth. Even left the dishes for me. Sth."

"I'm dreaming." Francis rose from the bed, joints cracking. His movements were strained as he slogged through the clutter to get the lights.

"Oh, Frank, no lights, please. You'll ruin any chance at sleep we have left."

"I won't sleep now." Francis struck the switch and the room flared. All of the brooding objects, so brash and ill-mannered in the dark, seemed to cower when unveiled: the oak writing desk footing the window, the boxes beside it, the pestering clock that still hung above their bed despite the whimsical time it kept.

"It's you," said Francis, baffled. "Philomena."

Philomena rose slowly on her side, planting her fist into the mattress for support. "Frank. Sleep. *Please*." No sooner had she spoken than a firm glow took her husband's eyes, a look so sage and odd it made Philomena rise entirely from the bed, her dark feet falling to the carpet as she modestly gathered her dress to her body.

"What is it, Francis?" she said. "Has something happened?"

Francis was still pinching the light switch, his unsteady fingers making the room flicker a little. Finally, he shuffled a few steps from the wall and in a nervous gesture ran his palms over his snow-flecked Afro. The room was dense with the scent of roses.

"Come here, Phila. I want to see you." Her red dressing gown hung on a nail slanted through the white wooden door, and as he reached for it the door drifted ajar. Peeking into the hall with the pained expectation of these last few weeks, Francis yanked down the robe and held it out to her. "Here, Phila. Come."

"What happened?" she said.

Philomena had always been slow to daunt and even slower to please. Yet her black eyes had taken on a tension Francis was anxious to quiet. "All's fine, Phila. Now come get this robe and we'll set down a pot of tea." He was bewildered at the control in his voice.

Francis watched his wife carefully flatten her gown on the bed and rise with a grace that was half her age. Her lucid brown skin was still alert, if not a little dry. She'd been a stout woman all her life, but lithe in the waist and joints, the way, thought Francis, God should have made all women. When she took the robe from his hands, he started. Her flesh was peppered with musk, with rose oil. Pausing, he pressed her gently in the small of her back.

"You lead," he said.

The kitchen, the sloppiest room in the house, and so rife to cue argument, was a dim yellow by the light of the range. She must have turned it on when she'd come in. A swarm of half-washed dishes clotted the sink and cut awkwardly through the greasy suds. Francis had shoved the tap aside, and its measured drip resounded like someone drumming his knuckles on steel. Above the fridge's steady buzz, the smug whine of a fly could be heard. Drunk on the waste most probably, thought Francis, and he shed a regretful look at Philomena. It was shameful that after so many weeks away from the solace of her kitchen, his wife should return to this. He didn't have to see her to read the grim line her lips made. But she held her rebuke and cautiously sat at the low table facing the window, her back to the clutter.

Francis hastened to push in her chair. "You comfortable? Cold? Let me get the heat." There was an awe in his voice he couldn't suppress. Francis shuffled to the windowmost corner, a sudden pain in his hip. He rubbed at the nagging pinch through his pajamas. Winded, he placed his palms on the ribs of the water heater before leaning to turn it open.

"Your hip bothering you?" said Philomena, that bland harassing quality back in her voice, as though it caused her great strain not to nag him. And it was as if, after all these years, her aggressions were finally made clear to her, for she coughed benignly and chanced a tactful smile. "Has Dr. Pfeffer's Elexadrine kicked in yet?"

"Some," said Francis as he troubled the knob, "but you know how it is."

"But don't I," Philomena laughed. "I'm five minutes away from calling Nancy's witch doctor. Five seconds." Francis shot her the same odd look she'd gotten in the bedroom, and Philomena quickly dropped her eyes. There was a smattering of papers fanned out across the table, and Philomena rifled through them. She pulled one out and, glancing absently at it, said, "And what are these—bills? Don't tell me you've spent our life savings on another car. Don't tell me you bought something besides the new mattress." Now I've got him, she thought. Let him explain that one.

Francis paused at the heater, tapping a rung to test the heat, then leaned briefly on it before coming to take a sensible seat across from her. His walk, deliberate and arthritic, was only outdone by the strain of sitting. Philomena flinched, then rose from her own chair.

"Sit down, Phila," he said gruffly. Then softer, "Please." She felt him studying her as he wriggled to catch the most restful position. "I can't believe it," he said. "My god."

"Oh, stop it, Frank, and tell me what's going on. You can't just sit there gawking and not tell me what's wrong. For god's sake . . . take a picture."

Francis heard his granddaughter in Philomena's last expression, and this realization brought on a wan smile. But the look on his wife's face made his own grow staid. "The mattress," he began, "I bought because I just, I couldn't, I *wouldn't* sleep on the old one. I . . ." Francis caught his wife's face. "After you'd gone, I couldn't do it."

Philomena was perplexed. "You couldn't call, at least?"

Francis leaned forward to grasp his wife's hands; they were cold and rough. "Philomena, you died. You've been dead for three weeks now."

Philomena smiled wryly and tilted her head. When her husband remained solemn, she pulled her hands from his. Of the many thoughtless things he'd said or done—the missed anniversaries and birthdays, the biting comments, those three secretive months he'd left the bed cold—this was the worst. Fundamentally, infinitely, the worst. She pressed a hand to her fine mass of hair, and, glaring at Francis, it was as though she could finally confirm the thing that had been troubling her these long years.

"Phila." Francis flexed his hand on the table. "Phila, you know it. You know."

Philomena glared at him.

Francis stretched across the table and mildly shook his head. He could see the pain in his wife's features, the terror, the anger there. A desert settled in his mouth. "Philomena," he said, "on God's word. On my mother's grave; on our parents' graves, bless their souls." He paused and cut his look to the table. "Philomena, I'm so sorry. I'm so sorry."

Francis watched a tremor unsettle his own hand and, in a lapse of detachment, wondered whether it was grief or age that had put it there. Looking up he caught Philomena watching it, too. Her face was blank, and by this Francis concluded she'd chosen not to believe him. Their marriage had nurtured a similar trend, and her look brought the hurt of it back on him tenfold. He took his hand from the table.

In the corner, the old heater ticked to life. Francis watched his wife's eyes stray to the left of his elbow. Her face broke.

"God." Philomena drew her legs up slightly and curled toward the doorway. "God." Her tears were fitful, and reminded him of his own from the days before. He kept to his seat. Philomena lowered her knees, traced a steady hand down her skirt. She sat upright in the chair and, coughing short into her fist, brought her wet eyes to rest on his. "How?" she said.

Francis folded his hands on the table. "You had a heart attack. Coronary thrombosis."

"No, how. Where was I?"

"You were on your way to Nancy's house. She waited till half past six, then called over here to see what was keeping you. I was out back working on the Alfa, so I didn't get the call." He paused, less from guilt than an acute need to get the details right. "Nancy started to walk over, and on her way she found you leaning on a tree. You were grabbing your left arm, complaining of pains, flashes, and such. Nancy didn't know how serious it was and walked you back to her place. Considering how advanced your case was, it was a miracle you could walk anywhere, Dr. Pfeffer said. But she sat you down and called that quack of a doctor she sees, Neuman, Neumer. Nancy insisted he made house calls, that's why she called him. Well, he came, anyway. At this point Nancy tried me again, but I was still out. Dr. Neumer looked you over, and it's angina, he says. You died at his back when he turned to leave. Nancy. Sth. *Pfeffer* is our doctor. Well, she called me again, and this time I was there because I'd come in for tea. Then I ran over and . . ." His voice drifted.

"Were the children there?"

"No," said Francis. "Nancy had the sense to get them to the neighbor's."

"Do they know?"

"Yes. There was a funeral."

Philomena's eyes grazed the room as she strained to recall even the briefest detail, the taste of a rose, something. Finally, she looked to Francis. "Was it nice?" she asked.

"Two hundred roses. As many people." Francis smiled. "One of the biggest gravestones in Alberta."

Philomena nodded, as though the whole of it seemed a sensible business to her. She was ruefully aware that, as in life, the onus to praise him sat like a goad at her back. She set her lips in a firm plum stripe and said, "Thank you."

"Oh, Phila, don't be like that. Not now."

Philomena glanced at the table. "Are these my papers?"

Francis licked at the flutter in his lips. "Some. Medical records, life insurance, your will. There's also the lawsuit papers for Dr. Neumer— I'm still trying to decide on that. Nancy and I are barely speaking on that point."

Philomena chuckled. "You're both so headstrong. In a battle of wills you'd both die trying to best the other." Her last words rattled her, and she clipped them short with a leaden smile. "Don't let this drag on for something that no longer matters. Take it from one who knows."

There was an open anguish in his nod, and Francis cleared his throat. "Well, we know which side she gets it from," he said, smiling tiredly.

"I'm just a start," Philomena said. "You've won Mr. Stubborn these thirty years running."

"Behind every principled man there's an even worse woman. Remember Joan Majors next door?"

Philomena made a sour face. "I suppose you're right on that account. Nearly ran that man into the ground, with her orders."

"No. I'm talking of how stubborn you were when it came to her laying out our bushes."

Philomena was at a loss to recall this. Francis arched his back in a prim imitation of his wife, and propping a hand at either side of his sharp hips, cried, "We express our full regret!"

"Our full regret—that's right! Well, Ms. Maudie's entire world would've come crashing down, all for a few inches of property. What'd she expect?"

Ms. Maudie was Francis's mother, a slight, spry woman of ninety-four whose last years had brought on the desire to cloak herself in the perfect sleep. It was the final and most lasting of her manias. On the call of nine o'clock she'd throw herself in bed with an agility that failed her other times of the day and, fixing her eyes on the stucco ceiling, would wait for sleep with a hard-worn patience that was almost Christian. Francis recalled how she'd place Nancy's stopwatch at the edge of her bed, timing each night and nap in a disquieting show of preciseness. Then she'd drop off like a stone. When she woke, she'd scramble for the watch to see if she'd met *Canadian Living*'s suggested lengths of time for catnaps and slumber. But since she could never remember exactly when she'd gone to bed, and the watch she'd set hadn't taken because she didn't know how to work it, she assumed herself successful, so that rising from sleep became a constant act of genius.

These were the things you could laugh about, Philomena said wryly. Then there were the times she'd steal all the money she could find in the house, once splitting Nancy's prized frog bank, and, clipping the bills to the ceiling fan with laundry pins, scream, "It's raining money!" when it all shot off. Followed by the time she'd attempted to slip her fist into the register at Moe's, so that she'd have more to rain down on her. Then there was the incident with Joan Majors and the hedges.

Joan had wanted to uproot the fat line of hedges that separated the properties. Francis had been mildly put off, but acquiesced. When Philomena emerged from a tense day in Nancy's room helping her sound out and translate her French readings, she found Ms. Maudie squatting with her face to the living room wall.

"Maudie, what's happened?" said Philomena.

Maudie didn't answer, but smiled to herself, lisping shyly under her breath.

Philomena tried again. "*Ms.* Maudie, what's wrong? Why you facing the wall?"

Ms. Maudie explained that because they were going to cut down the bush, she could no longer stray outdoors. "I'm sorry," she intoned, "but you're just going to have to find someone else to drive in the horses."

Philomena laughed (they were as far from owning horses as they were from the moon), but when she discerned the real fear in Ms. Maudie's words, a twin sense of anger and grief washed over her. She strode over to the Majors's, where she found Joan already on her knees tweezing at the more bullish branches.

"And now I recall," Philomena laughed, "that just the sight of her made me so mad, Frank, so mad on your mother's behalf. I always got the feeling she never liked Ms. Maudie, despite what she may have thought of the rest of us. I walked over to where she was bent over pruning, those fat legs squishing out of her shorts, and I was just going to give it to her." Francis had lost the pleasure of her voice these last weeks, and he closed his eyes. "So I strode over to her," continued Philomena, "but I was nervous, and somehow my head was swimming with Nancy's French translations and such"—and here

she laughed—"not that I'd picked up any French, just the stupid way
they phrased all the English, formal-like. So I walked up and told her
that it was our family's humblest, no, dearest wish she'd stop at once,
that we expressed our full regret, but that this whole scenario must
cease to continue, upon Ms. Maudie's orders. I didn't even let her
argue. Two weeks she gave me the blind eye. Two weeks."

"She hated you," said Francis.

"Didn't she. Well, she always said I was 'taut as apples.' Now she
knows."

"Amen." Francis laughed softly, then his eyes grew dim. "Have
you seen Ms. Maudie? Where you been."

Philomena frowned. "I'm just like Maudie now. No short-term
memory."

Francis nodded. "By god, when she was sharp, she was sharp,
though. Mind like a steel trap. Never a detail faltered. Do you remember when we met? I brought—"

"Kofi's party, San Francisco. The Americans put a man on the
moon. You walked in with Maudie on your arm and I thought you
were a gold digger."

"And I thought you were a schoolgirl. I pulled Kofi aside, I said
Kofi, who's that schoolgirl on the couch? And he gives me one good
look and says, Francis, for a Stanford scholar you're not very bright.
That's no schoolgirl, that's an accountant! An ac*coun*tant, he said. I
was bowled over, you looked all of twelve years old."

"I still do. The skin of a six-year-old. Taut as apples." Philomena
scratched at her forearm and a spray of flakes salted the air; after
hanging for a moment like motes of dust, they settled in a frost on
her thighs. "Glory," she breathed and bucked her chair out to wipe
the skim of ice from her knees. Her eyes were alive with panic and
wonder. Somehow she'd have to kill that fine conceit of believing
herself alive, that the bonds of reality, gravity, and feeling still had

some power on her. And what might have seemed a glorious freedom to another only distressed her. She glanced at Francis.

His one good eye was tuned sharply on his wife, though if even his boss (the most caustic and badgering of men) had strove to convince him of the sudden icy frost clinging to his wife, he'd still claim he'd seen nothing. Her return he could take, somehow, but not this. Blinking deeply, he said, "I forgot the tea. You must be cold, with this old heater." As he began his strained rise from the table, Philomena rose herself.

"I'll get it, Frank. Lord knows I haven't been a help in this kitchen for a while." Anything to kill the cold in her skin. She walked to the overgrown mess and shoved the clutter aside. Hoisting the rusted kettle under the tap, she was aware of how remote it felt in her hands, how odd and charged, like the shocks Nancy and Maudie used to sting her with after scuffing the living room carpet. They'd spent an awful winter, the four of them taking shelter from the ice storm that had emptied the town—a time when the line between family and burden had grown thin. Philomena set the kettle on the burner's rings.

Thirty-four years of marriage had paired their minds, and it was no great surprise when Francis said, "Can't winter get awful?" as his wife took her chair across from him. "Remember when we were all cooped up inside and the snow just kept coming down—oh, it was treacherous. Nancy and Maudie running us up the wall."

Philomena smiled. "Ms. Nancy Heronimous Cordelia-Lime Torto. I remember. After Maudie, who'd had another attack and just become *Ms.* Maudie."

"Ms. Maudie Felicia Torto, Esquire. Driving us nuts with their demands." Francis spared a laugh. "More than anything, they wanted to ride in the Alfa. It was a hell of a time explaining, no, it's a summer car."

"Well, you *had* just spent our savings on it."

The room quieted, and they listened to the sound of the kettle ticking as it warmed at Philomena's back.

"Well," said Francis. He wouldn't go that road with her. Not today. "A horrible winter," he said. "And I think that was the time Nancy stopped doing her homework. Yes. And we got a call—"

"The call from Mr. Meyers, the guidance counselor." Philomena leaned back and chinned toward her husband. "And you were out that night, so I answered. And he says to me, he says, 'We at Aster Middle School mean to offer our sincere condolences for your family's tragedy.'"

Philomena had been baffled. "This is the *Torto* residence," she said.

"Yes, Mrs. Torto. We're all extremely sorry, and very concerned on Nancy's behalf."

Philomena touched a hand to her throat. "Something happened to Nancy?"

The line's static had thickened, as though the man were passing the phone to a fresh ear. "The elder Mrs. Torto has passed away, that's right?"

"Ms. Mau—Nancy's grandmother?"

"And for such a thing to have happened right in the house—"

"Ms. Torto is fine." Philomena couldn't pare the dry astonishment from her voice. "What on earth did Nancy tell you?"

The man had cleared his throat, rightly stunned. "Why, she told us her grandmother had been murdered in your guest room."

Francis slapped his palm on the table and laughed. "Can you imagine it? And he bought every word the child said. My god."

Philomena shook her head. "You had to wonder who he thought we were. Maudie being murdered in her sleep. What was Nancy thinking?"

"Nancy's judgment never was too keen," said Francis dourly. "Well, Maudie passed on soon enough after that anyway. But we knew it was coming."

The kettle began to lisp slightly. Francis glanced at his wife, then turned to watch the gloom lifting at the window. He had the sense his wife's eyes strayed this way, too. The spring of Maudie's death had been a trying time. The air was limp, the ground still hard with a stubborn frost; it was as though even the weather conspired to keep things harsh. Philomena had just sold Francis's Alfa Romeo, and their speech was minimal. Nancy had long ago refused to be the go-between. Ms. Maudie was fighting out the last of her cancer. The old Ford then quietly died, and because of the lack of transportation, it was necessary to climb the steep hill in a raw breeze to reach Aster General, rather than confound a sleeping neighbor to take you there. People became accustomed to dozing at rare hours of the day, such was the air of darkness that hung over the old town. Francis and Philomena went separately, and he knew that she wondered if he even went at all. And it's true, it had been difficult for him, sitting at the bedside of the woman who'd borne him and now had to inquire at each visit who he was. But he went, and after he'd gone he found he couldn't go home. His office became a round-the-clock refuge, a place where his way of grieving met no scrutiny because none of them knew. Except Anne. In the dimness of those gray months, when Francis was starved for cars and the company of others, Anne had helped him pick out new colors. Autumn Red. Cerulean. Chrome Moon.

Then Maudie had died and he'd sobered. Six o'clock found him sitting behind one of Philomena's hot meals one day, and he followed this life for an unsteady but decisive five months. Finally, when he spoke of his plans to buy back the Alfa on installment, her reaction (which he'd feared with the ire only a husband knows) was the first return to simpler times. She'd held her tongue and motioned him to bed, cupping his body with her own. He hadn't known how to thank her.

Francis turned from the window to his wife. There was a shade of purpose in her eyes.

"That spring was a terrible time, at Maudie's end," she said. She fixed him in the eyes. "But we couldn't all be blessed with your charms. Had I your charms, you can only bet that I, too, would have taken my nights elsewhere."

The room went leaden for a minute, then the silence was split by the thin cry of the kettle.

Francis struggled from his chair and limped to the stove to cut the heat. Behind her, Philomena could hear him filling two mugs. The dull hiss as two tea bags hit the scalding water. She heard the hollow scrape of the sugar pot, then the sound of his fallen hem as it grazed the linoleum. He placed her favorite blue mug in front of her.

Philomena ran a finger along the mug's rim, then brought it to her lips.

"Cinnamon?" she asked. Across from her, Francis nodded. Philomena cleared her throat, brooding on her mug. But what was the use of it, though. Tiredly, she placed her steaming tea on the table. "And how's the car running?" she asked.

Francis glanced at his wife's hands. "Alright. It's been out in the drive too long without a cover, though. So much has rusted out."

The banter between them came easily, diced as it was with the envy of better days gone. Francis laughed as she retold the story of Ms. Maudie's murder, the drama of Joan Majors and the bushes, and Francis told one of his own, from the years before San Francisco. His father had been a diplomat, and Francis had inherited a desire for travel. Philomena knew all this, and yet she listened with a patience that made it new. If not for the familiar kitchen, and the haste of life, they might have been dating, with that first thirst for all things un-known. Slowly, dawn filled the kitchen.

They sat in silence for a time, then Philomena laughed quietly. Frowning, and with a mild wryness in her voice, she asked, "Where was I?"

Francis hesitated. "You haven't said anything these ten minutes."

"Were the children there? Do they know?"

Francis hesitated. "Phila."

"Don't let this drag on for something that no longer matters. Take it from one who knows."

Francis pressed back into his chair, offering his wife brief, timed answers while she rode the arc of their lives a second time in the same words, the same turn of incident.

Francis felt his flesh grow cold, the stammer of his hand on the table. He couldn't hold her eyes. Finally, he began to listen with the same patience she'd shown him this night, and the sensations sub-sided. Even in her confusion, her face was beautiful, and it was as if with each repeated phrase he began to know exactly what she'd meant.

Philomena talked on, then paused. She frowned, and then a shy smile took her features. "It's six o'clock. Time for my walk."

Francis glanced to the window, then brought his eyes to rest on his wife. They looked a long while at each other. Francis lowered his eyes and nodded.

Philomena rose and walked to the doorway. She wanted Francis to come to her, but was at a loss to ask.

Francis moved toward her with his broken gait. Lurching at her shoulders, he gripped her broad body with a strength that quickly spent itself. Her body felt cold and hard on his, like a doll's. Impul-sively, he crushed his lips against hers and drew out a kiss so dry, so awkward and brisk, it left a stunned frost on his lips.

"You taste of roses," he said.

Philomena smirked. "You don't say."

Francis leaned away and looked at her. Her smile was curt, and when she turned from him it was as though she'd traveled a distance of miles, her body just a gesture in his dim, dim vision. He shuffled toward her.

Philomena halted and gave him a harsh look until he stopped.

"To the porch?" he said.

The thatched porch chairs, worn and splintered by years of fine company and many a Sunday taken outside to dine in the good season, were painted by a fall of leaves. The air was sharp so early, and Francis was reminded of the gifts retirement would bring. Philomena slowly took in the street, breathed deeply. Backing down the first step, she smiled at her husband.

Francis chanced a step forward. "Mind Ms. Maudie for me, alright?"

Philomena considered this. "You mind Nancy." She stepped to the sidewalk and, setting her lips firm, turned to make her way up the hill.

Francis stepped from the porch to watch her. Though her tread was heavy, she didn't once look back, and she stopped only briefly to lean against the tree that she'd collapsed against three weeks earlier. Her red gown flared and thinned in the distance, and then she was gone.

SUSAN AUSTIN

Michener Center for Writers

AT CELILO

My husband has not been sleeping well. He tells me this is something that happens to men his age. He says so without frustration but with conviction, to let me know he always knew this thing would come and that I should have known it, too. Jack is older than me but not that much older. When he does sleep his sleep is full of work, so much work he gets no rest at all. Jobs he'd never do in the waking world. Stringing fence line through sagebrush country so lonely he's happy to have a fly lick sweat off his sunburned chest. Shoveling a well pump out of the snow.

"It's a terrible dream," Jack says. "The thirst is crushing no matter how much snow."

In one dream he stumbles down a steep and narrow drainage choked with alder and clematis vines. In the rush of water he can't hear himself calling out. He crashes through spiderwebs thick as chewing gum and he fears he's the catch. He feels constantly threatened by bears although he never sees one. The fear is in his skin.

"Sexual dreams," I tell him, but he waves off this idea. He doesn't like to attribute so much work to sex.

What Jack mostly remembers about his dreams, however, is walking all over looking for me.

"But I'm right here," I say.

Jack says he'd rather lie awake than spend one more night walking down dead-end corridors in a shopping mall.

"That doesn't make sense," I say. "I hate to shop. You'll never find me in a shopping mall."

"It doesn't have to make sense," he says. "I'm looking for you. That's what counts."

I called the acupuncturist this evening. Her name is Clarissa; it's just the kind of name I expected. Jack has not slept a whole night through in over three weeks. He does his dreaming early and wakes in the middle of the night to take a pee and cannot go back to sleep. At first I restricted liquids for six hours before bed. "No water. Nothing, Jack," I said. And then he shovels a well pump out of the snow all night long, like Tantalus standing chin-deep in a pool of water, but when he parts his lips to drink, nothing but sand and wind, a terrible hot dry wind. Nothing, my husband said, not even the snow, could assuage his thirst.

I ask him what he does when he can't sleep. He says he goes out into the den and sits on the sofa.

"Do you lie down?" I ask.

"No," he says, "I just sit there."

This, for me, is worse than the dreaming. In his dreams, Jack has always done things without me. Like death, it's somewhere I cannot join him. When I was younger, I had no need for heaven; now I see the advantages. It's more comforting than believing Jack and I, rein-carnated in future lives, might pass each other on the street and, except for the charged air between us, a sense of something familiar, will fail to recognize one another. In his dreams Jack meets with people I do not know, sometimes women. He smiles and says it's not so, but I know this cannot be true. The first years we were together he was like a puppy chasing after rabbits in his sleep. He made soft woofing sounds, his penis rising up all on its own, making a little pyramid out of the sheets. In the morning I would ask him conspiratorially if he had dreamed of me during the night.

"No," he'd say. "I don't think I did."

Once he played golf with the Dalai Lama and he played really well, so well he almost beat his Holiness. Birdie for birdie, it was the Dalai Lama's last putt on the eighteenth hole that took the round. We both laughed because Jack has never in his life played a game of golf. This is worst of all. That he learns these things without me.

"What do you think about when you're sitting on the couch alone?" I ask. He shakes his head to mean nothing. I hate this. I have the same damn penny burning a hole in my pocket.

"But you must be thinking about something," I say. "Not even you can rid your mind of every thought."

Already fatigued by my line of questioning, Jack says, "I only think about sleeping."

The acupuncturist does not charge extra for the night call. The minute she walks in the door she says she can see how badly we need her help. Jack's *Wei Chi* is on the loose, worn out because it cannot find a way back inside his body to rest at night, leaving him at the mercy of wind and heat and dampness.

"Dampness, ha!" I say. "The chinook winds have been blowing now for three weeks." I dislike this woman immediately for that *we*.

I take that to mean I have failed my husband in some deep and un-forgivable way.

"I fix him chamomile tea," I say. "Warm milk. I get up in the middle of the night and stand over the stove stirring, stirring, pick-ing at the dirty cuffs on my chenille robe. I feel like my mother when I do that. Can I help it if I fall right back to sleep?"

The acupuncturist smiles and feels for Jack's pulse six times on each wrist. Perhaps she is one of the women my husband meets in his dreams. Now she wishes to repay the favor.

"I rub his temples," I say. Sex sometimes does it, but I don't tell the acupuncturist this. Jack falls asleep right afterward and then I'm the one left wide awake.

The acupuncturist asks Jack to take off his shirt and he does. She asks him to take off his pants and he does that, too. She tells him to lie down on the bed. The palm of her hand hovers above his belly. All he is wearing now are his boxer shorts. Jack may be sixty but his bi-ceps are as big around as sixteen-ounce cans of whole tomatoes. His stomach is taut as a trampoline.

"Do you feel cold sometimes?" the acupuncturist asks.

"Yes, sometimes," Jack says.

"So now you're feeling cold," I say. "How could you be cold and me not know it?"

The acupuncturist excuses herself for a minute and leaves the room. Jack whispers to me how warm her hand felt. "Almost hot," he says. "She wasn't even touching me and still she's hot." As if Clarissa has a fever, poor dear.

She returns with an extra pillow off the couch and fluffs it and slides it under Jack's knees. She sits beside him on the bed and opens her kit, which is nothing more than a dull brown plastic tackle box filled with cotton balls, alcohol pads in neat foil pouches, and needles. She asks Jack if he's ever had acupuncture before and he shakes his head no. She looks at me. I smile back nervously. My husband goes wild-eyed when she slips that first long needle out of the sterile package and into the assist and then taps it hard and quick until it breaks through the skin between his thumb and index finger. Later, he'll tell me it didn't hurt at all.

I expect to see blood but there isn't any. I say, "Did you know when horseshoe crabs bleed they bleed blue blood? Well, it's true."

The acupuncturist makes little stabs with the needles under Jack's skin. She pokes around until she finds *the spot*. It makes my stomach turn just to watch him that way. Sometimes when Jack is sleeping he says he's walking around through a burned-out city. Dresden, he thinks. He has a cut on his scalp but he doesn't know how he got it. Everything is, or has been, on fire. Whole sides of buildings have collapsed and he can look, floor after floor, into other people's lives. These people go on doing what they are doing as if nothing bad is happening at all, as if they know better than he that this is only dreaming. In one apartment a man and woman are making love. The woman is wearing a ruffled apron and the man has got her pressed up against the kitchen table. A covered pot jumps and spews foam all over the stove. The woman is holding a wooden spoon in one hand and she's using it like a jockey's crop against the man's thigh.

"And you keep watching?" I say.

"Sure I do," Jack says. "At least until I know it's not you."

He goes on looking all over the scorched city. The acrid air burns so it makes his voice hoarse. He can't call out anymore. He passes a café where coffee is still steaming in cups but no one, no one is in sight, dust and debris so thick he writes his name on every table.

"To let you know I did come looking," he says.

In a bombed-out store window, he presses his face against the shattered glass. He is relieved to discover the amputees are only mannequins. He is certain he sees me shopping, the dream world a whole other disinterested land. Finally he frees the store entrance of rubble and opens the door and runs inside and when he puts his hand on my shoulder, it's not me after all, it's another mannequin named Claire. She says she's searching for a black party dress.

"It's exhausting," my husband says to Claire. "I feel exhausted."

"Well, you are," she says.

Jack closes his eyes. I am surprised how well he is doing. He was against the whole idea at first. Hocus-pocus, he called it. Now listen how he answers *yes* and *sometimes* whenever the acupuncturist puts a suggestion in his head. He has needles in his legs and several in each hand and one square in the soft part of his belly, the *Sea of Chi* the acupuncturist calls it, just below the navel. The needle jiggles, rising and falling with each deep breath. I've seen my husband naked for how many years and still I have never seen him like this.

The acupuncturist says Jack's insomnia has to do with his heart. The heart is made of fire and without rest the mind wanders about feeding the flames. She puts a needle in each ankle near his Achilles tendon, the *Supreme Stream,* to balance the fire in his heart with water. When she taps a needle just above his hairline and one in the crown of his head, I say, "I'll just go fix us some tea."

From the kitchen I can hear the two of them talking. I know the acupuncturist is kneading with her fingers some part of Jack's body before she taps in a new needle. Her voice sounds soothing. I hear her say, "It happens all the time. Most people are frightened by sharp things, truth."

I put the tea water on to boil and look at the clock. It's 10:03 P.M. For a while my father woke every morning at 3:03 A.M. He'd open his eyes and sigh, sensing it was too early, and then the clock on the bureau said it was so. For a while he woke at 3:03 A.M., and then it changed for some unknown reason, but a reason regardless, to 5:11 A.M.

Five-eleven A.M. was better, my father thought, but still it was odd. Another week or two would pass, until he'd wake and read the clock and discover a triplicate of integers. It went on like that for a number of years. My father's faith was forged out of numbers, out of a curious mathematical axiom that proved to him we don't create reality but rather discover it.

When my father woke at 3:03 A.M. or 4:44 A.M., he got out of bed and went into the kitchen. He'd light up a cigarette and make some instant coffee. He didn't want to disturb the rest of the household, but his lungs weren't built to manage the added load of tar. We heard his coughing through the heating vent. I never knew what it was he did out there until after I met Jack. On weekends, after Jack came home from Vietnam, we sometimes drove from the city out to my parents' house to visit. My parents still lived along a stretch of the Columbia River called Priest Rapids. In those days Jack could sleep right on through the night, woofing and building pyramids, and so could I. But sometimes the noises from the kitchen would wake us. It seemed to me as good a time as any for sex. But it made Jack nervous, my father coughing in the yellow kitchen under blinking fluorescent light. Nothing wrong with the old man's hearing. Instead, Jack got up and searched around in the dark for his clothes and put them on and went out into the kitchen and sat with my father.

"What do you two talk about out there?" I asked.

"Get up and find out," Jack said.

"You'll stop talking if I show up."

"What makes you think so?"

In the fall of 1956, when I was ten, my father took me to a place on the Columbia River called Celilo. He told me, What you see now, you'll never see again. It was as if the river, shore to shore, was unraveling. It wants to run away from itself, I told my father. It's running toward the sea, he said. Men on rickety wooden platforms no more than a foot wide leaned out over the riotous water. They were scooping dip nets into the spray and mist and sometimes coming up with a salmon. They weren't so much above the river as in it. I asked my father who these people were. He said that one of their leaders had proclaimed the young men of his tribe should never work. Men who work cannot dream, and wisdom comes to us in dreams. My father worked every day except Sunday and on Sunday he mowed the lawn. He slapped his hands on his thighs and laughed. I was never certain what he was laughing about, the idea of not working, or never dreaming. My father said you can unmake a life the same way you can unmake a river. That spring the dam was completed and within six hours Celilo Falls went underwater.

The air duct added a tinny sound to Jack's and my father's voices. I imagined them sitting across from each other in that terrible light, my father dabbing the tip of his cigarette in the ashtray, swirling it around and making a little cone of ashes, my husband drawing squiggles on the newspaper with a ballpoint pen. Sometimes I heard them laugh, and then my father would start in coughing, and soon after I would hear the water running in the sink, and then I was all right, being left alone, because I knew it was Jack holding his hand under the tap waiting for the cold water, before he filled a glass and gave it to my father.

I asked Jack, "Do you sit across from each other at the table?"

"Where else is there to sit?"

"Do you talk about the weather?"

"Yeah. And building projects. You have to know everything?"

"Do you ever talk about the war?"

"Sometimes," Jack said.

I waited for him to elaborate but he never did. Those early mornings, their voices were water flowing over smooth rock. I would listen for the doves to start cooing. When the doves started in, I knew the night had almost passed.

When the tea is ready I set two cups on a tray and carry it to the bedroom. I turn the doorknob, careful to be quiet, and a wild idea enters my mind. What if Jack is off somewhere dreaming of his acupuncturist? In a shelter of trees above where the creek flows down the beach at Shifting Sands, the rain steady but so light it doesn't even disturb the surface of the water. At Celilo. But these aren't Jack's dreams at all. They're mine. We live whole separate and private night lives.

I open the bedroom door and find the acupuncturist slipping the last needle under the fold of skin between Jack's eyes, the *Yin Tang*, his third eye, the *Hall of Impressions.*

"That should do it," she whispers. "We'll just let him cook for a while." She holds her hand gently on his forehead. When it is clear he is deep in sleep she follows me back into the kitchen. We sit at the table in front of our teacups. The night feels bright and accurate.

"Is he dreaming now?" I ask.

"Probably he's dreaming," the acupuncturist says. "What do you think he's dreaming about?"

"Fences," I say.

The window is open over the kitchen sink, the wind in the leaves like the sound of rushing water. "His mother slept all night to the sound of talk radio and didn't wake until after the coffee was brewed," I say. "After Jack's father died, we had to buy her a new coffeemaker with a timer, otherwise she might sleep all the way past noon."

The acupuncturist tells me the needles are really a supporting medicine. That the acupuncture only supports Jack's own desire to sleep peacefully through the night. She is youngish and pretty. I worry that maybe Jack was right—it is all hocus-pocus. The acupuncturist stirs her tea with the tea bag and then looks for some place to set it. The clock ticks on the kitchen wall. I jump up and go to the cupboard and take down a small plate and when I pass by the open window and look out, I see stars. What stars they are I don't know, except for Fomalhaut, the mouth of the great southern fish. When I was young I knew a boy who believed that the souls of the dead rose up into the sky and became stars. The souls of his ancestors, birds and deer and salmon. He didn't want anything to do with the fluffy cumulus of days. Give me the night sky, he said.

Fomalhaut is twenty-five light-years from Earth. The white mouth of the fish I see in the southern sky tonight comes to me from as far back as the end of the Vietnam War. I say to the acupuncturist, "You said sometimes the needles talk to each other. Is it possible for them to talk, say, person to person? If you fill me full of needles and put me to sleep, might I go off where he's gone? Could we end up there together?"

The acupuncturist looks amused. "It doesn't work like a telephone switchboard," she says. "Why would you want to do that?"

We sip our tea. I listen for the end of the chinook wind. I say to Clarissa, "He says it might be Dresden where he's going in his dreams but I don't think it's Dresden at all. I think it's Saigon. I think Jack is on his way to Saigon and he's looking for a woman but it's not me."

Jack does not stir until the acupuncturist touches his forehead to pull the last needle out from between his eyes. He turns his head my way and I can see that she has done good, the acupuncturist; Jack looks serene. For a moment his expression becomes thoughtful, as if he is trying to recall something he'd meant to say, and then he closes his eyes again and falls back to sleep. The acupuncturist packs up her tackle box and latches it shut. She refuses my tip for the house call. She says Jack should sleep on through the night, and she's right.

When he passes the 3:03 A.M. mark, I begin to think about the doves cooing, the copper in a horseshoe crab's veins that turns its blood bright blue. I stretch out on the bed beside Jack, careful not to disturb his sleep. He stirs a little when I do this, but then he settles down. He is lying on his back. His cheeks puff out with each breath until the air escapes in a watery sigh. I close my eyes.

Nothing can be heard above the pounding river. There was a boy I knew named David Cloud and he drove me all the way from Priest Rapids to Celilo to welcome the salmon home. David Cloud said he was a dreamer but he didn't have to tell me that, I could see. He just laughed and said, "White men don't know how to dream." The falls had been swallowed up years before, the river muddy and fretful. He touched my cheek with his hand. It frightened me for a moment to feel his hand against my skin; if this was only a dream then I could go home and do what I said I would do, which was to wait for Jack to come back from the war. I understood then what my father meant when he said lives could be unmade the same as a river. David's hands were tough from working in the cannery, stiff and sore from slicing open the pink bellies of salmon. I said, "Be careful, you'll end up with bird claws, no use to you at all." He laughed again and said that was okay; by then he would have a set of wings to match. David Cloud. He was right. That day David drummed his body against mine, to the beat of thundering falls, so that the river would always be there, he told me, flowing just beneath the surface of my skin. It was said that when David Cloud was shot out of a helicopter gunship over Núi Bà Den, the sky became thick with feathers. But in this dream David is fishing. The river is so huge it spits all over us, dampening the curls so my hair falls in straight strands down my back, my white blouse not meant to be wet all the way through. David Cloud sure doesn't mind. I follow him to the edge of the catwalk, as far as I can go, because I know I am only dreaming, and somewhere out there Jack is dreaming, too. David carries his dip net onto the spindly platform that overhangs the foaming terraces. He is in the heart of the river now, just below the falls. He leans way out. Both hands grip the net. He hauls it back and forth through the froth and spray. All around, his people are feasting and dancing. They have been hungry for a long time and now the salmon have come back home. Their singing is the sound of a river dreaming its way to the ocean. David looks back and smiles, to be sure I am proud of him, a big fat salmon dangling from his net. I call his name. David Cloud, I say, but there is no answer above the untamed river. I have lost him to the falls. I feel a hand on my shoulder. I think this must be David and breathe a sigh of relief, but when I turn around it isn't him at all, it's my husband, Jack.

We wake at dawn to the sound of doves cooing.

Jack says dreamily, "I never saw the falls before the dam."

"It's been such a long time," I say.

"It's odd," he says, "but when I was over there I actually wished there was someone else. In case I couldn't come home to you."

My hair has left a damp spot on the pillow, but Jack looks rested. He stretches, as though he's done a good night's work.

"Do you want to stay in bed?" he asks. "Sleep in late?"

"Let's."

He tucks a few loose strands of hair behind my ear. Where we are going is still uncertain, but the river is singing.

KATHARINE NOEL

Stanford University

APRIL

Another windstorm had knocked out the farm's electricity, so the dining hall was lit by candles. In two months, they'd lost electricity three times. Angie liked how the flickering light made the movements of the Staff and Residents oddly holy, investing the smallest gesture—emptying a cup, unbuttoning a coat—with grace and purpose. In the candlelight, the tremor in her hands was barely visible. One of the things she hated about lithium was the way she shook, as though she were seventy instead of seventeen. This half-light meant she didn't have to pull her sleeves over her hands or turn her body so that it was between other people and whatever she held. Angie didn't know what she was going to do about the trembling when Jess visited this afternoon. Keep her hands in her pockets, maybe.

"Eggs and bacon," said Hannah, folding back the foil from a pan. She lifted the serving tongs. "What can I get you, Doug?"

"Yeah, yeah." Doug was sitting on his hands; his long legs knocked against the underside of the table.

"You want both?"

"Yeah." As he reached for his plate, a coin of scalp shone at the back of his hair where he'd begun to bald.

Hannah was Staff, one of the college students taking a semester off to work at the farm. She'd told Angie that she would write a paper at the end and be given course credit by the Psych Department. Most of the college students looked biblical, with their long hair and rough shirts, but Hannah had crew-cut hair and overalls. She wasn't pretty, but she was graceful, and that, combined with her thinness and short hair, made her stand out in a way the prettier students didn't.

She finished serving and closed the tinfoil back over the pans. Doug had already wolfed down half his food, and he held out his plate anxiously. "Can I have seconds now?"

"What's the rule, Doug?"

"Not until six forty-five."

"Yeah, I don't think everyone's up yet."

Doug put his hands under his thighs again. He rocked forward. "I used to have a car. A Honda Civic. It was green. They're good cars, aren't they? Aren't they?"

"Damn good cars," Hannah said. Angie liked that Hannah talked to Residents, even the most floridly psychotic, about whatever they wanted to talk about. Most Staff insisted on reality-checking every two seconds.

The milkers came in, stamping snow from their boots. Sam Manning poured himself sap tea from the samovar. He had gray hair, cracked hands, wrists so wide he could have balanced his teacup on one of them. Sam was the only Resident who milked—the other milkers were on Staff—and so he'd been down to the barn already this morning. He sat down next to Angie. When he reached for the sugar bowl, she felt cold air on his sleeve. His boots gave off the sweet, murky smell of cow shit.

"The big day," he said.

Angie nodded and looked away. With Jess's visit only a few hours away, thinking about it made her feel like she had something sharp caught in her throat. They hadn't seen each other in three months, not since Angie had gone into the hospital back in New Hampshire. Sometimes, Angie couldn't bring her memory of Jess's face into focus, which gave her the crazy fear they wouldn't recognize each other.

"They're good, they're good, they're *good cars*. They're good cars. They're good cars. Mine was green. Not too slow and not too fast. Not too safe and not too unsafe. Not *too* safe. Can I have more bacon?"

"She said six forty-five," a Resident said reprovingly.

"She said, she said, she said bedhead."

Hannah shrugged lightly. "About ten more minutes, Doug."

The door behind them opened, bringing the din of wind. Cold air rushed into the dining hall; the candle flames hunched low, wincing. The residents who'd just come in had to struggle to close the door.

"Do you ever see any of your old friends?" Angie asked Sam. "From before you got sick?"

"Before I got sick was a long time ago."

"But do you?"

"I'm not like you." He turned his big hands over, looking neutrally at the dirty nails a moment before looking up at Angie again. "I've never been good with people. Really my only friend is my sister."

Angie still hadn't gotten used to the way people here said agonizing things so matter-of-factly. *He couldn't stay married to a mental patient. My mother says it would have been better if I wasn't born.* Angie said, "You have lots of friends here. You have me."

"You were asking about outside, though. You're nervous about your friend coming."

"Not really," she lied. Jess had been her best friend since second grade. Up until the breakdown, they'd seen each other almost every day. Now when Jess called on the pay phone, Angie sometimes whispered, "Tell her I'm not here."

Hannah yawned, covering her mouth with the back of one hand, blinking as her eyes watered. The yawn went on so long that she looked embarrassed by it. Gesturing toward the long table behind her, she said, "I've been up since four making bread. It's still hot, if anyone wants some."

"I fed on dead red bread, she said. She said, come to Club Meds in my head." Doug rocked forward, then back. "Is it lemon bread?"

"Just regular bread. Wheat bread."

Doug shook his head, making a face. He was too tall to sit at the table without hunching, and his knees hit against the underside, making the plates jump. "Sorry, sorry." He hunched even more. His scalp showed, waxy, through his thinning hair.

Nurse Dave had the med box. He poured pills into Doug's cupped palm: Klonopin, a green pill Angie didn't recognize, the same yellow and gray capsule of lithium she took three times a day. She looked away. Their movements were shadowed on the wall behind them, Nurse Dave straightening up, Doug remaining stooped as he reached for his water. The nurse watched Doug swallow his pills, then handed Angie her envelope, which she tucked beneath the edge of her plate. She'd only just gone from monitored to unmonitored meds, which meant no one watched her take them. She wanted to wait a few minutes, to make being unmonitored matter.

"An engine is a thing of beauty," Doug said.

A Resident muttered, "Here we go."

Hannah kept her voice casual. "What did you do last night, Doug? Did you watch the movie?"

"An engine is a thing of beauty, a thing, a thing, thing of *beauty*. In*jec*tor, *in*take *man*ifold valve spring *timing* belt *cam*shaft *inlet*

valve com*bus*tion chamber *pis*ton skirt alternator *cool*ing fan *crank*-
shaft *fan* belt *oil* pan gasket oil *drain* plug oil *pan air* conditioner
com*pres*sor—"

Hannah glanced at the clock: It was only six forty but she said,
"Do you want some more bacon, Doug?"

"*Fly*wheel *en*gine block ex*haust* manifold exhaust *valve* spark plug
rocker arm spark plug *cable* cylinder *head* cover vacuum diaphragm,
distributor *cap,* in*jec*tor, *in*take manifold valve *spring,* timing *belt,*
camshaft, *inlet* valve, com*bus*tion chamber, *pis*ton skirt *al*ternator
*cool*ing fan crankshaft." When someone rose, their shadow—huge
and flickering—leaped up and slid across the east wall, stooped as
they scraped their plate, straightened to set the plate in the sink. Doug
rocked forward in his chair. "Fan *belt* oil pan gasket oil drain plug
oil pan air compressor—con*di*tioner—compressor flywheel engine
block exhaust manifold. Inlet *valve.* Combustion *chamber. Piston.*"

At seven they went into Morning Meeting. Everyone wore jeans
and work boots at the farm—Residents' usually newer and nicer,
Staffs' more likely to be worn and mended. Angie and Sam found seats
together. Across from them, a Resident in a denim hat licked his
chapped-to-bleeding lips, over and over. Staff whispered something to
him and he stopped for a moment. Aside from the attendance sheets
balanced on the resident advisers' knees, Morning Meeting reminded
Angie of the Unitarian Church services she'd gone to with Jess and
Jess's parents: folding chairs, announcements, singing with guitars. To
the east, against the mountains, the sky was purple with dawn.

They sang with heavy emphasis:

> *Left a good* job *in the* ci*ty,*
> *working for the* Man *every* night *and day.*

Some Staff were knitting, needles clicking softly. One of the biblical
college students had taught Angie how, but she knit only where
no one could see her—lithium worsened her natural clumsiness. It

would be nice to have something to do with her hands, though. Sitting here gave too much room to think, so that Morning Meeting often turned into a half-hour meditation on ways she'd fucked up. The last time she'd gone to Jess's church, she hadn't slept for three days before. She'd drunk a mug of vodka before church, trying to calm down, and the combination of mania and alcohol meant that she didn't remember much of the morning now. She did remember banners made of felt on felt—*joy, peace,* an abstract chalice. She remembered screaming with laughter at the stupid banners, she remembered during the service talking loudly to Jess, she remembered falling down after the service, suddenly surrounded by legs. The way the noise was sucked out of the room. By her face was Jess's mother's ankle, stubbled with hair. The silence after her fall had probably only lasted a couple of seconds, but it had seemed much longer to her. She saw each black hair on Mrs. Salter's ankle sprouting sharp from its follicle, each follicle a pale lavender indent, and under the skin the hair continuing down, ghostly, toward its root. Above the anklebone was a small scar, white as a chalk mark. Angie could see Mrs. Salter in the shower, rushing a pink razor up her calf—the sharp, coppery taste that came into her mouth even before she knew she was cut, the way that the cut would have flooded with blood, not red but pink because her skin was wet, washing in a pale, wide stream down her anklebone and foot, and the way she would have cursed and pressed the cut with her fingers. Angie reached out and touched the scar. In the moment before Mrs. Salter jerked her leg away, Angie could feel a tiny seam beneath the tip of her finger, as though someone had taken two neat stitches there with white thread. Inside the scar was Mrs. Salter's soul. The soul was just that small, tiny and white as a star. For one moment she understood the realness of Mrs. Salter to herself, how to Mrs. Salter the world radiated out from her own body, and she could feel that for every person in the room at once— she felt the room's hundred sparkling centers.

Mrs. Salter jerked her leg away.

The noise of the room had flooded back in. One of the noises was someone laughing, yelping wildly. Someone had said, "Is that girl okay?" Someone, Jess, had said, "Stop it, Angie, stop it, *stop* it." And then Jess had run out of the room and that had seemed even funnier.

Sam put his hand on her arm. "Angie? We're supposed to be going out to the truck."

Angie was bent over, arms around herself, face against her thighs. Nothing, she was thinking. Nothing, nothing could make her fall apart in front of Jess again. She would be okay as long as she was careful, as long as she kept her hands out of sight, as long as she kept her thoughts on track. As long as she focused on the small details, as long as she made that be enough, as long as she made that be everything.

They rode the half mile to the barns in the back of a rattling Ford pickup. On sharp turns the key sometimes fell out of the ignition. The wind had died down to an occasional blast, sharp enough to pierce through Angie's coat. Though the sun was weak, the snow on the ground shone. They jolted slowly down the road, past the Residences—Yellow House, White House, Ivy House—past the Director's House, past the orchard, which in the summer held beehives. The sheep lifted masked, unsurprised faces to watch them. The llama, kept to protect the sheep from coydogs, had matted hair and a narrow, haughty countenance. As the truck passed, he detached from the flock and jogged mincingly toward the fence.

At the cow shed, the college student turned off the ignition; the truck continued to shake for a minute longer. Angie climbed up onto the rusty ledge of the truckbed, jumped down heavily. Pulling her scarf over her nose and mouth—as she breathed she tasted ice crystals and damp wool—she went around to the passenger-side door. Her hands were clumsy in their leather gloves, and it took three tries to unhook the baling wire that held the door. When the wire slipped free, she took a few awkward steps backward in the high snow, opening the door. Sam Manning had been riding in the cab. He clambered down, and then together he and Angie wired the door shut again.

Coming in from the snow, Angie couldn't see at first inside the barn. Everything looked dim. Written above each stall were the names of the cow's sire, her dam, the bull she'd been mated with, and then the cow's own name: Molly, Margaret, Jenny. Angie helped to unclip the cows from their long chains and herd them out into the frozen side yard. Jenny went uncomplainingly, but when Angie went back for Margaret, she balked in the doorway. Angie hit her, then set her shoulder against the cow's heavy haunch and pushed. Margaret set her hooves, tensing back. Her huge eye rolled wildly. "Come on, stupid bitch," Angie whispered. Beneath her cheek, Margaret's coarse hair smelled of rumen, straw, manure, at once pleasing and abrasive. "Come *on*," Angie said, banging the cow with her shoulder. Margaret didn't budge, and then all at once she gave in and came unstuck. As though it were what she'd intended all along, she trotted out. In the yard, the cows crowded together, standing head-to-rump, their breath rising in dense white clouds. Angie unzipped her jacket and stood, hands on hips. Clouds of her breath—smaller than the cows' and more transparent—rose in the icy air.

Back inside, she pitchforked up yesterday's matted straw. Mixed in were crumpled paper towels, stained purple with the teat disinfectant the milkers used. The barn was warm; Angie took off her jacket first and then her sweater, working in a thermal top and gloves. Betsy turned on the radio, an ancient black Realistic balanced between two exposed wall studs, dialing until she found a faint heavy metal song, fuzzed with static.

"No voices," said Sam Manning.

"No voices," the team leader agreed. Betsy rolled her eyes, tried to find another station. Finally she turned off the radio.

"They're all going to talk *some*time," she said. "There's going to be *commercials*."

In silence, they used brooms to sweep the floor clear of the last chaff. Then Sam Manning hosed down the concrete. Sam was more than twice her age, someone she would never have even known outside the farm. In this odd new life, though, he was her friend, her only real one, the only person who laughed when she made a joke instead of looking worried. They'd first found each other on Movie Night because they both voted for videos that lost. They wanted *Chinatown* instead of *Pretty Woman*, *Do the Right Thing* instead of *Ghost*, anything instead of *Sister Act*. Angie went to the Movie Nights anyway—she had nothing better to do. She and Sam sat in back and made fun of the dialogue. *It must be hard to give up something so valuable*, the concierge said to Richard Gere, who blinked stoically.

When Sam was twenty, voices had told him to kill his twin sister, then himself. He'd come to her college dorm and stabbed her in the stomach. She screamed and rolled away and his second thrust went wild, tearing open her arm. He managed to stab her a third time, in the thigh, before a resident adviser got there and wrested the knife away. Sundays, his sister came to the farm, and they sat together smoking. She was also burly and iron-haired. Her limp was barely noticeable, but if she pushed up her sleeve, she revealed a knotty scar that ran from her right elbow down her forearm, almost to the wrist. There had been such extensive nerve damage that she couldn't use her right hand. It stunned Angie what could be lived around in a family: Surely it shouldn't be possible, their sitting together on the stone wall by the sheep barn. She'd seen the sister reach for Sam's lighter, dipping into his shirt pocket as naturally as if it were her own.

At nine-thirty, they took a break. Hannah drove down from the kitchen, swinging herself out of the truck cab. Her jeans were made up more of patches than their original cloth. She reached back into the truck for chocolate chip cookies and a thermos of cider.

The cookies were hot from the oven. The Residents and Staff stood in the lee of the barn, eating the cookies and smoking, ashing into a coffee can of sand. Angie, who didn't smoke, wandered over to the fence and watched the cows. It had gotten warmer; she balled up her scarf and stuffed it in her pocket.

Hannah came up beside her. "Why do you think everyone here smokes?"

"Everyone did at the hospital, too. I don't know why." Angie wiped the corners of her mouth to make sure she didn't have chocolate smeared there.

"It drives me——" Hannah cut herself off. "It's annoying."

Angie said shyly, "I like your jeans."

"Yeah?" Hannah looked down, considering them.

Angie's sweater snagged on the fence. She pulled it free, leaving a wisp of green wool in the rough wood. She rubbed her mouth again, in case there really was chocolate there. Suggesting to herself things she might say to Hannah, and then rejecting them, she pretended to be wholly absorbed in watching the cows. They looked miserable in the field, barely grazing.

Hannah said, "I was hoping maybe we could talk sometime."

"Yeah? I mean, sure."

"Before lunch? We could take a walk. Or this afternoon, I'm driving Town Trip."

Angie shook her head. "This afternoon I'm meeting my friend from high school."

"Time," the team leader called.

Hannah asked, "She's visiting?"

"I'm meeting her on Town Trip."

"Why doesn't she come to the farm?"

"I don't know. She can't come for very long." Actually, Angie had told Jess that only family could visit the farm.

"Angie!" The team leader pulled on his stocking cap and said to Hannah, "You're holding up my best worker."

Angie felt herself grinning with stupid happiness. She said, "I could talk after this. Before lunch."

They walked through the soft snow on one of the old logging trails behind the farm. Hannah asked her about getting sick and the hospital, which Angie'd only talked about with doctors and other patients. Telling someone her own age, someone who hadn't lived in the System, made her queasy. Still, she'd told the story so many times that the words came easily.

The day had turned beautiful, warm for the first time in months. When Angie said she'd been misdiagnosed in the hospital, Hannah stopped short. "They misdiagnosed you?"

"They thought I was schizophrenic."

"So they had you on—?"

"Mellaril? It's an antipsychotic?" Blushing, she told Hannah how Mellaril had made her neck and jaw muscles stiffen so tight that she couldn't talk. She told how sometimes she'd fallen out so badly she'd been put into Isolation, where she threw herself against the wall until aides arrived to sedate her.

"I can't imagine you doing that."

A fist in Angie's chest, tight for months, unclenched a little. "I can't either, really." She looked at Hannah for the first time and saw on her face neither pity nor revulsion.

Talking faster, she said they'd given her tranquilizers to counteract the Mellaril, how on tranquilizers the world stretched out thick and flat. Her words started tripping over each other, like when she was manic, and she said, "Slow down, slow down. I know I need to slow down." She hit the side of her head with her fist and grinned.

She told Hannah that parts of her past seemed to belong to other people, to a girl watching television without comprehension on the ward. Or a crazy girl who bit, who called her mother a fucking cunt bitch of a whore, who broke windows, who had torn her books apart, who had slept with people she didn't know. Hannah said *Jesus* and *Wow* and, twice, *It's the world that's crazy.*

Melting ice dripped from the undersides of branches. If Angie closed her eyes, she could hear the drops all around her, running together into a sound like tap water. She probably looked crazy, walking with her eyes closed. She opened them and said, "It's almost spring."

"People say spring's a hard time at the farm. A lot of people have breaks."

Angie glanced at her, but Hannah didn't seem to be remembering Angie as one of the group at risk for breaks. Trying to use the same casual tone, Angie asked, "I wonder why in the spring? I'd think, like, a month ago, when it was so gray all the time. And, you know, cold."

"Apparently the change does it. In winter people hold together as long as it seems things are going to get better. Then when things do start getting better—I can't explain it well. We had a training on it. They said until things stabilize again midsummer, April's the last good month."

They'd reached the end of the trail. Hannah turned to hug her and said, "Thank you for telling me so much. You're a very strong person."

Angie hugged her back tightly, and afterward, all through lunch, she talked to Hannah in her head. She clarified some of the things she'd said earlier. Sitting in the TV room, waiting for the Town Trip, she told Hannah silently about her younger brother, the way that he sulked and snapped on visits. She said, *You've seen him, right?* and in her head Hannah said, *I think maybe. Reddish hair?* She confided to Hannah that she hadn't taken her meds this morning. Maybe skipping a lithium dose would make her shake less. She was going to take a double dose tonight, as soon as Jess left.

Jess.

She was too wired to sit here. She had half an hour before the van left for Town Trip. Out on the front porch, she pulled her parka tighter around her body and started walking. Wind stirred up small eddies from the surface of the snow. She turned and cut up into the woods.

In the woods, the snow was deeper. Black tree branches rubbed together, moaning. The high snow made walking hard; she stopped to unzip her parka. She thought about lying down to make a snow angel, then—as she started to lower herself—thought maybe there was something crazy about lying down in the snow and straightened and went on.

Hannah lived in one of the small Staff cabins out here in the woods, little houses without plumbing. When Angie'd been on the Grounds Team she'd helped deliver wood to these cottages. She'd still been on the wrong meds then. Her few memories of the insides of the cabins had a dreamy, unanchored quality: a red blanket, a shelf of books, a propped-up postcard of a painting.

The clearing between Angie and Hannah's cabin was wide and very still. Thin smoke twisted from the chimney. She saw a small brown hawk the moment before it launched itself from the tree into the air. There was the soft thump of snow falling onto snow, the *hush, hush* of wings. Walking through snow had soaked Angie's pants to the knees and she shivered.

Just as she was turning to go, the cabin door opened. Hannah emerged, walked a few feet, drew down her jeans, and crouched. In the woods, everything looked like a pen-and-ink drawing: white snow, gray smoke, black trees, and the cold blue wash of shadows at their bases. And Hannah seemed drawn with ink, too, as she stood again, pulling up her jeans. Short dark hair, the white undershirt she wore, then the closing of the cabin door behind her.

The wind paused. Angie walked toward the cabin. From inside came the chirrup of the woodstove door. A log was thrown on the fire, and then there was a silence that stretched over the clearing to its edge, where the snow disappeared in the bases of trees. Where Hannah had been, the snow was pocked yellow. Angie felt oddly exhilarated. She crouched, using her teeth to pull off her mitten and put her hand above the surface, feeling warmth mixed with the cold air rising against her palm.

The Town Trip was to Sheepskill, thirty miles from the farm. Hannah parked the old van behind the health food store. Hitting the parking lot, the Residents were like a clump of fish being released into a tank, turning in place for a moment, disoriented, then separating. Two of the lowest functioners headed together toward Sheepskill's supermarket. Others walked in the direction of the drugstore or the record store.

Angie lingered near the van. Kicking snow from her boot sole, she said, "Today's the day I'm meeting Jess. Who I told you about."

"I remember." Hannah finished writing the names of Residents who had come to town, then tossed the checklist onto the front seat. "Are you nervous?"

Angie's stomach kept twisting, like a rag being wrung out. "No. I guess a little. I haven't seen her since before the hospital."

"It'll be fine," Hannah said, pulling the van door shut. She reached and touched Angie's arm briefly. Then she took two steps backward, waved. "Go on. It will be fun."

As a meeting place Angie had chosen The Daily Grind, Sheepskill's less popular coffee shop, where they weren't as likely to run into other Residents. Walking down Main Street, she tried to see the town as Jess might. The stores had high, square fronts and faux nineteenth-century signs, or else real 1950s ones. The banked snow was melting, filling the street with gray slush. In front of the gas station was a boy her age with a smudgy mustache, jaw raw with acne. He lifted a mop from a bucket of hot water, rolling the handle between his ungloved hands so the strings flared into a circle, then bent to swab the sidewalk. His body, beneath the blue gray jacket, was beautiful. In the cold air, clouds of steam rose from the bucket. A handmade sign advertised free maps with a full tank of gas.

The Daily Grind was at the top of the steep hill. The slush made walking difficult: With every step, Angie slid half a step back, arms out at her sides for balance. Even though she did physical work, she'd gained weight on lithium, and she reached the top of the hill breathing heavily. On the café's porch, while she tried to pull her clothes straight, a woman came out, holding the hand of a little boy. He had hockey player hair, cut very short on top and left long in back. The boy said, "Mom, I want—" and the mother yanked his arm, hard. She hissed, "I told you, don't say *I want.*"

Jess stood as Angie came in. Angie's fear that she wouldn't recognize Jess had been crazy: She looked so familiar that Angie didn't think *There she is,* but, *Oh.*

There you are.

Jess was tall, a swimmer with broad shoulders and bad posture. Her long hair was pulled back in a ponytail. As she stepped forward, Angie stepped back, then realized Jess had meant to hug her. They bumped together awkwardly, Angie's hands still in her pockets.

"You look great!" Jess said.

"The coffee's pretty good here."

"It's been so long since I've seen you!"

"Do you want some coffee? I'll get it."

"No, I'll get it." Jess reached back for her purse. "My treat."

Once, Angie would have said—what? Something sarcastic about Jess's generosity. She sat, then looked quickly around the café, relaxing when she saw she'd been right: no other Residents. Inside her pockets, Angie's hands were trembling, despite skipping her Eskalith. She needed to calm down or she'd sound like a mental patient: *You look great. The coffee's pretty good here.*

"Here," Jess said. "I got you a muffin, too."

If she gripped the cup hard enough, it stilled her hands. The coffee was black, bitter, and delicious. The farm didn't have coffee. On Town Trips, Residents bought jars of instant and brought it back. Tablespoons of dried coffee were a currency as valuable as cigarettes, more valuable than real money there.

There hadn't been coffee in the hospital either. The first morning last fall that she'd woken up on the locked ward, she had such a bad caffeine headache she'd shivered and vomited. She'd told the nurses she was dying, she had a brain tumor, she was descended from Scottish kings, and she was dying on a shitty filthy motherfucking ward. She took off her clothes and lay down on the floor of the bathroom. The small, cold tiles under her cheek had, for a moment, brought her shockingly back to herself ("Angie," she'd thought, "Angie. Angie. Angie. Angie."), but then the Nursing Aides tried to move her and she'd become terrified, scratching and biting, and that was the first time she'd ended up in Isolation.

Jess said, "This is a nice place."

"Yeah."

"Your brother probably tells you everything about school."

Angie shook her head. "Luke doesn't tell me anything. We've

never been exactly close." She stopped herself from saying, *And now*—

Jess visibly relaxed. She began talking about who had broken up, who had gotten into what college, the swim team. In the café were two geeky junior high boys playing chess, a woman with a sleeping baby, a middle-aged man sketching. No one had any reason to think Angie was anything other than what she appeared: a girl in jeans, drinking coffee with a friend on a Saturday. She tried to listen to Jess, but her attention was on the street outside the door, willing Residents to stay away. So she wouldn't turn to look, she held herself stiff. Each time the door opened, she felt herself jerk in her seat. Jess smiled at something she was saying and Angie told herself, *smile*. She was relieved to realize Jess, in her narration of the last three months, wasn't going to mention why Angie hadn't been at school. Jess said some of the cheerleaders had been booted off the squad for coming to a game drunk. She laughed. Late, Angie laughed, too.

Jess looked down at her cup. She picked it up and swirled it.

Outside, a car moved carefully up the street, headlights on. In the slushy snow, its tires made a sound like ripping silk. It was three-thirty in the afternoon, the light beginning to fade. Jess at last looked up. They smiled at each other helplessly. "More coffee?" Jess asked.

If she drank more coffee she would be sick. She could just hold the cup and not drink. "Sure. I'll get it."

"Sit down, sit down."

She sat down. Her hands were too trembly, anyway, to carry two mugs without spilling.

Jess bustled over to the counter, joked with the girl working. It was Angie, not Jess, who was usually good with strangers, but suddenly Jess had taken on the role of the Competent Friend. On the way back to the table, she raised one hand—holding a full cup of coffee!—and used the back of her thumb to push hair out of her eyes. She sat down, saying, "I'm so tired."

"I guess you had a long drive."

"Yeah, I'm really angry you didn't find a place closer to home." Jess was smiling but all Angie could manage was a hum in the throat, supposed to be agreement and laughter.

"Tired," Jess said again. She bent her head, resting it on her arms.

While her head was lowered, Angie said quickly, "The farm's like . . . My parents think I have to be there. The doctor doesn't even think I have what the first doctor thought I have. No one has a clue, really." It seemed true as she said it.

Jess sat up. "You must be so pissed."

"It's not so bad. People are pretty normal."

"In your letter you said they were pretty crazy."

When had she written Jess? "Well, some people. Not most people, though. I'm friends with this girl, Hannah, she's just taking a semester off from school."

"So it's like that? I mean, some people are . . . Some people need to be there but other people are just . . ."

"Just there." For the first time all afternoon, her footing began to feel sure, not just because she'd found a softened way to describe the farm that wasn't, technically, untrue, but also because next to Hannah, Jess would seem awkward and unremarkable. "I mean, I wasn't going to come back to school in the middle of the semester. I think what I had before was a nervous breakdown, trying to do too many things at once. Everyone freaked out, but that was pretty much all it was."

"You know, that's what I thought. I mean, it's not like you're psycho."

"The hospital will make you psycho, though." You weren't allowed to use words like *psycho* or *crazy* at the farm; saying them felt like throwing off heavy blankets. "I was just talking to Hannah about how when I was in there, at the hospital, everyone was treating me like I was really sick, my parents were all"—she made her face solemn—"and everyone was saying I'd have to take meds, *medication,* forever. You begin believing it."

"In the hospital, I should've come see you."

"No, you shouldn't have."

Angie felt the conversation set its hooves and stall. She said something she'd said to Hannah: "When I think of the hospital, I don't know who I am."

Jess said, "What's that supposed to mean, you don't know who you are?"

"I mean it's confusing. I think about things I . . . Jesus. I mean, it's the world that's fucked up."

Jess pushed some crumbs into a line.

"I mean, isn't it?"

"I don't know. I guess so. I don't know."

The door opened and shut. This time, they both turned. Sam Manning, stomping ice from his boots, raised his hand in greeting.

"Who's that?"

"A Res— Someone from the farm." At least Sam was normal. Wasn't he? She had the time he stood in line to think about what she would say about Sam, but her brain felt slow. She raised her coffee and found she'd drunk it all.

Near them, a little girl was kneeling on the floor. Two women talked at the table above. Periodically, one of them called down, "Are you okay, Liza?"

The girl didn't respond. She had straight bangs that fell into her eyes and a windup toy, an alien with arms hugged to its body and three eyes across its forehead. The little girl wound a key in its side and it ran awkwardly, body pitched forward so that with each step it teetered, seemed barely to catch itself from falling.

Angie said, "They always make aliens look just like humans with one thing different."

"What?"

Angie's hands were jumping on the mug. She put them between her knees, pressing to still them. "Do you mean what did I say or what did I mean?"

"Which thing is different?"

"I don't mean there's a specific thing, I mean they change something."

"What are you talking about?" Jess looked suddenly on the verge of tears. "You're not even acting like you're happy to see me. I don't know what's wrong with you."

"Nothing's wrong with me!"

Jess flinched and looked away.

Sam was making his way over. He had a shambling walk—was that weird?—and blue down vest (weird?) and carried his mug carefully, watching to make sure it didn't spill. "Hey, Angie."

"Hey."

There was a silence, then Jess introduced herself.

"I know," said Sam. "I've heard a lot about you."

"You have?" Jess raised an eyebrow at Angie, who looked away. Jess asked Sam, "Do you want to sit down?"

"I guess, for a minute." Sitting, he looked around the café, cracking his knuckles. On his right hand, the fingers were stained dark yellow with nicotine. "How long was your drive?"

"Three hours," Jess said. "The roads were pretty good."

"You were lucky. Last night we had a windstorm."

"In New Hampshire, we had a windstorm last year that killed two people. A tree came down on their car."

Angie relaxed a little. This was a normal conversation. She was pretty sure. Sam asked about the colleges Jess had applied to, and Jess listed the places she'd gotten in and the places she hadn't. She thought she'd go to Bates. Had he gone to college? He had. Tufts University. "But I didn't—"

Angie blurted, "What do you think Hannah does on these trips?"

"Hannah?" Sam turned toward her. He was so big and so slow-moving. He said, "I saw her at the record store. I'm actually supposed to talk to her later. She said she already talked to you."

"Talked to me?"

"For her paper."

"Her paper."

"Her psych paper. She said you guys did an interview this morning." He looked at her, then frowned. "Are you okay?"

"No. No. I just . . . Right." An interview. She lifted her mug—no, all gone. She put it down. Too hard—it skipped and started to totter and Jess grabbed to steady it. Jess and Sam had identical expressions on their faces. They looked like her parents had begun looking at her last fall, wary and assessing. She laughed loudly. "You don't have to look like that."

"Like what?" Sam asked.

"Like I've just run over your dog."

"I don't have a dog."

Angie laughed again. She rolled her eyes at Jess, then saw that Sam was watching her. She froze, halfway through the motion, mouth still open, eyes wide.

"Okay," he said. He pushed back from the table and smiled weakly. "I guess you girls need time alone. I forgot how long it's been since you saw each other."

Jess said, "Stay, it's okay, we've had forever to talk."

Sam shook his head. Angie remembered how he'd said his sister was his only real friend. She hated the emptiness of his life. When he stood and said, "Well . . ." she let him walk away.

At four, ten minutes before the van would leave, they stood outside the café saying good-bye. The light had become grainy; in a half hour it would be dark. Low above the latched black branches of trees, the moon was a pale fingernail against the equally pale sky. A parked car, finned and low, its headlights left on, floated at the curb like a blind fish.

"I have to go," Angie said.

"It's good to see you."

"Good to see you, too."

Suddenly, too late, Angie felt how much she'd missed Jess. They used to say good-bye like this, lingering at a corner. They'd call each other sometimes ten times a night. For a moment, it seemed like homesickness would knock her down.

"Well, bye," Jess said.

"You have a long drive."

Jess shrugged. She bounced her keys in her gloved hand, looking off. Then she looked at Angie. "You're okay, right? Are you okay?"

How many times removed was she from okay? She nodded, tightening her coat.

As Angie started down the hill from Jess, she could see—spread out through Sheepskill—other Residents, straggling back singly and in pairs. She saw the whole town as a pattern of streets, glazed with late-afternoon light, leading to the van. When she turned, Jess was still standing in front of the café, watching her. Angie gave a hearty, whole-arm wave, the kind people on boats gave to people on shore.

At the van, she had to wait while two other people got in. When she put her hand into her pocket she found, still unopened, the envelope holding her meds. Pretending to cough, she bent and dropped the crumpled packet in the snow, quickly burying it with her foot. As she straightened, her face burned, but no one seemed to have seen. Ahead of her in line, Doug chanted, "Thing of beauty, thing of beauty." Someone else—low, so Hannah wouldn't hear—said, "Shut up, Doug," and he did.

Angie walked hunched over through the van to a seat in the back. Two Residents talked loudly. Hannah asked, "Julie, is your seat belt on?"

"Yup."

"Angie? Seat belt?"

Out the window, the air was lined as though with sleet—the last few moments between dusk and true evening.

"She's got it on," someone said.

Hannah backed and feinted, backed and feinted, turning the van around. Then they drove slowly out of the lot. Angie leaned her head against the cold, rattling glass. The passivity of being in a van made her feel like a small child, as though it were years ago and she were riding the school bus. In second grade, Jess had had a brown rabbit coat, so soft that Angie had found excuses—the bus going over a bump—for her hand to brush Jess's sleeve. They'd been best friends for months. During math time, they drew insulting pictures of each other naked. "This is you," Jess whispered, drawing salami-shaped breasts on a straight-sided woman. "Well, this is *you,*" Angie whispered, and scrawled armpit hair onto her own picture, pressing so hard the pencil lines shone silver.

The van turned a corner and Angie saw the real Jess, head down, walking to her car. Angie started to duck, but Jess wasn't looking her way. She had her parka hood up and her arms around herself for warmth. As Angie watched, she broke suddenly into a run. She was still hugging herself and she ran awkwardly, body pitched forward so that with each step she teetered, seemed barely to catch herself from falling. In the near dark, there was only a moment when she was going; then she was just gone.

BRAD VICE

Sewanee Writers' Conference

CHICKENSNAKE

Somehow the chickensnake had managed to climb up the twenty-foot steel pole and into one of the hollowed-out gourds the farmers had hung there as birdhouses for purple martins. Now the snake was coiled up around an empty nest, hugging it as if to keep it warm. Only the chickensnake's head stuck out into the world, as if the snake itself were frozen in the process of hatching from the shell of an egg, but every so often it would taste the air with its tongue to show it was still alive. The snake had lowered the clear membranes across its eyes and had puffed the glistening scales along the back of its neck to catch the last of the fleeting sunlight. Being deaf, the snake paid no mind to the flock of fussy birds screeching about its head, somersaulting left and right, swooping toward the snake's slightly upturned nose yet never daring to touch it. For the first time ever, the chickensnake was on top of the world looking down.

Below, Hazel Trull was backing the three-quarter-ton truck up to the mouth of the old barn when he noticed the martins. "Look over there," Haze said to his father, pointing to the storm of birds turning circles around their homes.

Haze's daddy stepped out of the passenger side. "I wonder what they're so upset about?"

The martins weren't mere pets or yard decoration. Like the cats that miced the barn, they earned their keep. One martin could eat its body weight in mosquitoes in a single day, and they often picked off tobacco worms and cut worms that devoured the tomatoes and corn. But it was hard not to feel a certain gratitude toward the martins' beauty. When the sunlight caught them just right, their black feathers took on a purple sheen, like transmission fluid or wine. Haze and his daddy walked to the back of the barn to get a closer look.

It was August, and Haze's daddy was wearing a long-sleeve workshirt to protect him from the nettles in the square bales of fescue the two were hauling out of the field. There had been a drought for much of the summer, and the bales were light, scraggly, and coarse. Against his father's warning, Haze had discarded his own long-sleeve shirt and White Mule work gloves in hopes of getting some relief from the near hundred-degree heat. Now his bare arms were cut up, his hands blistered. He would have put the gloves back on if his daddy weren't so quick to say, *I told you so.* Ever since Wayne, Haze's older brother, had died in the spring, Haze's father had been watching him like a new mother cow, never letting him out of his sight. No longer was Haze allowed to go walking in the woods alone or swimming with his friends down at the channel. When Haze's daddy wasn't farming, he was the Kennedy High School principal. When Haze entered the seventh grade next fall, it was going to be like baling hay all year long, one *I told you so* after another.

Without Wayne there to help out, Haze had to do all the groundwork himself. Drive the truck, hop out, throw a bale of hay into the bed, run around the other side, toss up another bale, get back behind the wheel and drive across another terrace, then start all over again. Haze's daddy stood in the back of the truck, silently stacking the bales into a tight pyramid, occasionally telling Haze, *you need to get a move-on, the sky's going to open up on us.* They were racing the storm clouds already on the horizon. After a two-month drought, the weatherman had surprised everyone by predicting thunderstorms in the afternoon. If the hay got wet out in the field, it would mildew and turn sorry when put into storage. Haze's uncle Poochie had said he was going to take a half day off work to help out, but it was almost dinnertime now.

Haze's daddy was the first to spot the chickensnake. "I ain't believing this," he said, pointing toward one of the gourds on the right. "Look." At the top of the pole, under the wheeling birds, was a crisscross of planks. Ten gray gourds hung from each plank, five on either side of the pole. With the last of the sun still shining bright it took a moment for Haze's eyes to adjust, but then there it was—the evil-looking head of the snake protruding from the second gourd on the right.

"How do you reckon he got up there?" Haze asked.

"Climbed, I guess."

"Can a snake climb straight up a steel pole? I would have thought it'd be too slick." Haze knew that snakes used their scales for traction, but they needed something to grab on to. Haze had once seen a man on television lay a timber rattler down on a large pane of glass. The reptile had become helpless and just flopped around.

"Evidently, this ain't your everyday snake."

"Chickensnake?"

Haze's daddy nodded. Chickensnakes were fond of creeping into barns and henhouses to eat eggs. A big one could swallow whole chicks. But there had been no chickens on the farm for years, not since Haze's grandfather, Lonzo Trull, passed away. He used to keep banty hens in one of the old mule stalls in the barn, but after he died Haze's daddy sold the hens. "I've already seen the cats kill two little ones this year," said Haze. "I wonder where they're coming from? There must be a bed of them around here someplace."

"Yeah, well this must be the daddy. Go into the house and fetch your gun."

Haze made his way across the gravel drive, onto the front porch, and then down into his parents' bedroom. He took down the little .22 caliber Remington bolt action from the gun cabinet, then grabbed a handful of shells from a candy dish at the top of the case. Haze hadn't touched the rifle in weeks, not since Wayne had been shot in a hunting accident. Wayne was killed by Mr. Parker, a seventy-five-year-old neighbor who'd been a childhood friend of Haze's grandfather and so had always had an open invitation to hunt on their property. Mr. Parker had shot Wayne in the face with a 12-gauge shotgun at close range. Ten years ago the old man had become eligible to purchase a lifetime hunting license for $50.75, and no one had bothered to check up on him afterward. At the hearing, the old man had admitted he was "confused" when he shot Wayne, even though he understood that Wayne was not a deer or turkey. Mr. Parker was a World War II veteran and was suffering from undiagnosed Alzheimer's, and there was no telling what kind of electrical storm had boomed through his brain when he killed Wayne.

Touching the Remington, once again Haze imagined how it must have happened. First he sees Wayne's face, his gray-blue eyes peering out from under his baseball cap. His brother wasn't handsome, but good-natured, pleasant. Wayne is walking through a stand of loblolly pine with a pump spray can used to poison pine beetles. He looks sort of like an alien in the surgical mask and thick plastic goggles he wears to protect his lungs and eyes from the pesticide. Then out of a thicket comes Mr. Parker shouting in an almost foreign-sounding language. Wayne is just about to lower the mask to say hello when the old man pulls the trigger. The pleasant, not-quite-handsome face is erased by a tight pattern of buckshot. The nose, the cheeks, the brow, everything is a bloody mess, everything but the eyes. The soft parts of the eyes are protected by the goggles.

The doctor gave Wayne's eyes to a little boy in Birmingham. Wayne had signed an organ donor card at college and hadn't bothered to tell anyone. The donation had upset Haze's parents, but it had given Wayne's wife, Loanne, a certain amount of comfort. Occasionally she talked to the little boy on the phone. Loanne was three months pregnant at Wayne's funeral. And now Mr. Parker was in a nursing home, blissfully unaware he'd ever done any harm.

Holding the gun gingerly, for a moment Haze pictured himself carelessly pulling the trigger and shattering the windows in the bedroom. He thought how horrible it would be if he lost his mind and went outside and shot his father in the face.

Wayne had died about a month after Haze's birthday. The Remington was a present from Uncle Poochie. Poochie was the Kennedy town constable and had all manner of firearms both in his home and in the tiny office he occupied in the courthouse. The day Poochie had given Haze the rifle, they had gone on a crow hunt together. Haze liked to listen to his uncle Poochie talk about the places he'd been overseas in the military or about what the farm was like thirty or forty years ago when his grandfather was running things and they raised cotton.

"You know, when I was your age there used to be Gypsies around here," said Poochie as they stepped over the mill creek that separated Haze's daddy's property from his uncle's. "They'd come in wagons and ask for work. Only they didn't want to do anything hard like pick cotton. Gypsies always wanted to paint your barn or something." Poochie was a tall, thin man, not nearly as big or strong as Haze's daddy, but when he talked to Haze, it was *to* him and not *at* him. "They buried a baby around here somewheres. One of their women was pregnant and ready to deliver and so your Big Daddy told them that they could camp out here until it was born and the woman was ready to move. I think he half expected it was some sort of trick. But it wasn't. There was a miscarriage. They buried it in the woods near the creek and that was the last we ever saw of them. There are a few Indian graves around here, too."

"Indians?"

"Yeah, buddy, before the government moved them out, this part of Alabama was Choctaw territory."

Poochie pulled a tiny cassette player out of his field jacket and pressed play. The tape inside began to screech and caw, and within moments a murder of crows spiraled above their heads. Poochie watched as Haze shouldered the Remington and fired toward the treetops. One crow fell dead through the branches, but the others flapped away before Haze could reload and get another shot.

Later, Poochie tied a strand of baling twine around the dead crow's feet and hung it up in a pecan tree next to his own house. "Look here, Haze," said Poochie, knotting the twine. "I know boys just want to go out and kill everything when they first get a gun, but you have to be careful. You can kill all the crows you want. They eat up everybody's corn and run off songbirds. Jays are mean as shit, too. You know what Big Daddy used to say about them?"

"No, what?"

"Every time he'd see a blue jay, he'd say, 'Jays go to hell on Friday.' So kill them, but don't let me catch you shooting songbirds—no bluebirds, or mockingbirds, or whippoorwills. They're good luck and don't do anybody any harm. Okay?"

"Okay. How long you going to leave that crow hanging there?"

"As long as it takes his friends to figure out they ain't welcome here." Poochie reached back into his field jacket and handed Haze the cassette player. "Kill as many as you can."

Within a month Haze had hunted down over a dozen crows, and three or four of their oily, black-feathered corpses swung outside every window of the farm. It made Haze feel good to know he was protecting his family property, and it made him a little sad when the crows finally grew wise and refused to answer the call. By spring, Wayne was dead and Haze's daddy wouldn't let Haze go hunting anymore. The crows returned. They bullied the bluebirds away from the yard and pecked kernels of Silver Queen that Haze and his daddy had set out for roasting ears. Sometimes at night Haze would dream about Wayne's funeral. In the dream, the pallbearers would carry the heavy mahogany casket from the church to cemetery, except someone had planted towering rows of silver queen among the headstones. On the edge of the first row of corn was an open, bottomless grave. Just before the pallbearers lowered Wayne's coffin into the pit, thousands of crows would rush out of the hole like bats out of a cave.

When Haze stepped out on the front porch with the rifle, he saw his daddy standing in the door of the old corncrib filing a hoe. Some years earlier, when it had become more convenient to buy feed corn from the grain elevator in Vernon, the crib had been converted into a toolshed. Walking into the crib was like walking into a tiny museum of agriculture. Between the massive scaffolding of dirt dauber nests, the walls were decorated with four generations of tools: axes, crosscut saws, Kaiser blades, cricket plows, can-hooks, obsolete tractor parts, and rotten leather mule skidders. Many of the tools, old and mysterious looking, had purposes the boy couldn't fathom.

By the time Haze had made it off the front porch, his father was walking back toward the barn. "Here." Haze's daddy offered the hoe to Haze with one hand and reached for the rifle with the other. "When I shoot him down, if he's still moving around you get him with this."

Haze held on to the gun. "Did you check on Loanne's kittens when you were in the crib?"

Haze's daddy looked up at the sky. "I don't have time to worry about any damn cats right now."

That morning at breakfast they had eaten only cold cereal because Haze's mother was going to drive Loanne to the doctor for a checkup. Everybody was surprised and grateful when Loanne decided to live on the farm and not move back in with her parents in Starkville. Haze's mother had tried to get her to move into the house with them, but Loanne liked living in Wayne's trailer. She was attending nursing school.

Haze's mother had refilled her cereal bowl with milk and handed it to Haze. "Take this out to Whore Cat for me. I don't want her to go out hunting for something and leave her new kittens alone. Loanne's got her heart set on keeping those cats, and I don't want anything to happen to them."

"What does she want with kittens?" Haze had asked.

"Well, she says she wants to keep them in the Lonzo house to keep down on the mice." Wayne's trailer was only a few feet from the run-down house Haze's grandfather had built before the depression; they used the old house as a hay barn in the wintertime. "But that's just an excuse. Don't you know she's lonely down there all by herself? I bet she brings one of them into the trailer with her by the time the baby's born." Haze's mother made a face. She didn't think much of living with cats or dogs in the house, but she was for anything that would make Loanne content.

Haze had carried the bowl of milk to the back porch, where the cats often slept curled up in peach baskets, but Whore Cat was nowhere to be found. Whore Cat was the oldest and wildest of the farm cats, and she had earned her name by constantly dropping litters under the Trulls' house. She was an ugly, skittish animal, an ill-patterned calico with pink wobbly teats that testified to her countless pregnancies, but she was a fierce hunter who lived off mice, lizards, and the leftover cornbread and pot likker the Trulls dumped in a hubcap next to the barn. Haze liked having the cats around the farm; the comings and goings of their quiet society made the place feel alive and slightly mysterious. The cats were always slithering in and out of the house's cinder block foundation, conducting secret meetings behind the chimney and under the living room floor.

Haze had eventually discovered the litter in the crib, lying on an oily T-shirt at the bottom of the ancient corn-sheller. The corn-sheller was a three-by-three cedar crate nailed to the wall like a trough. Attached to the right side of the cedar box was a crank that looked like an oversized sausage grinder. In the days before it was cost-effective to buy feed grain by the truckload, a farmer would make feed by placing cobs of corn into the mouth of the crank and turning the handle. The teeth on the wheel inside gnawed off the kernels and left both the loose corn and the naked cob at the bottom of the crate.

Inside the empty crate, the kittens had been licked clean and looked like three glistening moles. What little fur they had was speckled yellow and orange, and he could see the pinkish gray flesh of their bellies expand and contract as they breathed. Whore Cat was gone, already on the prowl. She had moved the kittens into the crib for safekeeping, only Haze didn't think the crib was all that safe. Owls sometimes roosted in the rafters during the day. Thinking of Loanne, Haze had covered the corn-sheller with a stray piece of roof-

ing tin. He'd pushed it flush to the crank and promised himself he
would keep an eye out for Whore Cat's return so he could let her in
to nurse. He'd left the bowl of milk on top of the tin, and had
promptly forgotten about the kittens until he saw his father sharpen-
ing the hoe in the doorway.

"Let me have the gun," Haze's daddy said.

"Can I try and hit it?"

"No, you best let me do this. I don't want you cracking one of my
birdhouses open."

My birdhouses. Haze's daddy made out like the whole farm belonged to him. "Come on, Daddy, please?"

Haze's daddy rolled his eyes. "I am too tired and in too much of a
hurry to argue with you. All I know is, if you miss, I'm going to take
that gun away from you for good."

Haze blinked slowly and finally exchanged the rifle for the hoe.
Just then Poochie's patrol car pulled into the drive, slinging gravel.
The car door slammed. "Yo, Floyd!"

"Over here on the backside, Pooch!" Haze and his daddy waited a
moment as Poochie made his way around the barn. Haze was surprised to see him still in his uniform.

"Where you been, Pooch? The sky's going to open up on us in an
hour or so."

Haze's uncle held up his hand. "Hold up. Lois called me about an
hour ago. There was a wreck after Loanne and her left the hospital.
Lois is okay, but they're having to operate on Loanne. You better get
over there as quick as you can."

Haze's daddy looked at Haze, and then at the hay field. "Is it serious? I mean, the baby?"

Haze's first thought was that somehow the wreck had damaged the
baby's eyes, and wasn't it a shame that they had already given Wayne's

eyes away to that boy in Birmingham. Then he could see by the expression on his uncle's face that it was more serious than that, and he thought about the dead Gypsy baby's lost grave in the bottoms of the mill creek.

"Look, Loanne's momma and daddy are already driving to the hospital. You better get over there, too."

By then Haze's daddy looked pale and dizzy. He closed his eyes and shook his head and Haze thought he might swoon. Just looking at his father made Haze feel queasy.

"What's with the rifle?"

Haze's daddy frowned and straightened. He pointed to the martin gourds where the exhausted birds were losing control of their circle. "Look up yonder, Pooch."

Poochie's sharp eyes spotted the snake immediately. "God almighty."

"I have to get it down and then we'll go." Haze's daddy shouldered the rifle and squinted. The rifle was too small for him; he looked like an overgrown kid who had refused to give up a toy.

"You want my pistol?" Poochie unlatched the safety strap on his holster.

Haze's daddy shook his head and there was a small ping from the Remington. The martins scattered. The snake jerked its head back into the gourd, leaving only about an inch of its belly poking out of the opening. "I hit it." Haze's daddy's face grew angry. "I just didn't kill it."

Haze wanted to say something smart like, *Boy, I sure hope you don't crack one of my birdhouses,* but he knew better.

"There's still a little of him sticking out, Floyd. You want me to take a shot?" Haze's daddy shook his head, shouldered the rifle and fired. Grazed again, this time the snake had had enough. In an instant it had tumbled out of the birdhouse and unraveled itself in the air. Time stood still as the three men marveled at it—the flying snake—four feet of airborne serpent sailing toward them. Haze was shocked when the snake landed inches away from his boots and began to crawl. The boy had forgotten all about the hoe in his hands.

"Kill it, son!" yelled Haze's daddy.

Haze struck at the snake's head. The hoe blade missed and the snake veered. By the time Haze had the handle up in the air again, the snake was past him, headed for the barn. If the snake got under the barn, it would get away for sure. It managed to get its head into the tall Johnson grass next to the barn's corner when Poochie materialized, grabbed the snake by the tail, and lifted it up in the air. Constricting the massive muscles in its body, the chickensnake curled upward and bit deep into Poochie's hand. Poochie cursed and flung the snake away.

The snake hit Haze's daddy square in the chest, and Haze was stunned to hear his father scream. The boy was tempted to laugh, or to scream himself. But Haze's daddy quickly stamped his foot down on the middle of the twisting snake's black-and-yellow body. The snake reared its head and opened its jaws to reveal a glistening pink mouth. It struck, first at Haze's daddy's steel-tipped boots and then at his denim-covered leg. "Come here and kill this damn thing!"

Haze rushed toward his father, holding the hoe like a spear. First he knocked the snake away from his father's leg with the flat of the blade, and then with a swift hack he beheaded the creature as easily as chopping off the head of a milk thistle or a morning glory. The headless snake became electric, a self-knotting rope that tangled and untangled itself, spinning around and around in the shorn pasture.

"Damn things are nothing but nerves," said Poochie holding his hand, blood dripping through his fingers. "See that yellow belly, chickensnake for sure."

"Give me that." Haze's daddy reached for the hoe. He pressed the flat of the blade down on the writhing snake and pressed until the corpse was relatively still. Then he reached down and picked up the open tube of snake and began squeezing and massaging it with both hands. A yellow beak emerged, and then the whole head of a martin fledgling, its purple downy feathers slick with chyme. It looked as if it could have been one of the snake's own young. The fledgling fell to the ground near the snake's severed head, then another and another.

"Three little bitties," said Poochie wistfully.

"I could feel them under my foot when I stepped on him." Still holding the snake in both hands Haze's father began to weep, just for a moment. He offered the dead snake to Haze.

Haze took it, felt the dry scales slide over the reptile meat as he closed his hands around it. "What do you want me to do?"

"Nail it up on the barn, high, somewhere the cats can't get to it. That'll keep any more of the bastards from taking up around here."

"What about the hay?"

Haze's daddy shrugged his shoulders. The black storm clouds had closed in, as if the sun had decided to set early. "Let it get rained on, I guess. Hell, let it come a flood. That's all I know to do."

Haze nodded, walked his father and uncle to the patrol car, and even opened the door for his father. When his daddy slumped into the passenger's side, Haze had never seen his old man look more defeated, not even at Wayne's funeral. Poochie hit the siren when they made it to the highway, and it gave Haze a quiet sense of relief. Finally he had a moment to himself.

Haze wondered if he could get the last load of hay off the truck before the rain hit. First he'd nail up the snake and then he'd at least try to get the hay into one of the mule stalls. Haze opened the crib door to look for a hammer when he was hit with the stench of spoiled milk. Whore Cat was standing on top of the corn-sheller, and she had knocked over the plastic cereal bowl Haze had left for her. The cat was mad and bleeding from a fight, maybe with another cat.

Her right eye was filling up with pus. She hissed at Haze when he stepped into the doorway.

"Oh, god, cat, what have you been into?" Then Haze remembered the dead chickensnake he was holding in his hand. Haze dropped the snake outside the door so it wouldn't make the cat nervous. He continued to speak to Whore Cat in a hushed voice, and the more he talked the more she seemed to recognize him. She began mewling, making it clear she wanted to get to the kittens and nurse—*who was fool enough to put this tin between me and my brood?*

Haze picked up the cat and cradled her gently in his left arm, being careful not to hurt her swollen teats, which were damp with blood. Then Haze flipped off the tin with his right hand. He was just getting ready to place the mother cat in with her kittens when Whore Cat screamed and bit him, sinking her teeth into the flesh between his thumb and forefinger. Haze dropped her to the floor. The kittens were no longer asleep on the oily T-shirt. In their place lay the chickensnake's mate, curled up on the kittens' bed. The sallow yellow swirls along its body were grossly distended. After such a large meal the snake was logy and could barely find the energy to open her eyes.

Haze stood there for what seemed like a long time before he puzzled it out, how the snake must have crawled through the cornsheller's crank, dropped down on the blind kittens, and smothered them in their sleep. After she swallowed them, she was too swollen to crawl past the crank's teeth. Haze had set a perfect snake trap, using the kittens for bait.

Haze picked up a stray ax handle, but he couldn't bring himself to crush the chickensnake's head. What was he going to tell Loanne? What was he going to do with the snake after he killed it—nail it up on the barn with the kittens still inside? He didn't have the stomach to cut them out. Haze felt like one of the old tractor parts on the wall, useless, just taking up space. For the first time since Wayne's funeral, Haze was alone on the vast farm, and he didn't know what to do. Behind him, Haze heard more mewling. He turned. The dead chickensnake outside had drawn the attention of five or six cats from the barn. The big tawny tom was licking blood from the open neck of the corpse. The tom looked up at Haze with blood on its nose, as if to say, *Get used to it.* Then he clamped down on the snake with his jaws, dragging the headless body backward under the crib.

That's when it started to rain. The cats scattered for cover. Heavy drops beat down on the crib, reminding Haze of the tin roof over his own head. Like the snake in the corn-sheller, he felt trapped. He balled up his fist, squeezing blood out of the deep cat bite. Cats have filthy mouths, his mother would have said if she were here—infection, rabies, cat scratch fever. She would have ordered him to wash his hands and treat the wound with peroxide on the spot. Yet Haze felt powerless to move, paralyzed by his own stupidity. He stared out of the crib as the rain began to soak the hay.

When he found the strength to turn from the door, he lifted the ax handle. He inched toward the sheller, then peered over into the corn trough and poised the handle just over the sleepy snake's head. Reluctantly the swollen snake began to uncoil, the newborn kittens weighing it down like tumors. For a moment, Haze felt a pang of sympathy for the snake in a way he knew his father never would. No real farmer wasted sympathy on snakes. But after all, it was only a snake, doing what snakes did. Haze felt sorry for it almost as much as he felt sorry for himself. Crushing the snake's head wouldn't change the fact that Whore Cat's kittens were dead, nor the martin fledglings neither. No matter how many snakes he crushed or crows he shot, he could never stop the world from eating itself.

HAL HORTON

Fine Arts Work Center in Provincetown

The Year Draws in the Day

Quentin fell in love in June—he was washing dishes at the time and looking through the window and across flowerbeds at the residents on the patio, speculating in an idle way about their probable life expectancies versus those of the flowers. It wasn't their impending deaths that preoccupied him, exactly, but the physical decline, which is the harder thing to imagine: easier to picture himself turned blue gray and getting humiliated, undergoing the casual abuse suffered by objects or dead fish—gaffed out of a pool of formaldehyde, carved open by medical students, thrown away piece by piece, liver, intestine. Being an object, being dead, isn't bad.

Dwayne knelt to stack dishes in the chrome-plated sterilizer as Quentin handed them down. The rain had just let up. Dwayne caught his eye and for a moment looked up at him, smiling. Quiet, he mouthed softly, and it was.

There is space for ten residents here. The residents are residents and not patients in order to make them feel at home, although it does sort of highlight the fact that they'll be here until they die. There is space for ten, and the average stay—because insurance companies won't pay for AIDS-related hospice stays anymore until the very end—is twenty-eight days. It makes for heavy turnover. Usually there are at least five or six volunteers around as well, cycling through in weekly shifts, nearly 150 volunteers in all, which for instance explains the eerily hygienic-looking garden: People frustrated because they can't offer any real help instead come in and do things like give massages, perform little folk-music recitals, cook elaborate meals— pull weeds for the dying. Quentin's job is the same as that of most of the guys his age: He cleans up and changes bedclothes and hangs pictures, moves big objects, but mostly he's here just to talk with the residents, be young and cheerful and handsome, smile back when they flirt.

He and Dwayne had just met on that day back in June, and maybe it was their gentle, wordless courting amid the dying, but Quentin had never wanted anyone so much. Dwayne was older, maybe thirty, and wore long, plastic-braided extensions—something he admitted shamefacedly when anyone complimented him on his hair. Quentin thought this was kind of charming. Together they took a sweet-smelling chemical to the countertops and began to talk about the residents, their quirks and infections mostly.

You think it's true, Quentin asked Dwayne, do you think most people die as they lived? This was a line from the volunteer coordinator: a tiny, energetic woman who worked sixty hours a week, who seemed always on the edge of anger but always just short of it.

Dwayne said, No, not at the end. That's just a way of saying it's them dying and not us. Something to keep us from bleeding with them. Dwayne smiled as if half apologizing for an insult. He'd been at this since the eighties. God knows your body's only got so much blood, after all, I mean, you can't bleed with everyone. But, really, there's really only three or four ways people are when they're dying from this.

It was a hot spring in Portland this year. Cory, a loud former cabbie, always in a lavender track suit, was still alive back then. He used to hold court afternoons on the patio. He was a bear, and stayed fat a long time, and made it through the summer, almost. And Trevor, and a woman named Jane who only lived out the day, both in wheelchairs, with thin, papery skin against their bones and wrinkles like crinoline or old fruit. Their skin was horrifying to see, initially, but to Quentin it lent them a certain dry nobility. They stared up from their eye-hollows at the sky and said what they could rasp out, most of it disjointed or disappointing. Their voices seemed uninhabited. He washed dishes and watched through the open window, and when the sun broke out they all stared, stunned a little by the sudden radiance of all the wet flowers Quentin couldn't name. He might have gone on indefinitely thinking about it like kids do—one day you just fold your hands over your heart and sort of evaporate—but it was really much worse, it was usually very bad, and this seemed all mixed up with the unreality of his sudden good fortune, which made him feel a little mindless, even though nothing had happened yet.

By mid-October the affair is over. And the residents are all dead—before Quentin knows it, all dead and the year almost ended.

This was what Dwayne had told him, back in spring: One kind goes out like angels, really, talking to everybody, saying proper good-byes to everybody, all that kind of thing. And that's hard, but it's also affirming, you know? Even if they do it only because they're aiming to get into heaven, like just in case. And another kind is bitter, and angry, and I'm not saying I blame them 'cause it is bullshit, after all, what, thirteen years in. I'd be real mad, I'm sure. This guy named Darius was like that, no family, no friends, he went down cussing, that was hard. And then some people are just afraid, and for me that's not so hard because you can do something, talk to them, at least be in the room with them. And then there're those that are so out of their minds, or so drugged up that they're just not there. Or maybe they are there, but they want nothing to do with the world anymore. They don't want you talking to them or feeding them, because they've got some business in their heads they need to take care of. And those kinds are easy.

Early fall, with Jerry dying and after two weeks Claudio dying still, Claudio to his gills on morphine and his face still wet with pain, with one of the two Johns shuffling on his walker, and Frank bitching, bitching always about something, his eyes lacquered with mucus but in good health otherwise. Today, the second Wednesday in October, 1994.

John, not the bedridden John but the John with the walker, the John who last week looked at him across the half-filled dining room, and shouted: Quentin! and then as all eyes turned: You make me quiver!—this an act of defiance, his jaw and maybe the rest of him trembling but his eyes not—this John corners him in the kitchen. He carries a bottle of lotion. John leans his waist against the walker. My hands get so chapped in this weather, he says. Here, give me your hand.

My hands are fine, Quentin says. There is nothing to do. What can you say? This is the John who says it would be so nice to be touched sometimes, touch is nice, you know? This is the John with a quarter bottle of lotion running off his hands, taking Quentin's left in both his own, feeling the wet places between Quentin's fingers, which are now so lubricated they drip on the floor. John, with quivering hands, with his eyes closed.

Olivia, another volunteer and a friend, comes up behind him later and whispers: Quentin! You make my ovaries tremble! and before he starts laughing he can feel his shoulders relax and fall and the fixed smile drop from his face.

This is how he goes into it. He'd had blood drawn the first week in October, and now, Friday of the second week, Quentin waiting, thinking how bad and the unbearable worst part of the bad is that it is standard, a rite, with Charlie here holding his hand—Charlie big and dopey and in a relationship, reliable, employed, the right person to bring. A galoot. He's harboring a stupid crush for Quentin still— an ex-boyfriend, not implicated. The part that makes it hard to sit here is how common it is, not so much that numbers are tragic but that something so bad could be so ordinary. How he goes into it: In his mind as he sits down and as the doctor smiles and opens the folder and as Charlie squeezes his hand he tells himself you tested positive you tested positive you tested positive you tested positive so when she says, You've tested positive, Quentin, the effect is so strange, not at all like he'd thought it would be. The moment seems pivoted above the possible responses, as if he has slipped into a dream and from this dream must remind himself that this is waking life, and it is true, the doctor talking about prescriptions and so on, but reality, life, these things are shifting, revealing themselves as less substantial somehow, or maybe it is that awake and asleep are false distinctions commonly made, made in a wrong way, blurred. He stands to walk out and Charlie rises to take his arm and Quentin says, No, let me go, I know you want me to stay but let me go, and he sounds so calm that Charlie lets him go.

But Charlie follows him out to the street. Reality comes into focus for Quentin soon afterward. Although the rest gets hazy, he will sharply remember Sixth Avenue Southwest in sunlight and himself standing in the middle of it, light glinting on chrome bumpers and hubcaps, and a car stopped and patiently idling a few feet in front of him, Charlie stepping from the curb, and the sun on the pavement at noon.

Charlie takes Quentin home and puts him to bed. He has long periods of sleep, followed by brief periods in the dim antechamber of consciousness, the phone off the hook. Quentin hadn't known how much sleeping could be done. If you sleep in long enough, you'll be tired on waking, tired and able to sleep more, for days. He comes awake without any of his dreams intact and drifts for a while, his body immobilized and his eyes barely open. His anger turns over slowly, without anything to fuel it, as if it is idling.

Later, he wakes to knocking and four or five people calling his name, and he realizes he still has hold of the edges of a sweet dream, which turns mawkish and sickly as he remembers it: He'd composed a list of all he hoped to accomplish in the years remaining and then accomplished them, and at the end of the dream he is launched by friends and family off a proscenium stage, crimson and sky blue, down into the orchestra pit, his mind at peace and his earthly accounts settled.

The voices depart, and sometime later there is a rattling in the lock.

Teddy appears in the kitchen: Quentin, there you are, here he is, thank you, he's fine, thanks so much. The superintendent leaves; Ian and Charlie are here, and A. J., and Michael of all people, his mustachioed angular face and a white kerchief on his head, looking like some old turbaned movie star that Quentin wouldn't really recognize because he never watches old movies. Teddy's older, neurotic boyfriend. Tallulah Bankhead is the name that Michael brings to mind.

Dwayne couldn't come, baby, says Teddy. You going to get yourself up out of that skanky bed and come out dancing or what? Michael's come to clean up your whole place while we go out to, I don't know, you want to go to Panorama? Teddy is short and hairy and balding, dapper, a bank teller. His and Michael's relationship is long-term and terrible. Teddy's told Quentin all about it: finances, positions, everything.

Quentin says, No, meaning Michael can't stay and clean. The air is choking, half-eaten food everywhere, spilled ash, a strong smell from the bathroom. His clothes are thrown around, stained with the dried residue of his half dreaming.

You were thinking these are optional activities my friend Teddy is listing for me to do this evening, says Teddy.

Michael, thin, severe, his health failing, kneels by Quentin, touches his arm, kisses him, expresses all his sympathies and everyone's fears and how happy cleaning will make him. You have to get up, Quentin, he says.

Hey, Quentin, say A. J. and Ian, stepping carefully across the floor, awkward in the general mess.

You had me so scared, says Charlie. Now Quentin puts it together, what all six of them have in common, why Dwayne hasn't been invited.

We're going to commiserate, Quentin realizes.

You got it, Q., says A. J., who is seeing Charlie now. We're going to go cry in the beer pitcher.

We'll pass it around until the beer gets all thin, says Charlie.

I can't, Quentin says limply.

Aw, come on, Ian says. You look good all sort of roughed up and scruffy like that. Ian is not seeing anyone. Come out with us, he says.

Up, up on your feet, Teddy prompts. He drags Quentin up from bed naked, and Michael shrieks a little and helps pull clothes onto him.

Not that shirt, says Teddy.

Quentin has always despised gay culture as openly as he dares, which Teddy claims is due to Quentin's latent homophobia, but which Quentin has always maintained is just good taste. After Teddy's sidewalk dithering over which place to go (more or less in a row: leather, striptease, Latino, and sort of upscale wood-paneled professional, with ferns, which for some reason is always filled with Oregon cowboys) and Quentin tired and swaying on his feet, they've decided on here. The music sounds like a funeral dirge backed with Morse code. Latex and vinyl clothes, the visible use of hair-styling products, mass-market cologne. Quentin has to concentrate fully to keep down his anger, a sensation like holding off nausea. A. J. and Charlie are dancing a few feet away with a sweet, self-conscious awkwardness. Ian and Teddy have him cornered in a booth: Talk to us, Quentin.

I shouldn't have come here. He looks out across the dance floor. The sort of men who follow facial skin-care regimens, consumer fetishists, all massed together in a rut. There seems to be a kind of shimmering, as if Quentin can tell the virus is moving among them, passing through them like a heat-mirage.

Silence is no good, says Teddy. Silence is bad. It sucks for you, you didn't deserve it. Say that.

Teddy. I've got nothing to say.

But we're here to make you talk. You'll feel better.

Quentin says nothing.

Well, let me tell you. You're looking all pissed off, you're trying to be pissed off at someone—the world—even, but actually you're pretending you're angry so you don't feel despair and hopeless wretchedness and all that. How's that for good news? I was like that for, oh god, the first month, do you remember, Ian? Teddy can put more emphasis on each word than most people manage in an entire sentence: I was angry at the planet, he says. And then, lightly, But then I got over that and wanted to die right away for, oh, about six months, I'd say. Cried every day, all day. And then I accepted it and I'm fine, and life is fabulous once again. Listen, Quentin, we're here to break you down so you can speed the process along. We don't want you to have to wait until spring.

Drink, Ian says.

Teddy, I'm leaving. I should go. I'll get a cab.

You're staying, baby, because we love you. Tell us. Tell us how it feels.

And Quentin begins, I got to—I—and when he starts crying he's taken by surprise, the choking in his throat and the water running down his nose, and he feels wide-eyed and panicked at his sudden inability to speak.

Two pitchers later he is good and drunk. He and Charlie are leaning on each other, bawling, talking about the time when they were dating, two years ago for about two weeks, and the other three are wiping their eyes and laughing. Quentin feels violated, exposed, and better, resentful that he feels better. He wants to kill Teddy and at the same time he is grateful and in love—completely unattracted to him, but also in love, with all of them. He snuffles back his snot.

This is when Ian pushes him on the shoulder, and says, Look, Quentin. So many beautiful guys.

He is right; they are beautiful, caught in halos of transience by the rotating lights, a field of them, like a field of flowers, like a phalanx of men moving through a bright Greek sunlight, like images of dead war heroes, or the forgotten selves of old men, beautiful and frozen and captured here in their youth.

They abandon the car and stumble back to Quentin's, shouting in the streets, and fall asleep together, the six of them piled on his bed in his immaculate one-room apartment, their clothes stinking of smoke. In the morning Michael cooks breakfast, and Quentin laughs along with them, at the bitterness of it, the materiality of being alive, the joy; on this morning, everything feels extraordinary, and he thinks he has learned the key to holding on to this feeling, this dispensation—he is going to feel this way, this kind of relieved gratitude, every day for the rest of his life, and he will treat his body like a fragile egg and feel like this for years, and then maybe forever: He is not at all sick. He could head out the door and run ten miles and be fine tomorrow, sore but fine. And he does this, when they leave; he takes a long run in the light and constant Portland rain.

He calls and explains to his boss why he's missed a week and a half of work, and he gets his job at the café back. The halo of this feeling is such that he even thinks a certain barrier between himself and the residents at the hospice will be gone; he will no longer feel as if he is on the other side of some unbridgeable gap, unable to register the existence of their emotions; and so, on the next Wednesday, the first week in November, he returns to volunteer.

Jerry's dead, Claudio's dead, the bedridden John's dead, a woman named Nancy and a man named Scott have come and have died already. Frank's still slowly deteriorating. What was his insurance, that we get to watch him die by inches? says Olivia. Today Todd, who is mostly blind, threw up in the entryway, a pitiful little trickle, and then collapsed into it. Today Gabriel, not a resident, had a heart attack watching his lover Bill die.

Dwayne stopped returning calls that second week in October. Today Quentin discovers that Dwayne's switched to Thursdays. The other volunteers miss Dwayne and ask him how Dwayne is and he has to smile and say he doesn't know.

Javier this week tells the volunteer Reiki therapist (already a painfully shy woman) he was responsible for giving Diana Ross and Barbra Streisand their first breaks into showbiz. Quentin thought Javier was being mean—the kind of sarcasm that's meant to communicate: Don't ask me who I was before I got sick, you fucking bimbo. He's known Javier since he started volunteering here six months ago, watched him weaken, watched him unravel, missed the Wednesday at the beginning of September and came the next week and saw Javier forty pounds lighter, gone from looking reasonable (passable, Quentin had thought) to looking like a corpse. Not something you can say, nothing to say. How are you? becomes loaded. Javier's been here forever, which is to say six months; the other residents call him the queen bee. Quentin goes now to find him, to give him shit for bullshitting the Reiki therapist. Javier sits in the room with the big-screen TV and looks out, roughly, to the middle of the room. Javier has not been giving anybody shit.

He has lost his mind and he has become a star.

So I hear you got Diana Ross started—against his will starting to do the math in his head; Javier can't be older than forty-five—Yep, is the reply. How'd that happen? Quentin asks him.

You haven't heard this story?

Tell me the story, Javier.

Well. You see. My grandfather was in the Crusades.

Quentin can't believe that this could be dementia. He wishes he had paper to write it down. He sat once at the bedside of a sixty-year-old black woman and listened to her talk about the horse-faced man in her medicine cabinet. (Don't you worry about the fantasies in my head, honey, she'd said.) The Crusades, Javier says, the thing about the Crusades was there weren't any women. The men all fucked each other. Javier's the rightful heir to the crown of Britain because of his grandfather; when he was born they wanted to get him on the throne, to get some life, some oomph back in the royalty; when he was five the Secret Service cleared out his preschool room and played him tapes of the voices of Jack Kennedy and Jackie Bouvier and asked him if he thought they'd be compatible. Rose Kennedy had wanted to be extra sure.

I was so creative as a child. They had tests, you know those tests? And I was at the top, at the highest of all of them. Look . . .

Javier's taken to carrying around a picture of himself.

Look at that face. You can just see the creativity, like it's all lit up.

Quentin takes it from him. He's said nothing; he had wanted to stop him and say you're joking, right? This isn't happening, right? because they'd been friends before now, he and Javier. Javier used to tell him stories of the Castro of the seventies, for hours, and of the eighties when it became like a horror movie, people disappearing all around him. But now Javier has given himself what he most wanted from life.

The photo is a big studio portrait, the old kind, on thick paper, of Javier as a five-year-old boy.

By the time Quentin's shift is over, Doug is ready to go, his family of stout relatives around him, supportive and weepy. Doug, a charming and ugly man who managed miraculously to stay overweight until the end, a former male escort–service owner, just last week a kind and gentlemanly chain-smoker. Now sequestered in his room with family. And the next day passes, and most of the week, and Quentin has forgotten to mark it, to speculate that by now Doug must have died; by now they've arranged the funeral; he is probably sunk into the ground by now.

Fast-food work for the college graduate is how his friend Jana describes their job. They work at a Portland chain trying to one-up Starbucks by offering espresso with anything you could think up to have with it, outside of whiskey and beer. Thankfully, everyone else who works there is gay, or at least into disco, except Jana, whom Quentin thinks of as a punk before punk got marketed. Because everyone knows. Quentin takes pills twice a shift. All the employees are cool about it. But he cuts himself early one morning on his first week back, stupidly, while shaving lemon rind for two romanos, and the manager—a normally hypercompetent, slightly older Arts M.A. woman, neurotic at work but generally totally mellow if you get her high—is right next to him, bent over and stacking ice cream into the freezer chest and she sees it happen, and she stands up from the freezer and says Quentin? in the escaping wisps of cool.

Quentin takes his hand in a cloth and comes within two feet of Jana at the register. Lemons are off for a while, he says.

The manager has found rubber gloves and is scrubbing the area and spraying it with what looks like Windex. Get, she says, get a bandage, go. And right then, in that space behind the counter, it becomes clear that all the prework 7:30 Republicans in line for their stinking fucking tall skinny lattes are lining up at a cage and all the hope he'd had seems like a lie told to himself and he wants to bleed into people's coffee.

He bandages it heavily, although it's small, and spends the rest of the day jerking espresso, mechanically, for not enough money to get anywhere ever—he has a reasonable record at a sadly expensive school and like everyone else couldn't land a career-type job to save his life in this town. And he's tried. Portland is flooded with humanities graduates like himself. Espresso-chain jerk is never anybody's first choice. Health insurance doesn't kick in until six months, and then Quentin will have to hang onto the job for the eight thousand it puts toward his pharmaceuticals. And maybe make regional manager, just in time to kick off.

Death as passage. Dying as a piece of the process of living. The professional grieving counselor is in the lounge. The John with the walker, who is newly bedridden, has talked about her for weeks; sometimes she counsels him over the phone. A middle-aged woman, ethereal, heavily eye-shadowed, pendant with raw crystals, rocking back and forth on her feet as she talks. The residents and Wednesday volunteers are gathered. John has been gurneyed out for the occasion with his IV and his spattering of lesions, and in the lounge she sketches death in bright colors, in lines of hope, all left vague enough not to be offensive to anyone, no matter his or her personal beliefs. They are probably in for creative visualization work later, pen-and-paper exercises geared to self-exploration. Completion of the circle, she says a few times. Professional grieving appears to be on the way to establishing its own religion. To Quentin, she is a bad actress declaiming her lines, and yet for the moment there seems something sincere in the way she thrusts herself upward at a phrase of inspiration.

Yes! says the bedridden John. He lifts one emaciated forearm, a young man aged past embarrassment, regarding the turned heads with a wavering smile. Yes, he repeats, and his eyes are held steady as he says it, as if he means to deny the option of mistrust, of sarcasm, to those gathered to hear.

The very next day, Thursday, late at night, a phone call: The nurses want Quentin to come and sit with someone, a brand-new resident who's having seizures and is also what they call active, which is to say actively dying. It could go late into the night. Quentin's spent long periods hand-holding the semiconscious but has never witnessed the end. Usually residents are surrounded by family and friends, a lover maybe, in the final hours, and so the volunteers last see the residents quietly disappearing into their rooms, and then later the funeral parlor bags emerge.

They need someone to come in just to sit and watch, because he's been falling out of bed. Bring a book. And when he gets there Dwayne's shift is just ending, and amid the forty donated flower arrangements they face off. Dwayne has been avoiding him. Dwayne is looking around at the floor, shifty-eyed, awkward, busted.

Quentin says, I'm coming to sit with a new guy. Ben.

Ben, right, says Dwayne.

How hard is it going to be?

Dwayne looks at the door, nodding, thinking.

Easy. Easier.

He can't tell Ben's active. He thinks there's usually shaking or something, a death rattle. Ben is about Quentin's age, he'd guess, early or midtwenties—he can't say how he can tell unless it's by the softness of the skin because Ben's hair is mostly gone and his skull shows through his face and Quentin thinks he could almost put the fingers of one hand around his biceps. Ben's asleep, or tranquilized. Quentin pulls up a chair. On the chair is a book, which lies open to a poem he recognizes: one of those homoerotically charged First World War–era odes to a dead soldier. He read it late in high school. Ben can't have laid the book there on the chair himself, but no one here would have been stupid enough to read it to him. Dozens of people would have been that stupid, of course. He puts one hand on Ben's forearm, opens his own book but doesn't look at it. The bars at the side of the bed are up. He's on an IV with clear fluid, but nothing more complicated. There are dark, raised, sarcomata-like slugs crawling up his forearm. They call what they do here "palliative care." Quentin wonders if he can talk still. Sometimes people can't talk, to tell you what it's like, which must be particularly bad. He hopes Ben's drugged. Quentin thinks he's always known it would be like this—that most people die in remarkably unbearable pain and don't always lose their minds first, either—but that he's been fooling himself. Liver failure, he thinks. Pneumonia. No, he'd be on a respirator, wouldn't he? Cryptococsomething, long Latinate names. Cancers, lots of options, lots of organs. Anything, blood poisoning caused by stoppage of the bowels, toxoplasmosis, combinations of things. Seizures could be, what's the word—strokes. But that wouldn't be killing him, necessarily. Could be a student, or was, looks like he is or was intelligent. Handsome probably, if you fill out the face.

His eyes are open, Quentin realizes, and they regard him in either dumb pain or hatred, and he tries to jerk his forearm from under Quentin's hand but it is the arm with the IV and it is taped to the bars at the side of the bed, and now he is jerking all over, and he's making inarticulate sounds in which the pain is evident. Quentin knocks over his chair running for the nurses. They hurry, but even as they hurry Quentin knows that they're hurrying for his sake, Quentin's, because there isn't any particular need for it.

Together they watch him for a while until he shudders and goes still, his forearm still solidly taped. The nurses say they'll have to leave the drip in for a few more hours. They go.

The next hours are hard.

Quentin tries to read, but someone is inside there—he senses it like a physical attraction, a magnetic pull in his stomach—and there is nothing to do. He feels as if he's incurring guilt by witnessing. The enmity the dying feel for the well has poisoned the air.

He hopes Ben's delirious, drugged, something—pain ought to have reduced the form lying before him to something no longer properly human. So that the pain becomes free-floating, not experienced by someone in particular. Or so that he dies like Javier, believing he got what he wanted in life, but Quentin cannot imagine what, for Ben, this might be. There has to be some compensatory mechanism in the brain. At least at the end—a neurochemical burst of white light, maybe. Quentin could almost believe it. Maybe you do go out dreaming your whole life in a flash. Maybe a long, glowing tunnel like you read about. He pictures it in Ben's mind: Ben reverting to a ten-year-old and flying with his arms outstretched—something like a bobsled run or a water slide would be good. Death is really a waterpark. Quentin laughs at this, and hears the mucus in his throat—he's been crying without realizing it. Ben stirs in his bed, and then his eyes roam the room wildly for a moment, to locate the source of the laughter.

Hello, Quentin says, smiling, his voice thick.

As they fix on him, he can see a shift in the eyes—as they narrow they become transparent—and Quentin can see through them for a moment, to the anger that is in some way satisfied, or recompensed, to have found someone crying and not laughing after all.

JENN MCKEE

Pennsylvania State University

UNDER THE INFLUENCE

I had just reached the point where talking to my ex-wife, Maggie, on the phone didn't throw me into a spiraling depression when our twenty-two-year-old son, Max, killed a man.

But I didn't know that right away. Maggie called me to say that we had to make the trip to Ann Arbor immediately, and that there was an emergency with Max—but that he was okay. So I waited for her on the front porch of my Kalamazoo boardinghouse at 4 A.M., a queer time to be awake. Everything assumed a rough, gray texture at that hour—the velvety blueness gone along with the moon's night-light glow—and all living things existed in a strange holding pattern, preparing to either enter into, or begin the descent out of, consciousness and daily life.

I lit a cigarette and watched for Maggie's headlights. Water dripped from the rusted gutter above, and a drizzling rain fell, the kind that made an umbrella feel like an overreaction. The weather reminded me of Max at age seven, wearing his too-big yellow slicker and stomping his boots into driveway puddles while waiting for his bus.

I had packed nothing for this trip, not expecting to stay long, and having fallen asleep again in my clothes I hadn't needed to get dressed. A stretched-out sky blue sweater hid a stripe of mopped-up salsa on my white button-down, and my black slacks were now a faded gray, with the knees worn to the point of start-up holes. I kneeled a lot at work while painting sets and marking dimensions on fiberglass and wooden slats.

Maggie, of course, had thought it hilarious that I was preparing for a production of *Who's Afraid of Virginia Woolf?* while we underwent couples counseling. "Let's pretend that we made Max up. That he doesn't exist," she suggested once in the car on the way over. But I told her we were paying the psychologist way too much to be playing gags.

Headlights moved fast down my street, and Maggie's green Volkswagen Beetle swerved to the curb in front of the boardinghouse, brakes squealing. I flicked my cigarette into the yard and rushed down the front steps so she'd see me and refrain from blowing the horn and waking my fidgety landlady, but Maggie didn't even look toward me. She honked twice. I jumped up and down, waving my arms, and then walked faster, imagining my landlady at the window, pulling back a pink lace curtain. I'd been there only a couple of months, and she seemed unsure about how I was going to work out. Maggie wasn't helping.

I opened the Beetle's passenger door and got in, immediately smelling pine-scented car deodorizer. The crown of my head touched the ceiling, so I had to slouch down, my knees crushed against the glove compartment. "I was right on the porch, for god's sake," I said. I groped blindly for the lever to adjust the seat.

"There's no light. How am I supposed to know whether or not you're ready? You could have fallen back to sleep for all I know."

The tires squealed as Maggie turned the car around, and I ran my hands through my salt-and-pepper fright wig of hair, slicked down with mist. Maggie was wearing turquoise nursing scrubs—she must have been interrupted during a graveyard shift at the hospital—and her shoulder-length, dark blond hair was pulled atop her head. Her eyes never left the road, even when I first got in. "What happened with Max?" I asked. "You never said."

Maggie accelerated, then pulled up to a stop sign, her hand on the gearshift. A charm bracelet tinkled on her bony wrist. She'd had it since she was in high school, but I hadn't seen her wear it in years.

"He was in an accident." She looked both ways and stepped on the gas.

"Is he okay? What happened?"

"He's okay, but he hit someone."

"Another car?"

"No, a pedestrian."

I curled my fists together underneath my sweater to warm them, and pulled my gold wedding band up and down my finger. "How is he?" I asked.

"They didn't know yet." Maggie reached down to click on the radio. Janis Joplin's "Piece of My Heart" started playing from the doors and dash, and Maggie tugged at her ear then, as she always did when she was nervous. Her profile showed itself in rhythmic flashes, the lights along the highway flooding the car's interior like a slow strobe. The indented lines around her mouth and across her forehead had become more prominent recently, but her eyes showed no sign of tears. This was to be expected. Maggie had cried only once in her adult life, as far as I knew, and that was because of the physical pain of childbirth.

I, on the other hand, cried during all kinds of films and theater productions. Maggie would snap open her stiff purse and hand me a small Kleenex pack. Her thoughts were almost audible in those moments: "Pull yourself together, Gary. It's just a story." But she had *always* been tougher than I was.

Her mother had died of a strange, rare sort of heart failure when Maggie was still an infant, and when her alcoholic father died five years before our separation, she had been estranged from him long enough to throw out nearly all his possessions and photos, except for one: a sun-faded, framed picture taken on a South Carolina beach. Her father held baby Maggie in front of his body like she was an expensive vase he wanted to touch but couldn't think of buying. Next to them stood Maggie's mother, blurry and stooped over in a blue-and-green-striped one-piece swimsuit, smiling big behind horn-rimmed sunglasses.

Maggie didn't display the photo, but kept it well-hidden. When we started having serious problems, I searched through previously unexplored parts of the house, looking for answers, or at least something to cling to. I found the photo then, in a white stationery box hidden at the back of a shelf in the hall closet, buried under kite string and mailing tape, and I wondered if Maggie kept the photo for comfort, or to fortify herself anew with anger and bitterness.

I cracked the Beetle's window an inch, feeling the wet chill of early morning, then cranked it back up. Nothing was said for a long time. I just stared out the windshield at bottom-lit billboards for restaurants and cheap hotels and gas stations and listened to the tires thunk across stretches of poorly patched pavement.

Maggie broke the silence first. "Have you talked to Max lately?" The question was full of accusation.

"A couple of weeks ago. He told me about classes. Some movie he saw."

"Did he seem upset about us?" she asked.

"When did you last talk to him?" I countered.

"Two days ago. He told me he has a new girlfriend."

"Did he seem upset to you?"

Maggie reached for her purse in the space between our seats and rooted around inside it for gum. She found a pack, but all the paper wrappers stood empty. "Goddamn it," she muttered, and tossed the empty pack over her shoulder.

"Even if he was upset about the divorce, this was an accident, Maggie," I said. "It had nothing to do with us."

She kept her eyes on the road and nodded. "Well, there's nothing we can do until we get there. So let's talk about something else. What play is going up now?"

"*Twelve Angry Men.*"

"Well, that may not bode well," she said, deflated, but then she suddenly brightened. "Or maybe it does. At the end, in the movie, Henry Fonda convinces them all that the guy's not guilty, right?"

Nodding, I described my set ideas to her, explaining that it was sterile and cold and realistic. As my hands formed the shape of the backdrop in the air, my ring glinted with a flash from a passing streetlight.

Maggie looked at me. "You're still wearing that?"

Her bare fingers curled tight around the steering wheel. She had stopped wearing her ring when we started counseling, and we fought about it. What were we even going to counseling for, I asked, when she seemed to have made up her mind already? She said that taking off her ring didn't mean that she'd made up her mind, but that the ring didn't represent our marriage to her. Instead, she said that the ring had come to feel like a leash, one that I could tug on to keep her from going too far from where I was and what I wanted. It didn't make any sense to me. My ring always felt like a life preserver, spinning across rough, cresting waters toward me—a lumbering, flailing, drowning figure.

I slouched down in my seat and shoved my hands back into the sleeves of my sweater. "I haven't taken it off yet."

"Why not?"

I shrugged. My initial reaction was to say, "Nothing legally states that I have to remove my ring," but it echoed too closely to, "Who's gonna make me?" So I said nothing. Maggie smirked and shook her head.

The truth was, the divorce had not yet become fully real to me, and it was just too hard to talk about it, so I put off all the explaining. I didn't want everyone's clucking sympathy. Just two weeks earlier, Tom and Sheila Kramer, a married couple who taught with me in the theater department, had asked me along to dinner after striking a set, and they suggested that I call Maggie to invite her. Torn between telling them the truth and my intense need for normal company and conversation, I went to the backstage phone. As they watched me from several feet away, I dialed our old number and pressed down on the receiver's cradle to carry on half of a conversation to the sound of silence—then a dial tone—pretending to receive fake news of Maggie's not-too-serious illness.

"I didn't even get to talk to Max," Maggie said suddenly. "He was being checked out for injuries at the hospital, so an officer called me."

"So you don't know whether he's been getting enough protein."

Wincing, I regretted this immediately. It was a dumb comment, inappropriate, and this wasn't the time for a running gag. A few years before, when Max came back from working at a summer arts camp, he announced that he had become a vegetarian, and when he left for college Maggie had worried about his nutrition, asking me, after we spoke with him on the phone, whether it sounded like Max was getting enough protein.

She looked at me now from the corner of her eye. She might as well have had the word *idiot* tattooed just above her eyebrows as a constant reminder of what she thought of me.

"But he's fine, you said, right?" I tried to recover.

"Yes. As far as they could tell, he's going to be fine."

I hunched my body into the small seat, feeling like a folded lawn chair stored for the winter. Rubbing my eyes, I decided to pretend to take a nap. We still had an hour and twenty minutes to go, and the thought of more strained conversation was unbearable. So I closed my eyes and listened to the engine's steady hum, occasionally opening one eye to look at my ex-wife. Her fingers tapped out of rhythm to the radio, and she blinked excessively. I knew she was frightened and tired, and I was, too. But we'd gotten past a point where we could comfort each other. Anything we did now only aggravated one another, so we played the well-adjusted divorced couple, with my physically uncomfortable pretend nap and Maggie's symbolic "taking of the wheel" feeling like improv theater roles that were still being workshopped.

Outside Max's hospital room, a tall black police officer stood next to Maggie, who had her hands on her lower back. She looked miniature standing next to the cop, but sturdy, too. He could have shoved her and she wouldn't have budged an inch.

I had just bought a couple of candy bars for Max and me at the vending machines at the end of the hall when, in response to the news from the officer, Maggie's hand flew up to her mouth and her eyes widened. The cop then headed into Max's room.

I hurried down the hall, candy in one fist. Maggie didn't say anything at first, so I waited. Finally, with her hand still in front of her face, she said, "The man Max hit just died."

I clenched the candy, unsure whether to hold Maggie or leave her alone. The chocolate was starting to melt in my grip. "But it was an accident."

Maggie looked down at my hand and pulled a Butterfinger from it. She unwrapped the end, then stared at the chocolate, not eating. My hands gripped the remaining candy bar more tightly as I curbed the urge to reach for Maggie. She spoke again. "Max had been drinking."

She stood rigid, her hand still holding up the opened Butterfinger, as I awkwardly blanketed my body over her. At the sound of Maggie crunching off a bite, I pulled away and swiped at my eyes with the pad of my thumb, studying her stony, stunned expression. Certainly as a nurse she had to turn off emotional attachments, but she looked stuck to the floor where she stood. I guided her by the elbow to the waiting room, into chairs that made a deflating sound. Maggie hadn't seemed to blink in the last minute, but everything that I thought of saying would be wrong or stupid, so I stared down at my Hershey's bar, sliding the silver foil-wrapped chocolate back and forth through its brown sleeve.

"I didn't even know Max drank," I said aloud, expecting Maggie to roll her eyes and say something like, "He's in college. Of course he drinks, Gary." But she said nothing.

On the television screen above us, cartoon bears with symbols on their bellies—a heart, a rainbow, a flower, a dark cloud with rain-drops—spoke in slow, high voices about planning a surprise party for a friend. A four-year-old girl with staticky black hair and purple footie-pajamas sat cross-legged on the floor a few feet away from us, her face cranked up toward the screen.

"Wasn't he in SADD in high school?" I asked.

Maggie dropped the Butterfinger on the armrest and stood, wiping her hands on her scrubs. "I'm going to go talk to him."

"Do you want me to come? Maybe I should." I leaned forward in the chair.

Maggie didn't answer, but walked away. At the sound of the doorknob to Max's room clicking into place behind Maggie, I saw how it would all happen—the newspaper articles bordered with Max's senior high photo and a current one of him in handcuffs. Smiling images of the dead man with his dog, then the sight of the killed man's somber-faced family lined up on a bench behind the prosecuting attorney's desk. I stood and started walking, following signs down hallways, finally ending up in the hospital gift shop.

I moved around the tiny store as if sleepwalking, passing inflated foil balloons fastened with ridged pink ribbon, two rows of greeting cards, shelves with old Whitman Samplers and shiny bags of lemon drops and butterscotch disks, and a box filled with clearance-priced stuffed animals. I picked up a plush, fat orange cat that had suction cups on the end of each paw. It wore a purple headband, a bored expression, and a white T-shirt that read, NO PAIN, NO PAIN. I brought it to the counter to pay.

On the walk back through the airless, white, fluorescent-lit hallways, nursing shoes winged by me, and I remembered that suction cup stuffed animals were meant to be stuck to the inside of a car's back window and realized that getting this for Max, when he wasn't going to be driving for a long, long time, was stupid. With each step closer to the waiting area the thing looked more ludicrous in my hand, and I wondered if they did returns in such a small gift shop, or if I should give the thing to the girl in the purple pajamas.

The accident would have been hard for anyone to deal with, but for Max it would be particularly hard. Max was like me. All his life he'd had difficulty accepting responsibility, though he had a fierce conscience. One night, when he was about five, Maggie and I were watching television. We heard a steady stream of water from the bathroom. Suddenly Max came out, leaving the tap and the bathroom light on. His cheeks were wet with tears. He said something, but we couldn't understand the words through the hiccups and deep moans. We sat him on the couch between us, and Maggie pushed his hair back from his forehead to try to calm him. Max tried to tell us again, and all that we could glean from his sentences was that he had taken some sort of change purse from the playroom at our church. Weeks before, he had presented it to Maggie as a gift, saying that he won it for being so good.

I stepped toward Max's room, guarded now by the cop, who stood there with arms crossed. Through the vertical rectangle of webbed glass in the door, I stared at Max sitting up in his bed, head between his raised knees, long fingers laced behind his neck. Maggie stood next to Max's bed, pushing his hair back from his forehead, and I squeezed the stupid suction cup cat behind my back.

I tossed the toy into a nearby trash can and then entered the room. Hearing me come in, Maggie straightened her back. She crossed her arms and looked from me to Max, biting her thumbnail, and my son raised his face. His eyes were red and puffy and tearstains dotted his blue hospital gown like rain. He was trying to muffle sobs; small hiccuplike sounds came from his throat. I was on the brink of losing control myself; if I rushed him, Max and I would burst. So instead, I placed my fidgeting hands in my pockets, feeling the other candy bar I'd stuck there. Then I walked slowly to the side of the bed. I stared at the black stitches on his forehead, rubbed a comforting hand awkwardly along his arm, and watched Maggie pull tissue from the box on the dresser and shove it firmly into Max's hand.

"It was an accident, Max," I said, offering the only words of comfort that came to me. I felt Maggie's reproachful eyes on me then. "What?" I said. "It *was* an accident. Wasn't it?"

But Max just stared at me and blinked wide, his breath loud and rushed as a long-distance runner's.

Days later—long after Maggie and I had gone to Kalamazoo to pack some clothes and come back in separate cars—as we drove back from court to our Ann Arbor hotel, I was still struggling for the right words. Max's hearing was over, but the judge had to decide on sentencing, which could range anywhere from two to eight years in prison.

The fast food on my lap smelled up Maggie's car, and the onion rings felt hot through the grease circle on the white paper bag. In my head I rehearsed things to say to Maggie. "At least he didn't run from the scene. If he had, he'd be looking at a lot more time." But then Maggie, I knew, would just get disgusted with my glass-is-half-full approach to life. Instead, having no better ideas, I asked, "What are *you* going to eat, Mags?"

Maggie shrugged. "I don't know. I haven't really thought about it."

"Do you want me to get you something? It'd be no trouble."

"No thanks."

"Are you sure?" I pressed, not even remembering what we were talking about. I just wanted to keep filling the tight air between us with words.

Maggie stopped at an intersection, waiting for the light to change. A strip mall stood on one corner, a dry cleaner and real estate office on the other. We were a good ways from the campus area now, in an older part of town. Maggie turned off the air-conditioning, so the question that came in the ensuing silence seemed startlingly important. "How do you feel about all of this?" she asked.

"With Max?"

Maggie didn't look at me, but nodded, staring up through the windshield at the light. Her eyes looked tired and resigned. The car lurched forward again. "I mean, what do you really think will happen?" she asked.

I gripped the armrest on the door. "He'll be okay. He has to come through this. He has no choice. Life goes on."

"Why do you think he drove after drinking? He knows better. I know he knows better. He's smarter than that. But I haven't had the nerve to ask him. Have you?"

I shook my head and said no, and then we were quiet. We passed the second-run theater I had been to two nights already, and I saw the sign for our inn, which stood next to an interstate. A good spot for a clean getaway.

Maggie suddenly spoke again. "Have you looked at the family in the courtroom? His parents? His girlfriend?"

It had been impossible not to. The mother was white-haired and rigid, occasionally glancing toward Max with eyes closed in cat-slits. The father, gray-haired with black glasses, was no larger than his petite wife, and he dabbed at his red eyes with an ironed, stiff white handkerchief. They never spoke, almost as if, like me and Maggie, they had split up and had been brought back together only to see this one last tragic event through to its conclusion.

The dead man's girlfriend appeared to be in her late thirties, with a bloated face that was powdery and pink. A black barrette held back her shoulder-length, dark hair. She often wore the same white blouse; with ruffles at the wrists and neck, it was something that had been out of style for years.

"And there are others in there, too," Maggie continued. "Lots of people that he worked with sit in, and friends and neighbors. While you're off in the bathroom or outside having a smoke, I overhear them. I hear them sentencing Max themselves. It's just like it always was, all over again."

Maggie entered the inn parking lot, pulled into a space, and stepped hard on the emergency brake.

"What does that mean?" I asked.

Maggie shoved her door open, making a "forget it" gesture with her hands, and climbed out. She turned back toward me, but didn't bend down to look at my face. All I could see was her gray business suit, and I heard her voice as if from far away. "You getting out?" she asked.

Paralysis had struck me in the passenger seat. I imagined Max in an orange jumpsuit, with cuts on his face and catatonia in his eyes. Five foot ten and small-bodied, he would struggle to be left alone in prison. I'd seen shows on television—documentaries—that talked about how some cells allowed so little privacy that you had to defecate in the open, yet at the same time, they were isolated enough to make you talk to yourself for company. My mouth hung open, but no words came.

Maggie's hands rested in fists on her hips, and then she threw them open at her sides. "Okay," she said and closed the driver's side door. Her heels clacked against the concrete but soon grew faint. I leaned my head against the window, and though I wasn't in the least religious, I prayed in whispers for Someone to give Max another chance.

When I finished, I pulled my burger from the paper bag in my lap. As people came and went in the parking lot, I ate the cold, greasy food, though I tasted none of it.

There was a knock on my hotel door, so light that it could have been for the adjacent room. Through the peephole appeared the back of Maggie's head, hair damp on her shoulders. She'd never come to my room before. Hadn't sought me out once in the week we'd been there.

Maggie turned around fast upon hearing the door, startled, as if she'd hoped not to find me. "Oh, hey," she said, and her elevator eyes, half-closed, took in my unbuttoned shirt and loose tie. She paused, then finally said, "Would you mind if I just hung out here a while? The housekeepers are cleaning my room."

I stepped back and waved her in. She wore baggy jeans and a dark blue sweater now, which made her seem different from her austere courtroom persona, reminiscent of Kim Novak in *Vertigo*. In casual clothes she seemed more vulnerable, more familiar.

She sat in one of two hard, high-backed chairs that circled a small café-size table, and she spread her fingers on the tabletop as if she were trying on rings. Her eyes shifted to the bed, where the newspaper lay in half-folded sections. "I should have brought something to read," she sighed.

"Do you want a section?" I asked, sitting on my hands at the bed's edge.

Maggie looked back to her hands on the table. "Depends. What are they saying about Max?"

"Nothing new. What I read seems more focused on the—" I didn't want to say the word *victim*. That made it sound like Max had intended the man's death. And saying *dead man* was out, because even though that's exactly what he was, I didn't want to have to imagine the coffin and procession and black clothing and yellow flowers. Talking about the poor man was, for Maggie and me, an intricate dance, one we would rather sit out than risk clumsily treading on each other's feet.

"What did they say about him?" Maggie asked.

"Just..." I began, then got stuck again. Funeral images still scrolled in my head, though I hadn't said the words. My voice shook, and I cleared my throat. "I don't know," I said quietly. "You can read it if you want."

Maggie gestured a dismissal, closing the subject. "Who's covering work for you?"

"Tom and Sheila are getting started from my sketches so that when I come back, things should be on schedule."

"Well, that's good," Maggie replied, nodding her head. The air in the room felt tight, too many hot molecules packed in and tossed around a space too small. Maggie rubbed one ankle over the other, like a cricket without sound.

"Do you ever—"

"What?" I asked. "Do I ever what?"

"With this whole thing. Do you ever wonder if we did something wrong?"

I fought the urge to say what both of us expected me to say. My lips almost formed the words without me thinking about them: "No, of course not" and "It was an accident." Instead, I admitted that I had wondered, especially while watching the events in court. "Small things that seemed insignificant before keep cropping up," I confessed. "Like when Max found our stash."

Maggie and I had left a play at intermission one night eight years before, at her insistence—it was an absurdist drama, and Maggie didn't see any point in theater that she couldn't relate directly to her life. When we came home, we found Max standing atop the washing machine. His hand was inside a cigar box on a high shelf; two roaches lay on the dryer. He froze when we entered, paralyzed with his hand among sealed Baggies of pot—a bronzed pose of guilt.

"But we talked to him about that. And we never had it in the house again. Besides, worst comes to worst, having an occasional joint wouldn't necessarily make Max have poor judgment. Hell, we've done the stuff off and on for twenty-five years, and we've never"—she stumbled, then bulldozed ahead—"killed a man. We've got to get used to saying that and quit hiding around it. It was an accident, but Max killed a man."

The words pounded me like a left hook. Something about hearing them from Maggie's mouth made the thing unalterably real. I turned my face away and heard Maggie leave her seat. She settled on the floor beside the dresser that held the chained-down television, and she propped her feet up on the wall, so that she looked like an overturned chair. She started doing sit-up crunches, blowing out and counting with each pull upward. I clicked on the television, flipped past coiffed local news reporters behind desks, then settled on a Bugs Bunny cartoon. Maggie rested for a second, then crossed one leg over the other and pulled one elbow to her knee. Watching her, I rallied the courage to ask, since a part of me thought she wouldn't hear anyway: "Have you been happier?"

Maggie stopped and stared at the ceiling, breathing hard. "Since we split, you mean?"

"Yes. Has your life been better?"

Maggie stayed lying back, fingers laced behind her head. "I think in some ways. Yes. Generally, it's been a good thing for me. I'm in the best shape of my life. I'm reading more and trying some things I probably wouldn't have before—do you know that I went caving a couple of months ago? Spent four hours in this cave, crawling through tiny, dark spaces like a worm. Got so dirty you wouldn't have recognized me," she chuckled.

"I'm not happier," I said quietly.

Maggie raised herself up and stretched her arms behind her. She avoided looking directly at me. "I miss things sometimes. It's not like everything just goes away. I may be cold, Gary, but I'm not inhuman."

"Tell me one thing you miss."

Maggie sat down in the hardback chair, face red with exertion. She thought for a minute. "I miss you running your hand over my hair and telling me good-bye while I'm still dozing each morning. And how you'd take the sections of the paper you knew I wasn't interested in to work with you and leave the rest for me. I always thought that was sweet."

I muted the television, but felt teary, so I cracked a joke. "I was hoping you'd say 'your earth-shattering sexual prowess,' but no, huh?"

Maggie smiled politely—our fragile familiarity now shattered again—and looked down. "No," she said, quietly.

We got stuck. Our eyes, by habit, fixated on the glowing television screen as I switched channels. On the local news, a picture of the dead man from Max's accident flashed on the screen. I turned up the sound. There had been a vigil, and many community members were calling for the maximum possible penalty. "Seems like a dream," I murmured. "I still can't absorb this whole thing."

Staring at the screen, Maggie asked, "Do you ever find yourself agreeing with them?"

"Who?" I asked, turning down the sound.

"The people calling for the maximum penalty."

I clicked off the television. "No."

Maggie's voice sounded low and unfamiliar, and the room had dimmed so that her face wasn't clearly visible. "I know he's our son, Gary, but he was reckless and killed, by all accounts, a good, decent man."

I walked to the vanity next to the bathroom and stood in front of the mirror, not knowing what I had come for. I switched on the light and looked at my brush on the counter, then raked its hard plastic teeth through my hair. "Well, you've done it, Maggie," I said.

"Done what?"

I thudded the brush against the counter, then turned and began moving around the room, turning on all the lights. "Having a conversation in the dark makes me feel like I'm in a Dash Hammett novel or something," I said. Though I didn't look at her, I knew Maggie hadn't moved.

"You said I've done something. What have I done?" she asked.

The mattress crunched when I sat, and I stared down at my hands. "Parents are supposed to love their children unconditionally. That's parents' rule number one, the one you're never supposed to break. And you have."

"I have not. I still love Max."

I shook my head. "Then you can't want him to rot in prison, when he's still a kid, for something that was an accident and that he feels terrible about."

"I can have conflicted feelings, Gary. This isn't black and white. Max knows what he's done and regrets it, but is that enough?" I didn't respond, didn't look at her, so she continued. "Gary, grow up. Max both blames us and feels sorry for us about our divorce, among other things. Aren't we allowed to feel conflicted about him? About what he's done?"

I tugged a sheet across my lap and met Maggie's gaze. "But when I hear that phrase—the victim's family—the first thing I think of is *us*," I said.

Maggie threw up her hands and looked around my room. "I thought I could be honest," she said. I searched her face; I wanted to tell her that she could, but I wouldn't have meant it.

Maggie pursed her lips, stood, and walked to the door. "Thanks for the company," she said, not looking back. "See you in the morning." After she was gone, the room felt different, like the house had the night I gripped the handles of the suitcases she had packed for me. Everything was still in its original place—worn furniture, the mail stack, clothing on hangers and folded in drawers, trash in twist-tie bags—but it suddenly seemed like a dummied-up model version. Like a strange family might walk through any moment.

The next day the judge sentenced Max to two years. Later that afternoon, in Maggie's hotel room, she and I made love for the first time in over a year. My body and skin remembered Maggie's like a favorite song in that cramped, dim, crummy room. Although we automatically assumed old positions and habits, there was an urgency and a yearning in our movements that had been missing toward the end. Maggie pressed her hands against my back, striving to read its scars and freckles like Braille, and I kissed parts of her that never struck me as important during our marriage—temples, shoulders, wrists, ankles, toes. I had missed them, and by laying my mouth on them I staked a claim, like an astronaut who plants a flag in the craggy surface of the moon. I wanted permanent access to Maggie again. I wanted these body parts to belong to me.

When it ended, I rolled onto my back, naked atop coiled, sweaty, thin white sheets. Maggie pulled on a long T-shirt and walked to the bathroom. I heard the toilet flush, and then Maggie stepped back out to the vanity, turning on a light to wash her hands at the sink. The curves of her short, muscular legs, her small feet, her angular shoulders, and the curled tips of her blond hair made her beautiful. She smelled like lavender, as usual, and I crushed her pillow to my face, breathing it in deeply. "Well, now what?" I asked.

Maggie brushed out her hair in short, tough strokes and looked at me in the mirror. "What do you mean?"

"Us. I mean what happens to us?"

Maggie scooped up her hair behind her head and twisted a rubber band around a stubby ponytail. "I am going to get some sleep right now, and then I'm going to go see Max again," she said.

My modest smile faded. "Okay. But we've got to talk about this sometime."

Maggie turned and walked toward the bed. My arms spread wide to receive her, but on her way, Maggie bent to pick up my jeans, my sweatshirt, and my hiking boots, and when she arrived at the bed she set them down.

"You can't go to your room naked," she said quietly.

My face burned. I started to speak, but closed my mouth again, staring across the room at Maggie's clothes, spread in piles around her small, brown leather suitcase on the floor. Finally, I asked, "I'm supposed to go?"

"I think it would be best."

My eyes fixed on a water stain on the ceiling, a brown-rimmed cloud of damage. As a kid, I had planned to grow up and fight crime, scale buildings and rooms with suction cups roped to my hands and feet. I wanted now to climb up the walls of Maggie's hotel room, use vacuumed air to position myself on the ceiling like a bat, then watch Maggie, try to figure her out, and wait to see if she tried to talk me down or even noticed me. Or I'd linger to see if she would simply call the desk for another room, turn off the lights on her upside-down ex-husband on her way out, and shut the door with a firm pop that would, in its small way, kill me.

"Was this nothing?" I asked, my voice loud.

Maggie sat on the bed's edge, her back to me. "Don't you remember the night of your mother's funeral? After being surrounded by death for days, we had this... urgent kind of sex." She paused and stared into the mirror, watching my face in the glass across the room. It seemed like the only way she could look at me.

"We needed each other today," she continued, filling silence. "It's been hard watching Max go through all of this, and knowing that he's going to have extremely difficult years ahead of him—all because he was careless and made a mistake—seems too awful to be real."

I stared back at the ceiling and shrugged. "Why do all of this, Maggie? Why fight inertia?" I asked. "Don't you think these coming years of visiting Max and imagining what he's going through every day are just going to make us need each other more?"

"I'm sure there will be times when I wish we were together. But we can't fall into that trap."

I grabbed my pants, shook them out, and shoved my feet through the dark tunnels of the legs. I'd pulled my pants up to my waist before I realized they were inside out, the white pockets drooping like linen wings. I sat back down and pulled off the pants, hoping that Maggie hadn't noticed, but knowing she had. "What's happening up ahead that you must be free of me?"

Maggie leaned forward and set her face in her cupped hands. "I don't know, Gary. Maybe the Peace Corps. Maybe scuba diving in the Keys. Maybe training to lead bicycle tours in Europe. I don't know exactly, but I know that I need to be disentangled right now in order to make myself happy."

I yanked the pants up above my hips again, fastening my belt. "The truth of the matter is, Maggie, that you can only disentangle yourself so much. You can divorce me and push me away, but you can't do that with Max. You can't divorce Max, and no matter what kind of wanderlust or midlife thing you're going through right now, you have to do everything you can to help him," I said, pushing my fists through my sweatshirt's sleeves.

Maggie went into the bathroom, and the lock clicked. There was no other sound. She just went in to wait for me to go. I finished dressing and stomped to the bathroom door, intending to leave with a biting, clever comment, but upon reaching the spot, I said nothing. I stared at the white door, trying to see or imagine Maggie through it while listening for sound. As a child, Max had often rushed into the bathroom—the only room with a lock on it—in order to avoid confrontation or punishment. But this was a first for Maggie.

I raised my hand once, intending to pound on the door until I got Maggie's ire up and drove her out, but my fist stayed in the air, poised next to my head. Instead of pounding on the door, I opened my hand and rested my palm against the cool surface. I set my ear against the door, too, but heard nothing. After a moment, I crept toward the hotel room door to leave, but stopped, staring at Maggie's open suitcase again. Suddenly, without thinking, I shoved everything in sight into the bag, zipped up the sides, and took it with me.

The late-afternoon sun shocked my eyes and seemed to expose my theft to the world. I felt like a naked cave dweller, walking awkwardly among foreign-feeling terrain.

I knew she would come after her belongings as soon as she realized they were missing. I tossed my own things together in my room and carried the load out to the car. I checked out, then drove around Ann Arbor, watching in my rearview for Maggie's green Beetle. I would eventually head home, but that was the obvious path, so instead I pulled into an A&W, calling my order into a small silver squawk box. While waiting for my food, I unzipped Maggie's suitcase, which stood in the passenger seat.

The bag didn't provide much to go on at first. The casual stuff she'd worn in the evenings, after court, presented no surprises—T-shirts, sweatshirts, jeans—and a large, clear Ziploc bag held her travel toothbrush, toothpaste, hairbrush, floss, and shampoo. But in one pocket I found a silky black thigh-length nightgown. This was something I had never seen. I held it up by its spaghetti straps, imagining Maggie's body inside it. She had never been one for lingerie. She had always slept in a T-shirt or, during the coldest months, in flannel pajamas. After Max turned four she'd never slept naked, in case he needed something in the middle of the night.

I was still holding the nightgown when the waitress knocked on my window. I rolled the window down halfway, letting her hook the tray onto its edge. She looked about seventeen, and her eyes quickly registered the nightgown in my right hand. Clearly she had made a mental note to tell the others inside about the pathetic man holding women's lingerie in the blue Ford. "Need anything else?" she asked, barely containing her laughter.

I tossed the nightgown into the suitcase, where it fell into a soft heap, and told her no.

But I stared at the nightgown while I ate. How long had Maggie owned it? Had a lover given it to her as a gift? I hadn't even tried to date anyone since we'd separated, hoping that things would work out. But she had found a new, more effective way to hurt me—luring me back to reject me all over again—and I was sick of trying to understand. If all she lost was a suitcase full of clothes, she would be the least damaged of all of us.

I drove the hour and a half home then, singing along with a Johnny Cash tape while trying to think of things to send to my son in jail.

When I arrived at my boardinghouse, I stepped lightly on the uneven sidewalk and tiptoed up the stairs. My landlady had entered my room while I was gone—my mail was stacked neatly in a pile rather than fanned out on the floor below the slot. But everything else was as it always was. The lusterless green and white floor tiles in the kitchenette. The nearly empty, dark wood cupboards on which the doors hung open. My recliner and sixteen-inch television in the living room. The yellow walls bare, except for pale squares where previous tenants had hung posters and pictures. And the strange smell of sour milk and laundry detergent.

Maggie's nightgown shrouded the top of her suitcase.

I turned on the television to hear voices, to feel like I had company, and unpacked my own bag. I hung up my suit, which would need dry cleaning, and dumped everything else into the laundry hamper next to my twin bed. We'd bought the hamper just before Max was born, and even though it hadn't been near diapers and baby powder and lotion in years, the sight of it always brought their smell to mind.

After putting my toothbrush and shampoo and comb and mouthwash in their proper places in the bathroom, I fell into the recliner. The nightgown's slick fabric felt cool on my fingers, and again I imagined Maggie's shoulders beneath the thin straps. Unless another crisis struck, I would never get to touch her skin again. But she had never allowed—never would—real access to herself. I ran the cool fabric across my cheek, then dropped it onto my face from above my head. My eyes closed and I inhaled lavender, hearing the wind buck against the small window in my kitchen. And then an idea overwhelmed me.

I unbuckled, unzipped, unbuttoned, and pulled off clothes and stretched Maggie's nightgown over my head. It was small, and once my arms were through the straps the nightgown rested above my chest, tight as a sausage casing. I pulled and squirmed, and one strap popped. The seams strained and could have given at any moment, but my will to make something of Maggie's mine, to have and ruin something of hers, was critically important.

In the bedroom, while standing at the full-length mirror, I froze at the sudden loud knock at my front door. All the landlady needed was to see me in a woman's black nightgown and I would be out on the street with my spare furnishings.

But when I tiptoed toward the door, something told me it was Maggie. And then her voice came through the wood. "Gary? Come on, Gary, I saw your car out back. I know you're home." I didn't answer. Standing in her black nightgown, I stared at the shaking door. I wished for Superman X-ray vision to see Maggie's vexation through the knocker. "Gary?" she asked, more quietly. She sounded pitiful, more like a lost child than I had ever heard her, and for a moment I thought this wasn't about the clothes at all.

The knocking stopped then, and a small thunk sounded, as if she had leaned her forehead against the door. I considered answering, or opening the door. I was aching in sympathy for her self-imposed isolation, but then numbness overcame me. She had made me, after more than twenty years, a little more like her, a bit tougher, and even when her quiet, ragged breathing and moaning and muffled sobs could be heard coming from behind the door, I could not, for the life of me, raise my hand to the knob to let her in.

DYLAN TAI NGUYEN
92nd Street Y

PEACE

At first glance she mistook his handwriting for barbed wire. The tail of every other word hooked into the head of the next, forming a taut snarl that twisted and slanted and jerked its way across the page. In other places his script slackened, the ink fading, the characters thin, wobbly. If it took only seconds to notice these details, it was because by now his penmanship had become as familiar as the lines in her palms, whose trails her fingers traced nightly before bed. In his initial letters four years earlier, his cursive had been vigorous and smooth. As she began disentangling the first few lines—"Don't worry about me, love. I'm happy here. I am happy."—the thought crossed her mind that she was holding something forged, and she skipped to the bottom of the page. She felt better when she saw his signature there: the tail of the *y* in "Huy" surging upward, sturdy, the same as always. The night they first met, twenty years earlier, in 1959, he had lifted her hand, opened her fist, and then carved his name—a trail of heat—onto her palm.

"My love," he continued now, "I've never felt more patriotic. I work hard for the common good and I am happy here, very happy. The Americans were wrong after all." And now his words began to stumble below the lines. "Your brother Ty—have you seen him lately? He, too, is working hard, I'm sure, in the New Economic Zones. But maybe you can take the children to visit him. He's their favorite uncle, a role model for all of us, the perfect Socialist Man." In actuality, Ty lived in a place called Angels' Breath, Pennsylvania. There, Suong knew, he received no letters from the middle of a northern jungle. There he counted profits from his electronics store; listened to the twilight songs of birds not frightened away by curfew sirens; raised boys without expecting that they'd leave home some day in camouflage uniforms with sleeves too long. What her husband was really saying in that letter screened by prison guards, Suong understood. She quit her business selling *che* pudding on the Saigon sidewalks, gathered coarse clothing, chopped off her hair, and the next morning disappeared into the southern countryside.

Her three sons remained with their grandmother. They lived on Equality Street, where the houses had drawn curtains or closed shutters, in the city that had been renamed and soon was plagued by drought. With Suong gone, the boys found it hard to sleep. *Tet,* the Lunar New Year, was almost here. And so every night they tried to dream of their parents' faces—although not even the oldest boy, Binh, could recall any details of their father's face. They tried to dream of red envelopes bearing *li xi* money, of candied persimmons and sugared lotus seeds and dried coconut shavings, too. But sometimes at curfew, other times near dawn, most often in the middle of the night, a pounding on the door would startle them from sleep; next came a fusillade of voices, and they'd hide underneath the threadbare covers that did nothing to cool their sweating brows or their tingling skin. Ten days before the New Year this was the explosion they heard: "Open up! Open up now. We are looking for Lam Thi Hong Suong, bourgeois doctor under the old puppet regime, wife of the convict Ngo Truong Huy—Ngo Truong Huy the subversive poet, the former journalist of Western propaganda, the Director of Documentation in the Agriculture Ministry of the rebellious government. I ask you once again, old woman, where is your counter-revolutionary daughter? Where is she hiding? She's been absent from her study sessions with the Association of Liberated Women."

"As I told you three nights ago, sirs," their grandmother said, "the comrade is *not* a counterrevolutionary. She's away visiting a cousin with cancer. Will be back soon, real soon."

"How soon, old woman?"

"Sirs, there's nothing in that closet but ration coupons and some useless books—"

A door slammed.

"*How soon,* I said."

"I'm not quite sure."

Something was hurled against a wall. Glass shattered. Their dog yelped twice, gave a growl, and, after what sounded like a kicking noise, whimpered.

"I'll ask you one more time: You have absolutely *no* idea when the reactionary will be back?"

"No, Sirs. Soon—that's all I can tell you. We're getting worried ourselves."

"We?"

"Me and my grandchildren. They're sleeping—"

"Dang, check inside."

Approaching the bedroom now, in boots that pounded the floor like a hammer on an anvil, was a dark uniform crowned by a military cap. When the children saw the silhouette of an elongated arm unzip the netted canopy that screened their bed from mosquitoes, they bit their tongues and feigned sleep—the youngest, Tuan, did not re-member that people asleep still needed to breathe. They felt their covers being tossed into the air: a gust on their arms, legs, toes. A flashlight singed their faces, then crept down their necks and torsos. Tuan was still holding his breath as the uniform moved over to their mother's empty bed. A rustle of sheets, a curse. Tuan's chest felt like it would explode. After ten seconds of silence, the boots walked away, and Tuan released his lungs, gasped air, and reached for Binh's hand.

In the living room there was a slow bumblebee buzz: pages being torn from books. Then, a different voice, a mousy one, called out, "Hey, what do you got to eat, old woman? Treat your guests to some holiday grub."

"Quiet, Duc!"

"Sorry. A little hungry, that's all. I haven't eaten in two days."

The leading voice again, in his piercing Phuc Tinh accent: "This cousin with cancer, where does she live?"

"Outside Hanoi, sir, the same as I told you last time. Suong and she were separated for so many years during the war that split our country apart, the war caused by the American invaders."

"And the comrade's name?"

"Lam Thi Muoi."

"All right." He cleared his throat. "Good enough. Just remember, old woman: We'll be back *soon.*"

In the morning, as the grandmother swept the floors and taped up chair legs, both Tuan and the middle brother, Ha, asked once again where their mother had gone. "Your comrade," the elderly woman replied. "I mean, your *mother* will be back soon, real soon." To them she spoke without an affected northern lilt. Voice sprightly, she added, "Get ready for school, okay? It's the last Friday of the month. We might get meat for dinner tonight." The boys raced to see who could reach the bathroom first.

Binh sat on the sofa mending the books last night's visitors had strewn across the floor. He imagined that the scraps of paper he was taping together were orphans and parents, reunited after a storm. Binh, at fifteen, had already grown to resemble his father with the same tall, wiry frame. But from the man's face he had inherited only one feature: lush and dark eyebrows, like twin dragons guarding the entryway to the imperial palace of his eyes. These were the brows, folklore claimed, of a military leader, a national hero. Binh had once shocked his parents by reciting from memory, couplet after couplet, the first two hundred lines of *The Tale of Kieu;* he was five at the time. Since then he'd learned at least three thousand poems by heart. He believed that the poets *spoke* to him. And he liked to speak back, joining his voice with what he imagined were theirs, reciting without stuttering or slurring his syllables, which he was prone to do in company. He believed, too, that words had a certain sincerity, an integrity that no one should tamper with. He loved to recite his father's poems most of all. Within the past year, however, he found that several of his father's best verses had slipped from his memory. He bit his lower lip now, trying to remember an elusive couplet from a poem his father had written called "Waterscapes"—but then he heard his grandmother announce that it was time to leave for school.

The sky was cloudless, the air so dry it smelled of metal—a tinge of copper or iron. Over the former capital the heat hung thick as a curtain. Dust from unswept alleyways and dirt from parched streets cast a brownish haze that invaded eyes and made skin itchy. As she ushered the children to school, the grandmother trailed in back, alongside Binh, while in front walked the two little ones. At the end of their alley the grandmother stopped moving and wiped the sweat from her forehead. "No rain now for fifteen days," she said.

"I thought it was only fourteen," said Tuan.

"You're wrong," replied Ha, who was a year older. "Because you're wrong, that means you get punished!" Ha started to tickle and punch his little brother. The two boys were soon screaming and grabbing hair. Tuan called to his grandmother for help.

The elderly woman did not answer. She was thinking of their mother as she spotted Ton Nu Thien Huong, the woman from Can Tho selling *hu tieu* noodles. The merchant was squatting on the corner, her legs compressed into an **M**, behind a tower of stacked bowls and a pot with steam rising heavenward. To her left was a wooden box in which she stored her coins. When she spied the grandmother, she fumbled with the box's lid, flipping it up and down, open and shut, as if fanning an invisible customer before her. It was rumored that when asked how much a bowl of her noodles cost, she'd declare, "Just a bit of change," and then, her eyes narrowing, "or one bar of gold. Take your pick." Then she'd glance downward, at the wooden lid, the underside of which, if you looked carefully, showed an abstract painting of palm trees sprouting from a cluster of islands, on the shores of which rested a slender fishing boat. As the family walked by, she locked gazes with the grandmother, and the grandmother nodded back.

Ha and Tuan were still scuffling, one of them stuck in a headlock. Then, with one gentle word, the grandmother got them to stop acting like typical boys. "Boys." Binh sighed. For some time now he'd been distancing himself from his brothers on their morning route, hoping his grandmother would take his aloofness to mean that he was too old now to be escorted to school. He longed for growth and transformation, for passage to the other side. But who would be there to receive him? To confer the honor?

On Democracy Boulevard the family passed the four-story house formerly owned by Suong's brother, Ty, now occupied by the Minister of Foreign Relations. On the second-floor balcony the new owners had draped a red flag in the middle of which was a star the color of the sun. It was at this point every morning that the grandmother slowed to a leisurely pace. Binh knew that she did so to give the boys a good view not only of what had been their uncle's mansion, but also, across the street, of the hospital where their mother once taught pediatrics and of the Ministry building where their father worked until 1972. The grandmother said nothing as they strolled past these landmarks; neither did she so much as turn her chin in their direction.

On the street once named after a former emperor, but now called Insurrection Road, the family saw, peeking from behind a curtain, the fat, rosy face of Nguyen Thi My Le, and then, appearing beside it, the grayish face of her identical twin, Nguyen Thi Thu Van. Both women had married foreigners, in 1954. During the early and middle stages of the war, when Van's health prospered and Le suffered from cancer, Van had nursed her sister's every need, often neglecting her American husband in the process. In 1973, however, their fortunes reversed: Van was struck with tuberculosis; her American husband left her to go back home. Le's cancer went into remission. Without hesitation, Le invited her sister to move into her house, against the wishes of her Russian husband.

Except for some shrubs with withered leaves, the Saigon sidewalks were treeless. In their place bloomed the stumpy limbs of veterans, the vegetated faces of lepers, the gourdlike stomachs of dust children. Some of the last group, the *bui doi,* were brownish-haired street urchins who'd been abandoned by single mothers during the war and had thus spent their days holding up signs in English: "Lookin for Papa Addason" or "Anyone no Mr Mark Glassco from Oregone?" Lately, though, they knew not to use such language. They all had dull eyes, filled with the listless look of children who were always hungry and thought they deserved it. Hoping for eye contact or a nod from a passerby, they huddled in clusters like ragweed. Occasionally, though, especially when cadres asked if they were infected with enemy blood, the dust children dispersed, squinted to make their eyes more almond-shaped, tried to blend in with the air.

"Excuse me," a dust child no older than five called out as the family passed. She tugged at the grandmother's sleeve until she stopped. "I can cook and clean. And I don't eat much."

The grandmother avoided the girl's eyes and nudged her boys along.

At the intersection of Reunification and Happiness Roads, waiting around for customers and fanning themselves with newspapers, were bronze-skinned pedicab drivers, a few of whom bore poetic names like Hoang Kim ("The Golden Age") or Quoc The ("National Prestige"). The latter, a cousin of Ngo Truong Huy's, had been a member of Saigon's National Assembly. Not a single bribe—not even a platter of fruit—did he accept while in office, and when Saigon fell he found himself with not enough money or influence to get out of Vietnam. Now, released early from camp because he'd mastered the art of appearing mute, he spent eighteen hours a day pedaling this Secretary of the Party branch, or that Director of Social Programming, or a teenage cadre and his girlfriend, many with first names like "Two," "Three," or "Six." This morning Quoc The was taxiing an obese Russian woman with a flowered parasol over her head. He was pedaling arduously. His hunched back, Binh thought, looked like a tortoiseshell.

At this point, too, the grandmother always slowed down their walking, sometimes even waiting for Quoc The to return from his route. Binh knew that the grandmother did this because Quoc The's face bore a vague resemblance to their father's. It had been three years, eleven months, and four days since the boys had last seen their father. In 1976—after writing to twelve bureaucrats, pleading with ten of them face-to-face, meeting surreptitiously with eight policemen and four minor cadres, and paying a special tax to every badge she encountered—their mother had been able to arrange a visit to Long Thanh Reeducation Camp #3. At the time their father had yet to be transferred up north, since Hanoi had not yet been able to prove he had spied for the CIA. That afternoon, as Binh now remembered, the four of them had stood behind a barbed wire fence. They jostled for position with other families, squinting across a dusty field toward a cluster of buildings. The air reeked of fuel and exhaust from the buses that carted wives and children from all corners of the south. When someone elbowed Suong, to her surprise she elbowed back, harder. Babies were crying. Children coughed up dust. When a guard came out of the building known only as Building A, a short woman began to wave. "Sister, that's a cadre. Are you blind?" someone whispered, and the woman, to everyone's dismay, started laughing—and then crying. Suddenly a boy fell into the bags at Suong's feet, and so Suong began counting them frantically. They'd brought five bags and four boxes—containing food, medicine, clothes, and, most precious of all in the economy of bribery, cigarettes. They'd been barred from bringing games, rope, sharp objects, weapons, books. In front of Building A, five uniforms were now swinging open the first of four metal gates.

And then they appeared: the disappeared. They came out en masse, floating away from the building with the corrugated tin roof, floating through the dust toward the barbed wire fence. They appeared to be fading, then coming into view again, a mass of half-naked figures with skin like the leather of old sandals, figures now blending together, now separating, all floating. Binh surveyed the field, focused his eyes hard. There was someone whose eyebrows resembled his own, but he was advancing toward another family. Another someone, whose slope of shoulders looked so familiar, but no, the figure drifted toward a woman in a gray scarf.

Then suddenly, Tuan pointed. Binh remembered thinking, *How did he find him before I could?* At the time he felt like crying. In front of them now, his silhouette crosshatched by wires, was a shadow-man. Up close, his skin had the sheen and texture of stale rice paper. Binh remembered his mother's arm snaking its way through a chink in the fence. The arm snagged, jerked; three streaks of red on tanned flesh. But the arm kept extending itself, as if on instinct, toward the hand, a web of bones, on the other side.

Tuan was kneeling. He was trying to remove a pebble stuck between the shadow-man's toes. Because one question still barbed itself in the folds of Binh's mind—*How did he find him before I could?*—Binh was too ashamed to look his father in the face. He found himself absurdly counting the ribs jutting out of the figure's midsection. When the shadow-man finally spoke, it was to Suong, and his voice was tinny. On his breath was the sour smell of spoiled rice, and Binh tried not to wince.

They had only memories. The afternoon of April 30, 1975, Huy had gone into hiding, and in a panic that evening, Suong burned all their photographs. Many nights Binh recited the man's poetry by candlelight, hoping for a vision other than that of two columns of ribs. Sometimes he imagined that the ribs were not slivers of bone, but instead the crescent-shaped feathers—the coverts—on a pair of white wings. Sometimes he resented his father—for having loved Vietnam too much not to have escaped in 1975, for having left the family with no money, even for having worked for the losing side. Other times—was it not true that his father's face and some of his

poems were disappearing from Binh's memory?—Binh was convinced that it was he, the son, who'd been abandoned.

The front gate of Independence High School was draped with a black-
and-white poster projecting a face with intense eyes—eyes "full of
promise," his fellow revolutionaries had always said. As his little
brothers said good-bye to Binh, the grandmother patted Binh's shoulder and said, "Don't be too smart in class, okay? Just blend in." When
she saw a school official staring in their direction, she managed, by relaxing her brows, to smooth the wrinkles on her forehead.

Inside the school gates, Binh joined his classmates in performing
calisthenics to the beat of Communist slogans. In the classroom he
did his best to pay attention, smile, raise his fists at the correct time,
to clap and clap until his palms turned red. He followed the cue of
the Society of Red-Handkerchiefed Youth—student leaders who'd
earned the honor of overseeing the communal cleaning, leading
group discussions, and monitoring the patriotism of their peers. Binh
was taking notes now while his history teacher lectured: "Ho Chi
Minh remains all around us. Like the glorious sun shining on the
rivers and deltas of our homeland, like the sun warming the air you're
breathing now. As Uncle Ho said, 'Nothing is more precious than
liberty and independence!'" All these words Binh scribbled in his
notebook. He stared at them, trying to compare them to the winged
verses that fluttered in his head. Many of the words were the same:
homeland, liberty, independence.

After lunch he was summoned to see the principal. He joined
twelve other students inside an office that was ripe with the lardy
smell of *lap xuong* sausages, the principal's favorite snack food. They
took a seat on the floor as the principal, scanning the room, counted
heads. The principal could barely suppress a grin. Any public-speaking
opportunity excited him. As a boy he'd known how to spell only his

first name, which was "Two." His schooling was interrupted in the first grade, when his father died, and onto his shoulders, the shoulders of the only son, fell the job of paying the family's debts, of sowing and plowing the land that, for countless generations, his family had lived on and sweated on and died on but had never owned. At sixteen he joined the Revolution, where he learned to spell *Giai Phong Nhan Dan* ("The People's Liberation"), Ho Chi Minh, and his own last name.

The principal licked his lips and took a deep breath. "You're here, my good Socialist children, because of a very special honor. You won't believe how fortunate you all are. You won't believe it!" He fixed the part in his hair and continued, "Next week the Minister of Education is visiting our school all the way from Hanoi, to celebrate *Tet* a little early, and I've decided that in the welcoming assembly you thirteen will get to accompany him onstage. What do you all think of that?"

A chorus of "We are proud, sir."

"What was that?"

"We are proud, sir!"

From the back of the pack and with a fist high in the air, a girl yelled out: "Long live the People's rule!" Her bare legs were ringed with craters. Ringworm. To express her fervor even more, the girl tightened the knot of the red handkerchief around her neck. Then, finding it difficult to breathe, she began fanning herself with both palms. The only fan in the room, amid the Cuban cigars on the principal's desk, benefited only the administrator himself and a few students sitting in front.

"This is a big honor for our school. So listen carefully as we vote to see who does what at the assembly." He stopped to swat a mosquito, then wiped the creature's body, mingled with his own blood, onto his slacks. "Since Tran Van Ba is quite tall, maybe he should get to carry the flag. I'm not sure, though. What do you all think?"

"The flag is a symbol of our glorious revolution!"

"I nominate Tran Van Ba as flag bearer!"

"Me, too!"

"I third the motion!"

There were no dissenting votes. Soon they decided, also unanimously, who would deliver the *Tet* greetings; who would lead in the singing of patriotic songs; who would recite a poem called "Celebrating Our Increased Agricultural Productivity Due to the Auspiciousness of the New Economic Zones"; who would perform a different one, titled "On the Merits of Peaceful Intervention Into Cambodia, To Save Our Neighbors From the Horrors of the Pol Pot Regime"; and one more, in classical *luc bat* meter, called "You Chinese Aggressors, We Are Taking Heed of Your Shenanigans Near Our Border!" The principal then proclaimed his hope that the Minister's gift to the school would be a set of math books from Romania, so that Independence High students would no longer have to copy the teacher's lessons onto pieces of paper and glue them together as the semester progressed. After a round of applause lasting three minutes the principal added, "And so, the biggest honor is left to Ngo Hoa Binh, since we haven't elected a task yet for him. Stand up, nephew."

Binh rose.

"Today is Binh's lucky day. First, let me announce that just this morning the faculty voted Binh into the Society of Red-Handkerchiefed Youth. No, no, hold your applause, nieces and nephews. What's more, since Binh is our top student, with the most eloquent writing skills, he'll deliver an autobiographical speech at the assembly, to show the Minister of Education what lies in the heart of an exceptional Socialist student, to show him how you've all struggled but managed to endure." The principal licked his lips twice, and his face beamed. "Come here, nephew."

Binh stepped forward. After the principal placed both a red hand-kerchief and a three-page essay in his palms, Binh bowed his head. "Read it over first, and then you can practice your speech on us." "Thank you, uncle." As he skimmed the first page, Binh furrowed his eyebrows in the exact manner his father had done in 1973 upon hearing that his poems had been officially banned by both the Hanoi and Saigon regimes. When he finished, Binh did not look up.

"Okay, nephew. Now speak. Speak with passion."

Head still lowered, the boy only shifted his weight a little. There was no sound in the room but the whirling of the fan.

"Nephew?"

Still no reply. Binh squinted at the three pages—written in red ink—and skimmed them for context. After the section welcoming the Minister to Ho Chi Minh City, after the four paragraphs de-scribing the heroic deaths of his two brothers in 1954, at Dien Bien Phu, the battle that "overthrew those barbaric French oppressors, sending them home wounded and crying craven tears," and after one passage consoling the Minister's family for these deaths, the speech ended with "And now, I, Ngo Hoa Binh, would like to take this op-portunity to publicly condemn the crimes of my reactionary grand-father, Ngo Truong An, who studied ophthalmology in Paris with the French colonizers, and of my bourgeois mother, Lam Thi Hong Suong, who was a doctor under the old puppet regime and served as President of the Volunteer Medical Corps in the puppet army. Most important, I am here today to publicly denounce the crimes of my father, Ngo Truong Huy, subversive poet, former journalist of West-ern propaganda, former Director of Documentation in the Agricul-ture Ministry of the rebellious government. I take this moment to vilify them for their sins, for their blindness, but also to apologize on their behalf and to herald the rise of a new generation, one of independent-minded and clear-sighted Socialist Youth, one that will never shirk from any opportunity to serve their nation—in the classroom, in society, or in a neighboring nation. When I serve in Cambodia next year, I will do so with great pride, instinctual patriotism, and not an ounce of trepidation. I pledge allegiance to Uncle Ho. The Democratic Republic will triumph for one thousand springs! Long live Uncle Ho's legacy!"

As Binh stood motionless, the other students held their breath. His cheeks were flushed, his sideburns damp, the sweat on his feet making his sandals feel loose. The principal began to tap his foot. "Don't be coy," he said, ducking his head to avoid a buzzing fly. "We're family. Just read."

His teeth clenched, the teenager tried to look the man square in the eye, but couldn't. To his dismay the red handkerchief slipped out of his hand, and he had to kneel to pick it up. He felt himself closing his eyes in the hope that his father's face would appear to him just then. But under his closed lids he saw nothing. What he felt was an intense burn. He tried to recite in his head the mesmerizing music of his favorite couplet from *The Tale of Kieu,* but his memory stumbled over the first few words. Binh swallowed hard. Among the various changes that had occurred in his body this past year, he disliked most the new tendency of his voice to crack without warning—to croak, then leap away like a frog eluding capture. He swallowed a second time, harder, pushing down his Adam's apple.

"Nephew?"

Thirty minutes later a woman whose birth name was Vo Thi Bao Ngoc raced through the gates of Independence High, across the courtyard, and down the hall to the principal's office. This woman and Binh's mother had grown up in adjacent villas in Bac Lieu in the

1940s, shared nannies for two years, attended the same French private schools. Ngoc had even been present the day Binh was born, had held him in the delivery room and kissed him as if he were her nephew. Although Binh was unaware of these facts, Ngoc knew exactly who he was. Throughout the war, using a network of agents disguised as chauffeurs, mailmen, waiters, nurses, ushers, Ngoc had monitored his mother's every social engagement, every wedding and ball, read every editorial and poem his father published, even guessing correctly about those that appeared under pseudonyms. She had not spoken to Suong in fourteen years, not since 1965, when she chopped off her hair and changed her name from Bao Ngoc ("Precious Jade") to Bac Nam ("North and South"). That year, too, she shunned Harvard for Moscow University, and in an overnight marriage without firecrackers or guests, she renounced her parents and all her relatives and friends for new ideals and a husband. An illiterate revolutionary from Ninh Binh, her husband would become, after 1975, the principal of Independence High. Simultaneously she'd be appointed President of the Ho Chi Minh City Branch of the National Association of Liberated Women.

In the middle of 1975, Bac Nam had received a letter from Suong bearing two pleas. First, could she pull strings in Hanoi to grant Huy an early release from camp, or at least make sure that he would not be transferred up north? "I have nothing to offer you," Suong wrote, "since everything has been taken from us. Although circumstances have divided us, Ngoc, I humbly ask you to reevaluate my husband's alleged crimes." Suong then reminded Bac Nam that, after making a speech outlining his proposal for land redistribution in the southern provinces, Huy had been ousted from Saigon's Agriculture Ministry in 1972; that he had been on the verge of resigning anyway, upon discovering the amount of corruption around him; that after 1972 he was merely a writer "dabbling with words, useless words." Next,

Suong reminded Bac Nam that their fathers, at least, had belonged to the same political party, that their grandfathers came from the same village, that they were still related by marriage. She ended with: "When we were young, Ngoc, there were times when I was not sure that you and I were two different people. I have nothing to offer you, sister, but peace. Peace, and the love we had for one another as girls. Please, Ngoc. I beg of you." The second request was less urgent: Could Bac Nam at least see to it that under the new regime Suong's sons would still be allowed to go to school? Suong then offered to meet with her in person, but the cadre refused. In her reply she wrote only this, her script fat and steady and dark: "Dear comrade, Universal education is a cornerstone of any egalitarian society. It is regrettable that some children of reactionary parents are being barred from schooling. I am, however, trying to change this. Rest assured. The children mentioned in your letter dated May 15, 1975, will be allowed to go to school."

Bac Nam had been rebuffing her husband's sexual advances since the Liberation. He had turned soft; he had picked up the habit of hoarding ration coupons, suggested they move to a bigger house, asked her to grow her hair down to her waist and wear a gold ring to match his own, turned obsequious to higher officials, too. To her horror he'd once even suggested that Hanoi should adopt more lenient reeducation policies. "The culprits we should be punishing," he'd whispered that night, "are the collaborators who left in 1975, the ones who pillaged from the poor. But they are no longer here. The French and Americans: They, too, have fled. Leave it to those bastards to make others clean up the poison they started. But the people still here, still loyal to the Fatherland, are our siblings. We have to love them as such, or they, too, will look for answers outside Vietnam. We must search for the truth in our hearts that will allow us to love one another again."

Her mind a blur of black that night, Bac Nam had been unable to offer a rebuttal.

But this afternoon, when her husband had called her with quivering voice and began, "Honey, what do I do now? This rascal Ngo Hoa Binh, he refuses to read the speech I prepared for him"—her immediate response was to hang up, skip lunch, and march straight to Independence High.

"You let him do *what*?" she was screaming now, behind the closed doors of his office. "You just stood there and let him spit in your face?"

"I roughed him up a little first—"

"You let a boy spit on you!" She slammed her hands on his desk. "Aren't you aware of his scholarly lineage? Don't you understand the symbolism of this? Don't you remember that he has Chinese blood?"

"*Quiet,* honey. The students are outside."

"He did this in front of your students? And then what? Did you kneel down like a peasant during feudal times, like a peasant woman on an *Indochinois* rubber plantation, like a peasant woman during My Lai—and *beg* him to stop?"

"No!"

"What, then?"

"I...Well." The principal raised an eyebrow, then blinked rapidly. "I pushed him around a bit, of course. And then I sought your advice."

"I can't believe this. None of this would be happening if you weren't so keen on currying favor with the Minister of Education. That corrupt bastard."

"I'm sorry, honey."

"How many peasants paid with their lives just so my husband can swallow spit from reactionaries? How many women ..."

With one sweep of her arm, she knocked the fan from his desk. She pursed her lips into a tight red line and closed her eyes. She turned her back on him. In that moment, although she could have passed for a Hong Kong starlet dreaming of a distant love, Bac Nam was actually trying to erase from her mind's eye the image of a steel cage with rusted bars behind which she had been forced to kneel and in front of which paced a blur of black-and-green fatigues, black leather belts, and black boots. She was trying to silence in her mind's ear the clank of a metal key turning, the creak of a metal door opening. The sound of belts unbuckling.

Bac Nam pivoted and faced her husband once more. "Call an all-school assembly," she said, her eyes flashing steel. *"Now."* Not waiting for his reply, she bulleted out of his office and down the hallway graced with pictures of military uniforms, ignoring the students who were studying the floor tiles and pretending they had deaf ears. Like the tank she had helped steer on April 30, 1975, the tank that had smashed through the gates of the Presidential Palace, she charged out of the building and into the fiery air of the city she'd devoted her entire life to liberating.

Twelve minutes later Independence High's twelve teachers herded 240 pupils onto the soccer field where they performed calisthenics every morning. The principal had canceled classes for the afternoon, the teachers announced as they arranged their flocks in seated rows on the ground. Secretly, the children rejoiced—until they noticed the solemn faces of the Society of Red-Handkerchiefed Youth, until they felt scalding ground through the seats of their shorts.

Standing on the north side of the field, as upright as the flagpole twenty feet in back of them, were the principal and his wife, and a teenager whose posture was no more slouched than that of the couple twice his age. In front of them were three empty chairs. The middle one had been placed four feet farther downstage, toward the south side and closer to the students. Bac Nam was holding a megaphone in her right hand. She raised it to her lips and said, needlessly, "Everyone quiet!" The flag slapped above her in the dry wind. "Quiet, please," she said again. Giving him a nudge, she told Binh to step onto the middle chair. She herself climbed onto the left stool, all the while motioning for her husband to take the remaining one. "Students of Independence High," she continued in her northern accent, which had once been southern. "Today you will witness and judge for yourselves the evils of colonization. This," pointing a foot toward Binh's legs, "is what the French and the Americans have done to the teenagers of our Fatherland. And now you, his peers, must help him purge himself of that most unnatural poison." With her left hand she held up Binh's essay, shaking the pages. Wrapped around her neck was a black leather belt imported from Sofia, Bulgaria.

For the next fifteen minutes only the spectators flinched, and even then, not very conspicuously. The teenager did not recoil. Not when Bac Nam ordered him to turn and face her. Not when she spat between his eyes. Not when the principal, on command, followed his wife's lead. And when she made Binh turn to the crowd and begin rehearsing the speech that immediately made him both an outcast and a hero, Binh's voice did not croak. His articulation was perfect. As he spoke, the clouds came out of hiding, they sailed across the white gray to embrace each other, and then, after what had been fifteen days of drought, a drizzle fell. The children turned content, thankful for the cool wet. Soon, the papers in Binh's hands clattered with raindrops, and the ink streaked down the pages like mascara. The saliva was washed from his face. Harder now the rain poured, hammering his cheeks, his lips, the red handkerchief around his neck. He was finding it difficult to read, and so he slowed down a bit. His voice remained strong though. His shoulders like concrete. In no time the flag with the star the color of the sun became so drenched, it hung from its iron pole like a flaccid curtain. By the time he reached the last paragraph, the papers in his grasp had become a pink mush, and the spectators in front of him were just dots and marbled stripes.

"Very good," Bac Nam whispered to him, after he'd pronounced the last word, which was *legacy*. To congratulate him she ran her hands all over his back, sloshing his sodden shirt. She stroked him blindly, missing the fabric, touching no one. "That was divine," she whispered, water dripping from the corners of her mouth. She offered him a smile. The rain subsided while she tousled his hair. "I'm proud of you," she mouthed.

And then, suddenly, her face changed. She curled her fingers into talons, swooped toward him, and, with a violent downward thrust, ripped his shirt. It snagged near the armpits, so she tried again, this time tearing from the bottom and up the seams. When that didn't work, she screamed, "Off with it!" and as Binh obeyed, she flicked the megaphone over her shoulder. Slowly she unwound the serpentine belt from her neck. The rain picked up again, falling obliquely now because of the wind. Binh's red handkerchief fell to the grass, followed by his tattered shirt. Bac Nam put a hand on his naked back. "Now raise your arms," she said. There was a brief pause. "And kneel. *Kneel,* I said!"

Then her voice sailed across the field, "We must reeducate to purge! We must purge to reeducate!" and she raised the belt over her shoulder, and she heaved a loud grunt, and she snapped her arm downward, and she whipped the back of the teenager whose first name meant "Peace," and she whipped the very spot where her touch still lingered, and she whipped, she whipped. With every lash of leather, a spray of water skidded crazily off his skin. The rain was coming down harder. On his flesh Binh felt coals, then a brief cool. Fire, ice, fire again. And yet, even as he heard the thunder in the heavens matching the thunder on his back, even as he heard her scream, "Ten. Twenty more to go," not a muscle in his body—the wiry body that was very much like the one breaking boulders and unearthing land mines and convulsing among electric wires and trying to survive on a handful of rice and a new poem a day, in Ly Ba So Reeducation Camp #5—not a single muscle slouched. Slap, smack. The skin on his face barely moved. "Eighteen." Throughout his reeducation, the teenager simply gritted his teeth and creased his forehead a bit. He imagined that he could be whatever he wanted, as his mother had once taught him, that he could be a water buffalo, strong, or a wooden door, stronger, that his back could be a steel roof, strongest of all, as his father was telling him now, the man's lips moving to reveal a row of bloody teeth. When the storm from Bac Nam ended, he looked out at the sea of students before him, his siblings in a new generation of Socialist Youth, and despite the sheets of rain, he did not feel blinded. Binh ran a quick hand through his hair, which had dampened into curls. And then, with rainwater on his cheeks and a look of *hoa binh* in his eyes, he announced, "My family. I apologize for my entire reactionary family." And then he joined in the clapping that reverberated through the soccer field. Speaking now with a voice no longer a boy's, he proclaimed, "To welcome the Minister of Education to Independence High next week, that will be the greatest honor of my life." It was then that he realized words did not need to signify anything; they could be as meaningless as an unseasonable drought and they need not last so long as bruises, they need not cut like leather.

OTIS HASCHEMEYER

Stanford University

The Storekeeper

SPLASH

Four days before the UN Security Council resolution will turn Desert Shield into Desert Storm, the team waits for the scouts on the south side of a dust-covered washout deep in the Iraqi desert. Their operation is illegal, but necessary. Hays, the storekeeper, a thin man with pinched, worried shoulders, slumps against a rock. It is 102 degrees Fahrenheit. Across from him, the shade reaches out, but because the team's pale desert camouflage best matches the sun-bright rocks, they sit in the sun. The radioman tells him the temperature, humidity, wind speed, and direction, as he does every hour, whether Hays needs the information or not. Humidity can slow down a bullet, but today the humidity is negligible. The wind speed is seven knots—light for the desert.

The rifle lies across his thighs. A beige cloth sticks out the muzzle as protection against the sand and dust. Sand fleas move through the hairs on his wrists and under the collar of his shirt. He reaches in his pack for more insect repellent, dabs some on his neck. The lens hoods on the scope are down, and Hays closes his eyelids, too. Sweat runs down his forehead and stings his eyes.

The scouts return. They have located an Iraqi observation post a little over a kilometer away. The guys say, "He's just up there smoking cigarettes. They left this guy on a perch."

The CO looks around. "Is there anything else up there?"

"He has a radio and machine gun."

The CO tightens his lips. "Hays," he says. "Splash the target."

Hays opens his eyes. For the first time, he is ordered to kill a man.

ACCURACY

I got my first rifle when I was ten. It was a .22—a gift from my dad.

He was the kind of man who could just look at a gun and tell what was wrong. He'd glance over, say, Son, the bolt's not locked down. And I'd think it was, but when I checked, sure enough, it wasn't all the way locked down. Or he'd say, The shot's right low—you're pulling.

My father was in charge of auto parts distribution in Arkansas, Oklahoma, Kansas, and Missouri, and he was often gone. I knew when he was home he didn't want to waste a lot of time teaching me how to shoot. He wanted to get out in the woods. So I practiced.

One thing I did was take a toothpick and tape it to a garbage can. I'd start walking backward until I couldn't see it anymore. Then I'd take one step forward and shoot it.

We hunted all over the wild country near our home in Sebastian County, Arkansas. My dad always seemed to know where the birds and squirrels were, though in truth he didn't care much for squirrel hunting. He didn't find it challenging. He preferred quail hunting. I thought squirrel hunting was sporting because the squirrels could hide in the trees.

One day, my dad showed me that deer hunting wasn't so sporting. We

*were out bird hunting. I remember some snow remained on the ground,
just in patches where the shade stuck. He held up his hand and motioned
for me to turn around. And I did, and there was a six-point buck about
fifty yards away. I stood there for a second. The deer stood there for a second looking at us. Then it ran off into the brush.*

I said, "Wow, that's pretty."

He said, "See why I don't hunt deer?"

I didn't, so I said, "No."

"Could you have hit that deer?"

"Sure, Dad. It's as big as a barn."

He said, "I rest my case." And that's the last we said about it.

1,219 METERS

The bolt action single shot .50 caliber M88 that Hays carries was designed in 1988 by Wes Harris, then master gunsmith at G. McMillan
and Co. of Phoenix, Arizona, to meet specific Navy requirements. It
is titled "a special application sniper rifle."

The weapon has an effective range of 2,000 meters (1.2 miles).
With tactical optics, it weighs in excess of 30 pounds. According to
G. McMillan's technical manual, the M88's purpose is to "provide the
user with a system capable of a high probability of a destructive first-
round hit on identified point targets." Hays's instructors at sniper
school called it the ultimate in overkill.

Hays rests the weapon against his shoulder and takes a small plastic case out of his shirt pocket. He removes earplugs and screws them
into his ears, muffling exterior sound. He flips the switches on the
scope that release the lens covers and scoots over to a low rock that
has an unobstructed view to the northeast. He folds out the gun's
bipod and places its feet on the rock. According to the scouts, the target is about a kilometer away. He levels the weapon. Crouching, he

moves his right eye to its sighting distance. Because the scouts' directions are good, he finds the man almost immediately.

The man has his observational post in the sharp mountains. He holds a military crest, a ridgeline below the actual crest of a hill. He has an excellent view of the low valley spread before him, but he is not silhouetted against the sky. Though a low row of sandbags lies in front of him, his head and chest are well within the reticle of Hays's scope. He is armed with what looks to Hays to be an American-made M60 machine gun. Above his head, he has fashioned a sunscreen by draping a beige cloth over two prongs stuck into the sandbags behind him. The sunset casts the red sandstone into a deeper red.

Hays adjusts the split-image focus that is the range finder. Green numbers in the lower center of the sight compute the distance as Hays turns the dial midscope. The man's M60 leans against his shoulder. Because the image shimmers with the heat waves, Hays uses the sharp lines of the gun barrel to join the upper section—the man with a concave wrap on his head—with the lower—his shoulders and the hands resting passively on his weapon. When the two halves meet, Hays sees the range is 1,219 meters.

The man turns his head in Hays's direction. For an instant, they look at each other. Hays does not move. The man's eyes remain unenlightened. On his ledge, from that distance, he cannot see Hays. The man puts his head down left and away, lights a cigarette. Then, he returns his gaze to the eastern horizon.

CURVES

We met in high school. I'd been playing football, been injured, and I decided to take the band bus. I looked back and saw her sitting in the back, and I said, goddamn, that is a good-looking woman. She was a majorette. So I got up and went back to where she was sitting. I sat down and more or less just told her, By god, we're going together.

Everything was going according to plan. She was a perfect mother and a perfect wife. For fun, we'd go dancing. She loved dancing with me, she said. She said she felt like she was in orbit. On a Friday night, we were out dancing, and I noticed a twinge in my left knee.

The morning after my wife and I had been out dancing, my knee quit. I fell on my face. I couldn't stand.

The doctor said, "Looks like you have some serious cartilage problems here. We'll scope it. Two hours, you'll be back."

An in-out patient deal. So we scheduled the operation for a Thursday. She was caring for me, perfectly wonderful. They took me into surgery and six hours later I came out of surgery.

Six hours later, I'm in the recovery room. And my wife is standing there, but she is dressed differently. I made a mental check to see when she could have done that. I didn't know the time—that it had been six hours.

"Well, there was a problem," she said.

I said, "Hi, honey. You look awfully nice. What do you mean problem?"

"The doctor says you'll be unable to walk for a while."

I thought, two or three days. "Well, that's no big deal," I said.

"Here he is. He'll tell you."

The doctor explained that at some point my kneecap had been crushed, and that while most of it healed, some bone chips got between the two bones and acted as an abrasive. They chewed the bottom off of this bone and the top off of that bone. He said I wouldn't be walking for six months to a year.

When he was done, my wife leaned over, gave me a kiss, and said, "By the way, I'm going out."

That's why she was dressed up.

Something happened when the doctor said I was going to be gone, unable to do anything. What I think is, she snapped right then and there. She blew a fuse.

It wasn't a full year after that, maybe eight months, when she said she was moving to New Orleans, and she was gone for good.

What I didn't realize, at the time was, during those months she was taking care of me, she did it, but she held it against me. That's what I figure, anyway. That's what it must have been.

And I was completely devoted to her and our kids. I always built everything around that premise. That was the way I was raised. That was the way my parents were raised. And then, out of nowhere, this curve hit me.

AMMUNITION

The team carries three types of ammunition for the M88: armor-piercing DUs, "whitey petes," and exploding ballistic tipped. Because Hays takes out targets only at great distances, he does not need much ammo. They carry one box of each type, each box containing twelve rounds.

Because naturally occurring uranium contains only 0.7 percent of the fissionable U-235 isotope, the process of extracting fissionable U-235 for commercial and military applications creates nuclear waste in the form of depleted uranium (DU). This is the principal ingredient of the DU armor-piercing round. DU is two and a half times more dense than steel and one and a half times more dense than lead. The density of DU makes it possible to have a smaller bullet, with less air drag, with the same mass as a larger round. The DU concentrates phenomenal weight onto a single point—more initial shock, more destruction. For example, the DU liquefies steel on contact and forces the molten steel out in its wake.

The white phosphorous round, "whitey pete," is primarily used for munitions and fuel. Phosphorous is packed around a titanium spike, and then the entire bullet is covered in a protective skin. As the projectile travels through the barrel, its protective material wears off, and air friction ignites the phosphorous.

The ballistic tipped round explodes on contact. The lead compresses a core of high explosive. This compression creates the heat that is the catalyst for the explosion. The ballistic requires less accuracy—even with a close hit, the shrapnel will kill or seriously injure. For this reason, the Geneva convention outlaws this round: more potential suffering. No one discusses the illegality of the round with Hays. The ballistic is necessary, like being there before the war starts is necessary.

The armor-piercing round is the most accurate of the three rounds the SEALs carry. After this first shot, Hays will take every other shot with a DU. For this shot though, because he is nervous, he uses a ballistic.

PLUMBING

My father called me about plumbing problems, and I went over. He met me outside. He took the grate from the side of the house and climbed into the crawl space. I handed through the toolbox and followed. We crawled along, ducking the girders and the joists. He led with the flashlight. I brought along the tools. I noticed we were passing the bathroom, but I only got suspicious when we passed the kitchen at the north end of the house. Finally he got down into the far corner and rolled onto one elbow.

I said, "Dad, why are we here? We're not here to fix the plumbing, are we?"

"Son, what are you going to do?"

"About what?" I asked. I really didn't know what he was talking about.

He said, "About your life."

He laid the flashlight down and its light faded off into the dark corner of the house, and all at once I saw that he was exactly right.

He said, "I've already talked to your mother, and we would be willing to take the kids."

He'd been in the Navy and recommended ships.

RISING

Hays supports the rifle butt with his left hand. The sweat has all but stopped dripping from his forehead, and he is glad for his eyes, but both his hands are perspiring. He knows he can make the shot, but he is nervous. All the man has to do is pick up the radio. He wants to make sure that if he misses, or the bullet just goes through a lung, it will take him anyway. He gestures toward the ammo box containing the ballistic rounds.

A gunner's mate hands him one. Hays puts the ballistic in his left hand and places his right hand, palm up, on the bolt handle. He rotates the bolt out of lockdown and slides it back.

He shifts the ballistic round from his left hand to his right. The round is nearly seven inches long and weighs one pound. He brings it up close to look at it, one last check for imperfections, and then, without thinking, he blows on it—purely ritual.

Because he doesn't trust the bolt to fit the bullet, he pushes it with his thumb, feeling it along the way, easing it into place. The shell's case head clicks when it meets the chamber. Hays slides the bolt forward and locks it down. Then, he taps the bolt handle to make sure it is locked down.

Hays has his left leg folded underneath him. His right leg is stretched out. He lifts his weight off the left. His movement is almost imperceptible. He rises. The rifle barrel comes down.

GOD

Since I'd completed two years of college and had a degree, I went to APG school. About the second week, Chief Petty Officer Pate called me into her office. Pate was a hawk-nosed warhorse, a grade-A ball buster. And a wonderful woman.

She said, "So, Hays, what do you want to be?"

Well, that's a good question. I mean, if I could be anything. And that's how it felt to me, being in the Navy at that time. So, I gave it a little thought. I said, "I want to be God." Pate looked like she didn't get it, so I said, "I want to be the guy they call."

She nodded. "You want to be a storekeeper," she said.

VARIABLES

Hays's scope does not have mechanical adjustments for Minutes of Angle and windage that would allow him to shoot dead-on in the crosshairs because should the scope go out of whack in the field it could not be reset accurately, and the weapon's accuracy is Mission Critical for the SEALs. If the weapon cannot be counted on, then Hays will not be Mission Critical either—which means he can get sent into dangerous situations because he is expendable. Still more important for Hays is that he have confidence the weapon will perform the way it always has. Therefore, the vertical range line and the horizontal windage line of the scope's reticle are calibrated with green marks for the DU round, white marks for "whitey pete," and red for ballistic. Hays eyeballs his adjustment with the red marks. He is the only variable, and he does not vary.

STOREKEEPER EXPLAINED

The ship I was on, the USS Saint Louis, *a 557-foot LKA, was in Sasebo, Japan. They were decommissioning the ship and parceling out the people. And me being the rate I was, an SK, I could pick anywhere in the world. I thought, I'll go to the supply center in San Diego. So that's what I did.*

A week or two later my captain called me over.

I took my little notepad. "Yes, sir. What can I do for you?" I figured he wanted cigars. You see, I could get anything.

He said, "Hays, how would you like to be attached to a SEAL team?"

I said, "What do you mean attached to a SEAL team?"

"They need a storekeeper."

"Where is it?" I asked. "Not Little Creek, is it?"

"Coronado," he said. "Two to three months max. They're short a storekeeper."

I said, "Great, I'll do it."

I packed my bags and a week later I was on Coronado. I found out that the previous storekeeper would sometimes take two or three days to fill an order. That's a problem with the SEALs, because they're used to getting what they want when they want it. Twenty-four hours is the rule.

So when I got there, I knew that the first thing to do was teach the team that I could do anything. If they get confidence in me right off the bat, I have the battle whipped. They'll all come to me and say, We need this.

Maybe my third day, the captain of the base, a type A personality cubed, called over and said he wanted Stinger missiles.

I said, "Sure. I can get you anything you want." But I thought, Jesus, Stingers.

But I'd be damned if I wasn't going to get them. Now, I'd been to Stinger school. I knew they had them at Pendleton.

I called them, said, "I'll send a helicopter." Whatever it takes to get that captain what he wants, I'll do. I'll send a plane.

They said, "You'll have to come yourself."

"All right, I'll be there."

I ended up getting an old gunship, a Huey, to pick me up and take me over to Pendleton. Had to sign all this shit. I couldn't believe how carefully they controlled those things. We were back by two in the afternoon. Went over to the captain's office.

He figured I was going to make some excuses. "Where did you want them delivered?" I asked.

He looked at me. I could tell he was surprised.

But that was my job. They ask for it. I get it. That's the way to be a storekeeper.

There was only one time I didn't get something in twenty-four hours. A SEAL comes in. He's enormous. He asks for boots.

"Sure," I said. "Right away. What size?"

He put his foot up on the counter. Size fifteen. That was the only time I didn't get something in twenty-four hours. Goddamn it, that pissed me off. I don't like to let someone down.

CALCULATIONS

The ballistic tipped bullet needs contact with a sturdy bone structure to explode. In humans, bone ossification is completed about the age of twenty-five. The last bone to ossify is the breastbone, the sternum. The target looks about twenty. Hays would like to take a sternum-to-spine shot, but the man faces due east. The bullet will be coming from the southwest at approximately a thirty-degree angle. He decides his trajectory should meet the target just below the man's right pectoral muscle. In sniper school, he learned that any torso shot with the .50 will neutralize a soft target from the shock alone. Still, he has never seen that, and he knows a good shot requires an exact target, not an approximation. Hays believes he can make out a shirt pocket. This is where he wants the bullet.

The acceleration due to gravity is 9.8 meters per second squared. His scope has been bore sighted at 1,000 meters. With the M88's muzzle velocity of 2,660 feet per second, the scope compensates for a drop of approximately 10 feet at 1,000 meters. Through the scope, Hays sees this as dead-on in the crosshairs; 1,000 meters is his zero distance.

From Hays's zero distance he elevates the crosshairs for the additional 219 meters. He uses the red calibrations on the reticle to adjust his Minutes of Angle for this added distance. The crosshairs settle on the man's earlobe. Then, Hays compensates for the man's elevation, which he calculates at 100 feet. Hays knows that a bullet's curved path is dependent on the angle of opposition between the bullet's velocity and earth's gravity; therefore, he sights high. He moves the reticle from earlobe up and left of the frontal lobe. The man inhales cigarette smoke deeply, glad, perhaps, that the shade has stretched out to meet him.

MIRAGE

When I was on the USS Saint Louis, *I was traveling around, winning marksmanship competitions. I had a specially built stainless steel Colt .45 Mark IV and, of course, I used an M16 rifle, too. To improve, I ordered the classified manuals on sniping—as storekeeper I could order whatever*

I wanted. I read them, but mostly they confirmed what I already knew. They did, however, give me more information on mirage.

When I was transferred to the SEAL team, I went where they went. One day they flew from Coronado to the Navy firing range at Pendleton and I was with them. They went out to take turns with a type of rifle that I'd never seen before. It was an M88, and they were shooting at something you couldn't even see. Anyway, I ribbed them a bit.

I said, "You need a scope to hit that?"

A gunner's mate had just missed. He said, "You're so good, grandpa, you take a try."

The other guys laughed.

The CO said, "Go ahead, Hays."

I asked what the zero was and he told me. So, I got down on my stomach and sighted. It was a type A1 silhouette—a black outline of a man on a white background. It was near a sign that told the distance, over a thousand meters. And I saw that the problem they had was the mirage. I read it and fired. The CO said it was a hit.

I said, "I know," cocky. I sure didn't say anything about the pain from the recoil, because there's not much that humbles a SEAL, and it's great to shut those guys up.

They were there that day to find a guy for sniper school, a sniper for Iraq. I didn't know that. I was only there on cross-assignment. They were supposed to cut me loose. And I was too old. And I didn't have the right psychological makeup—I was too logical. But I had to take that shot, to prove that I could do it.

MIRAGE EXPLAINED

Rising heat waves cause mirage. Late-afternoon mirage is worst because the sun's heat, absorbed all day long by the desert, is released.

While mirage can sometimes make a target appear to be where it is not, if read correctly it can tell the sniper where the target is and what the weather is doing at the target.

Because the man is isolated, he is an easy read. His image shakes with the rising waves—he is "scared." Behind him the mirage of the hill, a mirror image of the hill, reaches up and skates off to the north. The hill is scared in the same way as the man, with shimmering waves crossing both. The left side of the mirage flickers in and out, vanishes. From this, Hays sees that the wind comes from the left side, moving from south to north. The man's image skates left, too. He sits in a crosswind. From the angled ascent of the mirage, Hays estimates a ten-knot wind. The bullet's thirty-degree approach diminishes Hays's ten-knot adjustment by half. He brings his sight just left, over the man's shoulder.

The man has not finished his cigarette, and Hays does not want him to. When he finishes the cigarette, he may do something sudden. Hays knows; he used to smoke.

TEAM

There were twelve people on the team. Of course, no one was allowed to wear insignia. There was a radioman—RM, Second Class Petty Officer. He was in charge of talking to the people in Scotland, the guys looking at the satellite pictures. That was his job.

We had at least four or five gunner's mates, and they ranged in rate from Third Class Petty Officer to First Class Petty Officer. They carried M60 machine guns. They were in control of all the weapons except my rifle.

Two guys from operations. They were big guys. On a ship, operations specialists are primarily concerned with radar. They're the guys who write on those acrylic boards backward. Here, one of them was a painter. But actually, in the end, everyone got to paint.

Two CHT guys. On the ship, they would be plumbers and take care of the CHT tanks. Why see them out there as warriors? Well, there again, they had the build, the mentality.

We had a boiler technician. On the ship, his job was to take care of the boiler, obviously. On the SEAL team his job was to kill people. That was his job.

The rest of the team was comprised of boatswain mates. In the Navy, the boatswain mates are full-time drunk and disorderly. And these guys could shoot. Not as good as me, unfortunately.

Our mission was to paint. We got into a position about a mile away, depending on the size of the target. The laser was a box about a foot long, two inches wide, with a scope. The aircraft flew at thirty thousand feet, above the clouds. From there they dropped their missiles and bombs—the laser-guided ones. The aircraft would be past the target before the things even hit.

But we were there. We were putting down very specific radar information, just for those bombs.

It takes two men. One lights up the target. Usually he's lying down with the bipod set up. The other guy has an infrared reader. The guy with the IR sees what the radar's on and then he says, Stay right there. Even though the painter can't see the laser, he stays right on what's in his crosshairs. The bombs go only to the reflected signal, and we make it big with a spreading device, an aperture in the box.

We radio that we're set up and in position. They acknowledge the transmission. We wait. Then, we get a call that the missile's launched, or the bird's in the air, how long it will take to be there, and what direction it's coming from. Then we paint the target. After a little while, it blows up. And it was amazing because we would be painting a target, pretty close by, and the thing would just blow up. There was no whine from those bombs. We didn't see them. It would just fucking blow up.

SAFETY

The operation of the M88's bolt automatically flips the safety back. Hays also acts automatically. With a swivel of his thumb, he arches the safety forward.

TEAM EXPLAINED

I knew it was illegal, but I justified it because our mission was to paint specific critical targets. Really important targets. Not scud missile sites or something. Germ warfare, chemical warfare plants, beginnings of things like nuclear power plants that can be used to make plutonium. Really critical shit that they wanted destroyed first strike. If they went in and carpet bombed the targets, they were going to kill hundreds of thousands of people who didn't need to die. By painting, we were certain of hitting what we wanted to hit.

But as I lined up the shot, the thought that it was illegal didn't cross my mind. The thought that I shouldn't be there didn't cross my mind. The thought that this guy was going to die didn't cross my mind. The only thought that went through my mind was, I can't let this SEAL team down. I would be devastated to let them down.

SPLASH EXPLAINED

Hays's index finger touches the trigger at the center of the pad where his whorls peak. He exhales. He inhales. He is not concerned with remaining still. He concentrates on his projected trajectory. He concentrates on reaching out to his target. Because anticipation might cause him to flinch, he empties his mind of the future, of the inevitable, retina-jarring recoil. He exhales half his breath and holds—just for a moment. The trigger has a single-step, smooth-as-glass pull. Twenty-two milliseconds pass before the firing pin falls upon the primer.

At the blast, he is surprised. The bullet spirals out of the barrel as he takes the recoil like fluid into his chest. Involuntarily, he shuts his eyes against the impact.

The bullet leaves the muzzle of the M88 at over twice the speed of sound—a penetrating sound, in this case, which kicks up dust in a ten-foot radius around Hays. Everyone holds their hands over their ears except the spotter, who has plugs in his ears and watches the target through binoculars. Some of the team, those who stand in the sound wave's expanding path, feel the vibration in their guts. The sound spreads out and echoes off rock and the opposite bank and the surrounding hills. It echoes in their ears.

Meanwhile, the bullet's boat-tail is reducing air drag and allowing the bullet to retain optimum velocity. Involuntarily, Hays opens his eyes. The bullet meets the target in one and six-tenths of a second. The man is not surprised. He is unaware because the bullet meets him in silence.

The major destructive force of a small-caliber bullet is the result of a permanent wound channel—the circular path the bullet makes as it passes through a body. Because the sniper wants one shot to achieve his objective, he might choose to induce unconsciousness and eventual death with a hit to the vascular organs such as the heart or liver, or by cutting major blood vessels, such as the groin's femoral artery or the carotid arteries in the neck; however, a target may retain consciousness and muscular control for up to ten seconds. Therefore, a sniper prefers a hit on the spine—the higher the better—or better yet, a brain stem shot that requires hitting something about the size of a golf ball that sits at the base of the cranium. Snipers leave nothing to chance. They care only for accuracy.

Yet for Hays it is not the permanent wound channel that causes his target to splash.

The second way a bullet affects a soft target is through temporary cavitation, which is the result of the shock wave, the moving molecules that are the projectile's wake. It is this shock wave, produced by all bullets, that will cause a full beer can to explode, but leave an empty one sitting peacefully. The wake of the liquid is forced outward by the impact and bursts through the tin can. But because most human tissue is flexible, the shock wave causes only a temporary inflation and cannot be counted on for destruction—in general.

But because the shock wave is proportional to the kinetic energy of the projectile, which is a reflection of its velocity and its ability to retain that velocity, its mass, the prodigious shock wave that accompanies Hays's .50 caliber ballistic does not allow the tissue to retain its flexibility. Instead, the tissue absorbs the energy of the .50, expresses it through velocity, is forced outward like wake, and does not come back. The target goes splash.

This is what happens to the man: His chest splashes; his spine dents the lead; the high-explosive core compresses; the heat acts as catalyst; the solid powder turns to voluminous gas; the lead bursts outward.

The sound wave follows—crosses the washout, passes up into the hills, and over the perch to be lost into the distance forever. Hays snaps the lens covers down on his scope. He twists his earplugs out and places them in their case.

Hays does not cross the washout with the SEALs. The SEALs go up the hill first to make sure there isn't anybody hiding. Then they make a hand motion for Hays to come up. He stands on the edge of the site. There isn't a sound. He can tell they are amazed. He thinks, these guys are bad asses—for-real bad asses—and not a word crosses their lips. He knows the assumption is, you have done this, you are proud of it. Hays thinks the man looks like a big animal has come in and destroyed him—that his spine has been taken out like something reached in and took it out of him, laid it off to the side. And there is a strange smell. He knows it is the smell of death, plain and simple. He is not proud.

There is no way to clean him up. So, they leave him.

They move away from the washout, meander north. The red glow in the west sinks. The stars appear more brilliant with the passing moments, moving with the darkness from east to west. The cold comes. They walk three or four miles. The SEALs have on their night vision, Cyclops. Hays does not have one, so he follows behind, tracing their silhouettes against the pale desert rock. The wind picks up and then dies. For Hays the air smells clean, empty, even though he smells his own body odor and the insect repellent heating on his neck.

When they stop, they just stop for a rest. He opens his pack and eats some MRE—meals ready to eat. He stows the rest.

The CO motions, and they cluster for the briefing. Hays stays on the outskirts. He wants to seem like he is part of the group. He isn't really; his only job is to shoot. The CO talks about where he thinks they should be at the end of the next day. Then he asks the team how they think the day went.

"Well, the old man can shoot," one says.

Some others agree. Hays doesn't move. He does not say anything.

Afterward, he moves off and takes a cleaning kit from his pack. He opens the rifle's breech and takes out the bolt. He has a mirror, like a dentist's mirror, that he places in the breech. Then he shines a red light down the barrel. He looks at the mirror and the reflected light to see if there is any crud. There is. There always is. He pokes a brush through two or three times, then he puts down the rod, slips a patch in the slot, soaks the patch with Break-Free, pulls it through. It pulls out, twisting along with the rifling. He looks at the patch. He checks the barrel again with the mirror and the red light.

Seven years later the Navy calls him. They ask if he would like to come back and teach marksmanship. He won't do it. At thirty-nine he's back in college completing a psychology degree—not on the GI bill. He doesn't want any of that. His oldest daughter will attend university in the fall. His son has begun military school. His youngest daughter is competing in cheerleading competitions. All is well. But that is not why he won't take the Navy's offer. His vain hope is that time will push his memory to the vanishing point. Unfortunately, his dreams betray him.

At night he dreams repeatedly of the man smoking his cigarette, the man inhaling, perhaps because Hays is smoking again himself. Then he looks for the lack of surprise in the man's eyes. For some reason that is important to Hays, that the man didn't know it was coming. But as he watches, the image starts to skate away. That is generally when Hays realizes that he is viewing the man through a scope, that its reticle superimposes the image—crosshairs that for years were made from a black widow's silk webbing. In this, engineers followed nature. Hays follows those who believe that through intellect we might become sublime. Hays has no natural killer instinct. From over a kilometer away, there is no need. Instead, Hays calculates the distance, elevation, wind velocity, and direction. What he does is all intellect. And in a sense, his action is sublime, in that it is perfect. And it is through perfection that we find our closeness to God.

THE STOREKEEPER

It was when I was flying home that I decided to give up all my guns. My father had died recently. He wouldn't have understood my reasons. He'd say a gun is just a tool. Nothing more. Nothing less. And he'd be right. Still, when I got home, I took my son to the gun cabinet and said, "All these are yours now. You take care of them." The Mark IV, the over-under, all of them.

And he said, "I'll take care of them, sir."

I never explained to my son what my job was over there. A storekeeper, I tell him. He knows what that is.

FRANCES HWANG

University of Montana

TRANSPARENCY

Henry Liu lost his voice halfway through the trip, coughing so violently that his left side felt like he had pulled a muscle. Whenever he felt pain, he put his hand across his chest to reassure himself that his heart was still beating. He looked at the view as his wife drove, at the broken edges of mountains covered in snow and the turquoise lake where not a single fish lived because its waters were too cold. The mountains held a stillness that silenced him. They looked changeless and unreal with their tiers of snow, reflected perfectly in the clear green surface of the lake. It moved him to think how many thousands of years they had stood, worn silently away by wind and ice. He felt regret watching the lake slip past his window. When it disappeared from view, Henry felt as if he had been given a last glimpse of the world. He knew that he would be dead before the trip was over.

His sixteen-year-old son, James, slouched in his seat, playing his Game Boy. Alice leaned her head against the window reading a Russian novel for college—a thousand pages at the very least—by an author whose name Henry couldn't pronounce. His wife kept exclaiming at the scenery—*look outside, isn't it beautiful?*—and when neither of their children looked, she became angry, saying what a waste it had been to bring them, until his daughter put the novel down on her knee and gazed through the window. His wife drove the car in fits and starts, pressing down hard on the accelerator and just as suddenly releasing it so that the car kept lurching forward and slowing down. "Mom," James yelled, "you're making me sick! Stop it!"

"What?" she said.

"Your driving! It sucks! I'm a better driver, right, Alice?"

Alice picked up her novel and flipped a page.

"Mom, stop the car and let me drive!"

"You shut up," his wife said. "I don't want all of us to end up dead at the bottom of the cliff."

James gave a heavy sigh as he collapsed back into his seat. He glanced out the window. "Everything looks the same," he complained. He picked up his Game Boy, pushing his glasses back with the edge of a finger.

Henry rolled down his window, but his wife turned to look at him. She didn't like the wind hitting her face because the lady who sold her makeup said that moving air wasn't good for her complexion. So he closed the window, and they drove like that for another hour or so, the rented car smelling of vinyl, the way new cars smell, and the lukewarm air blowing in softly through the vents. Through the glass, Henry stared at the mountains taking up the sky, massive fissured surfaces that from a distance became faint blue outlines. He wanted to remember them, but it seemed impossible for his mind to remember anything so beautiful and vast. On previous vacations, he had bought a postcard or two to remind him of the places they had seen, but this attempt at memory now seemed like wasted effort.

A tickle crept into his throat, and Henry held his breath. He didn't want to begin coughing, but the itch blossomed in his throat until he felt he was suffocating. His eyes watered as he hunched over in his seat, coughing. His family watched him in silence. "How are you?" his wife finally asked.

Henry nodded, swallowing, his fingers touching his throat.

"Your father is sick." His wife sounded surprised, like she hardly believed it. Ever since Henry had lost his voice, his family talked about him as if he weren't there. What about Dad? his children would say. Poor Dad! Their regard made Henry feel his sickness even more. He would look at the lines of his skin, its cracked translucence, and wonder if he were becoming invisible.

His children liked to hear him croak. "He sounds like the Godfather," James said. "Hey, Dad, can you say, 'He sleeps with the fishes.' Say it, Dad." Henry just smiled. When he wore his gray jacket and pants, James and Alice addressed him as Don. "How's it going, Don?" they said and laughed together in the backseat of the car. They made their voices deep and scratchy. "You do a favor for me, I'll do a favor for you."

It was odd, but when he did speak, his family stopped their chatter and listened to his every syllable. He spoke so rarely that his words seemed to hold unusual power. Now, as they followed a winding road through the mountains, Henry lifted his hand up. His wife glanced at him. "Stop," he said. His voice was like dry wind, he felt his insides shaking. His wife pulled over to the side.

"Are you okay, Dad?" Alice asked.

"Okay," he whispered. "Water."

Alice found a bottle underneath a jacket on the floor and poured him a cup. Henry drank quickly with everyone watching. When he was done, he pointed to the mountains outside the window and then opened the car door to get out.

"What's he doing?" Alice asked.

"Dad's going crazy!" James said.

"He wants to see the view," his wife told them.

His wife and Alice got out and followed him to the overlook while James stayed inside the car. Henry stepped onto a large red rock to see the view. "Let me get a picture," Alice said to her mother. "Smile!" Her voice was buoyant in the singsong way that people spoke when taking photographs. Henry noticed that his wife was smiling without really smiling. Her face seemed to be resisting the wind. She kept blinking as she held her lips together, a colorful silk scarf surrounding her throat. Henry was struck by how old she looked as she waited for Alice to take the photograph. "Dad, turn around," Alice said. Henry shook his head without looking at her, waving his hand as if brushing away a fly. His daughter took his picture anyway, a side profile of him gesticulating on top of the rock.

"Why doesn't he want his picture taken?" Alice asked her mother.

"Don't worry about him," his wife said. She and Alice paused for a moment, breathing in the view. "So beautiful!" his wife sighed. Then, they turned and headed back for the car.

Henry set one foot on top of another rock. A burned oak tree rose from the rocky earth, its limbs twisted in the air. There were acorns hanging from the dried-up branches, and they were colorless as silver; they looked petrified. Henry thought it remarkable that the acorns had not already fallen. He picked up a small piece of rock, brick red, like a misshapen diamond, and pressed it into his palm. One side was crusted with dirt, leaving his fingers dusty and dry. It smelled like stale smoke, like ash, when he sniffed at it.

When he looked back to where the car was parked, he noticed that his family was staring at him. He tossed the rock to the ground and then spat along the side of the road, trying to clean his tongue of the taste of ash. When he was inside the car again, before they had even driven a mile, he turned to his wife, speaking to her in Chinese. "Please take me to the hospital," he said.

Three hours passed by as they waited in the emergency room for a doctor. As Henry had complained of chest pain, the nurse had taken his blood pressure and pulse to make sure he wasn't having a heart attack. She also drew a sample of his blood and sent it to the laboratory for results. His wife had dropped their children off at the motel after giving them permission to sign up for an ATV ride. Henry didn't like the idea at all, but his wife relented after James promised he wouldn't drive but would share the same vehicle with his sister. Henry knew, of course, that Alice would let her brother drive, but he didn't say anything to stop them.

There was a television in the waiting room, and he and his wife were watching the men's finals at Wimbledon. The screen was mounted so high, however, that it was impossible to follow the ball as it flew across the net. After squinting for an hour, Henry finally gave up and closed his eyes, while his wife continued to watch the game. He was tired of the heartless drama and the crowd, which demanded nothing less than perfection from the players.

With his eyes closed, Henry concentrated on the pain inside his throat. He wanted to drink something—hot tea with a couple of cough drops thrown in, a few tablespoons of whiskey mixed with honey and lemon—anything to relieve the soreness. The air had turned raw in his throat, as if he were breathing particles of dust. He had heard of people with asthma being able to breathe again after being submerged in water, and he thought once more about the lake he had seen that afternoon, its glacial stillness with not a single thing stirring below. He imagined lying on the silt floor, his nameless body edged in blue, drifting without words or sound along the empty bottom.

His wife shook his arm, and Henry woke up. He cleared his throat and sat up straight in his chair. Several people were looking at him. "You were snoring," his wife told him. His body felt cold and damp, and he rose shakily to his feet. "Where are you going?" his wife asked. He pointed his thumb toward the window. "Huh?"

"Outside."

In front of the hospital there were a few empty benches. Henry chose the one facing the most sunlight, so he blinked as he sat down. The sun felt weak against his skin, like the light was passing through him.

"You have a smoke?"

Henry looked up at a woman standing beside him. She was in her early thirties, with frizzy brown hair, and she wore the flimsy gown issued to patients. When she stepped in front of him, Henry could see that she wore another gown underneath, that one reversed to cover her back. Her right arm was attached to an IV drip, and she had dragged the metal stand along the cement walkway with her.

"What?" Henry asked.

"Do you have a smoke?" she repeated. She made the motions of taking a cigarette in and out of her mouth.

Henry shook his head, waving his hand.

A nurse wearing blue scrubs walked through the sliding doors and approached him. "Henry Liu?" she asked.

Henry nodded, getting up out of his seat.

"Actually, Mr. Liu, you can stay where you are. I just wanted to check on how you're doing."

"Okay."

"We're almost ready to see you. We're still waiting for the results from the lab. It won't be more than an hour or so."

"Nurse," the woman said, "got a smoke?"

"I'm afraid not," the nurse said, turning away.

"God, what does it take to get a cigarette around here?" the woman demanded. She paced up and down the walkway with the IV stand. She stopped by his bench and rubbed her shoe along the cement curb. "This feels nice. Henry, right?"

Henry looked over at her in surprise.

"Henry," the woman said again, "won't you talk to me?"

Henry tapped the base of his throat and shook his head.

"I know my body better than any doctor," the woman said, "but they won't let me smoke. I can't even drink my glasses of water. You know what they call my condition? Psychogenic polydipsia. Psycho fucking what? I said. Who would think water could be bad for you?"

Henry raised his eyebrows and looked at her.

"My ions are off," she said. "Missing electrolytes. The doctor said I was drowning."

The woman's eyes had a green fluorescence. When she spoke, her skin moved tightly along her face like she'd received a face-lift. Yet she couldn't have been older than thirty-five or so.

"You don't believe me, do you?" the woman said. "You probably think I need a new liver or something."

Henry cleared his throat. "How much water...?" He curled his fingers and made the gesture of drinking from an imaginary cup.

"A lot, Henry. I am addicted to water. The pills I take make my mouth so dry." A couple walked toward them from the parking lot. "Hey, excuse me, got a smoke?" the woman yelled.

"Sorry," the man said, and the couple passed by.

The woman pulled her IV stand closer to the bench and sat down beside Henry. "Guess how much water I drink."

Henry shrugged.

"Come on, guess."

In his lap, Henry stuck out his thumb and forefinger. "Two gallons," he whispered.

"No," the woman said. "I drink 452 fluid ounces each day. Three and a half gallons of water." The woman leaned her head back, tapping her fingers along the bench in spite of the tube that came out of her hand. She crossed her legs, bobbing one foot up and down, the laces of her tennis shoe dangling. Henry could see short brown hairs sprouting from her legs. His wife didn't ever need to shave; her legs were so dry they had a sheen to them, like cracked porcelain.

"Nothing more delicious," the woman said. "Everything has a taste except water. You know how hard it is to find something without a taste, Henry?" She began fiddling with the tube stuck on the back of her hand. "The other night I dreamed I was sitting in a restaurant with my ex-husband, Ronny, and it was like we were married all over again. The only thing he said to me was, 'I've flushed out my ears.' Then he proceeded to cut his bread into very small pieces. To be honest, I was more interested in looking at the menu. There were fancy things, a lot of French words I didn't know. But I remember one dish in particular. Encrusted Squab Stuffed with Goat Cheese. Can you imagine? All I wanted was meat loaf, but I couldn't find it on the menu. The more I looked, the more convinced I was it was my last meal." The woman caressed her IV with the tips of her fingers. It made Henry nervous, like she might yank the tube out at any moment. "I never wanted to have a taste for things."

"Lou Liu," a voice said from behind. Henry jerked his head up, saw that his wife was standing behind the bench. *Old man,* she had called him. Old Liu. His wife stared at the woman sitting beside him.

"Your wife, Henry?" the woman said.

Henry got up awkwardly out of his seat. He would have introduced them, but he didn't know the woman's name.

"It's time for me to pick up the kids," his wife said to him in Chinese.

"Oh, I know," the woman said. "That's Japanese, isn't it?"

"Okay," he said. "I'll be here waiting."

"What are you talking about, Henry?" the woman asked.

"Who is that?" his wife said, digging through her purse. Henry shrugged. His wife put on her sunglasses. "Don't forget about insurance," she said as she turned away. She walked to the parking lot, clutching her purse. Henry watched her recede into a horizon of glinting cars.

"Well, I have a better chance of understanding you when you don't say anything at all," the woman said when Henry sat down again. "How long have you been married, Henry?"

The question startled him. He stared down at his feet planted on the smooth, newly laid walkway. For his last birthday, his wife had to remind him that he was turning fifty-three, not fifty-two as he had imagined. Sometimes he caught himself drifting away only to be seized with panic that he no longer knew where he was. The years had passed by as in a dream, and he suddenly found himself sitting on this bench, speaking to a woman he didn't know, as he tried to remember his life.

"Twenty-two," he finally answered.

"Impressive," the woman remarked. "Ronny and I didn't last half that long. Love can turn ugly so fast. The simplest things about him made me go crazy. Like at night, when Ronny brushed his teeth, he used this curved metal thing to scrape his tongue. He liked showing me all the gunk he collected because he was trying to persuade me to use it. Whenever we went out to eat, he would inspect his glass. If there was the slightest water spot, he'd wipe it down with a napkin." The woman sighed. "It's the stupid, small things that make you hate someone. We parted ways, and then last summer a neighbor found Ronny. I never thought he would be capable of doing that. He didn't leave a note, just a piece of paper calculating how much he would have to fall. He was 189 pounds, and he worked it out that he would have to fall eight feet and two inches." The woman scratched her elbow.

"I know what you're thinking," she said, folding her hands over her stomach. "The doctors ask me all the time. Do you know what's going to happen to you if you don't stop, they say. Seizures. Coma. I don't know whether to believe them or not. I have such a terrible thirst." The woman paused to gaze at Henry. "You don't think my body would be telling me something that's wrong, do you?"

The skin along the woman's face sagged once she stopped talking. Henry wondered what it would mean to be like her, smoking her cigarettes, taking her pills, drinking her water. He had never been addicted to anything in his life. He imagined her arranging glasses of water neatly in a row. She would pick up a glass and begin to drink, and when it was empty she would pick up another, letting it pour down her throat, filling the folds of her stomach. She was trying to drown something inside of her, but Henry didn't think it could be done.

"It's the moments of pettiness that you regret," the woman said, "even though they reveal who you really are."

When the nurse came to get him, he rose out of his seat.

"So long, Henry," the woman smiled. She gave him her hand, brown and lithe, the nails bitten down to shapeless stubs. Her skin had a soft dryness, and her fingers clutched his own with nervous energy. He turned and followed the nurse back inside.

After taking his vital signs—measuring his temperature and pulse, his blood pressure, respiratory rate, and oxygen saturation—after taking his blood and submitting it to a laboratory for tests, after giving him a chest X ray and then a CAT scan, hooking him up to the cardiac monitor to follow the rhythms of his heart, it was determined that Henry had bronchitis. Henry laughed like a fool at the news. It wasn't too serious, the doctor said, prescribing for him the usual course of antibiotics as well as a cough syrup with codeine to suppress the fits and relieve the pain. Henry's family was sitting in the waiting room when he came down the hallway. He had a bracelet around his wrist, and he was holding a white paper bag containing his medications.

"What's up, Don?" his son said to him.

"How are you doing, Dad?" Alice asked.

Henry nodded his head and smiled. He'd taken his antibiotics and cough syrup already and felt like he was going to be better. "You drive?" he asked his son.

"Sure," James said.

"We saw a bear from the side of the road," Alice told him.

Henry's eyes widened. "A bear!"

"He had a white patch on his chest," Alice said. "He stood up on his hind legs when he saw us."

"Alice tried to take his picture," James said, "but he ran into the forest when he saw her."

"You kids," he smiled, patting his son on the shoulder.

Outside, the mountains had become a mass of shadows darker than the sky. Driving along the highway, Henry felt them closing in as the tiny car pressed forward. They stopped at a seafood restaurant a few miles from their motel. Henry felt hungry for the first time in a week and ordered two bowls of vegetable soup. Alice had brought her novel into the restaurant—she was at a good part, she explained, and had only a couple of pages left in the chapter. She read diligently until the food came and then placed her book facedown on the tablecloth.

Henry cleared his throat. "What kind of story?" he asked, pointing to the cover of his daughter's book.

"Oh!" Alice exclaimed. "It's hard to say." She bit her lip, revealing neat, childlike teeth. "It's about this young man who's innocent. Almost like a saint," she said, touching the spine of her book thoughtfully. "He's in love with a general's daughter, but there's also this tortured, fallen woman. She's beautiful and mad, all these men are in love with her, but she doesn't like any of them. One of them gives her a hundred thousand rubles, but she throws them into the fire."

"Sounds like a stupid book," James said.

"It's not," Alice said.

His wife cut off a piece of her salmon and put it onto Henry's plate for him to try. Henry couldn't help but notice the gentle slope of her hands, her maternal fingers and clear rounded nails. They had been at an ice-skating rink, he remembered, when he first touched her hand. She had clung to the wall, wearing a bright yellow dress— a dress, even though they were skating!—but he realized she had worn it for him, and as she tottered on her skates, he had taken her small cold fingers into his own.

His wife's jade bracelet gleamed in the light as she turned her wrist. The waiter came and refilled their glasses of water. Henry touched his glass, felt the beads of condensation along his fingertips. He thought of the woman at the hospital, imagined her lying awake at this hour, trying to forget the dryness in her mouth. Perhaps she swallowed her own saliva for relief, moistening her lips with her tongue. He lifted the glass to his mouth, his lips parted to receive its coolness.

Something clinked against his teeth. A pink mass floated upward his lips.

"Dad, my glass!" James laughed.

Henry saw a pink retainer sitting at the bottom of the glass he was holding. His family erupted into laughter.

"I put it in there for a rinse," James said.

"You know your father is getting confused," his wife said.

"I didn't see," Alice laughed. "Did he really drink from it?"

People began looking over at their table. Henry flushed, realizing he was still holding the glass of water in his hand. He felt a painful throb in his chest, as if his heart were swollen, but he knew that it would be years before it finally gave out. He could hear it beating louder and louder now as he set the glass on the table and waited for his family to quiet down.

CAIMEEN GARRETT

Florida State University

CIRCUITS

Our sex life suffered terribly the summer my boyfriend competed on the amateur tug-of-war circuit. He lost all interest—it was like living at the Jersey shore with a seven-year-old with a sixteen-inch neck and triceps swollen like horseshoes. Our landlord introduced him to the sport, and from the first beachside competition my boyfriend was hooked. After that, when he wasn't valeting at the Angler he was training, running, lifting—or sprawled out in Secrets, the bar that sponsored the Frayed Knots. When he did happen to be in the apartment with me, he was never still but constantly looking for ways to improve his pulling technique. He would test different kinds of chalk and household items that might improve his grip, leaving ghostly prints behind. In the doorway of our bedroom he would grip one side of the doorframe and lean back in a low crouch, perfecting his wide stance. When I decided to make the bed, I inevitably found his grip strengthener tangled in the sheets.

When we watched television, he would rub his palms across the top of a cinder block he kept by the couch to roughen them. He was trying to improve his grip. His hands, which had been quite handsome, were now completely callused. They seemed like entirely new hands and I wanted them on me. But though he would intentionally expose his hands to all kinds of harsh treatment, it seemed that touching me would ruin them. He often slept with his hands thrust into his armpits, as if he feared I would moisturize them in the night.

I didn't know there was a tug-of-war circuit. I didn't know that there were things called circuits. Apparently they were going on all the time without my knowledge. Why wasn't there a list of all existing circuits available to the public? I had talents. Certainly there was a circuit for me, and no one was telling me about it.

We had one intimate moment that first week of June—perfunctory on his part, like renewing a long-lapsed CPR certification, a bluff through something distasteful. I imagined a litany of reminders and directions flooding his brain, *head-tilt-chin-lift-head-tilt-chin-lift, locate notched rib.* A thalidomide baby could have counted on one hand the number of times we had conjugal relations after Father's Day.

Still, my boyfriend seemed fond of me, appreciative when I rubbed nongreasy sunscreen on his back and neck, careful to run a line down the part of his hair. He begged for cornstarch rubdowns after competitions, yet by the time I was kneading his hamstrings— the obvious portal for transcending mere physical comfort—he was asleep, a ribbon of drool soaking the pillow like the barren dialogue bubble of a dumbstruck cartoon. Sleeping, awake, I studied him for guilty gestures, stared at his dirty clothes puddled on the floor, expecting clues—Conversation Hearts hidden under thimbles—to reveal themselves if I just looked in the right place.

I was an assistant aboard the *Sea Rocket,* a tour boat that circled the bay hourly, and a few nights a week I did face painting on the amusement pier of the boardwalk, creating butterflies, peace signs, and Pikachus. It was license to cradle the jawbones of strangers requesting Grateful Dead teddies, prepping the skin with a dusting of baby powder that caught the fluorescence of the Tilt-A-Whirl and the Racing Flamingos and limned their cheeks in a curve of cilia down. I learned the trick eye doctors and makeup artists must perfect, feigning obliviousness to the forced intimacy of faces inches apart, directing my exhale down, seeing only the truth of skin.

Those anonymous cheeks, the salt air, the typical inflammatory factors of beach life, affected all my appetites. It seemed cruelly ironic that as my boyfriend's desire shrank, mine inversely increased. I found his new sport thoroughly erotic. It was absurd, vacuous—and totally primordial. The primal simplicity of the struggle, the quaint camp, the mental hygiene filmstrip of it all! I didn't want him to stop or choose between us—I just wanted to be part of it. I was fascinated with the rope. To be pulled apart. Fought over. I wanted to *be* the rope, or at the very least tied up with it. In bed I got into the habit of extending my arms overhead, crossed at the wrist, in easy reach of the beach wrap slung over the headboard. My boyfriend did not notice this maneuver. I tried my usual bag of tricks. My unusual bag of tricks. My illegal-in-forty-seven-states bag of tricks. But my boyfriend took no interest in anything beyond tugging—his rope, that is. Meanwhile, I couldn't floss my teeth without getting aroused.

The weekend competitions were erotic torture: five-man teams of tan young men, shirtless men in low-slung shorts that shifted to reveal the etched lines of their hip flexors, men pulling with everything they had. Perhaps this was the appeal—how everything, all of one's self was telescoped into one moment of pure concentration. I had little in common with the other war widows, flighty girls in tankinis who squealed like the studio audience of a cookware infomercial. I hid behind scratched Oakleys, feigning indifference as I flipped through waterlogged magazines, gazed down at bloated paperbacks whose pages arced like the tissue plumage of a Thanksgiving centerpiece. I'd heard on NPR that the dominant female wolf of the pack will try to stress out the other females so they don't ovulate. This was the attitude I took with the girlfriends. I thought I deserved to dominate someone.

Afterward we would sit in Secrets for hours, my boyfriend and the rest of the Knots performing vigorous autopsies of the matches, noting the subtle fluctuations of strength, waxing rhapsodic about the precise moment when they could feel that a pull was about to be won or lost, the powerlessness they felt in that moment just before a loss, as they foresaw being inexorably dragged over the dividing line. They would crunch numbers on cocktail napkins, plugging their one rep max for the bench press, the squat, the snatch, and clean and jerk, their stroke output from their latest ergometer readings—they would cram all these numbers into some equation that would spit out their strength in terms of bodyweight—*I can pull 2.4 times my weight for five sustained seconds and hold 1.9 over thirty, but if it goes more than three minutes I drop to .97.* They were like ants and they plotted the coordinates on XY graphs that showed strength relative to time. I would sit eavesdropping at the bar with my rum and Diet Coke, doing my best to translate their slang, catching an eloquence in my boyfriend's words that I'd never heard before, certainly not in his conversations about us.

I gave up all attempts at seduction and was too proud to broach the subject, though my frustration was hard to conceal. What was the point of living in beach squalor, with a bathtub so clogged with sand it took three hours to drain, in a place where the TV weathermen said the word *humiture* daily—what was the point of this sweaty hassle if not to have an unreasonable amount of sex? Why else would couples live at the shore? Instead of confronting my boyfriend, I sulked. I am not an attractive sulker. When he asked me to hand him something, I would start to give it but at the last second pull back, forcing him into a little tug. I played it cute, but after the second Scotch-taped twenty he became less amused. Then he wouldn't take things directly from me, but would wait until I put the salt shaker or newspaper down on some neutral ground like the coffee table. It was like hostage negotiations. *Slide the remote over to me. Nice and slow.*

July passed. My free time was spent alone in the apartment where I endlessly viewed the contents of our scant video library (holdings: five), which had mysteriously come to include the instructional videotape for the Garden Weasel, a piece of equipment that neither of us owned. It was while watching this tape that I discovered unwholesome uses for my boyfriend's Gripstrengthener.

One day in August, I was sitting on the pavement outside the King-O-Wash, balancing on my lap a vending machine lunch to match my vending machine life, thinking that this was my last summer of bad habits—come Labor Day I would wear SPF fifty every day for the remainder of my tiresome life, drink only the occasional glass of red wine, and never mash my face into a pillow again. As a summer of bad habits, this had been a disappointing one. My bad habits should have been used to greater effect, for a higher purpose, because sooner and sooner I'd be an old woman getting saltwater flushed through varicose veins, conceding to age in a skirted bathing suit that fooled no one. I peeled the cellophane back on my Handi-Snak crackers and spreadable cheese—I liked it because of the preparation involved, the little red stick for spreading purposes, the way I could lump the entire cup of cheese on just one of the crackers if I so chose.

I looked up from my cracker preparations to see the leader of the Frayed Knots crossing toward me, a comforter wadded under one arm. He was the anchor—rear man in the lineup who wrapped the rope around his waist and called out the cadence. With an audience he was all charm and obsequious gallantry, but I sensed that alone he was the sort of man who abandoned shopping carts in the lot instead of shepherding them back to the cart corral, the sort who could hold a camcorder steady as strangers were mauled by rottweilers or trampled by a petting zoo nag gone mad. I had a sense about people. My boyfriend had told me this unsubstantiated rumor that the anchor had a titanium nose due to losing the real one to an extremely rare nose disease. I wasn't sure what kind of metal titanium was, though I could picture its location on my classroom periodic table of elements, but, regardless, it seemed an odd choice. *Why not Gore-Tex?* was the thought I kept having.

"Crackers and pretzels," he said. "There's a nutritious lunch."

"It's 'hungry size.'" I gestured to the label and held the pretzel bag out to him. "Of all the sizes that's my favorite. So, do you think that somehow skirts on bathing suits are slimming? I mean, who do these women think they're fooling?" En masse the Frayed Knots were an impenetrable force, speaking their inscrutable twin language that excluded anyone who had not stepped over the event horizon of their little cult, but alone, individually, they were powerless, demystified, and my fear and discomfort dissolved.

"Is a rear spoiler slimming on a car? I don't think so." He looked down at me as though assessing the nascent figure flaws that would provoke such an inquiry.

He jabbed a pretzel at his mouth and began to beat the comforter against the pavement, shaking out sand that stung my calves and cheeks. I studied his nose, quite prominent in profile. You'd think if it were really fake they would have given him a nice, small nose in harmony with his chin and forehead, unless, of course, they were trying to replicate his God-given nose. I wanted to ask him if the titanium got hot and itchy under his skin, particularly during beachside athletics, and what he did to counteract that. I noticed large brown stains on the pink underside of the comforter—the result of something equal parts menstrual and murderous from the look of it.

"You know, I thought the custom merely involved the groom hanging the bridal sheet out the window, not prancing down the street with it. This is much more entertaining." I crushed my empty soda can. "Congrats on snagging a real live virgin. The suspense must have been excruciating." I had become snide in recent months—the summer had done that to me.

"An experiment gone awry. It's chocolate diptop, you know, Magic Shell. Ill-conceived from the start, really."

I didn't have time to prepare my mind to block the visual image this information produced. It was not an entirely bad image either until his girlfriend intruded—a dishwater blond with a penchant for toe rings, attractive in a straight-to-video sort of way. I followed him into the Laundromat.

"Don't you need cold for that, cold surfaces, for it to work?"

"Yeah, well I thought I had a way around that." I waited for him to elucidate, but he was silent as he rubbed a dollar bill across the top edge of the coin changer—a gesture I found attractive. "If I'm ever rich, I'm pumping money into diptop research. Make that shit work in all temperatures."

"You should really use stain stuff on that," I said. I picked up my bottle of Spray 'n Wash and blasted a dot matrix archipelago along the left hem.

He leaned against my washer, drumming in syncopation.

"You're an unbalanced load." He lifted his right hand to hit an imaginary cymbal, then resumed drumming. A stricken look must have passed over my face because he gestured to the control panel: UNBALANCED LOAD was lit up.

"I don't know what you got in here, but it's a-rockin'." He patted the belly of the vibrating machine.

I blushed, relieved that I had not been insulted and also because he seemed to be intimating something risqué about my laundry's behavior. He saw the opening and went for it.

"Could you take care of this for me? Do you mind?" he said, pushing his pile of quarters toward me, giving a pleading look meant to be simultaneously seductive and sympathy inducing vis-à-vis his helpless maleness. "I need to catch Greg at Mateo's before his shift ends. You're gonna stay with your stuff anyway, right?"

I looked down at the brown blot that in a Rorschach situation I'd ID as either someone wearing a nasal pore strip or a fat woman getting a very thorough Brazilian wax. A puff of air blew in as the door closed behind him, and I was left working the stain against itself.

I became disenchanted with the face-painting gig and my boss offered to transfer me to the balloon animal kiosk. I bought a book and practiced in front of the television. Twisting balloons is surprisingly sensuous; the fear that they might burst in your face adds an element of excitement, though they don't explode nearly as often as you might think. I learned the various different twists. I learned to exhale hot on a balloon, then rub like frostbite until it was coaxed into the bend of a swan's neck. I started off simple, dogs and swans, advancing to reindeer, penguins, bears holding tulips, pairs of lovebirds inside giant hearts. I discovered that I had an excellent sense of proportion in dealing with balloons. This pleased me, since I had no sense of proportion in any aspect of my actual life. I had an instinct for using up the length of balloon just right, never running out at the end. I did not produce three-legged dogs or tigers with atrophied back legs half the size of their front limbs. I twisted off one-, two-, three-inch bubbles with ease, always producing symmetrical animals with ears and limbs all the same length, balanced animals that could stand upright on their own, and soon the apartment was littered with them.

Finally the summer drew to a close. Soon my boyfriend would return to Temple to finish his MBA and I would meet fresh classes of ninth graders. I got it into my head that his desire would return—win or lose—after the final Tug-of-War Championship. As we headed to the beach that Saturday I felt optimistic. Maybe Labor Day weekend could be saved. Perhaps this all would end, dissolve away like a dream, my boyfriend realizing that I had been here all along, patient, loving, faithful, and still in possession of a great rack. The Championship, five heats in all, was carnal misery—match after match of barefoot men straining in the sand, screaming themselves hoarse as they pulled on a cadence. The sight of my boyfriend, fourth man back in the lineup, pulling with all his might, the inverted hearts of his calves tensing into sharp relief, the cords of his arms swollen like plaited bread—oh, it was just so wonderful! I tried to mute my ecstasy by looking away, but then my eyes fell on the team captain—a body you could sled on—and I had to mutter *"titanium nose, titanium nose"* to calm myself. The Frayed Knots made it into the fourth round, then lost after a grueling eight-minute bout. Though I wanted my boyfriend to win, it was more arousing when he lost. There was something about seeing him being dragged forward against his will, every fiber of his being straining against it—there was something about this that was just so hot.

We watched the rest of the competition, then stayed at the beach cookout for nearly two hours. I convinced myself that my boyfriend needed time to come down from the disappointing loss. At one point I noticed him leaning across a picnic table, arm wrestling with a teammate, the W of their arms separating overflowing bowls of potato salad and ambrosia. I glanced up at some skywriting blurred beyond intelligibility—*apropos* it seemed to read—then back at the table. My boyfriend was slowly releasing his opponent's fist from where he'd sunk it in the ambrosia. Hand released, the opponent put the back of his hand to his mouth and sucked off the clinging mini marshmallows and coconut flakes. *Oh no,* I thought, *I can see where this is going.* I walked toward the table, trying to affect a look of tragedy, which was nearly impossible with such a stupendous tan. My boyfriend smiled as I awkwardly seated myself on the picnic bench pushed too far under the table. He began to rub my inner arm the way he used to, but the feeling had gone out of it—he rubbed my arm like he was mining a vein.

We had walked the eighteen blocks up the boardwalk to Waverly, then one of the two blocks north to our apartment when my boyfriend spun around.

"I'm in need of fries. Smothered in cheese sauce. Be back in a sec."

He squeezed my sunburned shoulder, then strode off in the opposite direction. There was no suggestion that I come with him.

In the apartment I waited in the bedroom for his return. I waited in the living room. I waited in all the rooms of the apartment, which totaled three or four, depending on how you looked at things. Finally, I decided it was time for extreme action. Early in the summer, when I still thought my actions might have consequences, I had thrown myself on the mercy of Frederick's of Hollywood. I retrieved the shopping bag from my closet and pulled out the costume, still pristine in its cellophane sack. Looking at it now, I could see I'd been gypped. With a ten-dollar hooded gray sweatshirt and some crotchless panties, I could have easily duplicated this Unabomber costume. The only inauthentic details were the two melon-size holes cut to expose the breasts. I put it on and pulled up the hood—the dark curls sewn around the hood itched, and it was hot. The getup didn't seem as sexy as it had in the dressing room of Frederick's. The lighting there had been better. Fortunately Frederick's had taken its inspiration from the widely disseminated police sketch, not the actual disheveled Teddy K. That wouldn't have been attractive. I adjusted the tiny letter affixed to the hip so it laid flat. I slipped on the aviator sunglasses and things improved. Perhaps some thigh highs would help. I nervously paced, awaiting my boyfriend's return, conjuring up opening lines of postal dialogue, coy asides about letter openers. When he finally did come in an hour later with a giant tub of fries, I was in an undignified sprawl on the couch, trying to invent a balloon anteater. I jumped up and assumed the languorous position I'd practiced in the doorway of the bedroom. I couldn't bring myself to utter any of the dialogue I'd practiced, so instead I squeaked "Hi, sweetie, what took you so long?"

He threw himself on the couch, releasing sand from the cushions, and started to laugh.

"Oh, god," he said, "where did you get it?"

I explained about Frederick's clearance rack, and I laughed with him, because there was humor in the situation, and it is healthy for couples to laugh, especially healthy for them to laugh during sex, though I'd have settled for unhealthy sex at that juncture. After a sufficient laughing interlude I stopped so he could see it was time to get serious. But he just hunkered over his fries on the coffee table, popping them into his mouth.

"I've got something to give you or I'll explode." I tugged on the tiny letter, let the elastic snap against my skin.

"These fries taste like bone marrow." He flipped on the TV.

I turned the TV off, pushed the coffee table away, and stood in front of him.

"Don't make me go Luddite on your ass." I tried to keep an edge out of my voice. I palmed the remote control batteries, then chucked the carcass on the couch. He wasn't going to move; he wasn't going to do anything. I could see that now.

"Rape me, you isotope of your former self!" I ripped off my fake mustache and threw it at him. I was immediately embarrassed by this pathetic outburst, but beyond embarrassment, too. Besides, since I taught high school science, it was not so odd for me to use a word like *isotope*. Likewise, the Unabomber was a math and science guy, and clearly eccentric to boot, so I was still keeping in character there. He certainly could have made such a remark, though no doubt he would have tended toward more sophisticated comparisons.

My boyfriend stood up, banging his shins on the coffee table.

"You're tricked out as a terrorist, for god's sake." He picked up his tub of fries and hugged them in the crook of his arm. He slipped back into his sport slides.

He moved to leave, then stopped and held my chin. He searched my face, like candling an egg, holding it to the light to reveal imperfections. I thought he'd found something there—he moved a finger to my lips—but it was only to rub away a clot of mustache glue, and of all the sounds the next moment contained—the slap of his sandals, the moan of cars, the rotor wash of the fan ruffling the newspaper and sending balloon dogs skittering across the linoleum—I only listened for, and imagined I heard, the tiny flick of glue hitting the floor.

BELLE BOGGS

University of California, Irvine

WHO IS BEATRICE?

> *The ledge was the rim of heaven*
> *until it betrayed the boy's weight;*
> *surprised laughter, the only sound*
> *as he tumbled downward.*
> *Fate's duplicity: autumn's bounty.*
> *Arms met no resistance.*
> *He sank.*

It's her own self Bea recognizes most clearly in the poem. Her son isn't there at all, not really, though it is ostensibly—in a detached, just-the-facts way—about him.

"Farm Accident," the poem is called, and it nearly knocks her over, the accident of reading it.

For the past several months, Bea has been using her weekly trip into town to wander the perimeters of the university, lingering in a café over coffee-stained newspapers and greasy pastries after a morning of grocery shopping and errands or scouring the aisles of the natural food store for amber-colored plastic jars of herbs with mysterious functions and long names. Sometimes, when she feels lost and unanchored because she has no parcels, she buys postcards or key chains in the tourist shops. But she likes the used bookstore on the edge of campus the best, with its unassuming, musty smell, its cluttered and undemanding silence. Used Books. If she isn't careful, she can spend hours there as the milk sours and the cheese softens, paper bags dampening, green things wilting in the back of her pickup. She will look up from her collected pile of battered paperbacks, and it will be nearing dusk, the sun slanting low through glass panes onto dirty wooden floorboards. She'll pay the clerk, cram all her selections into her canvas purse, and rush home to unpack and refrigerate.

It's a harmless pleasure, these stolen hours, and certainly her husband doesn't begrudge her the time spent away from the farm. He doesn't look at *his* watch, if he is inside when she comes panting through the door, grocery bags gripped in her hands. He simply puts down his coffee mug, kisses her cheek, relieves her of her packages. If he is in a field or by the barn when she returns home, he lifts his arm in the air, a gallant, old-fashioned wave.

But, always, on the forty-minute drive back, she finds herself feeling guilty—picturing her husband's big rough hands gripping the tractor wheel or pulling a tough weed, or shielding his eyes from the sun—and before she knows it she is making alarmingly obvious statements to herself: "I love my husband. Of course I do."

It is not an affair she is having, nothing complicated or dangerous like that. It is a small, harmless pleasure, like throwing away pennies.

———

The day that Bea finds the poem starts badly, with a call from Glen's mother. "We can hardly wait to see y'all this Thanksgiving." Lucille is a woman who sees and addresses everyone as a pair, as we or y'all or you two, and who plans everything excruciatingly in advance. "Didn't he tell you we were coming?" The coffee burns while she talks to Lucille, and Bea gets behind in her carefully planned schedule. The truck starts with difficulty, and there is a light frost to clear with her stubby nails, though it's only late September.

Inside the grocery store, Bea steps in a concentrated orange juice spill, and they are out of walnuts and several other items on her list, which means she'll have to stop by one of the smaller markets, which means—

Bea slows her rapid, shallow breathing, taking a handkerchief from her purse, dampening it with spit, and rubbing it along the bottom of her sticky shoe. She has been working on cultivating perspective and distance. Since the accident and up until just about a year ago, any succession of small inconveniences would have reduced her to tears or rage, but now she closes her eyes and pictures herself in a detached way, as if she were perched somewhere outside and above her body, in the trees or among the grocery store's fluorescent lights. She remembered this tactic from an eastern philosophy class she took in college: "There goes Bea, walking down the street; poor Bea sitting in the dentist's chair; poor Bea with the orange-juice sneakers, it'll all be over soon." Isn't that how it goes: It'll all be over soon?

It takes concentration and tends to make her uncommunicative and distracted, but seeing herself that way, from a place far above and in the future, is the only thing that works. She doesn't tell Glen about it, or her mother, or anyone else. It is her secret conversation with herself, her private, morose pep talk, her compromise with insanity.

After searching out walnuts and condensed milk and Glen's castile hand soap, she does not have long to spend in the bookstore, but that's probably for the best, Bea thinks—the books are starting to pile up on her nightstand, and she does have things to do that afternoon. Just a peek at the classics, a glance at the poetry.

The poetry! She should have left that alone.

It's there in the new arrivals section, a hardback collection of poems by a local poet, a professor at the university. On the cream-colored jacket is a photo of the poet. Hair and beard threaded with silver, he wears a thick wool sweater. He has won a prize. Bea could have married a man like that, a professor—a prizewinner. She is the type of woman, she has always suspected, that men really like: lots of soft hair, pretty skin and teeth, a round and graceful figure. She dated professors; she could have been a professor herself even.

Bea took a poetry workshop as an undergraduate, though not with this professor, before she dropped out and married Glen. Her poems were not bad, she had always thought, until she workshopped them and found that they were horrible, full of trite imagery and plodding rhythm. People always said at least one good thing (wasn't that the rule?), and that was always the worst part.

But still Bea was not bitter or hostile toward poetry itself. It was a relief to get away from it, to escape from academia and sad words like *discourse* and *text,* to find herself in the arms of a good man, to marry and be a mother and a wife, and to be vindicated by the strength and honesty of a simple life, but now something pulls at her, makes her want to finish the degree. Things have happened to her, bad things. She is getting through them, and now something is telling her that she can return to college and the life of the mind. At least something has brought her here, to Used Books, where she stands thumbing through a poetry collection, giddy and reckless with words, the idea of them.

Bea, who doesn't believe in fate, only in accidents, could just as easily have missed the poem, or the entire book.

But "Farm Accident" gets her attention. It's a page-long, free verse poem about a boy who falls into a grain elevator and drowns.

She stays up there, above herself in the store rafters, and watches herself shove the book in her purse and walk out the door. She forgets the *Poor Bea, it'll all be over soon* part, so surprised is she by the theft.

There had been local media coverage. Accidents involving children are not uncommon on farms, but Henry's death was unusual in its cleanliness and, yes, its poetry. Peering over the silo's edge, he had leaned too far, toppling into the wide, dusty shaft, his mouth and throat filling with spiky hulls (*Stay away from the silos; stay off that ladder:* In his mother's long list of don'ts, no wonder those warnings were forgotten or ignored).

They did not find his body until days afterward. Bea and Glen and their two neighbors, Sarah and Jack, fellow farmers with children, rehearsed scenarios involving death and bodily injury and searched every one of their four hundred potentially dangerous acres. That first night, Jack and Glen headed out into the dark with flashlights while Sarah held Bea's hand and made weak, comforting tea. Every few minutes, Bea would think of a new possibility—the lake! Check the lake!—and for the two women, the night grew steadily more sinister. Farm boys don't run away, both women knew that. They lose arms in combines, disappear into the dark green of rivers and lakes. As young children, they discover chalky bricks of rodent poison in the corners of barns. They step barefoot near water moccasins and copperheads, pick poison berries, stumble upon hissing, rabid possums.

The news media was respectful, in its small-town way, of the parents of the drowned only child. They photographed the silo from a proper distance, asked neighbors for interviews, but left Bea and Glen to themselves. Bea was grateful, at first—she had wild paranoid fears about being revealed as a neglectful mother—but later, when she collected the few, single-column articles into an envelope and sealed it, she felt so lonely and unsatisfied that she wished for something bigger, someone to talk to or yell at or kick. Glen was too kind, too humble in his grief. "God has taken him away from us, Beatrice": He said that most every morning for months, not to her really but to himself, to his knees as he sat on the edge of the bed, to his feet in the shower, or to his eggs at breakfast. Glen believed in the God of the serenity prayer, the God of certain unchangeable things. Bea had always managed to avoid the subject.

That was six years ago, the beginning of a quiet, desperate war between them.

They had met at an AA meeting in town. At twenty-three, Bea was the youngest in the group, a recent college dropout living on leftover student loans. She had become a problem drinker almost without realizing it. And so one day she found herself sitting in a smoky Baptist vestibule with mechanics and store managers, with divorced mothers and businessmen and truckers—and Glen.

At first she was the center of attention, the new kid in class, and she was flattered by their eager, earnest support. Everything she said was okay. It was okay to drop out of school and not have a job and it was even okay that she drank too much, but there was no reason to drink, was there, once you realized that everything in the world was okay and could be taken like medicine in small, bitter sips. (Later, Bea would find it funny that she would be recovering for the rest of her life from eight months of moderately heavy boozing. Hilarious, considering all the other things there were to recover from.)

When one March evening a month into her recovery she saw Glen sitting across from her in the discussion circle, it wasn't love that filled her chest with such immediacy but the feeling of kinship. He was more than ten years older, but there was something welcoming and safe about his wry smile and unlaced boots, and later about the low sound of his voice and the smell of pipe smoke in his proffered jacket, as they stood outside in the parking lot. He was a place to go, and she—what was she?

"Lost," he told her, a few months after they married in a small outdoor ceremony, when she asked. "Also beautiful. Old-fashioned, I thought, but with a sense of humor about yourself."

Old-fashioned—maybe that was what she was supposed to be all along. A wife, a caretaker, *taken care of.* He never said smart, Bea realized, and that was a relief. College boys always told you that you were *smart,* right after they told you you were *beautiful.* With Glen smart was either implied or a nonissue.

Glen still drinks, though now he does it in secret. A few months ago, Bea found a bottle of Jack Daniel's in the barn behind some chicken feed. It was a quarter full, and she was surprised that the discovery didn't shock or upset her. Liquor no longer had power over her—she even smelled the bottle, to test herself—but her mental image of Glen drinking alone, the quick swigs he must take before coming inside for the night, was pitiful. When she looked behind the barn for more evidence, she found only shards of glass, stuck together with bits of label and glue.

He had been off the bottle only about five months when they met, so when they began their life together after the briefest of courtships (picnics on the farm, long walks—she let *him* take charge of things) it was with a careening sort of sobriety and wholesome energy. They never went back to meetings. They were cured! Within the year they were pregnant with Henry.

And what a joy he was to them. A new start.

———

Henry was a plump baby, handsome and jolly, his hair falling into loose, amber-colored ringlets. When they went for strolls in town, around the university, and Bea saw other women her age—childless and single, thin, ravaged by fashion and studying—she felt pride in her roles as wife and mother. She raised vegetables in the garden Glen tilled for her, breast-fed Henry until it was practically embarrassing.

Henry grew to be a thoughtful, dreamy boy, smart and amazingly capable of entertaining himself. He went for long treks into the fields or the woods near the house. He returned with sticks and rocks and leaves that figured in elaborate games he devised and played alone in his room. Everywhere he went, he left doors open behind him.

As he grew older and went to school, there seemed to be less and less for Bea to do. She took up the farm's bookkeeping, and though she found that she had no head for numbers, she stuck with it. She wished that she had stayed in school, maybe even gotten a master's degree and developed a field of specialization. She could have kept busy writing critical or scholarly articles about life in the late middle ages or about nineteenth-century French literature; she could have had the best of both worlds. If she had any faith left in her creative abilities, she would have written poems about nature, and the strangeness of life.

He lives with them still, six years after he drowned in the silo. He is no longer a thin, freckled ten-year-old, but a sixteen-year-old of mythic stature.

"Tall," Glen will say at dinner. "He would have been tall, like me. A varsity basketball player in high school, maybe." The basketball net that Glen erected in the driveway when Henry was five, moving it up a few inches at every birthday, remains at the ten-year-old height, just above Glen's head. When he walks under it, the gray rope brushes his temples.

"But he would also have been interested in books," Bea is careful to point out. "He loved to read, remember. I bet he'd be a good writer."

Bea has saved all of Henry's childhood books—from *Pat the Bunny* to *Call of the Wild.* She has saved all his writings and drawings, every chewed pencil. They are artifacts.

"He was interested in botany, too, and agriculture. He would have helped me plow this harvest."

"Yes, he'd be nearing college age now. I could have helped him with his applications, shown him around the university."

These discussions—arguments, really, though you wouldn't think it for their genial, conversational tone—appear out of nowhere, as if they have always been there, waiting to be plucked from the silence.

"A farmer," Glen will say with finality. "He may have dallied here or there as a young one, but eventually he would have been a farmer."

"A poet," Bea mutters. "A man of letters."

There go Bea and Glen, drinking ginger ale, playing tug-of-war with their dead son.

High above, up there with the good china, Bea is powerless to stop it.

Poor Bea. Poor Glen.

It's an easy resting place, these games. Bea thinks of them, driving home fast. On the way out of town, she passes Chinese restaurants, pancake houses, prefab realty offices. She passes rusty, dented pickup trucks loaded with pumpkins and yellow mums.

Why did she take the book?

She should throw it out the window, toss it into a ditch, but she doesn't.

That night after dinner Glen is mostly silent, studying a seed catalog. They sit in the living room, and she reads the poem—all the poems, in fact—stealthily, with quick glances at her husband.

Typical, she thinks of the poems. Some of them are about being married, some are about getting older, some are about remembering youth. Some are about the moon, and the tides, and the harvest.

"Been to the library," Glen says. He doesn't look up, and it has always maddened Bea, she realizes now, how he calls the bookstore the library. He knows she doesn't check out the books—they're here to stay, to collect dust and coffee rings and dog-ears. It's the same way he calls all feminine attire—skirts, blouses, softly knit sweaters—*dresses*.

That's a pretty dress.

"Bookstore," she says. "Used. Yes."

The rage. That's the part that's missing from the poem. At every harried mother, every whining baby in the supermarket or the bank. Then the flu symptoms, lingering months. Psychosomatic, the therapist said. Rage toward him, toward her husband, her well-meaning relatives for their dumb, kind words. Toward Henry, for not being more careful. Herself, for raising a child on a farm. The knowledge that nothing will ever, ever be the same.

She counts the poem's twenty-two lines. It's a beautiful poem, it has all the merits of form and thought she's been taught to recognize. Its lovely, hateful syllables roll right off the tongue.

She was assigned the writing of just such poems in her undergraduate workshop, she recalls. Find a newspaper headline; that's the title of your poem. Bea's own attempts were halfhearted failures gleaned from the *Lifestyles* section. Once, she wrote about the elation of a woman who, hating sex, prayed every day of her married life for widowhood and, after her prayers were answered, discovered the pleasures of carnal love with another man, a widower. That was from Ann Landers. Another time, she wrote about a recipe for low-fat potato salad. It is still Glen's favorite of all the ones she's shown him.

No one reads poetry.

She would tell him that, one day. She would walk right up to him, at some faculty symposium or coffee shop reading, and throw it in his face: poetry has about as much relevance in this world as—

Bea thinks about tracking him down. She can see herself shuffling her feet outside classrooms or walking fast behind him to his car, even squaring her shoulders and knocking on the door of his apartment or his house. What she can't see is her own earnest expression as she says, *That was my son,* or *My boy was the accident you wrote about.* (What if a kindness or a wariness around his eyes makes her forget what she's come for? What if he takes her hand, asks her in for coffee? Beatrice was always quick to fall in love, even with the worst kinds of traitors.)

She'd love to run away, if only for the opportunity to make up a new and more plausible identity. It's slowly becoming a strange footnote, her old self: Maker of lunches, late-night assuager of irrational, stalling fears ("Mom, what if I forget to breathe when I'm asleep?" "What if I get amnesia and forget my times tables?"). She is no longer a mother. Six years is a long time, enough time to make you forget, to dissipate all your tenderness and fervor into numb practicality. She used to be afraid that she would crush Henry's tiny ribs with her hugs; sometimes, a frantic desire to take him apart, to run her fingers along his every bone, would overcome her. She does not even kiss Glen with her tongue anymore.

Glen—certainly he does not have such thoughts. He would never run away, would never put himself in the path of disturbing poetry. He's a good man, a strong, good husband. Still, she cannot help but think that if Henry were the poet's son, he'd be at a violin lesson right now, and then she pinches her own hand—hard, leaving purplish marks—for thinking it.

She should show it to him. It's her responsibility as his partner, his wife; he should know. Leave it open on his desk, tear out the page and tape it to the refrigerator. Let *him* be responsible.

They go to bed early: nine o'clock. Bea pulls an old flannel nightgown over her head. It is patterned with tiny yellow and pink flowers. Glen sleeps naked. His body is hairy and coarse—it smells like castile soap and dirt. Bea lies on her back. Glen wraps his legs over hers, rests his hand on her stomach.

"Glen," she whispers. He is silent. *"Glen."*

"Beatrice." His voice is not sleepy, or impatient, or reluctant.

"I think I need some time away from here."

"I told you, after all the harvesting is done, we'll go away, I promise." He kisses the back of her neck, pats her leg. He has always been physically generous, attentive to her body. "We'll go on a trip."

That is not what she meant at all, but she leaves it alone. She turns toward him and nuzzles his neck, sniffing for whiskey.

A week later, on a Tuesday, Glen goes into town alone to check out a sale at Southern States. Bea knows that he will leave before eight and that he will be gone all day. He'll stop by Jack and Sarah's. He'll talk with the men in the feed and supply store. He'll have conversations, in fact, with everyone he sees—at the gas station, the tobacco shop, the drugstore where he'll buy a ham and cheese sandwich sometime before noon. On his way home, he might rent a movie from the bait and tackle place with its meager selection of National Geographic documentaries and years-old Steve Martin comedies.

Bea knows she should get up with him, should fry some eggs or should at least make toast and coffee, but she stays in bed late, as she has for the past few days. She needs time to *not think,* to focus, to be absolutely alone if she is to do what she has decided to do, and so she pulls the quilt over her head and turns onto her stomach, hoping, *knowing* he will leave her there.

When she hears the back door shut with a satisfying whoosh and click, she flings the quilt back and quickly gets out of bed. The truck starts—it always starts for him on the first try—while she pulls on a pair of jeans and a sweater. She can hear the tires throw gravel as he pulls from their driveway onto the main road and she walks down-stairs and into the kitchen.

There is a note stuffed into her coffee mug, which he has set next to the thermos:

Dear Beatrice,
Gone into town today. Back this evening—5:00?
Hope you're feeling better.
Love,
Glen

He writes in small, neat, regular print, like architectural lettering. Bea puts the note in her jeans pocket and pulls the dusty phone book down from its place on top of the fridge. She looks up the university listings and then "English Department." She dials the number listed there and gets a recording of a measured, female voice. *For English and Comp Lit listings, press one; for Creative Writing, press two.* She presses two. *For Anne Lockney, press one; for George Abrams, press two; for Simon Watts, press three.* She presses three.

Another recording, a man's voice, deep and soft: "Hello. This is Simon Watts with the Creative Writing Program . . . Please . . . leave a message." He sounds distracted and uncertain, as if something has caught his attention and caused him to forget what he was going to say. Bea thinks she detects a tiny "um," or perhaps nervous throat clearing. Before she can put the phone down the machine beeps and she realizes she has left a brief, blank message. What does it sound like? Breathing? A hurried jostling and then *click*? Or maybe nothing at all?

Worried that he might have caller identification, or the program that calls the last person back, and that he might actually use these things, Bea decides not to call again. She slides her feet into her sneakers, puts on her hat and coat, and leaves. The little hatchback that Glen doesn't like her to drive—it has several problems, among them a loose distributor cap and CV joints that complain with sharp turns—actually starts, and Bea is on the smooth main road before she marvels, laughs at herself. Of course he won't call her back. He's probably too busy, she thinks, hitting on undergraduates and scouring small-town newspapers for interesting tragedies.

She keeps driving, though, all the way into town. Without the heart to find a new bookstore, to start over, Bea parks on the street in front of Used Books. She checks herself in her rearview mirror—she's a mess, really, but what does it matter—and goes inside.

"Hello," says the owner. He is leaning over the counter, reading the newspaper spread flat there.

"Hello," she says, and continues toward the fiction section. Fiction—that's what she'll read. A new novel. Short stories, maybe. A classic or perhaps a quirky new contemporary.

"I've been hoping you'd come in," the man calls to her.

His voice is familiar, friendly, but she freezes. How, with books stacked floor to ceiling, books piled everywhere, would he have noticed *her*, stealing a seventy-page, eight-dollar book?

"Last week you bought Simon Watts's new work, I believe," he says. *Bought?* she thinks. "It says here in the paper he's giving a reading on Friday at the university, in the Hayes Fellowship Hall."

"No," she finds herself saying. She pretends to be searching in the bookshelf, running her finger along the titles. "Someone else . . .

must've bought it. Last week I didn't buy anything. I was in a hurry I think." Rising so easily to her tongue, the lie makes her feel almost giddy, powerful. She knows she will not yield to his kindness.

"Oh," he says, disappointed. "Maybe so. It's a lovely book, though."

Quickly, and with a growing, uncomfortable new guilt, she selects a thick hardback, *A Treasury of Russian Stories,* and glances at the price, sketched lightly in pencil on the first page. She walks purposefully to the counter, sets the book down, and pulls a twenty from her purse. "This'll be all today," she says.

He picks it up slowly, turns it over in his hands. "A fine selection," he says. As he makes change in the register, she peeks at the newspaper before him, tilting her head a little to read upside down. She can make out *Simon Watts, renowned poet, reads from his new work.* Without saying anything he hands her ten dollars and change, then carefully tears out the reading announcement.

"Would you like this?" he asks.

"Yes. Please."

He tucks it into her book, then puts the book in a bag and hands it to her, and she leaves. When she gets home, she is sure to park the car in the exact spot it was in when she left. The next day, when she sees Glen leaning under its hood, she'll feel surrounded. *What is with these people?* she'll think, of Glen and the man at the bookstore, and she'll resolve to go.

Bea gets up early for the rest of the week and makes breakfasts too heavy even for Glen: cheese-filled omelets, steak-and-egg scrambles, pancakes. She waits until Thursday night to tell him she's going out on Friday. She says she's having dinner with an old school friend. Of course he doesn't question her or object, and she grows so nervous before the reading that there is little room for guilt over going without him. She is protecting him, after all, by leaving him at home, by not telling him where she's really going, and why.

She arrives early, at seven instead of eight, wearing a white blouse and scratchy brown wool skirt. She has on earrings and her dressy coat. Through the hall's windows she can see men inside setting up the chairs. It's been years since she was actually on campus, and as she wanders the lawn she grows wistful and sad for her old self: a diligent student, attendee of lectures and readings. She thinks of the way her neck hairs would stand up when she heard certain lines, how sometimes she would even cry. She thinks of her body then, smooth and fertile, her eggs slipping innocently each month from their plentiful bank.

Across the street she can see a small, dim bar, and she walks there briskly to wait. It's not the same one she used to frequent, but enough like it, with its dark wood paneling, vinyl-upholstered booths, and school-related paraphernalia—pennants, team photographs, and signed jerseys—that she is both comfortable and unnerved. She sits in a booth by the window and surprises herself by ordering a beer. It's just a prop, she thinks. She won't drink it, but then she surprises herself again.

The beer enters her veins like honey, and as it warms her she considers strategies: a quiet confrontation after the reading? Or should she stand up when the poem is read, like a lawyer or an objector at a wedding? She wishes she had her own poem about Henry to read, something beautiful and fine that would shame him. She drinks another beer and feels almost light-headed.

At ten to eight she takes her seat in the back of the lecture hall. She doesn't see a single person she recognizes. The hall is full of students and academic types. It's lit with a warm, yellow light, and Bea feels her face grow hot as she sits and waits. A woman adjusts the microphone at the podium, taps it, and begins the introduction. She says what a wonderful poet and friend we have in Simon Watts. She talks about his other books, his awards, his most recent collection, and how nice it is to see him returning to his roots with a book that takes so much of its imagery, its *energy,* from local culture.

"Ha," Bea says under her breath. A couple of students glance back at her. During the applause following the introduction, she gets up quietly to go to the rest room, and when she returns finds that her seat has been taken by a young man with a nose ring. Simon Watts has already started to read, and she is relieved that he hasn't opened with "Farm Accident." He probably saves that one—the tearjerker—for his big finale, she thinks.

A few lines strike Bea, but mostly the words wash over her. In the pause between each poem she feels queasy waiting for the next. Each time she is relieved by a poem about a country egg deliverer or a woman or the smell of winter wheat, then is anxious again before the next one begins. The pattern of relief and anxiety makes her almost seasick.

She tries to focus on his face but is too far back. It seems that he isn't really looking at the pages as he turns them. *He has his own poems memorized,* she thinks scornfully. She looks around the room at the students, faculty members, townspeople. Their faces are upturned or lowered in various listening poses, mouths serious or half smiling with pleasure. She thinks of what it would be to read to a group of people and have them listen like that.

And then it is over. "Thank you so much for coming," he says, bowing his head a little. Everyone claps.

Bea is stunned. How could he not read her poem? It is after all *the best one,* the most moving of all the poems. People are talking now, chatting lightly as they file past her through the doors into the foyer, and she must turn sideways to be out of their way. She sits in one of the chairs near the back and watches Simon Watts gather his things into a satchel. He is smiling, talking to the woman who introduced him. What will she say as he walks past? Will she grab his arm, burst into tears, stick out her foot to trip him?

But she doesn't have to do anything; as if disturbed by some wind, by the very aura of her, he drops a stack of papers next to Bea's feet as he walks out and must stop to bend down and gather them. He looks at her briefly, and looking back at him she realizes that there is nothing she wants to say to him. Not a word.

Halfway home, Bea is no longer thinking about Simon Watts or his poems. She is thinking instead about what her own Henry poem, her own version of "Farm Accident," would have to say. Things every dead child's mother knows: the featherlight touches of police officers, on one's back, the pitiful smallness of coffins, the brightness of flowers, the vastness of houses.

And, as she walks through their unlocked doors and up the stairs, the innocent snores of husbands, years later, alone in darkened bedrooms.

The next morning is bright and cold. When she gets up, Glen has already gone into the fields. Bea notices that one of the poems she worked on last night, when she couldn't sleep, is missing from her desk. She is suddenly nervous and flattered, but then she notices it is not her own poem, a brief, unrhymed piece about her collection of lumpy, unfashionable shoes, that he has taken, but "Farm Accident," which she had copied in her own hand to get her started. She has lovely penmanship, a long, slanted cursive.

Well, she thinks with the resignation taught by all her years of recklessness, that's that. I've betrayed him twice now. He'll read it, he'll drink some in the barn, we'll yell and cry, I'll tell him about the reading, that he was right all along about our boy being a farmer, and I'll throw the book away.

———————

The morning passes quickly—she does the accounts, rearranges the pantry for winter, mops the kitchen floor. For lunch she makes roast beef sandwiches. She extends each task to slow and unnecessary perfection: She takes out all her jars and cans and wipes them down, spreads the mustard evenly to the very edge of the bread. She arranges the pink brown beef in artful folds. The lettuce she cleans and prunes and pats dry with a paper towel. She goes back through the books, erasing all the incompletely erased pencil marks. She dusts the top of the ceiling fan. Finding an old toothbrush under the sink, she scrubs the places where the cabinets meet the linoleum, where the faucet and sink basin grow brownish gunk. She washes windows, opens up the stovetop to get at old, burned crumbs. She scrubs her own nails furiously.

Glen does not come home for lunch. He does not come home for dinner, either, and by seven o'clock it is almost dark. Outside the window, the trees are black against a faint blue-and-orange sky. Standing in the doorway, Bea leans her forehead into the cool screen, making a dent. She always used to yell at Henry for doing that.

"Glen," she calls weakly, without emphasis or urgency. "Glen."

The sound of their rusty porch swing startles her: "I'm right here."

"How long've you been there?"

"Hmmm, an hour I guess. Since the sun started to go down. You should watch the sun set, Beatrice. I never see you watch the sun set anymore." There is something in his lap; he takes a sip of it, sucking the bottle wetly.

"I know you drink, Glen."

"I know you know. One day at a time."

"Since Henry—"

"Since *always*," he says. "Don't be disappointed in me, it was only a little before, and not much since."

"I'm not disappointed." Bea is still standing in the doorway. She can see only his outline, a slouching figure, short hair, shoulders still broad. "Come sit down," he says, and pats the swing. The screen door swings shut behind her as she steps onto the porch. She sits down and rests her head on his shoulder.

"I read it," he says. "I hope you're not mad I took it."

"No, of course not." Beyond a twiggy forsythia bramble, Bea can see the wire cages and broken stalks of the summer's garden. There is still the heavy smell of rotting tomatoes—she and Glen have never been particularly tidy farmers.

"It's beautiful," he says, and when she turns to look at him, his eyes are glassy-drunk, and she knows his mistake.

"No, Glen—"

"I mean, the way you compared the smell of the grains, the way you used . . . metaphors, or whatever. It was really . . . good to read."

"I didn't write it, Glen," she says. "I found it. In a book."

"Oh." Bea is sure that she can feel him growing angry and confused beside her. For a long time he is silent, taking apart the stiff, furry soybean pod he has pulled from his pocket. He shreds it meticulously with his thumbnail.

"Our boy," he says. "In a book."

Bea closes her hand over the bean pod in his palm. She can feel the wet green part, the living part, where his nail cut. She is right there.

JOHN MURRAY

University of Iowa

A FEW SHORT NOTES
ON TROPICAL BUTTERFLIES

I. *DANAUS PLEXIPPUS*—THE MONARCH BUTTERFLY

Last night Maya locked herself in the bathroom again with her copy of *The New England Journal of Medicine*. She likes to memorize the most interesting articles and quote them to her patients. She is a lover of small details, tiny pieces of information, maps, diagrams, and the tortuous skull anatomy of the twelve pairs of human cranial nerves. Maya is spending longer and longer periods of time locked in the bathroom, and I know that she cries in there because the wastepaper basket fills up with tissues. Her decision to become a neurosurgeon was partly an attempt to control the surrounding world, which she sees as unmanageable. It is the ultimate test of her ability to remain calm in the face of difficult, and often dangerous, clinical situations. She has buried herself so deeply in her knowledge of details that she cannot properly feel what is happening in her own life. I know that she needs me to reach out to her, but I can't do it. She does not understand how much she has hurt me, and I clam up whenever we are together.

At dinner I watched her eat chow mein, waiting for an opportunity to say something about what has happened to us. It is fall, my favorite season, and I thought aloud that the Monarch butterflies of central Texas would soon begin their annual migration. These remarkable butterflies follow the Sierra Madre Oriental south across the tropic of Cancer and then turn west over the neovolcanic mountains of Mexico.

"Can't you forget about butterflies for a change?" she said to me.

"I'm just interested. They *are* fascinating."

"We'd be better off if you were more interested in children."

"I'm not ready for children." I concentrated on my food.

"You may not be. But I am. I'm already thirty-eight and not getting any younger. And neither are you."

Maya is twenty years my junior, and we were desperately in love when we married. She was a resident, working for me as part of her surgical rotation. It was such a cliché—distinguished older surgeon, ambitious younger woman—that we kept our affair secret for three years. The illicit nature of it appealed to her. For months we met in the pathology laboratory at night when we were both on call—we got to know each other surrounded by jars labeled NORMAL HUMAN LUNG and CHRONICALLY INFLAMED GALL BLADDER. The laboratory was the only place where we could be alone and where we would not be interrupted. It had a strangely peaceful feeling—like that of a deep pine forest where all you can hear is your own breathing.

Before Maya I'd had a series of relationships with women my own age. These were comfortable and easy affairs, filled with companionable silences, safe dinners, and weekends away. But I was never in love, and I never married. I chose convenience over everything else, and I did not want to be too close to anyone. Seeing Maya in a surgical mask and blue paper hat, I was bowled over for the first time in my life. She was different in a way that I cannot exactly explain. Maya looked like someone with secrets. She was utterly self-contained. It was this sense of isolation that reached out to me.

Last night, after an uncomfortable silence broken only by the slurping of wonton soup, I said to her, "Perhaps we should try getting pregnant in the summer."

"You said that last year," Maya said.

"I mean it. You know I do."

"You don't convince me."

"How can you say that?"

"Because I think you're lying. That's how."

She is quite right. I have not thought about children. I am putting it off. After dinner, I had trouble walking to the kitchen to make the coffee—I had to hold on to the wall to get my balance. Maya told me again that I drink too much and I shouted that I could damn well do as I please. She followed me into the kitchen then and wanted me to hold her. "Just hold on to me," she said, "and put down that bottle, for a change."

Watching Maya operate on the brains of strangers brings back memories of my childhood. Last week I stood in an operating theater and observed as she removed a tumor from the head of a sixty-nine-year-old retired tax accountant from Queens. The care with which she used the bone saw, cauterized each bleeding capillary with a sharp hiss of burning tissue, and gently cut through the layers of dura surrounding the brain reminded me of my father when he handled his butterflies. Maya treats every brain she works on with such respect that I am always amazed that she manages to operate on them at all. Her touch is as light as that of a butterfly wing. Her hands seem to flutter and waft in the air, barely in contact with the solid stainless steel handles of her instruments. It is always a surprise when the brain opens up beneath her hands.

Maya is fascinated by the story of my grandfather, partly because she is from an Indian family and has a deep understanding of how important relatives can be to what we all become. And partly because she has a professional interest in the disease that eventually killed him. "He is the only man I have ever known who was killed by a butterfly," Maya says. She likes to hear the full story, and I have told her most of it, often at night, lying in bed. Telling the story has become a ritual for us. Sometimes I wonder whether she married me for it— for a piece of my legacy. Maya, like me, has an admiration for the spirit of my grandfather, who was driven by a desire to understand the world around him. He was a man obsessed with butterflies, and sometimes an obsession is the only way to live. "You come from butterfly people," Maya says, "and you are a butterfly person."

In September 1892, my grandfather chopped off his left thumb with a butcher's cleaver because he could no longer use his hands. The force and accuracy of the blow were sufficient to remove the thumb cleanly at the level of the first metacarpal joint. This violent and painful act was the result of what my grandfather described as a "compulsion that could not be denied."

I imagine my grandfather examining his own thumb with scientific dispassion. He wrapped the bleeding stump in a handkerchief and drank half a bottle of whiskey to numb the pain. The thumb and bloody cleaver were left on the kitchen table, where they were discovered by a housekeeper. There is nothing more alarming than a severed digit with its fine hairs and fingernail—so vividly human— and the housekeeper dropped the tea tray she was carrying when she saw it. A doctor was called and the thumb collected, and my grandfather was escorted to New York Hospital where, under chloroform, a surgeon made crude attempts to reattach it. There was no such thing as microsurgery at the time—the instruments and techniques were unavailable—and the procedure was unsuccessful.

If the accident happened today, of course, the result would be very different. I would have had the thumb back on in eleven or twelve hours and my grandfather would be using it again in six weeks. I have a natural affinity for the detailed work that is needed for microscopic surgery of this type. I have always enjoyed details. I am sure this comes from my grandfather, who was a cataloger by nature. He was famous for his collection of butterflies. He had hundreds of them from all over the world pinned to felt boards in glass-fronted display boxes. As a child, I spent hours looking at rows of these brilliantly colored insects. They were vivid and exciting to me. Each splash of turquoise, mother-of-pearl, and burnt orange represented a distant tropical forest that seemed impossibly lush and colorful. My world, New York City, was gray and brown. I grew up looking at oily concrete, cast-iron railings, and slabs of fatty corned beef on white bread.

My grandfather's thumb became a part of our family folklore because—true to his nature as a collector—he demanded that it be preserved in formaldehyde. He came home with the severed digit bobbing in a small glass jar and put it on top of his desk. It sat there for many years. My father kept it after my grandfather died, and I grew up looking up at the thumb. It was the only connection with my grandfather that I ever had.

As children we were not told how he lost it, and so I created elaborate scenarios in my mind to explain its removal. He was an unknown but exotic man to us, notorious for his trips to remote and wild countries. As a young man he wore emerald waistcoats and carried a walnut hunting stick capped with a silver Monarch butterfly, *Danaus plexippus*. His house was filled with artifacts that included the dried scalp of a yeti—a leathery dome covered in tufts of black hair—and half a dozen shrunken heads. These small dry heads, shriveled like raisins, but with their essential features intact, made me feel as if I understood something profound. They represented a dark and violent part of my grandfather's past that was never discussed. They were all dark native heads with shocks of long black hair, with the exception of one that had a brilliant red beard and was clearly European—a small brass plaque screwed onto the back of the scalp said CAPTAIN CUTTER, 19TH BENGAL LANCERS CAVALRY REGIMENT. I hung the unfortunate Captain Cutter in my bedroom and showed him off to my friends. He was an impressive sight to twelve-year-old boys and earned me a reputation for being dangerous. I lay awake at night staring at Captain Cutter's dismembered cranium and imagining the terrible scenes that must have preceded its removal. I am not a morbid person by nature, but I possess a vivid imagination. I'm a daydreamer—a worrying quality in a surgeon.

Sometimes I wonder whether my grandfather's thumb was the reason that I chose plastic surgery. Perhaps I have always wished I could have reattached his lost digit. I have the thumb in front of me on my desk as I write. It is surrounded by swirling motes of particulate matter and seems to be moving slightly in invisible currents and eddies. I consider it to be a kind of talisman—whenever I travel for any length of time, I take it with me in my luggage. A customs official at the Bombay airport once found the thumb during a routine search and fainted.

Two years ago I realized that I could not let Maya disappear from my life. We were bobbing in an apartment complex swimming pool in Manhattan that smelled strongly of chlorine, the only people in the water. Dark blue tiles surrounded the edge, and long lines of orange floats marked swimming lanes. It was late and we had come from the hospital.

"You're risk averse," Maya said, blowing water through her nose. She had just finished several laps of breaststroke and was hanging in the water in front of me. Droplets of water gathered on her eyelashes.

"No more than most people," I said.

"You get upset if you don't eat breakfast at the same time every morning," she said, ripping the yellow bathing cap from her head and shaking out her hair, "and you've lived in the same apartment for twenty years, even though you hate it."

"I don't hate it."

"You'd rather not live there."

"So?"

"You're terrified of change."

I could see the blurred shapes of Maya's legs treading water beneath her and little flashes of reflected water on her cheeks. The lights in the pool were turned out suddenly, leaving us floating in the dark, with just streetlight filtering in through the windows. A maintenance worker's footsteps faded away.

"I'm organized and logical, that's all."

"No, *I'm* organized and logical. And I can take risks. You go to the same restaurants, have for years. You're terrified of traveling. You get worried if I'm more than a few minutes late—you imagine the worst."

"I do imagine the worst."

"I grew up in a large family," Maya said. She floated toward me and I felt her naked breasts against my chest. She flung her bathing suit onto the edge of the pool. It landed with a wet slap. "In a large family you have to take risks to be noticed. I was always trying to better my brothers. Screaming for attention. I had to assert myself."

"There's no doubt that you can be very assertive." She moved herself against me, and I felt her fingers, those delicate surgeon's fingers, fluttering on my shorts. She loosened them and pulled them down to my ankles with her feet. She wrapped her legs around me, and I felt scratchy pubic hair against my stomach.

"That's why I smoked. And why I had sex with a boxer." Maya's hair floated behind her like oil on water.

"You had sex with a boxer?"

"He claimed to have broken his nose twenty-three times. He was nineteen, I was sixteen. I brought him home with me. My father was a pacifist, you know, believed in nonviolent protest and all that. When he saw that I was going out with a boxer he was speechless. He didn't speak to me for months. I only did it once—to embarrass my parents. This boxer—he was only nineteen, remember—was already losing his mind. He couldn't remember my name from one minute to the next. Kept calling me Mandy, Molly, and so on. I was laughing the whole time I was with him. We did it in the training gym. Right on the edge of the ring. Under the ropes."

"So this makes you assertive, I suppose?" My first sexual experience was terrifying and involved a geneticist, half a bottle of vodka, a darkened room, and a borrowed apartment. I left before she woke up in the morning and never saw her again out of embarrassment.

"You're still afraid of losing something, aren't you?" She floated on her back with her legs clamped firmly around me.

"I'm afraid someone's going to come in through that door and find us," I said. She had begun rubbing herself against me.

"You act as if everything is about to be taken away. So you try not to invest in things. You've tried to avoid investing in people. How many real friends do you have?"

"I've got friends." She was moving rhythmically against me now, and the water had begun lapping gently against the sides of the pool.

"I don't see them. You avoid getting too close to anyone."

I spent my childhood ordering my collection of butterflies. Family, genus, species. I was devoted to the act of putting the world into ranked order. I could recite my grandfather's collection from memory. I remember hearing children my own age playing outside on the street as I lay on the floor of my bedroom, feeling lonely and different. But I felt safer away from them.

"I'm close to you," I said as she slid down my body.

"And I'm a risk," she whispered.

"I suppose you are." It was there, in that warm pool, with Maya's gasps echoing in the tiled space, that I suggested we get married. It was my first real risk in years. When the lights came on again, we were blinded instantly, and fell away from each other as if under a police searchlight.

My grandfather came into a substantial fortune in rubber and tea from his father's family, who owned plantations in India. He was a gentleman scientist. Sepia-toned photographs from the period show him to be a small, compact man with enormous muttonchop whiskers and staring eyes. I have made a close study of his diaries, big heavy volumes bound in calfskin. They make fascinating reading. He kept daily records of his life from the age of twelve. He had a tiny, cramped hand, and I have to get down near the dusty yellow paper to make sense of his words.

He became an amateur naturalist of some standing. His money allowed him the freedom to travel, and he spent a great deal of time in remote locations in South America, Africa, and the Pacific. He was enthralled by the highly colored species of the tropics and his diaries are full of his trips to butterfly breeding grounds all over the world. He collected beautiful examples of *Ornithoptera victoriae victoriae,* the Queen Victoria Birdwing, from the Solomon Islands, and of *Papilio antimachus,* the largest butterfly in Africa with its distinctive black and orange coloring. The specimens were transported on beds of cotton wool in airtight cast-iron cylinders. He spent weeks cataloging his finds according to the taxonomic classification system and then mounting them in display cases. The bodies were pinned through the thorax with such care that even today most of his specimens have six legs, proboscis, and antennae intact. Until he went mad, my grandfather was a patient man with a steady hand.

Somehow butterflies became the center of all of our lives. My father grew up with them, was given butterfly nets for birthdays, and knew the Latin names of the *Papilonidae* family of tropical butterflies before he started school. My grandfather took him to watch the fall migration of the Monarchs when he was little more than a baby, bundled up in wool, with dimpled elbows and knees. It infected my father, and it infected me. There is something about the transience and the beauty of these insects that gets into your blood. "Butterflies are a metaphor," my father said to us, "for life. Beautiful, fleeting, fragile, incomprehensible." Even as a young man, I understood this. I collected them like my friends collected baseball cards and stamps— each one had a personality to me. There was something free and audacious about these flimsy, absurdly colorful insects that was appealing. What possible purpose could a butterfly have other than to brighten up the world?

I have tried to explain this to Maya. But she is the daughter of a physicist from Pondicherry who emigrated after Partition, and she inherited his brain. Everything needs a physical explanation for Maya—the world is nothing but a mass of electrons, neutrons, and quarks—each with clearly defined rules of action and interaction. My abstract love of insects is lost on her. She grew up in Washington, D.C., cut her teeth to the music of Elvis Presley, and learned to drive during the last days of the Johnson Administration. She understood the first law of thermodynamics before her first kiss. Maya is a mass of cross-cultural contradictions—Levi's and saris; Twinkies and dhal; David Bowie and Mahatma Gandhi; *Kama Sutra* and *Casablanca.* She lives on cappuccinos, wears leather pants, and voraciously reads biographies. She has none of the elaborate superstitions of her parents, but since we returned from our honeymoon, she has started getting emotional during her period.

"Here I am bleeding to death," she said last night, "and you don't seem to appreciate what is happening to me."

"Nothing's happening to you," I said.

"Life is running out of me. Don't you understand? All my eggs are drying up. You're so cold. I'm shriveling like a flower in the sun."

"You're being emotional," I said. She was crying into my shoulder.

"Yes, I am. I want to have a child. It's as simple as that."

Maya has long, thick eyelashes that I sometimes think can be heard rustling against her cheeks when she blinks. She wants to believe that the brain is nothing more than a machine that can be serviced, faulty parts ripped out and replaced—thoughts and emotions little more than functional circuits that need good spark plugs and a starter motor. She looks like a wrestler in her tight surgical scrubs with the round thighs she inherited from her mother. Her father died of a temporal lobe brain tumor that caused him to speak in tongues and have visions of Lord Krishna in bowls of Indian food. She sees her father every time she saws open a skull.

"You're worried about Mr. Oomman," I said to her.

"It's got nothing to do with Mr. Oomman," she said with a jerk of her head. "Don't patronize me. It's about having a child, not about Mr. Oomman. I don't give a damn about Mr. Oomman. Mr. Oomman's brain is nothing compared to the current state of my ovaries. They're withering, I tell you. Withering! Withering like two pathetic grapes on a vine. And all you can do is bring up Mr. Oomman. Mr.

Oomman can go to hell." Mr. Oomman was a family friend of her parents and she was operating on him in the morning to remove a subdural hematoma—a relatively benign condition with a very high cure rate.

"Why is this so important to you?" I asked.

"How can you ask that?" Maya was sobbing.

"I just want to try to understand."

"If you don't understand now," Maya whispered, "then when the hell will you understand?"

She ripped the bottle of claret from my hand and threw it onto the ground with some force. It exploded into a blossom of pink liquid and glass on the kitchen floor. I turned and walked out of the room as quickly as I was able in my condition. As I came up the corridor toward my study, Maya ran after me. She was still carrying two chopsticks from the table, and she wielded them like daggers above her head—a small dollop of sweet and sour pork had fallen onto her upturned cheek. "Don't you walk out on me," she shouted at my back. "Let's get this decided. You can't keep hiding in your chicken shit room with those stinking butterflies. They're more important to you than I am. Your bloody butterflies and fucking Mister Cutter."

"That's *Captain* Cutter," I called over my shoulder.

"Whatever. He's a bloody shrunken head! You spend more time talking to the head of Cutter than you do to me! You and Cutter can go to hell." I reached the door and tripped on the rug as I entered the room, falling onto my knees. I caught my weight on my outstretched palms and waited for the dizziness to pass before getting up and locking the door.

My father took us every year to count Monarch butterflies as they streamed down the coast on their annual migration. He packed us all up in the Oldsmobile and we went to Cape May Point on the New Jersey coast. In those days it was a wild place. Sharp-scented forests led onto sand dunes and empty beaches—in September, bright sunshine appeared and disappeared from behind racing bundles of cumulonimbus clouds. Distant smudges of rain raced in from the sea and blew over quickly in sudden blasts that barely wet our hair. The breezes that came off the Atlantic were sharp and constant and filled our eyes with shell grit.

My father set up our lime green canvas tent with two bedroom annexes in sheltered clumps of pines. We built cooking fires and unloaded huge hampers of food that included potted shrimp, sardines, and armfuls of preserved meats—hams, lengths of salami, and pregnant blood puddings. My sister, Hannah, and I felt like explorers in a wild country. Each of us was issued a pair of binoculars, a magnifying glass, and a color plate of the mighty North American Monarch butterfly, five times life-size. Above us, bay breasted warblers, sharpies, Cooper's hawks, and tan peregrines hovered and plunged, soaring on violent coastal updrafts.

My father counted the migrating Monarchs for several years. The figures were meticulously recorded with red ink in oilskin-bound notebooks—every year he sent his data to the head of the entomology department at Princeton. He treated the exercise like a big-game hunt, wore Hemingway jackets with rows of front pockets, did not shave for several days, and rolled his own cigarettes in the open air. He became quite a different person for a short time. For most of his life he was a high school science teacher who saw everything as a set of first principles. He was a regular and ritualized man, not given to doing anything that had not been fully deliberated. But on Cape May Point, I was allowed to take occasional puffs on his taut little cigarettes. I still remember the feeling of loose shards of tobacco against my lips and acrid smoke on my teeth.

My father could have been on the savannah hunting wildebeest—indeed I have often thought of the butterfly migration as the insect equivalent of the famous migration of wildebeest down the Rift Valley in Africa. The African version is noisy, dusty, and terrestrial, while the North American version is utterly silent, clean, and airborne. You could live right under a Monarch butterfly migration and never know that it was happening.

One of the most amazing features of the North American Monarch is its ability to migrate fantastic distances to avoid the winter. How it does this remains a mystery. It was the sort of mystery that the naturalists of my grandfather's generation would have relished solving. They fly in vast flocks to the mountains of northern Mexico, where they perch in Oyamel fir trees three thousand feet above sea level, on the steep southwestern slopes. I have always thought that it must be lonely down there, in the Mexican fog, hanging from the limbs of those chilly trees.

In September 1937, my father brought along a college friend of his, Mr. Albert Gissendander, who worked with a firm of book publishers in Manhattan. He was a plump man, prematurely gray, who wore baggy linen suits that were stained yellow under the armpits. He broke his small wire spectacles on the first day and tied them together with a large wad of gauze padding. He had crooked front teeth and sharp bristles on his chin and consumed huge volumes of luncheon meats, often straight from the tin. My father liked him because he was one of those people who could call up a Shakespearean quotation for any occasion. He had a nasal voice and a precise flat diction that made the words lifeless and mechanical. In the evenings, my father discussed butterflies with Albert Gissendander and shared with him a hip flask of whiskey.

On our second day out, we began seeing the first of the Monarchs coming down the coast, bobbing and wafting like leaves in the sky above us. These flimsy insects make for a strange sight as they bounce through the air, especially when one reflects that they will continue this way for more than a thousand miles southward. It is a biological act that strains credulity. My father stationed himself in the dunes at the eastern end of the shore, and Albert Gissendander and Hannah at the other end, looking west into Delaware Bay. Even as an eight-year-old, Hannah was a better counter than most adults. She could maintain her concentration for long periods of time while standing absolutely still, and she had perfect vision. She had a small ring-bound notebook and pencil in one hand and a pair of binoculars looped around her neck on a thin leather strap.

I remember the day vividly. I was considered too young to partic-ipate, so I walked barefoot along the beach. A pale sun glimmered from behind a solid sheet of high white clouds. A tremendous gale was blowing along the front, and blasts of sand kicked up against my cheeks. The surf was flat and gray, with lines of foam gathering on the wet sand. I picked over strands of sea grapes, jellyfish, and chunks of frayed green rope and net shards thrown overboard from distant ships. The sand was cool and smooth against my toes. Because of the wind, many of the butterflies were landing on the beach to rest. I saw the tiny orange-and-black bodies clinging to rocks and clumps of sea grass, their wings opening and closing slowly. Some of them were landing on the water, too, sitting on the rippling surface behind the waves. Some of them were dying out there and washing onto the sand. I came back up the beach and slowly walked out on a long jetty made of cut granite boulders extending two hundred feet out from shore. I picked my way to the end of the jetty, hearing waves break against the rocks and crouching to inspect clear pools of water filled with tiny silver fish and the hard white domes of barnacles. Monarch butterflies were landing on the jetty, too, clinging to the rocks in flimsy orange groups, braced against the wind.

I was sitting out on the end of the jetty, balanced carefully on the rock, with feathers of sea spray blowing into my face, when I saw Hannah running out of the dunes. At first I thought it was a game. She had a short bobbed haircut with a high fringe; she seemed to be running toward me. I waved. She did not see me. Gusts of wind numbed my face and blew my hair into chaotic swirls. Hannah was wearing blue patent leather shoes with silver buckles. Her skirt blew out behind her as she ran, and her thighs were red from the wind. I realized then that as she sprinted *forward* she was looking behind her, at Albert Gissendander, who was lumbering after her out of the dunes. He ran with arms outstretched and was shouting something that I could not hear over the wind. He had his binoculars in his left hand. The leather strap was broken and dragged on the ground. Hannah ran down to the jetty and began climbing out toward me. She jumped quickly on the slick rocks. She was looking back over her shoulder when she slipped. Her arms grabbed at the air. She fell against a piece of sharp granite on which I would later find strands of her brown hair. She hit her head and then splashed into the water, and her fall seemed so instantaneous, such a momentary thing, that I expected to see her come up laughing immediately. I was perhaps fifty yards away. I had a last glimpse of her face as she went down— she was concentrating hard and her mouth was firmly shut. Without a sound she fell, down to those hard rocks, down into the clear, cold water of that September afternoon.

2. *ORNITHOPTERA ALEXANDRAE—* QUEEN ALEXANDRIA'S BIRDWING

One night in May of 1874, during a violent downpour, a man appeared at my grandfather's house in New York City. Unable to afford a hansom cab, he had walked all the way from the wharf district, and when he pounded on the door his thin dark fingers shook. He introduced himself to the servant as Thomas Gray. He stood waiting in the entry hall, surrounded by heavy vases filled with camellias. Water streamed from his slick oilskin and pooled at his feet. My grandfather, who was entertaining dinner guests, was called away from the table and came to the door dabbing his mouth with a napkin. Behind the heavy ginger beard and hollow eyes, he recognized his friend, who had left the country three years earlier on a Nantucket whaler, and whom he had given up for dead, drowned somewhere on the southern ocean, sucked into the belly of the deep like so many others.

My grandfather threw off the oilskin and embraced him. Thomas Gray was so skeletal that he had a birdlike quality. He walked quickly into my grandfather's study. His breeches were smeared with street mud and his boots were thin. He wore a rough nankeen jacket and a blue cotton vest. Long strands of hair, bleached white by the sun, hung around a jaw that had become thin and angular.

They had been the best of friends and had grown up together. They shared a genuine interest in entomology, which connected them even after Thomas Gray's family had lost their railway fortune in South American gold speculations. Butterflies had united them— a shared love of the insect world and a need to order, catalog, and list. They spent summers preserving specimens of *Saturniidae* that they found in groves of pin cherry, larch, maple, and walnut trees.

Thomas Gray was now a poor man struggling to build a reputation. He had left to make his fortune in the tropics, believing he would find insects that he could sell to museums and private collectors for a profit, while at the same time contributing to the natural sciences. As boys, both of them had read *A Voyage Up the River Amazon* by William Edwards and the journals of Charles Darwin on his famous voyage aboard the HMS *Beagle*. They knew of the astounding collections that Alfred Wallace had assembled in the island groups of the Pacific and were familiar with the theories of both Wallace and Darwin, presented separately to the Linnean Society in July 1858. My grandfather, who had a strict Protestant upbringing, was skeptical of the theories of natural selection and still believed that they could be disproved.

Thomas Gray spent two years in the Malay Archipelago and the Dutch East Indies, where he found jungles whose density and lushness paralleled the extraordinary variety of the insect life that he found there. He told my grandfather that he had collected over five hundred new species of butterfly, the same of beetles and flies, and several hundred of wasps, moths, and bees. He spent the last of his money on a return passage on a spice cutter out of Surabaya. They put in at Mauritius for supplies. The captain, sensing perhaps that Thomas Gray's collections were more valuable than Thomas Gray himself, had departed late one night with his collection while Gray was ashore. Two years of careful work, and all his dreams and aspirations for the future, went with the ship, out across the phosphorescent Indian Ocean. Penniless, he had worked his way back on trading vessels.

Now, standing in my grandfather's study, Thomas Gray was trembling violently. In the soft lamplight, my grandfather noted that his skin had a yellow tint. Later, unable to sleep, he would record everything that happened that night in his diaries.

My grandfather poured them each a healthy measure of brandy while Gray stood with his back to the fire.

"You will be pleased to hear that I have retained one specimen," Thomas Gray said to my grandfather. "I have kept it on my person, never wanting it out of my sight. You have never seen anything like it. I have had it with me for more than a year."

From his jacket he pulled a thick oilskin bundle, tied with a piece of hemp rope. He put the bundle on my grandfather's desk and unraveled it. Inside, wrapped carefully in sheets of sandy parchment paper, was the wing of a butterfly. It was just a single wing. It shone with a green and blue luminescence that seemed to pull light from the room. The wing was enormous—seven inches across from the lateral tip to the attachment point with the body. It shimmered on the dark oak of the desktop; it was mottled with black striations and partitioned into corrals of color that shimmered and flashed as the men moved it under the lamp. "Can you imagine the size of the butterfly it came from?" Thomas Gray inquired of my grandfather, who could not. It was the largest specimen that he had ever seen. It had a mythical quality that was difficult to believe.

Thomas Gray had been given the wing by a sailor who claimed to have found it on one of the tropical islands to the northeast of Australia, across the Torres Strait. The butterfly was so large that they brought it down with a shooter, the sailor said. They had fired three times before it fell to the ground. "This is the largest butterfly in the world," my grandfather wrote, "the dimensions of which cannot be believed."

"I want you to help me find this creature," Thomas Gray said to my grandfather. "What a find it would be. We would make our reputations. And we would make our fortunes at the same time."

Surrounded by solid furniture and dark teak paneling, they stood examining the wing for some time. I imagine the fire raging in the grate and blasts of rain pounding against the windows. My grandfather was entranced. Thomas Gray's eyes danced with fever and exhaustion. Later, after the guests had been seen to the door, and my grandfather had given Thomas Gray a dose of quinine, a hot bath, and a bed, he sat in his study and pored over his maps of the Pacific Islands. Everything else was swept from his mind, as if it had been carried away in the torrent outside his windows. "If this creature exists on the earth," he wrote, "then I am resolved to discover it." In his heart, he believed that the butterfly would disprove the theories of natural selection elaborated by Darwin and Wallace. "When there is only one of its kind," he wrote, "with no clear survival advantage to being of such magnitude and color, then it must surely have been placed here by a divine hand." This was the beginning of his obsession with finding the butterfly that would later be called *Ornithoptera alexandrae*, Queen Alexandria's Birdwing—the largest butterfly in the world.

Maya and I were having our wedding dinner with her parents when her father had his first seizure. Earlier that day we had gone to the registry office in Washington, D.C. We stood on blue fireproof carpeting for the brief ceremony. A handful of Maya's friends came and flashed photographs of us standing before the justice of the peace, a man older than I who had a set of poorly attached, clacking false teeth. Her friends threw rice at us as we walked out.

At dinner, with fork raised to mouth, her father suddenly went glassy-eyed. Drips of curry fell onto the tablecloth in front of him. His breathing became quick and shallow. Then he tumbled back in his chair and started jerking as he slipped sideways. His neck arched backward and his arms pounded stiffly on the floor. I could smell urine, sharp and acrid, when I bent over him.

I had always admired Maya's father. He had a rigorous mind and a sense of humor. He worked on subatomic particles and was a skeptic by nature. He could do differential calculus in his head and was passionate about old movies. "I will tell you in two words the most significant improvement in my life since leaving India," he said to me. "John Ford." He wore sandals all year, even in winter, and had delicate pink toenails and soft brown toes the color of maple syrup.

Maya drove him to the hospital herself, got the MRI scans and angiograms done quickly. There was a solid white ball filling the left temporal lobe of his brain, exploding into his head like some sort of celestial event in deep space. Her father had visions, saw lights in the sky, and heard voices from his childhood—his mother calling him inside, his father teaching him to read, distant coughs from his own grandfather, who was long dead. He cried like a baby. "For god's sake don't let me become a vegetable," he said. "Pull the bloody plug. That's all I ask. *Pull the bloody plug.*"

Maya assisted at his surgery. "It's my responsibility as his daughter. Who else can you trust? He knows I'll look after him."

"But he's your own father," I said. "How can you bear to see his brain? It's not something a daughter needs to see. How can you stand that?"

It was a seven-hour procedure in a cool operating theater resounding with the rhythmic clack of the respirator and the twang of taped sitar music. Maya shaved the head of her father smooth. His thick black hair fell onto the floor in clumps. Clear glass bottles at the end of the suction probes filled with blood and tiny pieces of connective tissue. I have never seen her colder or more isolated. In her protective goggles, double gloves, and green surgical gown tied behind her neck and waist, she looked prepared for battle.

I never saw Maya cry. She retreated into an inner place where she could dispense advice and give professional support. She made tea for her mother and brought dishes of rice and vegetables to the hospital room. She reassured her brothers and explained the pathology to them. Her white coat was wrapped tightly around her. "I have to take responsibility," she said to me. "I can't think about it. I just have to get on with it." She concentrated on the neuroanatomy, histological findings, and her father's intracranial pressure. Maya the clinician. I watched her slip away, slowly and for good reason, into a safe world somewhere behind her black eyes, somewhere behind those eyelashes.

As I get older, and especially at this time of year, I find myself thinking more and more about my sister Hannah. She understood butterflies. When my grandmother died, my father inherited the house, and we grew up in the creaking old place, full of dark wood, anti-macassars, plinths, and vases. Hannah was three years older than I was and I worshipped her. I remember lying on piles of my grand-father's Turkish rugs with her and learning the names of the objects and artifacts around us—Ethiopian wooden head pillows, rows of carved penis sheaths from New Guinea, garish yellow-and-red face masks from the Ivory Coast, the stuffed head of a salamander, one goatskin side of a yurt.

Hannah had a photographic memory. She knew all of the butter-fly names and species and could remember the notes from my grand-father's logbooks—"I saw the pink hind wings of two *Atrophaneura horishamus* in a clump of tropical climbing vine," she would quote, "mating in the sun." Hannah inherited my mother's chestnut hair and my father's buckteeth, which rested neatly on her lower lip and left red indentations there when she concentrated for a long time. She had stumpy fingers and thumbs that curled back to her wrists. If she had lived she would have had dental work, my mother said whenever she saw an old picture of Hannah.

Hannah took charge of me, led me around by the hand, and let me sleep with her at night. I never felt safer than in the crook of her arm, my face buried into her nightdress, smelling a strange mixture of pumice soap, milk, and burning hair. She dressed me up in her old dresses and tights, treated me like a doll, and took me for long walks with the dog in Central Park. I sought attention from Hannah, so I preferred being dressed as a girl, because it pleased my sister and be-cause it allowed me to accompany her.

Even as an eight-year-old, Hannah had ambitions that I'm sure my parents did not believe or think about. But I believed. In 1937, Amelia Earhart was in the headlines—there was a new acceptance of women as tomboys and adventurers—and Hannah wanted to fly a plane, too. She cried for days when Earhart's plane disappeared in the Pacific that July. And it was she who wanted to be a doctor, not me.

She had solid fingers and a light touch. She was able to concentrate on details for hours and was charming to everyone she met. I never had any of these qualities, but growing up, I tried to become more like her. By nature, I'm much more of an introvert—slow moving and unaware. I lose things, forget birthdays, put metal objects into microwave ovens, buy food that I never eat. Sometimes when I am alone, I feel like a kind of human chameleon trying to perpetuate the memory of a lost eight-year-old girl.

My grandfather would have looked for answers in the natural world, specifically in the biology of butterflies. There are interesting parallels to be found in the work of Henry W. Bates, a nineteenth-century English naturalist and explorer. I have perused his famous paper in the *Transactions of the Linnean Society in London* (1862), entitled "Contribution to an Insect Fauna of the Amazon Valley." Bates captured over one hundred species of *Heliconian, Ithomid,* and *Pierid* butterflies in Amazonia. He found that butterflies that were toxic to predators, and therefore had good defenses against being eaten, were mimicked by butterflies that had no defenses. These weaker butterflies changed their coloring and markings to match those of the stronger butterflies. By copying the appearance of butterflies that had natural defenses, they avoided attacks by predators. Bates's field observations began the study of mimicry in biology.

Biology is a powerful force that cannot be denied. I am a surgeon for my sister and because of my sister. And for her I learned to fly a plane, spent endless weekends with my stomach in my throat, fighting with the rudder while bobbing over the summer beaches on Long Island. Hannah would have enjoyed all that sky and sea and the little pink figures staring up from the surf far below as she buzzed overhead.

My grandfather corresponded with Henry W. Bates in the 1870s. He also had a lifelong friendship with Fritz Muller, the German naturalist who collected and observed butterflies in the Amazon. In 1879, Muller published "Huna and Thyridia: A Remarkable Case of

Mimicry in Butterflies," in the *Proceedings of the Entomological Society* (London, 1879). I have read the article several times. My grandfather owned a dog-eared copy of the volume, in which he made spindly marginal notes. The precision with which these striking butterflies can mimic each other's markings is astonishing. My grandfather was fascinated, and would later do his own experiments on butterfly mimicry. In the nineteenth century it was still possible for educated amateurs to make contributions to field biology. Driving these men was a certain curiosity of spirit that I admire.

In 1875, my grandfather sailed for the islands of southeast Asia in a four-masted iron sailing barque. Thomas Gray went with him. He was still weak and suffering periodic relapses of fever, but he was stronger than he had been and was determined to take part in the expedition. From San Francisco, they charted a southwesterly course that took them to Hawaii and then Guam, the Philippines, and the island of Borneo. Later they would loop southeast to the Solomon Islands and Fiji before returning west to Papua New Guinea.

In the pockets of his jacket my grandfather carried butterfly nets, bottles of chloroform, and a portable microscope with brass fixtures. He collected several butterflies of the genus *Atrophaneura*—there are striking examples of the red furry-bodied *Atrophaneura semperi albofasciata* in his collection. In the jungles of Borneo he found *Troides brookiana*—Rajah Brookes Birdwing—with its deep blue and green coloring. The second largest butterfly he found—*Ornithoptera goliath procus*—came from the Malaysian islands. One of his specimens has a nine-inch wingspan.

In New Guinea my grandfather hired a Dutch missionary named Rhin Postma to guide them into the jungle. The Dutch Calvinist was an alcoholic, with veined cheeks and heavy thighs. He wore stiff collars over his mottled red neck. Although he was familiar with some of the coastal tribes—groups who wore the plumes of parrots in their hair and decorated themselves with silver pearl shells—he had little understanding of the interior of the country. My grandfather looked at dark shimmering jungles and saw only butterfly habitats. They walked into the hills through morning mists and trees interspersed with kunai grass. Around them in the forests they saw giant crowned pigeons, pygmy parrots, cassowaries, and cockatoos. The dusk sky was rainbow-colored with flocks of darting parrots and kingfishers.

It was densely humid and they were beset by flies and biting insects. Thomas Gray continued to lose weight and was immobilized by fever. Rhin Postma was in no condition to hike through dense undergrowth. They decided to set up a temporary camp on the shores of a lake that the locals called *Katubu,* and let my grandfather press into the highlands on his own. "My friend is sick," my grandfather wrote, "and I am faster without him. The Dutchman is drinking too much and cannot walk well. I will be back in a few weeks. I cannot wait." He was unafraid of the unknown territory ahead of him. None of them knew what it contained or understood why he insisted on pushing ahead alone.

He continued with four native porters, haunted by visions of the largest butterfly in the world. Shortly after my grandfather left the lake, Rhin Postma abandoned the camp, leaving Thomas Gray on his own, sick and unable to move. He lay on a camp bed for several days in a state of delirium before he was killed by warriors from a mountain tribe, naked men with wild balls of feathered hair, who ran him through with stone-tipped spears. He was dismembered and the camp supplies taken. My grandfather was also pursued as he marched quickly on his short, thick legs, but was saved by his fire flints and his rifle. He was observed starting a fire in a few seconds with some dry grass and twigs, and once he shot a tree kangaroo with his rifle. The highlanders saw him as a figure invested with supernatural powers.

He and Gray were the first Europeans they had encountered. They approached him cautiously and examined his white hands, covered in fine brown hairs, with suspicion. The magnified images visible through his glass made people jump back in terror. His knives and fob watch, his microscope and other scientific equipment, and his fine brown hair and freckled skin were understood to be the trappings of something heaven-sent.

It was not a comfortable alliance. My grandfather was nervous, surrounded by spindle-legged men covered with thick scars, whom he could not understand. But standing in the heavy heat one day, he noticed that a warrior had the shimmering blue, green, and yellow wings of a butterfly strung from his neck. "They are wearing what I seek," he wrote, "and I know I have to befriend them."

He was taken to villages set in baked dirt clearings. Quick-limbed, potbellied children hid behind trees and pointed at him. He was treated as a guest, given food and shelter in grass lean-tos. They took him on hunting parties. He lived with this remote mountain tribe for several months. This was at a time when cannibalism was still widely practiced in that part of the world. Ritual marks were tattooed on his back. He learned to speak fragments of a mountain dialect that involved guttural throat sounds and clicking noises made by pressing the back of the tongue against the hard palate. When he made it clear that he sought the large insects that hung from the limbs of trees in the thick forest, he was taken to places where he could find them. In this remote and untamed place, among people living a different age, he found magnificent examples of *Ornithoptera alexandrae,* the Queen Alexandria's Birdwing. Over fifty butterflies were gathered and stored in caulked oak barrels.

I have read through the New Guinea volume—he recorded the daily routines of the tribe and made comments on what he saw. There were moments when he felt he could understand their lives and take meaning from them. It is clear from these pages that my grandfather also participated in cannibalism. Skirmishes between tribal groups were common; they were undertaken with long spears and wooden clubs. Victories were celebrated by roasting the bodies of the enemy and consuming their flesh. I recognize that my grandfather may have had no choice in the matter. The internal organs, including the brain, liver, lungs, and kidneys, were a particular delicacy. The brains were often eaten raw, and my grandfather consumed "the cerebrum of a poor unfortunate" on three occasions during his time in the mountains. It was a matter of survival for him—he had to participate fully or risk death, I can see that. I do not judge him.

When he walked out of the jungle, he found the remains of the camp by the lake and understood what had happened to his companion. He believed he had let Thomas Gray down. His hair was matted and uncut. He returned to the coast with a heavy feeling of loss and failure that he would never quite shake. He carried three species of worm in his large intestine and on his arm a tame cockatoo. On the voyage home, he wrote a long letter to the parents of Thomas Gray, but he never sent it. Instead, he went to see them in New York and gave them several specimens of the butterfly their son had gone to find. He knew that even this butterfly was poor compensation for a son. The cockatoo lost all its feathers, refused to eat, and was dead before the year's end.

3. *PARNASSIUS HARDWIKII* AND *PARNASSIUS MAHARAJA*—THE HIMALAYAN BUTTERFLIES

Seeing Maya's father after his surgery, I understood that we are more than just anatomy, more than just a set of structures. With his hair cut off, the long scar along one side of his head, and a spiderweb of tubes and wires emerging from neck, arm, and bladder, he was barely recognizable. He was paralyzed down the right side of his body and could not speak. Maya checked his intracranial pressure and muscle strength and examined his wound several times a day. There was something comforting about seeing his feet—small and delicate with their maple syrup toes sticking out of the bedsheets.

Although the man was paralyzed and swollen, his spirit had not left him. I felt it there with me, behind his eyes, which were dark and more understanding than mine. When I brought in a video of *Stagecoach,* I could sense his joy, and when his left thumb went up into the air, I could feel him there with us. He watched dozens of Westerns in his last days. We are more than just the sum of our parts, I said to Maya. I tried to break down her objective view of the human brain. His spirit was walking on some forgotten prairie, kicking among the tumbleweed, while his brain was less than complete.

We knew immediately that the tumor would recur. He had only weeks to live. At home, he tried to walk and fell over. Maya read physics journals to him. Maya's mother made him his favorite foods and fed him with spoons they had been given for their wedding. With a trembling left hand he wrote me notes that he didn't want his family to see. *Pull the bloody plug,* he wrote, and when I looked into his eyes, the eyes of his daughter, I understood my grandfather more clearly.

Toward the end Maya's father had more seizures. During the third and last of them he kicked himself off his wheelchair in the garden. When they found him, he was still alive, his face pressed down against the ground, as if he were listening carefully to insects in the grass. He wanted to remain outside. They laid him on a mattress under a clump of beech trees to stare at the sky through the white boughs. That was where he died, on a summer day, surrounded by bees, his forehead dusted lightly with yellow pollen.

In 1890, fifteen years after my grandfather's return from New Guinea, there were clear signs that he was going insane. He became obsessed with vaudeville, burlesque shows, and the circus. He had always been a quiet and meticulous man who believed firmly in Victorian morals and the importance of hard work and personal discipline. But in 1890 he began spending all of his nights in music halls—he saw over one hundred shows by the comedy team of Joe Weber and Lou Fields and went drinking with music hall comedians John T. Kelly and Peter Dailey. He spent days at the circus, becoming enthralled by the clowns. Because he was a wealthy man he was allowed backstage. He became acquainted with Dan Rice, the famous Civil War clown. He filled many pages of his diaries with sketches and descriptions of clowns—almost as if he were trying to make sense of the theatrical world by applying scientific methods as rigorously as he could.

He began asking circus and vaudeville performers home for musical and burlesque evenings—he staged several shows in his house on the Upper East Side, inviting wealthy friends and acquaintances from all over New York. There were displays of slapstick, magic tricks, funny songs, sight and sound gags. This new interest in theater was quite out of character for my grandfather, who had the personality and brain of a scientist, not an entertainer. But when he began participating in these shows himself, dressed in baggy suits and suspenders, flopping shoes, makeup and wigs, everyone realized that something was wrong.

He became a clown in real life—making gags and giggling at dinner, finding eggs and flowers in the hair of visitors, and installing in the living room a trick chair that disintegrated when one sat in it. In March of 1890, he induced a rhubarb tart to slide the length of his dining room table with a hidden magnet and a system of wires and pulleys. The dinner party consisted of "three Irish comics, a high-court judge, a physician of some standing who has pioneered the use of ether for minor surgical procedures, and the third cousin of Theodore Roosevelt." He reported that after dinner he bemused everyone (except the comics) with a trick bottle of tawny port that, although uncorked, would not pour. The cigars offered to the judge and the physician were of an explosive nature and resulted in "a very satisfying percussion that sent the smokers crashing back into their seats with a flash of gunpowder and a blast of black smoke."

My grandfather continued to document daily events in his diary. He was filled with a compulsion to "make flippancy of everything" and to "jest without restraint," recording that he often laughed uncontrollably for several minutes at commonplace sights such as a decanter of sherry or a conical pile of horse dung in the street. My grandmother must have been alarmed at the dramatic changes that she saw in her husband. My grandfather recorded that she packed several trunks and went to live with her family in Boston, leaving him to practice his tricks and gags alone in their granite-fronted house.

I sometimes drive past my grandfather's old house on my way to the hospital. It is a huge Victorian with four floors and servants' quarters. My father sold it years ago. Now it has been subdivided into offices and the ground floor is a health food restaurant. I'm sure my grandfather would have been amused by the waitresses in Ethiopian muslin shawls. He had been to Ethiopia—then Abyssinia—in the early 1870s. He had walked around the solid rock ramparts of the Coptic churches in Gondar hunting specimens of *Papilio dardanus* and *Papilio lormieri.*

After her father's funeral, Maya and I both needed to get away, so we spent a month in India. My images of India had been formed by an early love of Kipling. I had imagined turbaned infidels (black as night with crescent moon swords), tigers on leashes, and polite English conversations under fans pulled by emaciated fan-wallahs. The withered limbs, animals and death in the streets, and delicate children with staring eyes were a revelation. There are many butterfly species on the subcontinent, but it is hard to believe it when passing through the cities. I was keen to find specimens of *Parnassius hardwikii* and *Parnassius maharaja,* both of which live on the southern face of the Himalayas above 2,500 meters, but I never found the time to make any field trips. Maya bought me a white dhoti and the most dramatic and shocking lingums she could find, including an electric one that when plugged in flashed rainbow colors. I felt as young as I ever have felt. There was something invigorating about the place. It was chaotic, teeming with fecundity, as busy as a human beehive. After a while I forgot the squalor. One night as we lay on thin cotton sheets under a ceiling fan, Maya said to me, "You have the sexual energy of a twenty-year-old."

"Do you think so?"

"I do. I'm not complaining. But I wonder how you do it."

"I don't feel as if I'm doing anything. But I feel better being away from home. I feel a sort of freedom, I guess. Don't you?"

"Not like you. This is partly my home. I don't feel as if I've exactly escaped from anything. You know India. About one in five people you meet are probably related to me in some way, distantly."

"There's something liberating about being away from your family."

"I suppose there is." She rolled onto her side with her hands flat on the sheet in front of her. Indian pop music floated up from the street below and I could hear the distant bellows of water buffalo. In the dim light her black hair fell like ink onto the white sheets. Her feet and hands had been hennaed for our wedding and a complicated spiderweb of purple lines and flowers curved over her palms and the backs of her feet. There was a timelessness about this moment. I realized then that I could never really escape from my family at all. I carry them all with me.

We spent sweaty afternoons with members of Maya's extended family eating silver and bronze sweetmeats and talking about the quality of Indian pollution and computer software. I was accepted completely as an older man with a younger woman—in a society in which many marriages are still arranged, it was quite reasonable for us to be together. "It is more of an honor for me to be with you than with a younger man," Maya told me. We ate string hoppers and glutinous ice creams in outdoor markets. We rushed around like children, bought a carved teak chest and a set of solid brass doorjambs. I felt close to Maya then. She forgot about her father for a while. She put away her lists and schedules and I felt as if she were relaxing for the first time since I had known her. She joked that we should never go home and that we should spend the rest of our lives running a leper hospital. Maya told me the stories of her maddest relatives, where to stand on crowded buses, and key Hindi obscenities. The only thing Maya didn't tell me when we were in India was that she was two months pregnant with our daughter.

I would be a foolish man indeed not to admit that my surgical skills have begun to suffer because of my drinking. I now find myself drinking whiskey in my office, quietly and subversively, like a criminal, before my morning operating list. Two glasses of malt whiskey stop the alarming morning tremor and keep my hands steady. For an hour or two I feel as I used to feel in the morning—in command of my subject, calm and analytical. I swallow gulps of mouthwash and suck peppermints to mask the smell of my breath. And as quickly as possible after I have changed into my scrubs, I put on a face mask. I have always taken great pride in my work, yet now I feel reluctant and cautious, unable to enjoy what I do, unable to be companionable to the staff who work with me. I get away as quickly as I can—after a longer list I can think of nothing except the bottle in the locked lower drawer of my desk.

I can see that my skills have deteriorated, but I am convinced that it is not yet obvious to those around me. I notice a subtle diminution in the precision of my skin cuts. My sutures are fractionally less clean, less neat, more slapdash to my eye, but I am not sure this is noticeable to anyone else. Occasionally I drop instruments, something I have never done. All of this, I believe, is within the bounds of acceptable behavior. I am certain that I have not had a patient who has suffered as a result of my drinking. My record has remained good. There have been no complaints.

I recognize, too, that things are getting worse. Last week I was repairing several extensor tendons, severed in a motorcycle accident, in the right hand of a professional musician. I was working under an operating microscope. Two hours into the procedure, I fell asleep standing at the operating table. My head was leaning heavily into the microscope eyepiece. My hands, still holding the instruments, lay immobile in the open wound below me. I awoke suddenly and still have no idea how long I was unconscious. I assume that it was a very brief time. The resident assisting me was still by my side and did not say anything. The surgical nurse stood ready with the suction. I stood back from the table carefully and pretended to be thinking. I felt something akin to panic. When I had gathered myself sufficiently to speak, I told the resident to take over. I stepped aside and watched her complete the task. I stood there watching, ostensibly as a supervisor, although I paid very little attention to what she was doing. I had crossed some kind of barrier, I knew. I did not want to contemplate what would have happened if I had fallen. I did not want to think about those machine-sharp instruments in my unconscious hands.

It is time for me to take some concrete action, this is clear. I should go to the chief of surgery, Dr. Touli, and do the responsible thing. This is hard for me. I find it painful to discuss the details of my condition, particularly with a man ten years my junior, who has never possessed my level of skill. It is difficult to describe a weakness to a man whom I do not consider an equal. In truth, I believe that I should be the head of the department of surgery, not Dr. Touli. The reasons I was passed over for this position remain obscure to me.

4. *LIMENITIS ARCHIPPUS*—THE VICEROY BUTTERFLY

I can only imagine what my father thought when he saw Albert Gissendander heaving toward him along the beach. The fat wad of gauze on his spectacles was flashing in the sun. His mouth opened and shut noiselessly and he was waving the binoculars above his head. I stood at the end of the jetty and watched my father run. He seemed to move in slow motion, a tiny figure battling the wind, as if he were trapped under glass. It took him minutes to reach the jetty, by which time he had ripped off his jacket and thrown it behind him. He shouted at me with terrifying force, "Just stay here and don't move. Do you hear me? Don't move." I didn't move when I heard him cry out and jump into the water. I didn't move when I saw him wading back to the beach with my sister in his arms. Sometimes I feel as if I have been standing at the end of that jetty for fifty years.

Loss is a strange thing. My mother blamed my father and my father blamed the butterflies. The house seemed empty and lifeless. My parents were unable to talk to each other. My mother got a job as a secretary in a law firm and left us two years afterward for a man who sold theatrical supplies. In later years I would visit her and sit in a living room filled with wigs in plastic bags and stacks of Neptune forks. My mother became suspicious of science and logic. She started dressing flamboyantly, wearing makeup, and going to parties. She took up astrology.

My father never again looked at butterflies. We never again went to see the Monarchs migrate. He taught. He began a lifetime of renovating and remodeling my grandfather's old house. New plumbing was installed. Wiring was updated. Walls were added. He rebuilt his grief outside of himself in that old house, hammered and nailed it into place, as if his misery were something solid and visible. "We must prevail," he said to me. "We must go on." I read my grandfather's diaries and watched my father become a thin and dewy-eyed old man.

There is a grave, a shiny marble tablet at one end of a small earthy plot. Every week my father and I went to visit her, and in the summer I brought butterflies. I caught them in the garden and kept them alive in glass jars with perforated lids. Standing there among the graves, I'd let a butterfly out onto her headstone and watch it sit for a moment and then drift into the air and float off. When I think of butterflies I think of Hannah—there she is in front of me, a little sliver of color.

I saw Albert Gissendander once more in my life. I was an intern in the emergency room when he came in with chest pain. He did not recognize me. He lay with his eyes shut, holding an oxygen mask over his mouth and nose. His lips were blue. I asked him about his pain—it had come on while he was having a full English breakfast at a diner. The twelve wire leads of the electrocardiogram hung limply from his chest.

I placed my hands on his sweaty white skin and listened to fine crepitations in his lungs. He had a thin, irregular pulse. His heart sounded distant and muffled. It seemed to be beating underwater, like a deep-sea creature. "Will I be all right?" he asked me, opening his eyes for an instant. I inserted an intravenous line and gave him morphine. I imagined this body, propelled by this ailing heart, pounding along the beach at Cape May Point. His toenails were yellow and curled. We had shared something, this man and I, but I didn't feel anything. For a moment, I thought of telling Albert Gissendander who I was and watching his heart rate rise on the monitor. I could imagine it speeding up. I could imagine the peaks and valleys of his heart-tracing squeezing together, tripping over each other. "You'll be all right," I said.

I got him stabilized and he was sent to the coronary care unit for close monitoring. The next morning, when my shift had ended, I went up to see him. In the elevator I pulled my white coat tightly around my chest and did up all the buttons. I stood outside his room for some time, watching him in the bed. He was huge and white, lying beached in the bed like some giant aquatic mammal. I went into the room and pretended to study his chart. He looked at me benignly with dark moist eyes and did not speak. The cardiac monitor bleeped steadily. I stood for a moment at the end of the bed and then said, "I am Hannah's brother."

He regarded me silently and I was not sure that he had understood. But then he suddenly tried to speak. He pulled the plastic oxygen mask from his nose and mouth. His fat lips moved against each other, but no sound emerged. His eyes bulged. He was clearly in distress. He lifted one forearm off the bed and indicated that he wanted me to come closer. I bent down and put my ear to his lips. His heavy breath blew against the side of my face. "I'm a very sick man," he said in gasps. "You leave me alone." I stood hunched down with my ear to his face much longer than I needed to. As I left the room, I realized that I did not want to know any more. I did not want to cheapen the memory of my sister by talking about her with this dying stranger. I hoped that Albert Gissendander's memories of the past were vivid and alive, and that they would hasten him along his way. It is surprising how serious illness can sharpen the senses and bring the past into clearer focus—perhaps in the end he held himself accountable for what he had done.

My grandfather's hands began shaking and got progressively worse. He chopped off his thumb in frustration. The tremor became so severe that he was unable to control his arms and could no longer do fine work with butterflies. His memory began to disappear, and this was perhaps his greatest loss. It was his mind that had always sustained him. He began writing lists for everything that he had to remember each day. He shouted mercilessly at the nurse that his family had hired to look after him. As the disease progressed, he had increasing difficulty walking and getting his balance. Eventually he was confined to a wheelchair.

He had seen the disease in the highlands of New Guinea. The locals called it *Kuru*. There was progressive destruction of the brain, marked initially by moderately inappropriate behavior, which then progressed to diminished motor control and memory loss. The victims became ataxic and uncoordinated and were eventually unable to move at all. In six to nine months they could not speak or swallow and lost control of their eyes. Unable to eat, they often died of malnutrition. Only those who handled and ate infected human brains got the disease. In New Guinea the stricken individuals sat aimlessly in the villages, wild-haired and babbling.

Of course in those days nothing was understood about the neurodegenerative diseases caused by "slow viruses" or protein agents called prions. It would be sixty-seven years before Vincent Zigas and Carelton Gajdusek described *Kuru* in the Fore Highlanders of New Guinea—a form of dementia transmitted by contact with infected brains. And it was still some time before we understood other related diseases—Creutzfeldt-Jakob disease, scrapie in sheep, and the notorious bovine spongiform encephalopathy or mad cow disease. I have studied this collection of disorders. The end result is always the same. The brain is eaten away like Swiss cheese and there is no cure or treatment.

Maya is inherently interested in anything that eats away the brain. It is proof to her that we are little more than machines—noradrenaline, serotonin, and dopamine running through a set of circuits and pathways. Each loss of function has an anatomical correlate and this appeals to Maya's sense of order. There has been a handful of cases of transmissible neuropathies reported in neurosurgeons. They get the disease from operating on infected brains without appropriate barrier protection—a hole in a glove and a scratch on a finger can provide an entry point into the bloodstream. Perhaps a splash of infected blood into the eye is all it takes. There is nothing more tragic than a neurosurgeon who loses his or her brain. All that skill, all that intimate knowledge, all that manual dexterity, eaten away.

We were having afternoon tea with Maya's aunt and uncle when she miscarried. It was our last week in India. From the living room of their second-floor flat in Goa, I looked out over a beach covered in dull yellow sand. Shouts from a game of volleyball filled the afternoon—tanned young men in board shorts and ankle bracelets were playing to the music of Bob Marley, watched by thin women in saris at the food stalls. It was a sticky day and the tea was strong and milky. Maya clutched her lower abdomen and turned paler than I have ever seen her. She ran into the bathroom. Her aunt Priya followed. They emerged five minutes later with Maya holding a towel between her legs. "Don't ask," Maya whispered to me. "Please don't ask."

Her uncle took us in a rusty Peugeot to a private clinic with whitewashed walls set in a grove of waving palms. I had to half carry Maya up the front steps. The towel between her legs was already red with fresh blood. Her uncle ran off to find the obstetrician, who was his squash partner. I sat with my arms around Maya, watching an old man sweep the green concrete steps in front of us with a brush broom. I felt Maya slump into me. "I'm sorry," she said. "This is my fault. I should have told you."

The nurses were wearing winged caps and solid white shoes with laces. They found her a bed in a small room. I was quickly ushered out and told to wait in the dayroom, a linoleum-covered space in which twenty or thirty men and boys were watching cricket on a wide-screen television. They found me a chair in front of the television and I sat down reluctantly, not wanting to appear impolite. "This certainly is a compensation, is it not?" the man sitting next to me said through a wide grin. "Although we are in hospital, we have this magnificent television and a front-row seat for the first test match at Headingly. It is not to be sneezed at."

An hour later the obstetrician appeared and led me over to the windows. He was wearing a three-piece gray suit despite the heat. When he spoke it was with a strong Oxbridge accent—he sounded more English than my English friends. He had the air of a sportsman about him—competent games of squash and tennis, an occasional flutter on the horses, lifetime memberships to cricket clubs. His tie was monogrammed with two crossed polo mallets.

"I'm afraid she has lost the baby, old boy," he said to me.

"Nothing we can do?"

"Nothing at all. One of those things, I'm afraid. A spontaneous miscarriage. She'll be absolutely fine. I'm going to keep her for a day or two, just to keep an eye on her. I may have to do a D and C later."

"She hadn't told me. About the baby."

"Indeed. She may feel some guilt about that."

"I wish I'd known. Perhaps I could have done something."

"It's unlikely you could have done anything, frankly." There was a clatter of porcelain cups as a tea trolley was wheeled past. "There are only three things certain in the world," the obstetrician said. "Tea, cricket, and death."

I walked back to the room. Maya was asleep with an intravenous line running into one arm. Her hair fanned out on the pillow behind her. I walked over and put my hand against her forehead and watched her breathe through lightly parted lips. The linen sheets were starched and heavy. I could smell the new blood on her. I stood by the window looking out at chickens pecking the dust along the side of the building. A thin green lizard sat immobile, tongue flickering, on the wall above my head. I could hear children playing in the distance. For a moment I sensed the life everywhere around me, so constant that it was almost invisible. It is only when it is taken away that we notice, and that can happen in an instant.

My grandfather was never able to believe that Darwin was right. In his mind, the perfection of butterflies, their elaborate patterns and colors, exceeded the requirements of mere survival. "I cannot believe," he wrote, "that other butterflies notice the fine details that are seen on the wings of these creatures. To my mind, this is art for the sake of art. This is not just survival. It is something higher." After New Guinea, he gave many of his specimens to the Museum of Natural History in New York. He continued to spend summers collecting, but made no more trips overseas.

During the years before he became ill, he spent weeks out west in the plains states, the Rockies, and the deserts of Arizona and New Mexico. He took the whole family with him on some of these trips. These were happy days for my grandmother and their three sons, the youngest my father. My grandfather built a greenhouse at the end of his garden and made it a large butterfly breeding laboratory. He raised *Actias luna, Antherae polyphenus,* and *Automeris io* and looked for examples of mimicry among these butterflies. The year my father was born, 1888, he claimed to have proved that the Monarch butterfly is mimicked by the Viceroy butterfly. Unfortunately, his illness prevented him from publishing his findings.

He would have been pleased to see his own observations confirmed in the work of Jane Van Zandt Browner in the mid-1950s. She reported that in North America, *Danaus plexippus,* the Monarch butterfly, is mimicked by *Limenitis archippus,* the Viceroy butterfly, to obtain the protective advantage of the Monarchs' pattern and coloring. I have filed her article, "Experimental Studies of Mimicry in Some North American Butterflies" (*Evolution* 35 [1958]: 32–47) with the others in my butterfly notes. Van Zandt Browner noted this phenomenon in the population of New Brunswick Monarchs that undertake a fall migration to the mountains of Michoacán in southwestern Mexico.

When my father was four years old, my grandmother and the children moved back to live with her parents in Boston and stayed there for the last two years of my grandfather's life. My grandmother made no attempt to understand what had happened to her husband. Mental illness, in any form, still carried a damning social stigma, and it was never really discussed. Because my grandmother never understood the cause of his disease, she lived in terror that my father would somehow inherit it. She was wary of her own son, watched him carefully, and made him a serious child ahead of his time.

My grandfather never forgot Thomas Gray. Every year on his old friend's birthday, while he was still able, he released many hand-raised specimens, hundreds of them, from his greenhouse. A dense shower of speckled wings flew into the air around him as they tumbled into the sky. On this day he toasted his friend with whiskey and reviewed his butterfly specimens from the Pacific.

It was my grandfather's drive to possess the luminescent beauty of *Ornithoptera alexandrae* that had doomed him to a slow, progressive death. Somehow, when I look at the marvelous splashes of life and color that these butterflies still provide, I feel certain that he believed that it had all been worthwhile. I imagine him standing over his display boxes, magnifying glass in one hand and his diaries in the other, recollecting the days when he caught his remarkable specimens. I imagine him reliving the dark wetness of the forest, the sudden bursts of fluttering color, the dappled light through the upper canopy. He must have taken comfort in the long and ordered rows of butterflies in his collection.

Impotence is an emotionally charged word, but it is an accurate description of my current condition. I have not had an erection since we returned from India. Last week Maya hung over me in bed, straddling my pelvis, prodding my private parts as if they were a delicate archaeological find.

"I couldn't help but notice that there is nothing happening *down there*," she said to me.

"*Down there* is temporarily out of order," I said. Maya ran the tips of her fingers down my chest and put her mouth to my ear.

"Is there anything I can do about it?" she whispered.

"I don't know," I said. "I don't really think so." I have never had a problem with erections. Quite the reverse.

"It's me, isn't it?" Maya said. She slipped off me and sat on the bed cross-legged. "I completely understand. It's perfectly understandable." She was crying.

I lay rigid on the bed. "It's not you, it's me. I'm tired. I've been working hard."

"That's never stopped you before. You know it hasn't. You blame me for India."

"I don't blame you."

"You hold me responsible."

"I don't."

Maya got up from the bed and pulled on her robe. She stood over me at the edge of the bed with her hands over her face.

"How do you think I feel? I have to get up and go to work every day, just like you. I have to take all the responsibility. That's a lot to bear."

"None of this is your fault, Maya." I sat up on the side of the bed.

"You're terrified of taking responsibility for anything. That's partly why this has happened. Why can't you admit that?"

"Because I don't know what I feel. I don't know what has happened."

"You're drinking too much. Every night you drink."

In my mind I ran over the biological causes of impotence—vascular and neurological chiefly—none of which seemed likely in my case. And I love Maya. I seem to be in a state of paralysis. Everything is seizing up.

"I think it's psychological," I said. But Maya had already left the room.

My grandfather ended his own life in the summer of 1894. He was weak and had difficulty standing on his own. It is a testament to his will and persistence that he was able to get the rope strung from the heavy iron roof supports of his greenhouse. It was summer, and I imagine the garden around him swirling with dandelions and rye grass. He tied a noose at one end of the rope. It must have taken him hours to get up onto the top of the workbenches—he pushed equipment to the ground, knocked over pots, and scattered butterfly pupae around him. They found him hanging three feet off the floor. According to my father, the butterflies in the greenhouse were attracted to his hanging body. When they found him, his woolen suit was covered with red-and-black Viceroy butterflies, clinging to him from head to foot.

Last night Maya found the spare key to my study. I heard the key rattling in the lock and then she flung open the door violently. She was wild-eyed and had a hammer in one hand. Her cheeks were black with streaks of mascara. Maya has made a full physical recovery after India and easily held the hammer above her head. She walked quite calmly, with the hammer raised, over to my grandfather's butterfly display cases. Paradoxically, I found myself chuckling—she was wearing only her underwear and a pair of thick gardening gloves.

"These butterflies are a curse," she shouted. "Give me one good reason why I shouldn't destroy them all." She was swinging the hammer around her waist in broad arcs and was ready to strike.

"Maya, calm down," I said.

"One good reason. That's all I ask."

But I was unable to speak. All I could do was watch. And for reasons that I cannot explain, as I watched, I felt relieved.

Today I needed some air. I drove down the coast to look for migrating Monarch butterflies—the migration should begin soon. It was a beautiful September day, with stiff easterly winds and bursts of sunlight through racing clouds. Getting out of New York put me in such good spirits that I started singing in the car—a terrible rendition of "St. James Infirmary." My thoughts become very clear when I'm standing on the beach and facing the gray smudge of the Atlantic Ocean. I find myself walking for hours out here with my head tilted up to the sky. I barely notice the ground under my feet, stumble on tufts of sea grass, and turn my ankles in potholes and cracks in the sandy soil. Waiting for the butterflies is like waiting for old friends—I am impatient and anxious that they will not come at all.

When I arrived at the beach I went down to the ocean to feel the water. The first thing I do at the edge of the sea is put my feet into the waves. It is a superstition—I have to prove to myself that it is real and that I am here. It was a calm day and the water was flat and green. Rows of black-eyed sandpipers were running frantically on pink legs in and out on the surf-line. I felt self-conscious as I took off my shoes and socks and rolled my pants to the knee. Stepping carefully on soft, white feet that looked like a stranger's, I walked into the shallow water. Pebbles and shells shifted under my toes. As I looked down, my legs seemed like those of an old man—pale, hairless, mottled with subterranean veins and mysterious blotches—and it was surprising how removed from myself these pale limbs seemed to me. Long plumes of seaweed wrapped around my shins as I waded in. For the most part I feel as young as I ever have. But when I see my naked limbs, in bright sunlight, I am chastened, brought back to my age, my job, what I am supposed to be.

I decided to stay the night down here on the coast. I have found a small hotel where I can be anonymous. A group of Mormons is meeting here at the moment, using the convention facilities. I am surrounded by well-groomed people who practice polygamy. I managed to get a small suite with a writing desk and have pulled the desk over to the window where, in daylight, I can see out over the ocean. This afternoon I found a fish restaurant and ate fresh scallops for the first time in years. I haven't needed a drink today and am encouraged. There is a bottle of Black Label on the desk, and a glass of ice, but I am putting off pouring the whiskey. I find that I want to be clearheaded when I think about the past so as not to diminish it—I am too sentimental. I let things influence me too much. Hannah would have been more practical—would have told me to worry less and get on with important things.

As the sun went down this evening, I walked on the beach again. The sky was a raging pink in front of me. There are no Monarchs to be seen yet. When I walk beside these dunes, I sometimes think of Vladimir Nabokov, the most famous amateur lepidopterist of the century. He was obsessed with butterflies. One morning in 1941, he walked down a mule path in the Grand Canyon and found a new species of *Neonympha* butterfly. Up at the top, his wife, Vera, wearing a black dress with a white lace collar, also came across two previously unidentified species. Butterflies have the capacity for infinite variation. They are changing continuously. Nabokov would have agreed with my grandfather. He didn't believe that such beauty and perfection were required by nature for survival.

The average life span of an adult Monarch butterfly is four weeks. Four weeks to be a momentary burst of color and to reproduce. There is a painful transience to it all. They are nothing but a drop of color in the ocean. A fleeting moment that dazzles and blinds and then is gone forever.

It is fitting that I find myself by the ocean. I have wanted to sail for years. Being out of touch with land, carried on currents and winds that we cannot control, must be liberating. How enticing it is to imagine being at the mercy of the elements. There are boats out at sea tonight, flashing mooring lights toward the shore. It is reassuring to see them out there. And in those distant glimmers, across the coal-dark water, I can see my own past, drifting just out of reach.

BARRY MATTHEWS

Cornell University

EVERYTHING MUST GO

They are excavating the bodies at night, a few hundred yards away
from our house. The bright halogen from the spotlights seeps through
cracks in our closed windows and doors. It reminds me of alien ab-
duction movies, when a dark and quiet house is set upon by strange
light and noise, as curious aliens come to take away unsuspecting
humans. The noise is excruciating to hear because we know that caskets are being opened. A yellow crane lurches into view and then de-
scends below the windowsill, like a slow, confident beast attacking
helpless prey. The bodies themselves are shipped to Concord, without the caskets, to expedite the exhumation process. I stand in the
kitchen in my nightdress, holding my shoulders and gazing out at the
hazy light that hovers above the cemetery.

Weeks ago, a local undertaker was dragged off to jail after it was
learned that he was improperly caring for and disposing of the dead
bodies left in his charge. The specifics are vague to me now, but I

know that bodies were found rotting beneath the funeral home and that some families paid for embalming that never occurred. Around town they are saying that he even scavenged the clothing of some of the male deceased. A grieving woman saw him cross the street in a pinstriped Brooks Brothers suit she specifically remembered burying her brother in.

The digging is done at night so as not to alarm the townspeople. I don't see how the spectacle of large machinery operating during the day would be any less jarring than the commotion at night, but we're the only residents this far out of town. We're the only people being bothered.

The seminightly ritual of casket retrieval has started next door, and I suspect that it will give my thirteen-year-old son nightmares. His father, my husband, died a year ago. They were close, so this business with the errant undertaker hasn't helped any.

Evan has always had problems telling the truth. Before we moved to New Hampshire, when we were still living in Florida, the untruths began making themselves known. During the Barbra Streisand HBO special, he calmly explained to me and my husband that Barbra was rumored to have eaten one or two live babies. "That's why her mouth is so big," he said. Doug and I looked at him in disbelief, and he stared back at us coldly, certain of his own story. We laughed it off and told Evan that Barbra Streisand couldn't possibly be bothered to eat children, but my old vinyl recordings mysteriously disappeared during our move. On the drive up, Evan even leaned over and shut off the radio when "The Way We Were" came on.

Evan is an awkward child, and he has not adjusted to New Hampshire well at all. In Florida, he was one oddity among many. In New Hampshire, he's the only oddity in town. The older Evan gets, the more his strangeness manifests itself as an inextricable part of his person. It has become clear that everything he does and says is part of who he is, not some affectation that I can dismiss as part of his growing pains. He is serious and somber. He watches the morning news with adult attention, as if each story will have an appreciable effect on his day.

I participate in school meetings and volunteer at bake sales to show the other mothers that I am not embarrassed of my son. He is effeminate, prone to making sweeping gestures with his hands and laughing girlishly on those rare occasions when he can be moved to laugh. He is creative, intelligent, and unswervingly kind. Sometimes I might find myself standing in a group of parents, the children milling around us as we talk. I watch the pained expressions of other parents as they watch Evan—they are embarrassed for me. But I keep my face expressionless. It's Evan's choice whether or not he will change his behavior to suit the expectations of other people. I can't tell him how to behave. Since it is obvious I have no intention of changing Evan's behavior or of being embarrassed by him, the other parents think that I'm being cruel, that I feed him to the taunts of other children.

I work in the town library with Judy. She's in her midtwenties and completely out of place in White Creek, let alone in a small, quiet library. She dropped out of Dartmouth years ago and moved north to the surrounding countryside with no clear plan for her future. Most days she dresses in a skirt and heels, as if the library were a serious, moneymaking business.

Four months into the job, I can tell that Judy and I are fighting for a lost cause. Our only regular clients are the elderly, and they are dying out. I can count on one hand the number of people who come in on a weekly basis.

The building is a small, one-room brick bunker, painted white. Arched windows let in brilliant rectangles of light that fall just short of the stacks and vulnerable book bindings. We receive two newspapers and four magazines. New acquisitions are few and far between. The town has consistently voted against efforts to buy a few computers for the library. Some have suggested that we sell all the books and use the library resources to set up a scholarship fund for the town. *Why have a scholarship when no one has anything to read?* is what I want to say to the townspeople. Everyone thinks that if they keep throwing money at the public school, our children will miraculously become educated. It is a prospect as uncertain as the future of the library itself.

The move to New Hampshire had been planned months before Doug died. We realized that settling in Florida had been a mistake. We moved around uneasily in the sweltering parking lots and strip malls. We were New Englanders trapped under an awful sunlamp. The schools were terrible, the people were vacuous, the streets were dirty, and the vegetation was foreign and frightening. One afternoon Doug and I looked at each other from across the table without uttering a word, and we each knew what the other was thinking. We had to go. Doug gave notice at his job and we waited for the school year to end for Evan.

"Not one person has asked me where I'm from," I tell Judy one afternoon. "In six months, people keep smiling at me and winking."

Judy looks at me with a grave expression. "This is serious business," she says. "No one wants you to get hurt."

I look at her and look away. There's only one explanation. "Evan," I say. "Evan started a rumor." I sigh. "What are people saying, Judy? We have nothing to hide."

Judy makes me follow her across the lobby of the library to a corner away from the windows. Even though the library is empty, she whispers, "They say you're with the Witness Protection Program."

"Oh, for god's sake!" I say, loudly. Judy is shaken. "It's just not true," I tell her. "Evan told his classmates in Florida that his father and I were Wiccans, too. He told us that Barbra Streisand eats infants." Judy seems very wary of me, as if she cannot decide whether or not to believe me. She's probably thinking that I'm covering it all up and that I'll move away in the middle of the night to a safer hiding spot.

She watches me with large eyes. "There was talk of Cuban gangsters and a deal with the DA in Miami."

"My husband was a social worker. There aren't any Cuban gangsters in Jacksonville, Florida."

"I know what you're saying. I believe you," she says, patting my hand confidentially.

At first, I think I am losing my mind, but it becomes clear to me that Evan is using my makeup and replacing it with premium brands that he buys with his allowance. My purse is becoming inexplicably crowded with makeup and eyeliner that I don't recall buying. He replaces the colors as well. I realize one morning, while applying eyeliner, that almost all of the colors I've been using for years are gone. I look different.

It isn't something I want to talk to him about. It could be a phase or something more significant to him, but I think he'd rather just pretend that neither of us has noticed the new makeup. I do wonder how he buys the cosmetics without attracting attention. Does he tell the woman at the pharmacy that it's for me, or does he wordlessly put the makeup on the counter and show no apology in his eyes?

It took longer for me to realize that he was using the makeup on himself. I would never have suspected without looking closely at his face. He is a pro and uses the colors carefully. He looks angelic, pale-skinned with bright eyes. Without moving or speaking, remaining perfectly still, Evan is a beautiful boy. It bothers me that it took all this time for me to notice.

Because Evan used to insist on it, Doug would take him to work with him when he conducted nighttime volunteer training. He'd set Evan in a corner with construction paper and markers, torn magazines and glue. Doug lectured to idealistic college students, preparing them to assist the staff of a local methadone clinic, while Evan sat in the back of the room and made collages. It seemed strange to me at the time that Evan could be so content under those fluorescent lights, listening to Doug issue warnings about the erratic behavior of addicts. Doug didn't interact with Evan any more or less than I did, but Evan always wanted to be in close proximity to him.

And now, it's the two of us, sitting at the kitchen table soundlessly, with bed-mangled hair, unable to sleep with the noise and light from the cemetery. Caskets are being raised, workmen are shouting to each other. I stare at my hands and stir my tea over and over again. Evan huddles in his chair and leafs through a Sears catalog. There is a picture of a Christmas tree on the cover of the catalog, a family of four leaning into a pile of presents. The lights on the tree are exaggeratedly bright, like miniature halos.

Evan looks up. "The story about the undertaker isn't true," he tells me. "They're searching for Spanish gold." He returns to the magazine without waiting for a reaction from me. I open my mouth, but I realize that I have nothing to say. Spanish gold, I think to myself, why not? I close my eyes and lean back in the dim kitchen, waiting for the noise to end or sleep to overtake me.

I am driving Evan to school in the morning when I ask him, "Why are you telling people we're part of the Witness Protection Program? They think your father was a gangster."

He looks out the window and touches it with his finger. "I know it isn't true," he says.

"Why do you say it, then?" I'm not angry. I've gotten used to this lie and it feels harmless now, a mere slip of Evan's tongue.

Evan looks at his own hand and then at me. "It could be true and no one would know any better. It wouldn't change anything."

Of course, I think to myself, it is no less believable than the truth about his father. No less violent or strange.

A few moments pass before I say, "It doesn't help to tell people things that aren't true. After a while even you will have problems distinguishing between what's real and what's make-believe. And no one around you will believe what you say anymore." I say what a parent is supposed to say, but part of me wants him to hold on to his lies, nurture them. I want to tell him that he should do whatever it takes to make himself happy.

A week after the excavations start, Judy and I officially lose our jobs. We stand outside the library sharing a cigarette as a group of women volunteers hang a banner outside the grand windows of the town library: BOOK SALE, it reads, EVERYTHING MUST GO.

"I was going to sign out the valuable ones myself, illegally," Judy says, exhaling smoke. "All of the first editions and rarities." We watch as antiques dealers park on the side of the road and view the banner raising with interest. The morning of the book sale, the dealers will descend upon the library and strip it of any valuable books.

The educational books will go to the high school. Most of the fiction will be sold. Judy and I canceled the periodicals and disassembled the archaic card catalog system. On that last afternoon, the ancient library was filled with orange light and clouds of dust. There was so much debris floating around from our increased activity that it seemed as though the entire building were disintegrating on its own, giving up its molecules and disappearing, as if on cue.

The books will go, the building will become a storage facility for the high school sports teams, and I will be unemployed. The only place hiring within ten miles is the grocery store. I will probably have to travel at least an hour every morning to get to a job that pays well enough for Evan and me to be comfortable.

Judy has already decided to return to graduate school. "I can't stand not being around books," she says. "Undertakers stealing clothing, libraries being dismantled, Mafia refugees settling in. This place is too much for me." Judy extinguishes the cigarette on the ground with her foot. "I'll have to find a nice, small college town. Escape from all this excitement."

I look at the bright banner covering the library and shiver. EVERY-THING MUST GO sounds too final and all-encompassing, as though it's an imperative aimed directly at me. The banner tells me to hand it all over without a complaint. Not just the books and my job, but my son, my home, and my newfound sense of quiet. I've already given up my husband, so exactly how much is left to let go? And when it is all gone and I have only myself, what then?

I encourage Evan to apply to private schools. "We can only do it if you get a scholarship," I tell him. "And only if you want to." He wants to; I know. He'll be out of place no matter where he goes, but the White Creek Public School is so small that I know he feels conspicuous. We pore over the boarding school descriptions and applications, the glossy-covered promises for a rigorous, healthy education. I try not to raise his expectations, but part of me is just as excited as he is. I imagine him taking a step away from the safety we've found, into the world, and I suppose I admire him for it.

All of Evan's application essays are somehow about Doug's social work. Evan remembers the noble aspects of what Doug did in Florida, but has seemingly forgotten that Doug's life had been threatened, that he had been stabbed by a client with a pen, and that he eventually stopped being able to sleep, staring at the bedroom ceiling for hours every night.

After two weeks of the digging, I finally get the nerve to call up the police department and ask when the exhumations will stop. There are four or five towns involved in this particular civic venture—it is a *big deal.* I am told that the more digging that gets done, the more evidence will be collected. I'm assured that Ed Worth, our nefarious undertaker, will be put away for a very long time. I still would like to know, specifically, how much evidence will be enough. The sheriff tells me, "This will all be over. Probably another week."

So there's nothing I can do. I consider covering the windows facing the cemetery with heavy blankets or big drapes, or maybe sleeping with earplugs. I even consider trying to get a prescription for some barbiturates. None of these things would mitigate my daytime unease, though, the queasy pulling in my stomach when I see the covered machinery crouching by the gravestones, waiting for nightfall.

The sheriff offers to have an officer watch the house if I'm worried about the workers coming over or ruining my garden or anything of that nature. I bite my tongue before telling him that being watched by a policeman would be several times more terrifying than having a backhoe operator ruin my halfhearted attempt at a garden.

There is an accident one night. A small man with an unusually hoarse voice knocks at my door after 3:00 A.M. Of course I'm up, reading and drinking tea, pretending that nothing odd is happening at all. The man apologizes and takes off his baseball cap, as if he has come courting. "We called an ambulance, but this guy's bleeding really bad. He caught his leg on a saw."

A saw, I think to myself. Who gave these men saws? The hoarse-voiced man stays firmly in the doorway as I rummage through my linen closet for bandages and ointments. My hands full of first aid implements, I return to the door.

When he puts his hands out to take the supplies and I see how dirty they are, I say, "Bring him here."

Although the men try to not make a mess out of the house, a trail of graveyard dirt leads from the foyer to the living room. There are three of them: the small man, his enormous coworker, and the hurt guy. I put the cordless phone into the hands of the small guy and tell him to call back the hospital with the street address. The hurt guy is young—probably in his early twenties. The cut in his leg travels from his upper thigh around to the back of his knee. It looks worse than it probably is—there's a lot of blood, and his panic doesn't help.

"Oh, god," he says. "Can I die from this? Is this too much blood?"

"You're fine," I say, holding a washcloth against his skin. I've tied a tight cord around his upper thigh and have managed to stop most of the flow. His breathing is erratic. I see Evan at the top of the stairs and wave him back to his room.

"God, it hurts. Shit," the man says. His friends watch with serious expressions that do not help the situation at all. They should be laughing at him, poking fun of his clumsiness. Instead, they look like helpless boys, paralyzed with the sudden knowledge of a body's frailty. In fact, no one's life will be altered by this accident. The slip of the saw has not created widows or orphans. Within four months this man will be able to walk to California if he wants to.

"Oh, Jesus," he says. He's looking at the bucket of water beside him, at the bloody rags I've used to soak up the mess. Tears are forming in his eyes. He strains to catch his breath. "Goddamn." He closes his eyes and clenches his teeth. His entire body tenses and relaxes sporadically, keeping in chaotic rhythm with his panic.

I lean in close to him, grabbing his shirt in what I'm sure will seem like a threatening gesture. "You'll live," I say with my teeth clenched. "Stop whining so I can finish."

All three men watch in stunned silence as I start to dress the wound. I am thankful to hear the ambulance siren break through the quiet night. The wounded man's breathing is shallow as I withdraw from him, taking the bucket up in both hands. He will not meet my eyes.

Doug was murdered for our car, an '89 Honda with a rattling exhaust pipe. He was waiting for a green light in an empty part of Jacksonville, returning to his office from an HIV awareness workshop he was officiating at the community college. A woman in a Range Rover witnessed the crime. She had been driving around the area, lost, for ten minutes before she saw two men approach Doug's car while he was stopped at the light. It happened quickly. The men came at the car from either side. The man approaching from the passenger side slid into the seat and shot Doug in the shoulder. The other man opened the driver's side door and dragged Doug out onto the pavement. Instead of simply getting into the running car and driving away, the man held his foot on Doug's shoulder and shot twice, once in the chest and once in the throat. The shot to Doug's throat severed his head from his body. The car was discovered, stripped, in an empty lot in Tampa less than a week later. Four tires, a malfunctioning radio, the muffler, one of the side mirrors, the steering wheel, most of the engine, the transmission, even the first aid kit, tucked into the trunk in case of emergencies. The men were never identified or caught.

The three-week excavation finally ends the first week of October, and they try to make the cemetery look untouched. Bodies are returned to caskets, caskets are returned to the earth, and the ground is seeded for new grass. The soil over the graves swells up enough to be seen from the road. The cemetery won't seem as it was until the spring, but I'm simply grateful that it is over. Ed Worth is sentenced to many years in jail, and no one will ever completely trust the undertakers and funeral home directors who move here to take his place.

I keep the books in my closet as if I need to hide them from people who'd be looking for them. In fact, I have destroyed the cards that originally cataloged the books in the library. Books by John Cheever, Jane Bowles, F. Scott Fitzgerald, and Raymond Carver made a fairly smooth transition between the library and my closet in the month before the place closed.

I am certain that Judy has also taken books. I suspect she has been more ambitious than I in this regard, has perhaps been "rescuing" books from the clutches of antiques dealers for years.

I replace the books beneath my sweaters, and as I step back from my closet, all of the clothes shift and shake on their hangers in a tangled unison. I can't daydream myself out of my jobless situation. The want ads are rolled up on the kitchen table. I have been avoiding entering the kitchen.

This week I've been sleeping until one in the afternoon, leaving Evan to prepare his own lunch and wait for the bus without a good-bye kiss. The house seems huge without him around, and my steps echo eerily, so I've taken to wearing only socks, my feet sliding on the hardwood floors as I move from room to room.

From the corner of my eye I can see through the bedroom window to the graveyard. Those new swatches of earth in the cemetery are unnerving. It is as if there had been a war or an accident and many people died at once. The October sky is a uniform, foreboding slate gray. I don't want to be in this house.

———

There are children everywhere in front of the White Creek Public School, buses waiting at various points along the pavement. As I cross the parking lot, I see Evan on his own at the front of the building. He is sitting on the front steps, absorbed in thought. I have never seen him like this before, sitting so vacantly. This world of children, buses, and book bags moves around him as if he were a ghost. Looking at him, I can tell he feels incidental to the rest of them, and the thought is so painful I catch my breath. Coming closer, I realize that I'm seeing him at his most vulnerable, a way he would never want me to see him.

Looking up and blinking, he doesn't recognize me at first. When he gets to his feet, he actually turns a little, as if he were trying to get away. He thinks he's in some sort of trouble, that I've come to punish him.

"Mom," he says.

"Hey, tiger. I thought I'd save you a ride on that bus."

"It's cold," he says. His eyes are very far off. I don't want him to seem this way.

"Let's go for a ride," I say.

Before we left Florida, I asked to speak to the witness. The police advised against it, so I didn't press the issue. They found it morbid that I kept asking for details after Doug was buried.

I asked questions because I had to be there. I pictured him bleeding on the asphalt, eyes level with the car's tires and the shoes of his attackers, alone and completely helpless.

On sleepless nights I can close my eyes and lie down next to him on the hard pavement, the grit and dirt scratching my elbows and calves. Doug's blood flows beneath me and soaks my hair and back. His screams are deafening, the gunshots like cannons. My fingers cover his closed hand and I squeeze it tightly. I can hear the last of his breathing before the third gunshot rips his head from his body. After the screams and gunfire, the following silence is a roar of absence. Doug is motionless, the closed hand incapable of opening again. He still dies and I am just as helpless as I was when it actually happened. But I'm there, and neither of us is alone.

Evan is curled against his door, covered by a jumble of coats and sweaters that we keep in the car in case the heat acts up. He's fast asleep by the time we reach Portsmouth. His breath fogs the window. I leave my window open just a crack so I can smell the salt air, and I drive as close to the shore as the roads allow, taking deep breaths. I see enough of the ocean to feel small again.

Evan wakes up forty minutes into our return trip; the sky has let loose with a torrent of rain. He blinks his eyes and sits up straight. "Where are we?"

"Halfway home," I say. "You missed the sea."

He yawns. "Oh."

We stop at a gas station and I fill the tank while Evan runs through the rain to the rest rooms. The sky is deceptively dark. Water courses under my feet and beneath the car. A red neon sign from the window of the convenience store casts a pink glow onto the water. It makes me think of blood. I look away from the ground and quickly run inside to pay for the gas. I'm grateful to escape into the silence of the car.

Ten miles from the gas station it occurs to me that I never waited for Evan to come back to the car. The pile of clothing is still on the passenger seat, but the sweaters and coats couldn't possibly be mistaken for a person, a boy. I pull over to the side of the road and put my hand under the sweaters, as if Evan might be hiding there. I touch my forehead to see if I'm feverish even though I feel surprisingly calm as I push the pile of clothes onto the floor.

I pause just a moment before putting the car back in gear, a single moment. For a fragment of a minute I picture myself moving forward, without Evan, but then it's over.

I take a U-turn and drive back to the gas station as fast as the rain will allow. From a short distance, I see Evan standing there, without the shelter of the pumps, waiting in the rain. When I pull up beside him I see that his hair is stuck to his forehead and water courses over his face. He's soaked through his clothes.

"Get in!" I yell, although I'm sure he can't hear me. He pauses for a moment and then opens the door. He's so wet I can't tell whether or not he's been crying. I wipe his hair and face with a sweater while he sits there, limply.

"I'm sorry, honey," I say.

Evan is quiet. He looks straight out the window. I see that some of his makeup has rubbed off on the sweater in my hands.

"I am so sorry," I say.

Evan pushes his wet hair out of his eyes. "You almost didn't come back," he says in a whisper. He's shivering.

"Evan, that's not true," I say. I hold his shoulders and turn him toward me. "It isn't true." I mop his face with a clean sweater and he watches me with clear eyes. The heater blows a dry, warm stream of air at us and the rain patters loosely against the windshield.

I reach up and aim the rearview mirror at him. "Everything's streaked," I say, touching his cheek with my finger. I hand him my purse and he takes it cautiously. "Go on." He opens the purse and feels around for the right makeup, eyeing me suspiciously. "We're not going anywhere until you fix yourself," I say, smiling. He lifts his head and uncaps a tube of lipstick with one hand. I turn toward him and adjust the mirror so I can see both of us.

LAURA HAWLEY

Naropa University

THE GOOD LIFE

PHASE ONE: BLUEPRINTS

From our bedroom window we can see our neighbor's driveway. He lives to our right, up on the hill. His house is 7,500 square feet and there are usually six cars parked at the top of the drive. Terri thinks he lives alone, that he's around our age, maybe thirty-five, one of those upstart computer engineers from California. His driveway has horizontal grooves dug into the concrete from top to bottom. Our realtor tried to sell us on this feature, the heated driveway, but we passed. Our drive isn't that long, and it isn't too steep. Before we go to bed we make bets on which car our neighbor is going to take to work the next day. Terri always wins. She's figured out his routine: the BMW on Monday, the Explorer on Tuesday, the Land Rover on Wednesday, and so on. Terri's more observant than I am, or maybe I just like letting her win.

This neighborhood, Fox Run Hills—or so the red stone beneath the street sign reads—is considered upscale. Custom-built homes.

Nestled far back from Interstate 25. Spectacular view of the mountains. Ponderosa pine forests with vanilla-scented bark. Black squirrels and white-tailed deer. No bear problems. The occasional woodpecker. We set up a hummingbird feeder the day we moved in. These are our neighbors, the sub-suburban wildlife. Most of the lots around our home are vacant or have the skeletons of houses taking shape from a hole in the ground. A small photo album charts the growth of our house: the laying of the foundation, the pouring of cement, the erecting of support beams, the stuccoing, the placing of shingles. We show these pictures to coworkers, visiting family. We say, Here it is at six weeks. You can see the piping. As each new house evolves around us we smile like proud parents and make comments about how our fascia boards accent the green shutters and how those people across the cul-de-sac have no sense of color flow. I don't park my Volvo in the driveway. It leaks oil.

The Baptists own most of the land in this area. Anything not surrounded by a fence is theirs, and even the fenced-in land they probably owned first. When Terri and I drive past the Compound we look at the enormous windows of the main church and wonder which one our down payment paid for. As each new SOLD sign springs up on the empty lots, the Baptists get another window, skylight, or an additional parking space. We're not Baptist—I'm sure we don't even believe in God—and we can't help but feel a little cheated.

Terri and I, we're young, we're successful, we're the American couple our parents wanted us to be. We've made the risky transition from renters to homeowners, and soon to entrepreneurs. We plan to start our own e-business: maternity clothes and other essential items for the expectant mother. There's a niche for it. Terri enrolled at the local community college, where she takes courses on computer programming and Web design. She's the creative genius behind this. I'm along for the ride. She tries to make me feel important, asking for my opinion on particular brands of lotion and massage oils, clothes and exercise balls. But for now we only order samples and catalogs, sketch designs for the Web page. We pretend to be experts on the Internet and pregnancy.

The surgery came up during phase one of construction. We designed most of the house in the hospital room, during our first visit, when she underwent the preliminary tests. Inside: Corian counters, Emerald; gas fireplace; Jenn-Air dishwasher and grill-top stove; gas two-stage furnace; green suede sectional sofa; preassembled entertainment center with surround sound. Outside: Meadow Brook white paint with Hunter trim; riprap landscaping rock; terra-cotta patio stones; downspouts black-piped to the edge of the lot; brush-swirl finish on the drive; sandstone birdbath and a carved wooden bear wearing a red cowboy hat. We designed our dream home, and the next day returned to the apartment.

We're really lucky to have this house, which we watched grow from pinecones and weeds into a sturdy, insulated home with Ansel Adams prints on the walls, wedding pictures on the bookshelves, the grandfather clock in the hall. These are some of the features we passed down. From one angle our house resembles Terri, from another, me. My Time-Life aviation books, her assortment of potpourri containers and scented candles. Our house is like no other on the cul-de-sac, on Gold Peak Drive, in Fox Run Hills, on this side of I-25. That quiet moment of recognition when I park by the mailbox, knowing that I know all the secret corners in the basement, all the tiny flaws in construction, where to find the connector hose in the garage. Terri says she feels like someone handed her this amazing gift, and she's not sure how to thank that someone. So she keeps a close eye on dust, crumbs, old newspaper, dirty glasses. This perfect child.

PHASE TWO: CONSTRUCTION

The cat has had a complete, psychological breakdown. I didn't think cats could have breakdowns, but Terri insists they can. She says animals are more sensitive to disturbances than people, and it's a good idea to observe their actions as indicators of mood. Whose mood? What disturbances? She won't say. The cat, Nickel, has been watching the heating vents for three days. He crouches low and pivots on his front paws, his tail straight up in the air, the tip twitching back and forth. I've never heard him meow like this, a strange high-pitched squeal, and he smacks his jaws together like he's eating peanut butter. After a few days of this, I grab my flashlight, get down on the floor with him, and check inside the vent. Nothing. Only a nail, some dust, and what looks to be a small block of wood. Terri sits on the couch with her legs tucked up, a blanket around her shoulders. She sits there with the cat—when he's not scratching at the vent or pacing the house with his nose to the floor—and together they stare at the baseboards, at the fireplace. They flinch at every creak of the house. I watch Terri and Nickel from the deck. I smoke menthol cigarettes, which I usually can't stand, and watch them sit in the dark, their eyes glowing. Tomorrow I'll call someone to clean out the vents.

Maybe a housewarming party would help. This is Terri's suggestion. I don't think we need help. I'm fine with the house. Suddenly she isn't. She believes there is a ghost spooking the heating vents. We could have it catered, nothing fancy, some finger food, like crackers, celery sticks, sliced pineapple. Then why have it catered? We could put this together. She insists, and I give in. We make a list of prospective guests: the people she worked with before, the people she works with now, our old neighbors, her friends from college, at least the ones she remembers, her cousin that lives in town, and whomever I might want to invite. Except Frank. And what's wrong with Frank? She won't say.

Three days before the party, Terri swears a dish broke in her hands. She says she was getting it out of the cupboard and it split, a perfect crack down the center. Then she heard a series of cracks, and she found all the other dishes broken in the same pattern. She calls me at work to tell me about the broken dishes. I hang up the phone, sure that it's nothing serious. When I come home that night all of the cabinet doors are wide open, and Terri is sitting at the kitchen table, her eyes shifting from one cabinet to the next. We cancel the party.

The house is not haunted, at least not by supernatural forces. We have a mouse, which I've named Elvis. Terri thinks I'm making fun of her, since I tell her that her ghost is actually Elvis. She doesn't think this is funny. I set traps in every room and set one in every vent. Terri insists I use *deadly* traps, the ones with the spring. I want that thing dead, she says. The cat is useless in getting rid of the mouse, which we have seen only once, and then it was in the garage. Nickel continues to stare at the vents, but I can't figure out how Elvis could get inside the ducts. I've looked at the blueprints. I've traced every inch of pipe and wall space. Terri swears she can hear it, and she and Nickel wait patiently at the vents for any sign. I check the traps twice a day, once before work, once before bed. This is past amusing.

Sunday mornings we used to make blueberry pancakes and scrambled eggs. We'd sit on the deck of our new home and read the paper, smile at each other when we passed the Target circular. There is no civilized sound out here, only the birds. I bought a field guide so I can name the birds that share our Sunday ritual. The book is still in the bag. We have new neighbors to our left, and they have two golden retrievers.

We haven't performed our Sunday ritual for weeks. Instead, Terri sleeps until noon most days, the cat crooked on her pillow. She stays in her nightgown until 8:00 P.M. or so, when she changes it for a new one. Sometimes I stay in bed with her all day and we tell each other what we see in the ceiling plaster.

One morning I notice that our uphill neighbor has changed his driving pattern. Today he takes the Miata.

I don't want to discuss this, she says.

I add it to my list of things she doesn't want to talk about.

I wake up and Terri isn't in bed. It's two in the morning. I wait a few minutes, listen for a toilet flush, running water, but nothing. Nickel is on my chest, his paws pinned to my shoulders. He hisses, smacks my chin, then jumps off.

The rattling of something metal. I find Nickel in the living room, clawing at the vent. No sign of Terri. After checking every closed-off space in the house, including the pantry, I go outside. I walk barefoot down our short driveway, and I feel safe from broken glass and bottle caps. I want to laugh, until I see Terri in the driver's seat of the Volvo, parked by the mailbox. I knock on the window and she yelps, not a scream, but a yelp.

Terri? I say. What else do I say? The windows of the car are fogged, but I can see she's got my baseball bat across her lap, and she's in her nightgown.

Terri, it's me.

She wipes the window with her sleeve, tilts her head, and glares at me.

What do you want? she asks.

What're you doing out here? I ask.

She turns around and looks in the backseat, then checks the floor up front. She whispers something, but I can only see her lips moving. I try the door. Locked. I motion for her to roll down the window, but instead she speaks louder.

Did you look under the car yet?

I shake my head.

Look under the car, she says.

Terri, I say, come back inside.

The car! Look under the goddamn fucking car!

I get on my knees, then down to my stomach.

Do you see it? she shouts.

What am I supposed to be looking for? I shout back.

She says something again that I can't hear.

What? I say, then get up into a crouch. The door cracks me on the head and I fall over.

I heard someone walking on the roof, she says, and the car seemed the safest place if we got burglarized.

She stands over me with the bat on her shoulder.

Honey, she says, you're bleeding.

The Middle East peace talks; trade with China; the unusual amount of flooding on the East Coast; her mother; my mother; the electric bill; George W. Bush; Orthodox Judaism; geraniums or mums; a new squirrel-proof bird feeder; her increasing paranoia; Elvis the Mouse; Elvis the Ghost; Elvis the King of Rock 'n' Roll; the surgery; Nickel's annual vaccinations; her leaving open every cabinet door; my shutting every cabinet door; airline safety records; new patio furniture;

the surgery; subscription renewal to *The Gazette;* the cat's psychotic behavior; regular or decaf; *her* psychotic behavior; the problem with the ants; our neighbor's driving habits; the housewarming party.

A new house is growing across the cul-de-sac. Terri and I have walked around the lot, examined the foundation. Terri thinks this house will have a swimming pool. While we eat dinner the house across the street watches. It seems to be calling out to us, asking us to come in. I don't ask Terri if she thinks this, too, I know she does, I can tell by the way she stares at the wall separating us from the pine-needle landscape, the dusty pavement, the new house. She stares through the wall. In her mind that house grows paint, shutters, a decorative porch light.

She is wondering whether to place the sofa-sleeper near the fireplace or opposite the television.

The clock chimes and Terri's hand spasms, the heel of her palm smacking down on the edge of her plate. Roast chicken and mashed potatoes flip into the air, seem to hover for a strange moment, then fall with a dull splat on the kitchen floor. Nickel, lazy on the floor beneath my chair, hisses and bites my ankle. My leg jumps up, knee slams into the table, the silverware trembles, my water glass tips over. The three of us watch the water slide over the table to drip onto the floor.

Terri stands up slowly, her hand at her throat, walks to the wall separating our kitchen from the wilderness, and presses her body tight to it. She holds on to the wall with its spidery plaster designs and cries.

She would put the sofa near the fireplace. She loves to be warm.

A close encounter with the uphill neighbor. Behind our home is a regional park, but not a park with grass and swing-sets, a *natural* park complete with horse trails and red dirt paths. I run these paths twice a week. I run up to the two man-made lakes and run back. This is maybe three miles, but I have never checked.

I see a man running toward me along the path; he's in black shorts, black sunglasses, black shirt, black headphones. I move to the other side. He mirrors my move. I move to the center. He follows. From this distance a smile appears on his tan face. One of my regular fantasies is having a heart attack while I'm running. It's not an exciting fantasy, granted, but it occurs to me when I start to get short on breath, or when I can feel my heart beating too fast, what *I* consider to be too fast. I'll double over and hit the dirt. I'll start groaning, grab my left arm with a tight fist. A man in black will come down the path and smile at me. Sometimes he has a sickle over his shoulder, sometimes he hands me an aspirin. I watch the runner in black faking a swerve, grinning with large, white teeth. When he gets close enough for me to hear the electric buzz escaping his earphones, I remember that I need to rearrange the garden stones to accommodate the roots of the new mums we planted.

He circles around me and starts jogging in place.

I come to a full stop and wait for my heart to beat one last time.

Hey, neighbor, he says. I'm in 1685. Name's Tony Lorenzo. Lucent Tech.

Dennis, I say. Entrepreneur.

We shake hands. Sweat all over the place.

Well, gotta keep running, he says. Trying to beat my time. Come over later, we'll have a drink.

I nod and watch him sprint down the path toward the lakes.

Terri swears she found a muddy footprint on her white skirt, which she left on our bed, beside the open window. It wasn't her footprint, and it wasn't mine. I don't wear sneakers. We inventory the house and find only items we forgot we owned, rather than items that are missing. It doesn't matter. Terri knows what she saw, what that footprint means. What, she won't say. She packs a suitcase and says she's going to a hotel, and am I coming with her?

I say, This is our house, Terri.

This house is cursed, she says.

I say, It just needs to be settled.

It needs an exorcism, she says.

The Baptists came to the door this morning. They handed me a flyer for some church book sale, which I politely handed back. I pointed to the mezuzah on the doorframe. They said thank you and hurried back to their van. We're not Jewish, but it doesn't hurt to pretend every once in a while. I watch them drive away, the van kicking up dirt spilled on the road from the empty lots. I feel a little panicked when they disappear, and I wish I'd asked them to come in for coffee. When I go back inside the front door smirks at me. I make sure to slam it extra hard.

From a distance the two front windows could be eyes, the door a nose, maybe a mouth. The house has become a Cubist portrait, complete with drivewaylike tongue. It mocks me every time I return from work, from the store, from getting the paper. Something always appears to have moved. The planters lining the front steps are turned around, the red flag on the mailbox is up when I had left it down. The shutters wink at me. I find evidence of Terri's ghost in every room: her slippers in the refrigerator; her favorite bracelet, the one with the impossible clasp, in the spider plant pot; clumps of her hair in the cat food; her eyebrow pencil in my toolbox. I find Nickel asleep in the dryer when Terri calls to say she's not coming back to *that house*.

I love you, Dennis, she says.

Then love me here, in our home, I say.

I can't do that.

You told me you'd love me if we lived in the sewer.

Dennis, I'm sorry, but I can't.

She hangs up, and I walk out to the front porch listening to the dial tone. I wait for the operator's voice to instruct me to please hang up and try again, for a message from God, anything but this menacing hum. I stand here between the teeth of our home and search the darkness for any movement across the street. The new house is only a discoloration of the night. I turn off the phone. This is the sound of absolute zero.

It's time to say hello to the uphill neighbor. After our first encounter, I feel some obligation to be friendly. I am now myself and Terri, because Terri isn't here to be Terri with her careful social graces. Maybe I'm just lonely.

He opens the door, and this time he is wearing all white. This helps.

I thought I'd take you up on that drink, I say.

He smiles with those large, white teeth and invites me inside the house.

A giant white tiger skin rug takes up the whole entranceway, and there's no way to get around it without stepping on some part of it. Tony stands by the open door, so I am not sure where he stepped, and he makes no offer to help. I start to put one foot down on the sliver of white underbelly when Tony makes some sort of squeak, then shakes his finger.

Don't step there, he says.

Is it bad luck?

No, there's mud on your shoes, and this beast's value is up to ten thousand.

He kneels down and unties my shoes, slips them off my feet, and sets them outside on the front step.

Have a seat, he says, and motions to the living room.

I'm standing on the tiger's back in my bare feet and choking on air. This is a reaction I sometimes link to an incident at the age of five, when I wandered into an abandoned warehouse and soon found myself locked inside with all the darkness and echoes and monsters that accompanied it. Sometimes I connect it to my past life as a gladiator in Rome. The dead tiger in the entranceway supports this theory.

Terri says humans are not really creatures of habit, but animals that depend upon patterns. We build homes with rooms, she says, to maintain order. A house in Uganda is the same as one in New York. She's never been to Uganda, but she's sure they would at least separate the living spaces with cloth or some sort of jungle plant.

There are no walls in Tony's home.

I stand on the tiger's back, alone in an empty arena.

Everything in this house is black and white: white carpet, black couch, Formica countertops, black lacquer tables. The only color is in Tony's tanned skin. Even his hair is bleached white.

I like how the tiger skin feels under my feet, and I curl up my toes.

To the far right are a sectional sofa, entertainment center, end tables, plants, and the like. The sofa shapes that section into what might be its own room, square and conducive to socializing. Beyond the sofa section is the kitchen and dining room, with all the usual furnishings. Past the kitchen is a bedroom, where the dresser and bed create the same lines the sofa does, and next to the bedroom is what appears to be some sort of office space, again, with imaginary lines. Each section creates its own little room, and I wonder if he's set up some sort of invisible force field around them. The only areas in the house that are enclosed are the bathrooms, one in each corner. He has six bathrooms. From space, Tony's house must resemble a crop design with its hexagonal shape, and I wonder if the absence of walls has some strange connection to the cosmos.

Don't worry, Tony says. The architect paid close attention to the load-bearing walls. The key was to maintain a low-density ceiling, some sort of synthetic cement mixture. It's really quite stable.

He leads me to the sofa section where I sit on the short end facing the door.

Where are your socks? Tony asks as he walks into the kitchen area.

I don't have any clean ones, I say, and look down at my naked feet.

Where are your walls? I ask.

Tony laughs and says, Walls in the home lead to walls in the soul. Besides, I live alone. Just me and my environment.

It does feel communal, I say.

Unfortunately, walling in the bathrooms was a necessity. I did it primarily for the comfort of my guests. I seem to be out of wine. Do you mind rice milk?

Water's fine.

So, how do you like our little developing community here?

It's quiet.

He comes back to the sofa and hands me a glass of water with a lemon wedge curled over the rim. I rub my feet on the carpet and look for something metal.

So, you said you were an entrepreneur. In what business?

We're starting an online maternity store, I say. There's a niche.

He nods, sips his own water, and closes his eyes.

Right now I'm at Clairbridge, I add.

Another nod.

And you're with Lucent? What do you do there?

Classified. The things I do would blow your mind.

The seven-minute pause. Terri says that conversations last an average of seven minutes before everyone takes a commercial break. She says we're conditioned for it, that we're all the stars of our own TV dramas. I don't see myself as a star, maybe an extra, in a supporting role at best. In Tony's show he must play the president, or maybe the crocodile hunter.

Are you married? I ask. A ridiculous question. He said he lived alone.

He winks. I sip the lemony water.

My wife, Terri, just left. She didn't leave me, per se, really, she left the house. She thinks it's haunted.

In this black and white room, among the absence of everything that should put me at ease, I feel like a child. Tony leans back in his chair, crosses his legs, and nods with a soft indifference that is so comforting I tell him everything.

Remember, Tony says at the door, it's all about control. Take control of the situation.

I'm kneeling on the tiger skin, rubbing its head. I'll do that, I say.

He helps me put my shoes back on, then smiles with those large, white teeth bared.

Break it down to the basics, my friend, he says.

He hands me a container labeled EARTHGRAIN SUPER-NUTRIENT PACKED GRANOLA SNACK filled with what looks like ground coffee.

Here's some Diazinon for those ants. You can pick up some more at the Bug Man. It's off Baptist Road.

What isn't? I say, then wave and run my hand across the fender of his Land Rover as I head down the drive.

PHASE THREE: DEMOLITION

The Husqvarna chain saw I borrowed from Tony has a dull blade, and it began to buck and spin uselessly halfway through the wall dividing the bedroom and living room. A sledgehammer seemed to be the best alternative, and it does have its advantages, less noise being the most important. Even though I began removing the walls during the early afternoon, when my few neighbors were at work, the saw's roar scared Nickel out of his mind, and despite the protective headgear my ears rang for hours afterward. Now, I peel away at the Sheetrock with a crowbar, then knock away with the hammer, while Nickel watches me from the couch. He looks at me as if I'm a conquering hero, and I stop after each four-foot section to scratch behind his ears. His purr is not so unlike the chain saw's.

I leave the studs in place. My house is now a wooden skeleton, the plush furniture and state-of-the-art appliances spread throughout like lumps of tissue, the wiring exposed nerves, veins. I keep the electricity turned off, since Nickel likes to chew on the wires.

I sit with Nickel in the middle of the floor, rubble surrounding us. We are both coated in dust. We sit like this all night and we wait for something to happen. We wait for Terri to come home.

On the phone with Terri, the buzz of a bad connection.

What did you do?

It's gone, whatever it was, it left.

Dennis, what did you do?

I miss you.

What do you mean by *I took care of it*?

It's safe for you to come home now.

Ghosts. In the dark they slide around the studs, slip under the couch, curl around Nickel's paws. He growls and snaps his tail, glares at me, swats at me when I pass. I sift through the walls' remains, find rusted nails, scraps of paper, small footprints in the dust, not my footprints. I don't wear sneakers. Watch the refrigerator door swing open, a carton of spoiled milk floating in the air, tipping over, spilling onto the tile. Laughter. A package of bread falls off the counter. Nickel goes over and laps up the milk. In the morning the ants are everywhere.

Follow the thickest trail of ants outside. They climb up the wooden beams supporting the deck, then back down toward the trees. Sprinkle Tony's Diazinon along this trail, dump the rest of the container in the small mound, where they stream out in black ropes. Haven't seen an ant in two days, but found Nickel outside beside the trail. Even the ants won't touch him. How did he get outside? I don't leave the house. Terri would want to be here for his funeral; the only solution is to clear out the freezer and put him in, wrapped in a plastic bag.

Reverend Snider looks at me like I crawled out of the blackest hole in hell.

Sir, I'm sorry, we don't do that kind of thing.

You mean you *won't*.

No, I mean, we *don't*. That's a Catholic thing, and besides, it's essentially a dead rite.

Well, can you at least bless the goddamned thing?

Sir—

And my wife left me.

Would you like to freshen up a bit? Maybe then you can calm down, start to think rationally.

Rational? Christ, all I'm asking for is some help! Isn't that what you people are supposed to do? I've tried everything, please, you've got to help me. I need God right now.

A faith of convenience is a house without a foundation. Now, I suggest you go home and work things out with your wife. Seek God in times of plenty, and he will not abandon you in times of need.

How much do they pay you to spout that kind of bullshit? Fine,

fine, I'm leaving. If your God won't help me, I'll find another that will.

Tony and his absent walls. Terri says we all have our crutch. We invent ways to cope, and in the process of invention, time is irrelevant. She is a firm believer in the adage that to create you must destroy, and it is the destruction that restores order.

Terri and I were never religious. Even when the surgery came into our lives, we discussed it like choosing a new car. We were methodical, picked apart the benefits, the possible side effects. Our faith lay in the unbreakable logic of science, or so we saw it. Everything could be reduced to the common denominator, in this case the removal of all extraneous material. We factored the surgery like an algebraic equation. But that was months ago.

Today, Tony takes the Miata to work. The angle from this side of the street is not much different than the angle from our bedroom window. This new house in its infant stages of construction belongs to some couple from Texas. We never met them, but watched them survey the plot, then drive away in a Suburban. The Texas Cadillac. They don't come to visit their new house often, so I don't feel like I'm trespassing. I'm taking care of it. Breaking it down to basics. The naked studs and sawdust-covered floorboards ground me. Sustenance becomes primary. For food I go to Tony's GE refrigerator. Two days ago I saw him pull a key out from beneath the gutter, unlock his front door, then replace it. He'd never know I was in his house. I don't drink his rice milk.

During the day I run through the woods. I leave the trails behind and pay no attention to my heart rate. An occasional jogger appears, and I scramble behind the nearest tree, rock cluster. I sit by the ponds and toss pebbles, watch the ripples stretch and disappear.

Nighttime I return to my borrowed home, crouch on the floor, and stare at the house across the street, the Hunter green trim and Meadow Brook paint dead layers of my own skin. I am stripped and hollowed in this naked house frame.

A Federal Express van pulls up behind the Volvo. The driver emerges in his navy shorts and black socks, carries the white package to the door. He rings the bell, shifts the box from one arm to the other. Rings again. Sets the box on the step and lowers his head. He might be writing something. Knocks this time. He picks up the box and returns to the van. This white package, a blur of red lettering on the side. Inside are tiny bottles of massage oils, lavender-scented sponges, and catalogs from our primary supplier of maternity goods. I recognize the packaging like my own name. I watch the FedEx van circle around the cul-de-sac, turn right off Gold Peak Drive to Baptist Road.

Imagine smoke blackening the windows, the paint blistering away. The roar of the flames would not drown out the screams of the house. Nickel, safe and frozen between ice trays and steak. I crawl into the space that will soon become the bathroom in this house. Sleep an impossibility. Factoring the equation. Would fire fall inside or outside the parentheses?

I wake up to find her standing at the end of our driveway, her suitcase at her feet. She looks lost, like something dropped her here out of the sky and she's not sure what she should do. The house smiles at her, a nervous smile, the smile of an abandoned child, ready to forgive. She sits slowly on the suitcase. The early sunlight soaks her hair, and she is too beautiful to be real. I grab two studs, push my face between them, splinters in my palm, in my ears. I wait for her to turn around and see me, trapped in this wooden cage, but she only sits facing the front door.

We will be very lucky to have this house, which we will watch grow from pinecones and weeds into a sturdy, insulated home with Ansel Adams prints on the walls, wedding pictures on the bookshelves, the grandfather clock in the hall. These are features we will pass down to our house. From one angle it will resemble Terri, from another, me. Our house will be like no other on the cul-de-sac, on Gold Peak Drive, in Fox Run Hills, on this side of I-25. This perfect child.

I let go and walk out through the living room, slip between the studs that will soon hold its walls together. Gravel crunches beneath my feet and I smile, knowing that when I put my hand on Terri's sun-soaked hair I will be home.

CONTRIBUTORS

SUSAN AUSTIN is a graduate of the Michener Center for Writers at the University of Texas at Austin. She is currently working on a collection of short stories. She lives in Felt, Idaho.

BELLE BOGGS was born and raised in Virginia. She received her MFA in fiction from the University of California, Irvine, and is currently completing a novel.

ESI EDUGYAN is originally from Calgary, Canada. She has degrees in writing from the University of Victoria and Johns Hopkins University. In 2000, she was awarded a grant from the Canada Council for the Arts and was a finalist for the Fund for Future Generations Millennium Prize. She is currently working on a novel.

CAIMEEN GARRETT holds an MFA from Syracuse University and is currently working on a Ph.D. at Florida State University. She is finishing her first collection of stories.

OTIS HASCHEMEYER, a Stegner Fellow at Stanford University with an MFA from the University of Arkansas, lives with his girlfriend in a camper nestled in the narrow folds of the Santa Cruz Mountains. His work has appeared in *The Missouri Review, Fourteen Hills: The SFSU Review, Louisiana Literature,* and *The Alaska Quarterly Review.* He is currently working on a novel based on "The Storekeeper."

LAURA HAWLEY received her MFA in writing and poetics from Naropa University in May 2001. She was the recipient of the 2000 Jack Kerouac Award, and her work has appeared in *Fiction International.*

HAL HORTON is a graduate of the Iowa Writers' Workshop and a former fellow with the Fine Arts Work Center in Provincetown. He was born and raised in Alaska, where he now teaches snowboarding. He is (still) at work on a novel.

FRANCES HWANG was born in Virginia and now lives in Portland, Oregon. She recently earned an MFA from the University of Montana, where she won the A. B. Guthrie Memorial Award for her fiction. She received her BA from Brown University and her MA in English from the University of Virginia. She is currently at work on a collection of short stories.

BARRY MATTHEWS was born and raised in Vermont and holds two degrees from Cornell University. His work has appeared in *Blithe House Quarterly* and is forthcoming in *Micro²: An Anthology of Really Short Stories*. He lives and works in New York City, where he is completing his first novel.

JENN McKEE has previously published poetry in *Analecta,* as well as book reviews in *BookPage, Calyx, Harvard Gay and Lesbian Review,* and *The Centre Daily Times.*

JOHN MURRAY grew up in South Australia and trained as a doctor. His short story collection, *A Few Short Notes on Tropical Butterflies,* will be published by Harper-Collins in spring 2003.

DYLAN TAI NGUYEN graduated from Harvard and lives in Brooklyn. His fiction has been translated into Vietnamese, and his personal essays have been taught in courses on American Studies, Asian-American Literature, and Vietnamese Literature at a handful of universities, including Yale. "Peace" is adapted from the first chapter of a novel-in-progress called *The Disappeared.*

KATHARINE NOEL was a 2000–2002 Stegner Fellow at Stanford University. She is at work on a novel, *Halfway House.*

CHERYL STRAYED recently completed her first novel, *Torch,* which is set in northern Minnesota where she grew up. Her fiction and memoir have been published in *Nerve, DoubleTake, Hope Magazine, Oasis, The Slate, Carve Magazine,* and in several anthologies, including *The Best American Essays 2000.* She is a graduate of the University of Minnesota and Syracuse University and was a scholar at the Bread Loaf Writers' Conference in 2001.

BRAD VICE holds degrees in creative writing from the University of Tennessee and the University of Cincinnati and has published fiction in *The Georgia Review, The Southern Review, The Atlantic Monthly,* and *New Stories from the South.* He lives with his wife, Juliana, in Russellville, Arkansas, where he is completing a collection of stories tentatively titled *The Bear Bryant Funeral Train.*

PARTICIPANTS

United States

American University
MFA Program in Creative Writing—
Department of Literature
4400 Massachusetts Ave., NW
Washington, DC 20016
202/885-2971

Arizona State University
College of Liberal Arts and Sciences
Dept. of Literature—Creative
Writing Program
Tempe, AZ 85287
480/965-3528

Bennington College
Program in Writing and Literature
Bennington, VT 05201-9993
802/442-5401, Ext. 4452

Boise State University
MFA Program in Creative Writing
1910 University Drive
Boise, ID 83725
208/426-1205

Boston University
Creative Writing Program
236 Bay State Road
Boston, MA 02215
617/353-2510

Bowling Green State University
English Department
Creative Writing Program
Bowling Green, OH 43403
419/372-8370

The Bread Loaf Writers' Conference
Middlebury College
Middlebury, VT 05753
802/443-5286

Brooklyn College
Dept. of English—MFA Program
2308 Boylan Hall
2900 Bedford Avenue
Brooklyn, NY 11210-2889
718/951-5195

Brown University
Box 1852
Creative Writing
Providence, RI 02912
401/863-3260

California State University,
Long Beach
English Department
Long Beach, CA 90840
562/985-4225

California State University,
Northridge
Department of English
18111 Nordhoff Street
Northridge, CA 91330-8248
818/677-3431

Colorado State University
MFA Creative Writing Program
English Department, 359 Eddy Hall
Fort Collins, CO 80523-1773
970/491-6428

Columbia University
Division of Writing,
School of the Arts
2960 Broadway, Rm. 15 Dodge
New York, NY 10027
212/854-4392

Cornell University
English Department
Ithaca, NY 14853
607/255-6800

DePaul University
English Department—
Creative Writing
802 W. Belden Avenue
Chicago, IL 60614
773/325-7485

Emerson College
Division of Writing, Literature,
and Publishing
120 Boylston Street
Boston, MA 02116
617/824-8750

Fine Arts Work Center in
Provincetown
24 Pearl Street
Provincetown, MA 02657
508/487-8678

Florida International University
Department of English
Biscayne Bay Campus—
3000 NE 151st Street
North Miami, FL 33181
305/919-5857

Florida State University
Creative Writing Program
Department of English
Tallahassee, FL 32306-1580
850/644-4230

George Mason University
MS 3E4
English Department
Fairfax, VA 22030
703/993-1180

Hamline University
Graduate Liberal Studies—MS 1730
1536 Hewitt Avenue
St. Paul, MN 55104
651/523-2047

Hollins University
Department of English
P.O. Box 9677
Roanoke, VA 24020-1677
540/362-6317

Hunter College
MFA Program in Creative Writing
English Department
695 Park Avenue
New York, NY 10021
212/772-5164

Illinois State University
Department of English
Campus Box 4240
Normal, IL 61790-4240
309/438-3667

Indiana University
Department of English
Ballantine Hall 442
Bloomington, IN 47405-6601
812/855-8224

Johns Hopkins University
The Writing Seminars
3400 North Charles Street
Baltimore, MD 21218
410/516-7563

Johns Hopkins Writing Program—
Washington
1776 Massachusetts Avenue NW
Suite 100
Washington, DC 20036
202/452-1123

Kansas State University
Department of English
Denison Hall
Manhattan, KS 66506-0701
785/532-6716

The Loft Literary Center
Mentor Series Program
Suite 200, Open Book
1011 Washington Avenue South
Minneapolis, MN 55415
612/215-2575

Louisiana State University
English Department
Baton Rouge, LA 70803
225/578-2236

Manhattanville College
2900 Purchase Street
Purchase, NY 10577
914/694-3425

Manhattanville Summer
Writers' Week
2900 Purchase Street
Purchase, NY 10577
914/694-3425

McNeese State University
Department of Languages
P.O. Box 92655
Lake Charles, LA 70609-2495
337/475-5326

Michener Center for Writers
University of Texas
J. Frank Dobie House
702 East Dean Keeton Street
Austin, TX 78705
512/471-1601

Mills College
5000 MacArthur Boulevard
Oakland, CA 94613
510/430-3130

Minnesota State University, Mankato
English Department
AH230
Mankato, MN 56001
507/389-2117

Mississippi State University
Department of English
MS 39762
Mississippi State, MS 39762
662/325-3644

The Napa Valley Writers'
Conference
Napa Valley College
1088 College Avenue
St. Helena, CA 94574
707/967-2900

Naropa University
Program in Writing and Poetics
2130 Arapahoe Avenue
Boulder, CO 80302
303/546-3540

New York University
Graduate Program in Creative
Writing
19 University Place
New York, NY 10003
212/998-8816

Ohio State University
English Dept.
421 Denney Hall
164 West 17th Avenue
Columbus, OH 43210
614/292-6065

PEN Prison Writing Committee
PEN American Center
568 Broadway
New York, NY 10012
212/334-1660

Pennsylvania State University
Department of English
119 Burrowes Building
University Park, PA 16802-6200
814/863-3069

Purdue University
Department of English
Heavilon Hall
West Lafayette, IN 47907
765/494-3740

Rutgers University
Department of English
360 Martin Luther King, Jr.
Boulevard
Newark, NJ 07102
973/353-5279

San Francisco State University
Creative Writing Department,
College of Humanities
1600 Holloway Avenue
San Francisco, CA 94132-4162
415/338-1891

Sarah Lawrence College
Graduate Writing Program
Meade Way
Slonim House
Bronxville, NY 10708
914/395-2371

Sewanee Writers' Conference
310 St. Luke's Hall
735 University Avenue
Sewanee, TN 37383-1000
931/598-1141

Southern Illinois University
at Carbondale
MFA—Creative Writing
English Department
Carbondale, IL 62901-4503
618/453-5321

Southwest Texas State University
MFA Program in Creative Writing
Department of English
601 University Drive
San Marcos, TX 78666
512/245-2163

Stanford University
Creative Writing Program
Department of English
Stanford, CA 94305-2087
650/725-1208

Syracuse University
Program in Creative Writing
Department of English
401 Hall of Languages
Syracuse, NY 13244
315/443-2173

Taos Summer Writers' Conference
University of New Mexico
Humanities Bldg., Rm. 255
Albuquerque, NM 87131
505/277-6248

Temple University
Creative Writing Program
Anderson Hall, 10th Floor
Philadelphia, PA 19122
215/204-1796

Texas A&M University
Creative Writing Program
English Department
College Station, TX 77843-4227
979/845-9936

University of Alabama
Program in Creative Writing
Department of English
P.O. Box 870244
Tuscaloosa, AL 35487-0244
205/348-5065

University of Alaska, Anchorage
Department of Creative Writing &
Literary Arts
3211 Providence Drive
Anchorage, AK 99508-8348
907/786-4330

University of Alaska, Fairbanks
Program in Creative Writing
Department of English
P.O. Box 755720
Fairbanks, AK 99775-5720
907/474-7193

University of Arizona
Creative Writing Program
Department of English
Modern Languages Bldg. #67
Tucson, AZ 85721-0067
520/621-3880

University of Arkansas
Program in Creative Writing
Department of English
333 Kimpel Hall
Fayetteville, AR 72701
501/575-7355

University of California, Davis
Graduate Creative Writing Program
Department of English
One Shields Avenue
Davis, CA 95616
530/752-2281

University of California, Irvine
MFA Program in Writing
Department of English &
Comparative Literature
435 Humanities Instructional Bldg.
Irvine, CA 92697-2650
949/824-6718

University of Central Florida
Graduate Program
in Creative Writing
Department of English
P.O. Box 161346
Orlando, FL 32816-1346
407/823-2212

University of Cincinnati
Creative Writing Program
Department of English &
Comparative Literature
P.O. Box 210069
Cincinnati, OH 45221-0069
513/556-3906

University of Denver
Creative Writing Program
Department of English
2140 S. Race Street
Denver, CO 80210
303/871-2266

University of Florida
Creative Writing Program
Department of English
P.O. Box 11730
Gainesville, FL 32611-7310
352/392-6650

University of Georgia
Creative Writing Program
English Department
Park Hall 102
Athens, GA 30602-6205
706/542-2659

University of Hawaii
Creative Writing Program
English Department
1733 Donaghho Road
Honolulu, HI 96822
808/956-8801

University of Houston
Creative Writing Program
Department of English
Houston, TX 77204-3012
713/743-3015

University of Illinois at Chicago
Program for Writers
Department of English MC/162
601 South Morgan Street
Chicago, IL 60607-7120
312/413-2229

University of Iowa
Program in Creative Writing
102 Dey House
507 N. Clinton Street
Iowa City, IA 52242
319/335-0416

University of Louisiana at Lafayette
Creative Writing Concentration
Department of English
P.O. Box 44691
Lafayette, LA 70504-4691
337/482-6906

University of Maine
Master's in English Program
5752 Neville Hall
Orono, ME 04469-5752
207/581-3822

University of Maryland
Creative Writing Program
Department of English
4140 Susquehanna Hall
College Park, MD 20742
301/405-3820

University of Massachusetts, Amherst
MFA Program in English
Bartlett Hall
Box 30515
Amherst, MA 01003-0515
413/545-0643

University of Michigan
MFA Program in Creative Writing
Department of English
3187 Angell Hall
Ann Arbor, MI 48109-1003
734/763-4139

University of Minnesota
MFA Program in Creative Writing
Department of English
207 Church Street, SE
Minneapolis, MN 55455
612/625-6366

University of Missouri–Columbia
Program in Creative Writing
Department of English
107 Tate Hall
Columbia, MO 65211
573/882-6421

University of Missouri–St. Louis
Master of Fine Arts in Creative
Writing Program
Department of English
8001 Natural Bridge Road
St. Louis, MO 63121
314/516-6845

University of Montana
Creative Writing Program
Department of English
Missoula, MT 59812-1013
406/243-5231

University of Nebraska, Lincoln
Creative Writing Program
Department of English
343 Andrews Hall
Lincoln, NE 68588-0333
402/472-3191

University of Nevada, Las Vegas
MFA in Creative Writing
Department of English
4505 S. Maryland Parkway
Las Vegas, NV 89154-5011
702/895-3533

University of New Hampshire
Creative Writing Program
Department of English
Hamilton Smith Hall
Durham, NH 03824-3574
603/862-3963

University of New Orleans
Creative Writing Workshop
College of Liberal Arts
Lakefront
New Orleans, LA 70148
504/280-7454

University of North Carolina,
Greensboro
MFA Writing Program
P.O. Box 26170
Greensboro, NC 27402-6170
336/334-5459

University of North Texas
Creative Writing Division
Department of English
P.O. Box 133307
Denton, TX 76203-1307
940/565-2050

University of Notre Dame
Creative Writing Program
355 O'Shaughnessy Hall
Notre Dame, IN 46556-0368
219/631-5639

University of Oregon
Program in Creative Writing
Box 5243
Eugene, OR 97403-5243
541/346-3944

University of San Francisco
Master of Arts in Writing Program
Program Office, Lone Mountain 340
2130 Fulton Street
San Francisco, CA 94117-1080
415/422-2382

University of South Carolina
MFA Program
Department of English
Columbia, SC 29208
803/777-5063

University of Southern California
Professional Writing Program
Waite Phillips Hall, Rm. 404
Los Angeles, CA 90089-4034
213/740-3252

University of Southern Mississippi
Center for Writers
Box 5144 USM
Hattiesburg, MS 39406-5144
601/266-4321

University of Texas at Austin
Creative Writing Program in English
Calhoun Hall 210
Austin, TX 78712-1164
512/475-6356

University of Texas at El Paso
MFA Program with
a Bilingual Option
English Department
Hudspeth Hall, Rm. 113
El Paso, TX 79968-0526
915/747-5731

University of Utah
Creative Writing Program
255 S. Central Campus Drive,
Rm. 3500
Salt Lake City, UT 84112
801/581-7131

University of Virginia
Creative Writing Program
Department of English
P.O. Box 400121
Charlottesville, VA 22904-4121
804/924-6675

University of Washington
Creative Writing Program
Box 354330
Seattle, WA 98195
206/543-9865

University of Wisconsin–Milwaukee
Creative Writing Program
Department of English
Box 413
Milwaukee, WI 53201
414/229-4243

Unterberg Poetry Center
Writing Program
92nd Street Y
1395 Lexington Avenue
New York, NY 10128
212/415-5754

Vermont College
Program in Writing
Montpelier, VT 05602
802/828-8840

Virginia Commonwealth University
MFA in Creative Writing Program
Department of English
P.O. Box 842005
Richmond, VA 23284-2005
804/828-1329

Wayne State University
Creative Writing Program
English Department
Detroit, MI 48202
313/577-2450

The Wesleyan Writers Conference
Wesleyan University
Middletown, CT 06459
860/685-3604

West Virginia University
Creative Writing Program
Department of English
P.O. Box 6269
Morgantown, WV 26506-6269
304/293-3107

Western Illinois University
Department of English and
Journalism
Macomb, IL 61455-1390
309/298-1103

Western Michigan University
Graduate Program
in Creative Writing
Department of English
Kalamazoo, MI 49008-5092
616/387-2572

Wichita State University
MFA in Creative Writing
1845 N. Fairmount
Wichita, KS 67260-0014
316/978-3130

Wisconsin Institute
for Creative Writing
Department of English
Helen C. White Hall
University of Wisconsin–Madison
Madison, WI 53706
608/263-3800

The Writer's Voice of
the West Side YMCA
5 W. 63rd Street
New York, NY 10023
212/875-4124

Canada

The Banff Centre for the Arts
Writing & Publishing
Box 1020-34
107 Tunnel Mountain Drive
Banff, AB TOL OCO
403/762-6278

Concordia University
1455 de Maisonneuve Blvd. West
Department of English
Montreal, PQ H3G 1M8
514/848-2340

The Humber School for Writers
205 Humber College Blvd.
Humber College
Toronto, ON M9W 5L7
416/675-5084

McMaster University
The Commons Building—Rm. 116
1280 Main Street West
Hamilton, ON L8S 4K1
905/525-9140 ext. 24321

Sage Hill Writing Experience
Box 1731
Saskatoon, SK S7K 3S1
306/652-7395

University of Calgary
Department of English
Calgary, AB T2N 1N4
403/220-6431

University of New Brunswick
Department of English
Box 4400
Fredericton, NB E3B 5A3
506/453-4676

University of Victoria
Department of Writing
P.O. Box 1700, STN CSC
Victoria, BC V8W 2Y2
250/721-7306

University of Windsor
Department of English
401 Sunset Avenue
Windsor, ON N9B 3P4
519/253-3000 Ext. 2288

Victoria School of Writing
Box 8152
Victoria, BC V8W 3R8
250/595-3000